COURTHOUSE COWBOYS

A Modern Tale of Murder in Montana

by

P.A. Moore

Copyright © 2011 by P.A. Moore

This work is a fictional memoir based, in part, on true events. Names, characters, places, and incidents either are products of the author's imagination or used fictitiously. The author fabricated many scenes, conversations, and inhabitants of Kootenai County, Montana, by incorporating public information to create realistic detail. Numerous public documents of actual events, along with published trial transcripts from authentic cases, and various state and national news accounts, provided the basis for this story, as did the author's background, education, and experience as an attorney.

The expert medical and psychological information about childhood physical and sexual abuse, incest, and **Klinefelter's syndrome (KS)** is true and accurate. It is the author's primary goal in writing this book to educate readers throughout the world about KS, a common, rarely diagnosed, but treatable genetic disorder, that *affects 1 in every 500 boys born worldwide.*

ISBN-978-0-615-57677-0
Published by P.A. Moore, Inc.
First Edition: October 31, 2011
Second Edition: May 2, 2012

To my family, especially my beloved spouse, Jack: My world would not exist without all of you in it. In good times and tough times, at the end of each day, we have one another, in love and in faith, for all time.

Many thanks to Lyndsey Marshall and Mike Potter for their terrific cover design and production, with special thanks to Justin Marshall for his additional contribution.

Also, special thanks to my son, Jack, for serving as my shoulder angel throughout the years it took to produce this work.

"There is some soul of goodness in things evil,
would men observingly distil it out."

King Henry, in *Henry V*, William Shakespeare

PROLOGUE

The Growth of Cynicism

Norton, California – November 1996

LIKE MY CAR KEYS OR READING GLASSES, I've misplaced my soul somewhere between the Catholic Church and the courtroom.

Today a navy blue suit, matching pumps with three-inch heels, and a string of pearls decorate my tall, 43-year-old figure. Precisely shaped red fingernails tuck back a strand of russet hair into a coiffed bun centered on the back of my neck. My green eyes glare down a slightly crooked nose at the defense attorney rising from his chair.

"I'm glad your husband lost the election yesterday," the fat toad wheezes. "He doesn't have the integrity to be a judge."

A flush of fury creeps up my spine, its venom spewing out the crown of my head. I want to grab his tie, twisting it until his brown eyes pop from his smug face. I, Paige Sheehan Defalco, am unraveling. I take a calming breath. It doesn't help so I throw my yellow legal pad onto the prosecution table as I square off with this huge bloated lawyer who carries his arrogance on his sneer.

"Fuck you, Palmer!" I hurl the epithet toward him.

The fat attorney rears back, as if scorched by an oven blast. "What did you just say to me, Mrs. Defalco?"

I sense the court reporter scurry toward the door leading to the judge's chamber, seeking safety from my wrath. The judge has yet to take the bench. A few people mill around in the audience but now they, too, rush for an exit.

Rage radiates from my perfumed pores. My next words erupt over my glossed lips. "I told you to go screw yourself, Palmer. You're a piece of shit, and so is that ugly ass client of yours." I nod toward the blond-haired, tattooed little man sitting at the defense table, handcuffed and smiling at the unfolding drama.

Palmer, for once speechless, huffs an indignant breath. I open my suit jacket, spreading it back as I place my hands on my hips. I shift toward Palmer, crowding the pointy tips of my polished shoes against the toes of his scuffed brown wingtips. The corpulent slug towers over me.

I glare up at his pockmarked cheeks, but lean away from his distended belly. "Your law practice is a joke, and as far as *integrity,* Palmer? You don't have the balls to carry my husband's jock, let alone fill it. Jack has more integrity in his ear lobe than you have in your entire bulbous body."

The lawyer's skin glows magenta, but before he can respond, the bailiff enters, announcing the judge's arrival. I back off as the bailiff and I smirk at each other, united in our disdain for defense attorneys and the criminals they represent.

"Good morning, Counsel," Her Honor intones. "We are on the record in the case of People versus Harvey Junior--"

Palmer, the jerk, interrupts. "Judge, before we begin, I want to put on the record that Mrs. Defalco just told me to go fuck myself, right here in your courtroom." His sniveling whine grates through the silence.

Oh, for crapssake.

This son of a bitch just *tattled* on me. I roll my eyes as I sit down, not deigning to respond to such a childish display. I'm ready to call my first witness in the tattooed guy's preliminary hearing.

The judge pauses before replying, "Counsel, I am aware that Mrs. Defalco's husband lost a hard fought campaign yesterday in his bid for a judgeship. Now let's move on." Nodding at me, a hint of sympathy in her soft brown eyes, she continues, "Mrs. Defalco, please call your first witness."

Whether from last night's multiple martinis, a lack of sleep, the shock of Jack's election loss, or a combination of all three, I feel too weary to stand. Instead, I mumble, "The People call the victim, your Honor, the defendant's wife, who is in custody herself for refusing to respond to my subpoena." I tap my manicured nails on the table as the bailiff brings out the prisoner/witness.

This battered wife glares at me, her hatred for me second only to her terror of her ogre of a husband. He's tortured her for years. The day she tried to leave him, he heated up a butter knife on the gas stove. He held her down, laid the red-hot blade across the tattoo on her right breast that read 'Junior' - surrounded by a heart and arrow - and burned her. Then he ripped that tattoo off, sizzling skin and all.

I return her glare, ignoring the tiny speck of conscience that demands I let her go, that I forget about forcing her to testify against her will. But I hate her husband too much to let him walk free. If I don't plunge ahead, the judge will have to release him, and I cannot let that happen. Demonic crimes require drastic measures. I will do whatever it takes to win a conviction against this Hell's Angels-loving, methamphetamine-dealing, sadistic scumbag.

The victim has been safe in custody, more or less, but after today, she's on her own. Once she testifies, no one will protect her from her maniac husband. She'll have to hide again, begin again, find a new job in another community under yet a different name, all on her own.

Even if the ogre murders this woman after the

hearing, I can still send him to prison forever, so long as I extract the truth from her today, under oath. The smarmy bastard already has a contract out on her life, knowing that if I succeed, he's toast. As a deputy district attorney for Norton County, I've sworn to protect and defend those who fall victim to the bad guys. Yet today I'm just another overzealous prosecutor causing more pain and suffering for the maimed citizens I am supposed to help.

My life, like life for most prosecutors, breaks down to black and white. I am a good guy, along with everyone else in law enforcement. The criminals are the bad guys, along with their lawyers and the idiots at the ACLU. Nothing complicates this equation.

Whereas I once spent my college weekends at U.C. Berkeley releasing the downtrodden from jail on their own recognizance, I now savor the wreckage wrung from criminals I thrash in court. Bad guys sit handcuffed before me, faceless and nameless, their humanity reduced to their prison-issued, personal file numbers.

In mid-life, I struggle to recall my days as a liberal, protesting the Vietnam War, fighting against the injustice of race, gender, and class discrimination. Instead, I detest every one of these rule-breaking, society-destroying creeps. I know nothing of their personal life histories, nor do I care. My scorn extends to their friends and fellow gang members, sometimes even to their parents and siblings.

White, Black, Asian, Hispanic - they all look the same to me. I mock their ghetto homes, their jungle-cruiser cars, their gaudy jewelry, their oversized jeans hanging off their saggy butts, and their lice-encrusted, greasy hair. I laugh at the cops' snide observations of their arrests, and smirk at these prisoners in their orange jail jumpsuits. I snicker at their feeble attempts to explain to the judge why they committed their vile crimes.

They smell, these criminals - of incarceration, of poverty, of hopelessness. Often I hold my breath as I walk past the jail vent that vomits fetid air to the outside parking lot. I won't release it until I reach my brand new Suburban, where I can inhale the aroma of clean leather and air conditioning.

The Great Unwashed, one of my colleagues calls them, these toothless, acne-faced kids who awaken every morning with nothing to do, nowhere to go, little to eat, and a world of crime opportunities spread before them.

With their families fractured, often before they're born, the children of the streets cling to each other, their loyalty to one another the constant source of gang-related murders. Drugs and sex numb their fear of a future predicted to last only into their teenage years, when they're cut down by another's bullet.

Yet here I sit in court, inured to their tragic lives. The sooner they kill each other off, the fewer psychopaths I have to prosecute. I closely follow the obituaries in our local paper, waiting to celebrate the deaths of those against whom I've filed criminal charges. The younger they die, the less time they have to injure or kill the innocents.

"Mrs. Defalco?" I look up at the judge. She tilts her head. "Are you finished? Do the People rest their case?"

I blink, amazed that I've completed my questions, that I've rebutted Palmer's cross-examination, all in a near state of unconsciousness. Like driving long distances, I blank out in court these days, wondering occasionally how I arrive at my destination, to the conviction of one more evildoer.

My prisoner/witness sits on the stand, now finished testifying, still stabbing me with her eyes. "Yes, Your Honor. And the People ask the Court to release this victim from custody."

Turning to the defense attorney, the judge inquires, "Counsel? Any evidence at this time?" The porcine piece of crap shakes his head. "Not at this time, Your Honor."

I've won. The heinous little tattooed torturer now

faces trial and the rest of his life in prison. And his rat bastard defense lawyer will have to explain his client's conduct to a jury.

Perfect.

After the judge vacates the bench, I level one last malevolent look at Palmer as I leave the courtroom, heels clicking a brisk pace over the ancient linoleum floors. I'm weary of criminals and their obsequious lawyers. I've heard enough condolences about the election.

Inside my burgundy Suburban, I kick off my pumps as I debate whether to ditch out and spend the rest of the day at home, or drive across county to the office where I head up the Domestic Violence Unit. My fatigue reflects back at me from the rear view mirror. I convince myself the dark bags under my eyes result from smudged mascara.

I am a master of self-deceit.

* * *

As mindlessly as I perform in court, I drive toward my office rather than home. Not *my* office, I realize, after I've parked my land yacht in the employee parking space. Instead, I've driven to the Big House, the main office of the District Attorney wherein resides the man with all the power.

This man, however, is not the elected official. Rather, he holds the position of Chief Assistant. We mere deputies, his minions, refer to him as Lucifer. He seems to have dirt on everyone in the county and wields that knowledge with the flair of a Chicago politician. We suspect he even has dirt on God.

I greet the receptionists, skirt yet another brewing fistfight between two senior deputies, ignore my colleagues in the lunchroom, and beeline toward Lucifer's corner office. I knock, and he motions me to a chair as he gives the bum's rush to the person on the other end of the phone.

"Hello, Paige," he smiles, leaning back in his leather chair. "Tough break for Jack in that election. *The Year of the Woman*, my ass." He shakes his head in disgust.

I nod. If I open my mouth I might scream. If Lucifer shows kindness to me, I'll cry.

"So." He hesitates, likely sensing an emotional torrent lurks just under my pearl necklace. "How are things in the Domestic Violence Unit? I hear you could use some more help down there. We're a little short, but after the first of the year--"

I stand up, close his office door, and perch on the edge of my chair. "Joe, I'm done. I'm losing it. I told Palmer to go fuck himself in court this morning." I wait for his reaction.

He laughs then sobers. "Was the judge present?"

"No, of course not. I'm not *that* far gone." I run a finger along my pearls. "But it shows me that I can't do this job one more hour. Not with the kids at home, not if I want my marriage to last." Tears moisten my eyes so I look out Joe's window.

Joe isn't the kingmaker because he's stupid or insensitive. He surmises in a second that I'm lethally serious about dumping a promising legal career. "Paige, we've been close friends for nearly 20 years. We're like family. I've known Jack even longer, and we've all been through some tough times together." He sighs as a single tear escapes down my cheek.

Joe hates it when women cry. In the massive San Francisco earthquake in 1989, he and I stood together outside my law school as the city shook and buildings collapsed. Together we ran to his car and fled toward home. Nine hours later we arrived, but never once did I cry while he drove. I swallowed my terror, just as he did, because to do otherwise might have weakened his own resolve to get us safely to our families.

Indeed, I'm one of the few people in the office who

knows the real man behind the myth. While he is Machiavellian in his ability to outwit most of us, he loves his wife and children with the same passion I feel for mine and possesses more compassion than he'll ever express.

"In all these years, I've never asked for a favor. I've worked my ass off for you and mostly succeeded at my assignments." I suck in a shaky breath. "If you won't transfer me out of the unit *today,* to a desk job filing cases or some other mindless endeavor, I'm walking out that door and never coming back."

My demand is fortified by the fact that Joe's wife recently did just that - quit her career, packed up the kids, and moved the family to their condo in Colorado. She did this to escape the stress from contemporaneously parenting, working, homemaking, and volunteering. Joe now commutes to and from Colorado while he waits out the months to his retirement. Not a great set up, but three months earlier, when I'd taken my own kids to visit them, I realized how the peace in Colorado had rescued them from chaos.

Joe gazes out the window, his fingers steepled in front of him, calculating my mental state. Minutes pass before he returns my gaze. His frown eases into head-shaking resignation. "Go home. I'll move you tomorrow. I'll let you know where to report later today."

I sniff, grabbing a tissue from his side table. "Thanks." I head for the closed door but turn back. "I can't promise you I won't quit, even with the transfer. I just can't seem to keep it all together, you know? All the carnage by day and the perfect mom expectations at night rip me apart. You and Jack can separate work from home. But no matter what I do, these people haunt me. The battered victims, the bad guys, even my own kids."

Silence.

I open the door, glance one last time at the exalted offices on the ninth floor of the Big House, and sneak down the back stairway to freedom.

Within the safety of the Suburban, I exhale. I shed the old grease and body odor smell from the jail, kick off my shoes, remove my suit jacket, and rest my head on the steering wheel. A knock on the window makes me jump. Heart pounding, I see the concerned face of a public defender I both respect and dislike merely because he's on the side of the criminals. I push the button to lower the window, no smile welcoming his intrusion into my misery.

"Hey, Paige." The older man frowns as he gently touches my arm. "Are you okay? Can I buy you some coffee, maybe? I heard what happened with Palmer this morning." He shakes his head, chuckles. "Don't let it get to you. We all lose it from time to time."

When he smiles, his kindness further unravels me.

I swipe at an unwanted tear streaking past my nose. "Thanks. I'll be okay. I'm just tired from the election."

The lie rolls out, but the public defender is too polite to call me on it. He pats my arm and walks away. I drive toward home to avoid anyone else's compassion.

Passing the mall I wonder what the hell I am doing. When Jack learns that I quit the unit to assume a lowly desk job, and that I'm contemplating following Joe's wife to the sanity of some hinterland, he'll go ballistic. As it sits, our 17-year marriage nears divorce at least once a month. If I leave my career, move the kids from California to parts unknown, will Jack come with us, or throw in the towel? Worse, given the ever-shifting state of our relationship, does it matter?

I exit the freeway to the suburbs and wend my way through the back roads to home. This beautiful neighborhood boasts great schools, elite thinkers, demure politics, sophisticated restaurants, and hordes of money. For most people, life here spells success. It suffocates me, especially today, when I have to face Jack and my children with the news that Mom careens close to a nervous breakdown. Fight or flight? The fight in me wanes while the urge to flee expands with every panicked breath. As I pull into the driveway, my kids jump from the branches of our plum tree, delighted that I've arrived early, ahead of my usual late homecomings.

"Mom!" My son, Sean, only seven, streaks to me. He grabs me around my waist so tightly I teeter on my heels. My daughter, Claire, twelve, hugs me higher. I cling to them, the only beings on earth who matter to me at this moment. Eyes closed, I know I must protect them from the bad guys. I must keep our family together no matter the cost. Sane kids might come from crazy parents, and I suppose mine exemplify that theory, but they deserve better.

They deserve a mom who focuses on them first, whose smile doesn't mask fear and loathing, whose laughter erupts from joy instead of cynicism. I owe them a change of heart and a new playground where they can ride their bikes without fear of kidnapping.

As they run off to chase Bob, their new puppy, I grab my briefcase, say goodbye to the babysitter, and stand paralyzed in my recently remodeled kitchen.

One place beckons to me for reasons contrary to logic.

Montana.

* * *

"*Montana!* You want to move our family to Montana? Are you *fucking nuts*?" Jack Defalco explodes these words as spittle flies from his lips.

In the privacy of our bedroom, away from our children who sit glued to the television, I try to stay calm in the face of his wrath.

I'm desperate. "Yesterday our son said, 'Mom, you always tell us what a great childhood you had growing up in Colorado because you could ride your bike all over with no fear of kidnappers. We can't even go in the front yard of our house without a grownup.'" I pause before delivering the punch line. "Then he said, 'Mom, what kind of childhood memories will I have?'"

Jack runs his fingers through the top of his thick brown hair. "Oh for chrissake! We live in a great neighborhood, we make decent money, I'll be able to retire in six years on my full salary from the D.A.'s office, and you're on a high-speed career track at yours. The kids go to excellent schools, they play sports, they have friends here, and so do we. I don't see the problem."

Sitting on the edge of the bed, I clutch the duvet cover. "The problem is this: One of us sits at the bus stop every morning with a loaded gun between the seats to thwart any pedophile who might snatch the kids. Both kids are imprisoned in this palace of ours because we know where every sex offender lives within a 50 mile radius, and there are tons of them."

I stand, gaining a superior position in the argument through my much taller height.

"And look at our jobs," I march on. "Last week I nearly got shot running through the ghetto chasing a victim who I needed to testify in court. I'm trying to help this crazy crack addict by putting her boyfriend behind bars, and she's *running away* from me. We spend all day hanging around killers and child molesters, reading about macerated eyeballs and blood spatter patterns, and then come home at night and try to act normal - whatever the hell that is."

Jack glares at me, his hands fisted on his hips.

But I'm on a roll. "You and I barely speak anymore because we're so busy at work or running from one kid event to the next. Our friends are grossed out by our dinner conversation because neither one of us can stop talking about our cases. Like you the other night talking about that burned corpse in the dumpster or me discussing how much digital penetration into a vagina is required before it's a rape."

Jack stalks closer to my inferno, his voice lowers, and he half-kiddingly threatens, "If I had a tranquilizer gun right now, I'd dart you full of valium. You're crazier than a bedbug if you think this family will move to Bumfuck, Montana."

I sit back on the bed. "I know I'm screwed up, but it's nothing a shrink can fix. Don't you see that I've lost my conscience, my soul? I'm numb. I don't give a shit about humanity anymore - me, the Berkeley protester, the defender of the downtrodden, the voice for those who couldn't speak up for themselves. What happened to that woman who cared about people - not just crime victims, but *all* people?"

My hands shake as I reach for a glass of water near the headboard. Jack sits beside me. His left hand reaches for mine, both of our ring fingers sporting fat gold bands that declare our long ago commitment to stick together through the hard times.

"Here's the worst part," I let him weave his fingers through mine but can't meet his gaze. "In religious education, I was the teacher in charge of creating a Christmas project for the first grade. I bought little trees for them to decorate, complete with little ornaments and presents."

"Okay," my spouse responds, "now I'm really confused."

I stare into his intense silver-blue eyes. "The other teacher, when she saw my *trees,* raced to the store to buy little baby dolls we could wrap in swaddling cloth and put into cradles made from popsicle sticks. She looked at me like I was a heathen and said, 'Don't you think we should keep Christ in Christmas?'"

I rest my head on his shoulder as he puts his right arm around me, both of us struggling with my weird metaphor.

Moments later I sit up. "You know that scene in

Puccini's opera when the bad guy cries out, 'Tosca, Tosca, you make me forget God?'"

Jack, never an opera fan, shakes his head. "What's your point?"

"My point is that too many years living on the dark side, in the bowels of criminal law, have made me forget God. I hardly go to Mass because it interferes with my one morning off a week when I can drink coffee and read the *New York Times.* Seventeen years since I joined the Catholic Church, and I can't recall why I bothered. That's why I'm so lost and *that*," I stand and pace to the dresser before I turn back to him, "is why we're moving to Montana."

Resolved, I drop my shoulders, easing the tension embedded in those muscles.

"Because when I remember God, I'll find my soul again."

PART ONE

CHAPTER ONE

Soul Sister

Eight months later
Beartooth, Montana – August 1997

THE AMAZON STUD WOMAN, aka my new neighbor, Anne, poured us each another shot of vodka and clinked her glass to mine. "To soul mates finding each other in the wilderness."

Anne's nearly six-foot frame - lithe, athletic, and tan - swam through my vision. I raised my own toast. "To you, Anne, for accepting me for who I am."

Clink.

A week earlier Anne had introduced herself, arriving at my door clad in shorts and an exercise bra. "Gotta soak in the rays while the sun shines in Beartooth, which isn't for very long." Her blonde hair, bronzed skin, makeup-free blue eyes, and wide grin sang out serenity and inner peace. "I'm a Buddhist Unitarian, a physical therapist at the grade school, a recent and ecstatic ex-wife, a mom, and a sinner if you believe the old guy who plows the sidewalks."

The sinner part hooked me, so we'd met several times since. Anne excelled at every outdoor activity. An extreme skier, biker, hiker, kayaker, whitewater rafter, rock climber, ice caver, and horsewoman, Anne enjoyed every activity I abhorred, to wit, exercise.

She'd only moved to the neighborhood a few weeks before us and believed, as I did, that no other residents consumed alcohol or cursed. Tonight she'd slipped between our homes, glanced around for spies, crept in the side door, through my garage, and set the backpack-concealed booze on the table. The next hour of sipping freed us to share our virtues and vices, as only women can do, whether drunk or merely standing in line at the grocery store.

Anne leaned toward me. "So is your husband dumping you, or do you think he'll move up here some day?"

In early July, after driving with us 2,000 miles to Montana, Jack helped me unpack some household goods, kissed us all adios, and returned to California. To the safety of 'The Known.' He promised to commute every few weeks but made no commitment to move to Beartooth. He'd arranged to housesit at his cousin's mansion in a gated community near our old suburb. His new office location, across from the home of the Fairfax As, provided him with all the baseball and polish dogs he desired. His latest job assignment threatened death from boredom but no trials or stress, so life for Jack Defalco brooked no hardship.

I added more tonic to my cocktail. "Debatable. He misses the kids. He thinks I'm crazy, so who knows if he'll cave in to my latest effort at sanity. He hates Montana, loathes the idea of starting over in a community where he knows no one, and shudders at opening a private law firm where he's off the government dole." I closed my eyes, perhaps to shut out Jack's angry image or simply to stop the spinning of the room.

"Don't you wonder why you're here? I mean, of all the places on the planet, why Beartooth, next door to me? I don't believe in coincidence. We've met for a reason." Anne grabbed the tonic bottle. "The change for you must be incredible. From big city prosecutor to housewife folding laundry. From constant crime to safety and calm. From black-tie dinners to blue jeans and boots." Anne swilled her drink. "And not knowing a soul in Montana when you moved? I couldn't do it."

From a nice fat salary to unemployment.

I opened my eyes as I paused to consider my life's monumental course correction. "Tough to explain, but it's as if I *had* to leave. Something bigger pushed me. I had to let go and let whatever it was move me to where I needed to be." I shook my head. "I must be hammered. That makes no sense."

Anne's greater size metabolized liquor far more efficiently. "Of course it makes sense. Look, we both have eight-year-old sons who instantly became best friends. We both have black labs the same age that play together constantly. We're Democrats, feminists, and spiritual. Just go with it." She finished her last sip of vodka. "And open some wine while you're at it. We need to remember this moment, even if it's by the size of the hangover."

I uncorked a cabernet, grabbed wine glasses since I still believed drinking wine from a cocktail glass showed the height of poor manners, and poured us each a finger of red. "You know I'm the soccer mom for our boys' team, right?"

Anne nodded.

"The coach? Your ex? He's a little tightly wrapped."

At this Anne coughed, spewing her wine. "A little? He's a narcissistic ass. I don't know how we lasted as long as we did. On the other hand, he's a good dad and a great lawyer. If you ever decide to practice up here, you should talk to him."

"I'm not practicing law again if I can help it. I want

to live life as a normal person for a change. Except," I swirled my wine, watching it dribble down the inside of my glass. "I'm an addict, Anne. A trial junkie. Once that adrenaline flows, I'm out of control, you know? I'm not sure I can give up that rush."

Anne hesitated. "I don't know if you're meant to retire." She placed her wine glass on the table and used her napkin to dab up the scattered droplets. "There's something about you that exudes . . . I don't know. Competence? Like you're the one people turn to with problems because you're smart enough and tough enough to fix them."

Ouch.

That hit too close to home. Mom, the fixer of all problems. Ms. Defalco, the one to win the tough cases. Paige, the wife who could do it all, all at the same time. Anne just described the woman from whom I'd fled. How had that same woman trailed me all the way to Montana?

Refilling our wine glasses, I tossed back two gulps with new resolve. I would *not* let that competent, crazy, possessed female take over my body again. I *would* spend my days watching soaps, folding laundry, and making homemade pizza crust. I would not practice law, I would never defend a criminal, and I would suppress my craving for the courtroom.

As my eyes glazed over, Annie slipped out the way she'd come in. Since the boys were at a sleepover and my daughter long ago asleep, I maneuvered to bed where I held one thought.

This hangover's gonna be a bitch.

* * *

With Halloween just weeks away, Anne and I stared at the cornfield skirting the pumpkin patch. Our boys screamed at each other as they wove their way through the tall stalks. Within moments only silence marked their paths.

I ran toward the yawning quiet, yelling my son's name, the name he'd inherited from his grandfather. "Sean! Where are you? Sean!" I turned around seeking Anne. "Jesus! I should have known better than to let him go in there." My breath caught as Anne ambled toward me.

She wrapped a flannel-shirted arm around my shoulders and smiled at me. "Paige, what do you think is going to happen to them in a little corn field in the middle of Kootenai County? Seriously, do you think your son will get kidnapped in there?" She shook her head and squeezed me closer. "You need to get a grip, girlfriend. You're not in California anymore."

No shit.

I eased out a little carbon dioxide, sucked in a bit of oxygen, and let my hyper-vigilance lapse to my normal paranoia. "Okay, I'm an idiot. Except I can't shake it, this incessant terror that evil will befall my kids if I don't pay constant attention."

Anne wandered around the pumpkins to select one for carving. "You mean unless you constantly worry. When are you going to get the message that you're not in charge of the world? All you can do is live each day, in the moment, and let whoever's choreographing the universe work out the rest?"

I huffed as I attempted to lift one of the heavier orange orbs. "Don't get all Zen on me, Annie. That touchy feely crap works for you, but I'm Catholic for God's sake. That means I excel at worry and guilt. Besides, I'm in the middle of a spiritual crisis, so turning to a higher power doesn't help."

I didn't mention that the priest at our new parish also seemed to be in crisis, evidenced by his hellfire and damnation ramblings. The kids and I sat at Mass each weekend transfixed by the old guy's dire warnings that we were all doomed, a foreign philosophy in the liberal parish we'd left behind in California.

As Anne and I paid for our pumpkins, the boys careened from the cornstalks, laughing, dusty, and carefree. I froze as I studied Sean, watching the smile that creased his small, pale face. Hay stuck out of his blond hair, his blue eyes glinted back at the afternoon sun, and his thin arms and legs pin-wheeled around his torso as he played the wild child.

My son.

Carefree.

Able to leap tall squashes in a single bound.

For the first time in his young life, free to ride his bike anywhere around town.

Free to be a kid.

I glanced east at snow-dusted mountains, north toward Beartooth, west toward the sun lowering over the hills, and knew for the first time that I'd made the right decision. We'd arrived where our family needed to be. More importantly, I believed that Montana held my memories of God. If I could let go of the fear that pervaded every cell in my body, I could tap into that mine of spiritual salvation.

First, however, I needed to carve a pumpkin, finish sewing costumes, put dinner on the table, fold the laundry, help with homework, and prepare for another visit from my beloved but recalcitrant spouse.

* * *

Anne volunteered her ex, Tim, to accompany Jack as they took the boys around on Halloween, while she and I stayed behind to feed the sugar frenzy of other kids coming to our doors.

Hours later, we grownups toasted the holiday. "Here's to making it through another Halloween without hidden razor blades or poison in the candy," I offered. Jack clinked his glass to mine. Anne and Tim stared at us, their faces expressing the same dismay on those of our friends in California.

"What I mean is—"

Anne held up her palm. "Don't even try to explain." She turned to Tim. "Paige and Jack are recovering crime junkies. Paige actually allows her kids out of the house now, unescorted, so they can walk to school with their friends. It's a major step."

Tim's brows rose, a bemused look in his eyes. "Are you two going into private practice up here?"

Jack's "Yes" slid out a nanosecond before my "No!" *Damn it.*

I wanted to *appear* normal. "That is, Jack might open a practice, but I've retired from law to be a full-time mom." I looked to Jack for affirmation. Instead, he scowled. I stumbled on. "Of course it depends on money and whether or not Jack ever really moves to Montana." This last part I bit out somewhat harshly.

Tim, ever smooth, smiled. "More wine?"

I noticed Anne had retired to the couch. I excused myself to sit beside her. "What's up? Too much ex-husband for one night?"

Anne leaned her head back. "I don't know. I think I'm just old. Did I mention that when I biked over Malta Pass last week, I had to stop half way?"

I shook my head. "Geez, Annie, I couldn't make it a tenth of the way up that road, so you only biking half a million miles instead of the full ride doesn't sound like you're aging. Besides, you're only 47."

She chuckled. "Yeah, we're still sweet young things, you and I. In any event, I have my annual checkup tomorrow. Can you handle the boys at your house?"

"No problem. You're probably anemic from that brown rice and vegetable diet you're on. Cheeseburgers and garlic fries from The Bulldog. That'll fix anything that ails you."

* * *

Well, almost anything.

But not cancer.

The next afternoon, Anne relayed to me her diagnosis, advanced breast cancer. At the news I felt a hole burrow into my heart. My mother died of advanced breast cancer when she was 53 and I only 14, before chemotherapy existed.

Anne's wan face turned to me, tears streaming down her pallid cheeks. "So, Paige," she whispered. We held hands as we sat on her couch. "I guess now we know why you were sent to Montana, to drive me to chemo and watch over my boy while I fight this thing."

I placed my arm around her shoulders. Did I imagine that they'd grown thinner? "We're going to beat this, Annie. Between your friends, your doctors, my faith, our prayers, and a little luck, you're going to be fine." I swiped at my own runny nose with a tissue. "Just fine."

My confidence belied the terror that flooded every cell in my body, forcing me back on high alert.

CHAPTER TWO

A Christmas Murder

Kootenai County, Montana
December 25, 1997

FOR RICH TRUMAN'S FAMILY, Christmas 1997 shattered any belief they'd held in divine justice.

After celebrating the holiday with their children and grandchildren, Rich and Nina Truman hosted a party for their employees at the Swan River Inn in Shelton, Montana. Rich Truman was a popular Kootenai County businessman who had done well for himself and his family. Nina and he owned a lovely home set on wooded acreage near the small town of Whitehall, just a few miles south of the Shelton motel.

The couple began their life together as high school sweethearts, and recently marked 40 years of marriage. Best friends, compatible business partners, dedicated parents, and close confidants, they appeared inseparable to those who knew them well.

That night they took separate cars to the party so that Nina, exhausted from preparing for the day's festivities, could leave early. Nearly 60, the couple no longer had as much energy as they did when they were younger. After sharing a goodnight kiss with the love of her life, Nina left the party around 10:00 p.m. and retired for a well-deserved rest as soon as she arrived home. She expected Rich to return soon.

Rich left the party an hour later after wishing his employees a Merry Christmas one last time. The temperature hovered at 14 degrees, leaving the night air dry and crisp. It had snowed earlier, covering the ground with a picturesque layer of fresh powder. Weary but content, Rich thanked God his Christmas had been so full of treasure for his family and friends. Indeed, his family and friends *were* his treasure in life.

As he turned down the private road leading to his house, and to the home he took care of for his neighbor, Dr. Sam Jaffee, Rich noticed a car's headlights in the Jaffee driveway. The birch and tamarack trees, devoid of summer foliage, revealed a partial glimpse of the house from the road. Driving closer, he also spotted Jaffee's open gate, the lock and chain that normally secured it now lying in the snow.

Suspecting vandals, Rich pulled out his cell phone as he drove up the winding route to Jaffee's home. He noted fresh tire tracks in the snow and followed them to a small Ford Tempo parked near Jaffee's shed. The shed door stood ajar. Rich saw someone in the driver's seat of the Ford and thought he glimpsed another figure dart into the forest adjacent to the property.

As he pulled his pickup in front of the car, Rich's eyes caught 11:45 on the dashboard clock. He called 911, but when the call didn't connect, he realized he was out of cell range. Irritated, he left his phone on the seat of the truck, cautiously stepped out, and approached the driver's side of the car. He saw the driver raise both hands in surrender, but remained wary lest the driver pull out a weapon. This was, after all, Montana, where nearly everyone packed all manner of pistols, rifles, and knives.

Rich knew no one should be at Jaffee's house, especially late on Christmas night. The driver squinted from the truck's brighter headlights, a temporary blindness Rich counted on when he parked directly in front of the Ford. He fervently hoped to prevent the driver from aiming accurately if he had a gun, enabling

Rich to disarm him before the fool really did something dangerous.

Rich assumed he'd interrupted a teenage prank, played by typical teenage knuckleheads, looking for something to do on yet another boring night in Whitehall. The county's crime rate was one of the lowest in the U.S. and mostly involved DUIs, neighbor disputes, and domestic violence. Certainly, few residents risked becoming a homicide victim. After all, that's why so many Californians moved to Kootenai County. It was such a safe place to live.

The driver, a teenager, took off his gloves, still with his hands raised, and said, "It's okay. I'm safe, sir."

"You have any guns on you?"

"No, sir," the young man replied politely.

"Do you understand you're trespassing on private property?"

"Yes, sir."

"What are you guys doing here?" Rich inquired, in part to see if the kid was alone, or if, as Rich suspected, an accomplice had run into the bushes.

"Just fooling around, sir," answered the driver.

"What's your name?"

"Joe Smith, sir."

Rich nearly laughed out loud. "Where's the other guy?" he queried instead.

"He's out by the gate where you came in," the teen responded, now looking nervous, but confirming Rich's suspicions.

"Looks to me like you boys are burglars and I caught you in the act. Give me the key to your ignition."

The kid handed over the key.

Rich asked for the kid's driver's license, while he looked through the back window of the car. He spotted a revolver lying on the passenger side of the back seat. Rich opened the rear door, climbed in the back, and grabbed the gun, all in one swift motion. He pointed the gun at the driver and asked him if it was loaded, to which the driver, now angry, replied tightly, "Yes, sir."

Rich, growing angrier himself, told the driver to hand over his wallet. The teen complied. Rich felt tired, cranky, and cold. He hadn't planned on standing in the snow with some snot-nosed, little burglar. His wool plaid shirt, jeans, and cowboy boots were insufficient protection against this kind of cold. He wanted to go home, crawl in bed next to Nina, and sleep.

Still holding the gun, although no longer aiming it at the kid in case it accidentally discharged, he looked at the driver's license in the wallet. He quickly realized he knew this young man, or at least knew about him. The driver was a local hero, winning race after race in various wheelchair competitions. This would-be burglar was the same kid who had overcome personal tragedy and turned his paralysis, at the age of 11, into a talent and inspiration for other disabled kids.

Before Rich could ask the many questions that crowded his exhausted brain, the local hero pulled out a blued-steel .22 revolver from its hidden spot between the front seats. He aimed it at Rich's heart and fired four rounds at point blank range, all before Rich ever hit the ground. As Rich fell, the other revolver he'd taken from the Ford's back seat bounced to the ground. The car's ignition key flew into the air as the contents of the driver's wallet spilled onto the snow.

Rich looked at his own chest, at the blood pouring forth, and heard his breath coming in gasps. The echo of his own screams reverberated through the silence of that clear, winter night, as he desperately tried to move away from the car. But the driver, hands steady, leaned out his window and shot Rich two more times, emptying his gun. Still Rich crawled, away from the Ford, away from his killer, away from his imminent death.

He made it four feet before he sensed the presence of another person. Whoever it was, Rich could hear the newcomer crying, then scream at the driver, "Nick, oh my God! What have you done? What have you done? We need to get help! Call an ambulance! Oh, my God, Nick!" Rich heard more sobbing and then heard the driver order his cohort to finish him off. The kid who was crying refused and begged the driver, "Just go! Let's just go and get help!"

Rich Truman felt cold seep through his Pendleton shirt. He remembered when he'd put it on earlier in the evening, wondering if it was 'dressy' enough for the Christmas party. He thought of Nina sleeping peacefully across the way, and of his children and grandchildren, safe and sound in their own homes. He felt blessed they weren't with him, that he and Nina had taken separate cars. He wondered how she would cope without him.

Rich looked up at the Ford Tempo as the driver pulled the car forward. The wheelchair racer slowly and deliberately drew yet another gun, sighted down the barrel, and shot Rich one last time, even as Rich put his hand in front of his chest in a feeble effort to stop the bullet.

* * *

A few hours later, Nina awoke to an empty place in the bed where Rich should have lain. And then she sensed, as only wives can sense after decades of marriage, that something was terribly wrong. She called their son-in-law, Paul, who jumped in his own truck and headed toward the Truman's house.

As Paul approached, he, too, saw headlights at the Jaffee place, but they shone from Rich's truck. He cautiously drove up the long driveway, unaware that a terrified youth watched from the forest just beside the road. When he reached Rich's truck, the first thing he saw was his father-in-law's body, covered in blood, laying in a pool of blood-soaked snow. Paul called 911, and his call, unlike Rich's, connected.

As Paul waited for the sheriffs and an ambulance, still unable to comprehend why Rich died, Nina approached from her home across the way. He tried to stop her, to protect her, but she knew, somehow she already knew, that Rich was dead. She sobbed as she knelt beside her husband and kissed him. She held his lifeless body and repeatedly shook her head, denying the obvious.

The love of her life had been murdered.

* * *

The slaying confounded local law enforcement. Deputies at the crime scene puzzled over two sets of footprints left in the snow, one large and one small, both running in circular, incongruous patterns throughout the area. The prints trailed as far as a mile away, where they abruptly ended at the road. The investigators matched the tire marks left in Dr. Jaffee's driveway to tracks left at numerous, unsolved, storage unit break-ins around the county.

Yet even after chasing down multiple leads, even after accusing Nina and her son of killing Rich for the insurance policy he left, the cops failed to identity Rich's killer. So, for the first time in recent memory, the people of Kootenai County were afraid of something other than grizzly bears.

They were afraid of each other.

CHAPTER THREE

A Different View of Murder

Just after midnight
Whitehall, Montana – December 26, 1997

WHEN NICK STAGG NOTICED Rich Truman's headlights turn into the long Jaffee driveway, he quietly spoke into his radio headset. He calmly informed his little brother, Ben, that they had company.

Listening from his own headset, Ben, about to leave the house after placing his stolen treasures outside the window from which he'd entered, froze. He'd done just what Nick told him to do when he broke into the Jaffee house. He'd taken stuff he thought was cool: a roll of quarters, a hand saw with a pretty picture of Kootenai Lake painted on it, and a wooden duck decoy, brightly stained to resemble a Mallard.

Ben dropped the loot on the ground, clambered out the broken window, and ran toward the car. Without thinking, he changed directions, breathlessly whispering through his microphone to tell Nick he would run through the forest and meet him later at a certain spot on the road. Then Ben ran as fast he could into the trees. Still wearing his headset, however, he couldn't escape Nick's voice screaming at him to come back to the car.

"Ben, you come back here! You can't leave me! Get back! Stick to the plan, Benjie. It's okay. Just stick to the plan!"

Ben ran in ever-widening circles, then in paths back and forth, terrified of getting caught, terrified of his older brother's anger. He couldn't think, he could barely breathe. He wanted to run as fast as he could away from the house and the stranger who steadily drove up the driveway. Yet Nick's threats and screams finally penetrated his befuddled brain. More terrified of Nick than the stranger, Ben raced back to Nick's car.

Nick handed Ben a shotgun and told him to run into the forest. "When you get a clear shot, take it," Nick shouted as Ben took off running again.

Ben crouched behind a tree and watched Rich Truman's pickup wend its way up the snowy road. Nick's voice demanded over the headset, "Ben, don't you fail me now. You shoot this guy when you get the chance, damn it!"

Ben, in tears, scared beyond all reason, answered haltingly, "I can't . . . I can't do it, Nick. I can't shoot." He paused. "Promise you'll just give up like you said you would if somebody caught us."

Nick could hear Ben crying as the truck neared within yards of his own sedan. "Okay, Bro, okay, just calm down and be quiet. I'll take care of it. Stay out of sight."

I should have killed him when I had the chance, Nick thought grimly.

Ben was a pain in the ass, a crybaby who never caught on to Nick's plans. No matter where he sent Ben, Ben screwed it up. Nick briefly recalled the very first thing Ben ever took for Nick. Nick told him to take something of value from a neighbor's garage. Ben, weeping as usual, finally came back to the car with a rusted shovel. Worse, at the first house they'd burglarized two months earlier, Nick carefully explained to Ben he should steal anything with a plug so Nick could use it to beef up his personal computer. Nick considered himself an expert at computer technology.

Ben returned from the house, crying, but proudly

presented Nick with a toaster.

Nick shook his head to clear his thoughts of Ben's idiocy.

This is the moment I've planned for, for the last three months, he reminded himself. *If this guy identifies me or calls the cops, I'm killing him.* Nick made sure he hid another pistol between the two seats, then raised his hands in the air and removed his gloves, as if in surrender.

Breathe, man, he told himself. *Stay calm.*

Nick gave Ben one last command. "No more contact, Abe."

Abe was the crime name he'd assigned Ben, but Ben always forgot to use it, just like he forgot to use Nick's own crime name, Zock. Nick didn't know why he'd chosen those names. Maybe they reminded him of Cain and Abel.

Yeah, Zock and Abe, Cain and Abel.

How apt a comparison when he finally killed Ben and buried him in the forest. Then he'd use his little sister, Megan, as his legs. Even though she was only fourteen, she was much smarter than Ben and so much more loyal to her oldest brother. Besides, she had guts and didn't cry like a baby the way Ben always did. Nick smiled despite his nervousness and the bright lights from the stranger's truck glaring in his face.

As the stranger approached the driver's side, Nick yelled out, "It's okay. I'm safe, Sir."

* * *

Ben closed his eyes in relief as he saw Nick raise his arms in surrender when the stranger walked up. Ben never wanted to play Nick's crime games in the first place, and now he shook more from fear than cold. He just wanted to go home to his parents' house and sleep, but he didn't dare anger Nick.

Nick was Ben's best friend in the world, his lifeline, his protector. Ben realized he couldn't think things out by himself, make decisions, or readily comprehend what people said. Sometimes he could understand Nick, except when Nick gave him too many things to steal, or told him ahead of time how to break into strange places.

If people spoke in long sentences, all the sounds in Ben's head garbled the words. That constant roar of noise muffled the speaking world, but Ben couldn't silence it no matter how hard he tried. It seemed to Ben like a thousand television sets simultaneously played in his brain, but blared on different channels.

That's why Nick made him wear the two-way radio headset. Ben felt so stupid because he couldn't reason on his own or follow directions.

He felt his eyes tear up again and despised himself for acting like a girl. He hated himself anyway, for being so retarded and dumb; for making everyone mad all the time when he didn't understand; for looking like a scarecrow instead of a grown man; for his weird habit of smiling when he was scared or nervous. Ben hated himself almost as much as he hated his life.

That's why he had to be Nick's partner. He felt important when Nick counted on him for stuff. It gave Ben a purpose in life, a reason to get out of bed in the morning. At barely eighteen years old, Ben had nothing to look forward to - no job, no girlfriend, no place of his own to live, few friends, and no chance of ever going to college or being someone normal. There were times when Ben wondered what God had been thinking when he sent Ben to earth.

Ben's thoughts cleared only when he paddled his kayak down the nearest river. In those moments, Ben found peace from the chaos that constantly invaded his head. Remembering that his dad had taken his kayak away a few weeks earlier, as punishment, Ben allowed his anger to seethe. Still, the loss hurt less than the whippings.

Now, as Ben huddled behind the tree in the forest, he wished more than anything he could just ride down the river in that kayak - away from Nick, away from his parents, away from the world. Instead, it looked like he and Nick were going to jail for stealing. He couldn't imagine what punishment his dad would mete out for that, but he'd rather face his parents than Nick when Nick was mad at him.

The sound of firecrackers suddenly permeated Ben's brain, interrupting his memories and confusing him further. Did people shoot off fireworks on Christmas night? And then he knew, as only one brother can sense about the other, that Nick had done something horrible.

Ben grabbed the shotgun and ran toward Nick's car, tearing off his headset on the way. As he neared the Ford Tempo, he saw a man lying on the ground, blood seeping onto his plaid shirt, crawling slowly away from the car. He heard the man's screams and stared, horrified, as Nick shot the man two more times.

Ben heard himself scream, then sob, shouting at his brother, "Nick! Oh my God, Nick! What have you done? What have you done? We have to get help! Call an ambulance!"

Nick gazed at Ben as if at a stranger, then took out a .45 and held it out to his brother. "Take it, Ben!" he barked. "Finish him off! Do it! *Now!*"

Ben took it, but backed away from Nick and the murderous look on his face. He'd already set the shotgun on the trunk of Nick's car, and he now prepared to run.

Nick, knowing what a chickenshit his little brother was, pulled out one more revolver, a .357, and sighted down its barrel. He wanted to shoot Ben as much as finish off the asshole who'd nearly landed them in jail, but he needed Ben to clean up the crime scene and get away. Nick turned the gun toward the helpless human in the snow.

"No, Nick! Just go - just go get help!" Ben backed up further toward Truman's truck, setting down the .45 weapon Nick just forced on him.

The truck's lights illuminated his brother leaning out the driver's side window while he pointed his firearm at the victim. Rich Truman crawled a few more inches, raising his hand to his chest. Nick pulled his car forward and delivered a final shot.

That's when Ben Stagg ran for his life, and away from the killer he'd once called brother.

* * *

Ben plowed through the dark forest, into a nearby meadow, toward a pond frozen over with ice. Then he ran back toward his brother, around trees, through bushes, and finally stopped, panting and terrified. Ben had little stamina on a good day, none after witnessing his hero shoot an innocent stranger in cold blood. Through his noise-filled haze of confusion, he heard Nick's screams from the Jaffee place.

"Ben, come back! Don't leave me here! I need help! Help me, Ben, please help me!"

So Ben, as if on autopilot, responded as he always did when Nick begged him for help. He stumbled back to the car, and at Nick's direction, scooped up the scattered contents of Nick's wallet, along with a brown envelope covered in snow and the pistol Truman had grabbed from the Ford's back seat. He threw all of it onto the floor of the sedan's rear compartment. He grabbed the shotgun off the trunk of Nick's Tempo and threw that in the backseat, as he hurriedly jumped into the front.

Nick maneuvered his car around Truman's pickup

and raced to the highway, sped north to the next right turn, and careened toward their parents' home on Brander Road, undetected by man or dog.

Safe.

.

CHAPTER FOUR

The Devil is in the Details

Twenty minutes after the murder
Whitehall, Montana – December 26, 1997

SHIT! WE HAVE TO GO BACK, Nick thought in a panic as he stared at the spare key he'd jammed into his ignition.

As Ben shivered in the passenger seat, his sobs cutting the night's silence, Nick pulled the Tempo into the parking lot of a local business near the Stagg family home. He realized the dead man had dropped the main set of keys to Nick's car. Nick had grabbed a spare key in his glove compartment to restart his engine and escape.

Nick turned to his little brother. "Listen to me. You have to go back. That guy took my car keys, and they must have fallen near where he landed in the snow. If the police find them, they can trace the car to me." Nick's breath came in short, shaky gasps. "They'll arrest us and put us in prison. I can't let that happen. You have to go back to the body and get those keys."

Ben slowly raised his head, shaking it from side to side. He wiped his nose on his sleeve. "No way. I'm not going back there. I don't care if they put you in prison. You *should* go to prison! You just killed a man, and God is *never* going to forgive you."

"Just think about this for a second. We have to hurry. If the cops get me, they'll get you too. What will Mom and Dad say, Benjie?" Nick leaned forward and patted Ben's face, trying to get him to snap out of his shock-induced stupor. Ben jerked away, swatting at Nick's hand.

"I didn't do anything, Nick!" Ben shouted. "I didn't shoot anybody, I didn't kill anybody! Only you did that! Mom and Dad will forgive me."

Nick moved closer, his face inches from Ben's, confident he could manipulate Ben into returning to the scene. He remembered his brother's refusal to deliver the final kill shot and realized that was the first time Ben had refused any of Nick's orders or requests. Since Nick had decided he couldn't risk another drive back to the murder scene, Ben would have to go on foot. Besides, if the cops caught anyone, better to catch Ben than him.

Nick quieted his temper. "Yes, you did Benjie. You burglarized that house. You were there when I killed that guy. That makes you just as guilty as me. If the cops arrest me, they'll arrest you, too. So you need to calm down and go back there to find those keys. Now, Ben!"

Nick reached across Ben to open the passenger door and shoved on Ben's shoulder. As Ben unwound his skinny body to leave the car, Nick made a vow to himself.

I'll remember this rebellion, Little Brother. It just cost you your life.

* * *

Defeated by his inability to reason through to the truth, Ben climbed out of the car, into the freezing darkness. Nick had parked over a mile from the Jaffe house, so Ben needed to run through the forest to return to the body. Nick made him wear the headset, as always. His legs felt like concrete, anger washed his brain, while nausea roiled his stomach. He wanted to die and prayed God would take him before either the police or his parents realized what the brothers had done.

When Ben got to Truman's body, he shook violently as his sobs ended in huge gulps. He again used the sleeves of his coat to wipe tears from his eyes and snot from his nose, desperately trying to locate the missing keys. He couldn't find them, even with aid from the headlights of Truman's truck, which Ben had forgotten to turn off in his panic to leave earlier. Those lights also illuminated Truman's bloody corpse, a sight Ben hoped never to view again, even in his nightmares.

He spoke into the headset, telling Nick he couldn't locate the keys. "I'm leaving without them. I gotta get out of here."

Nick's voice screeched through the headset, "Find the keys! Find the damned keys! They can trace my car through those keys!"

"Nick," Ben pleaded, "They're not here. I've looked everywhere around the the . . . body . . . and there's nothing."

"Okay, listen to me. You have to move his body. The keys are probably under his body because he was holding onto them when he fell, and then he crawled. Just roll the body over until you can see underneath. Go on. You have to do it." Nick's tone was stentorian, yet laced with panic.

"I can't," Ben whimpered. "Please don't make me do that! I can't touch him. I can't even look at him."

"Do it. *Now.* The police could come any second. Do you want to spend the rest of your life in jail? Do you want the death penalty?"

Ben leaned over Truman's body and pulled on an arm. The body didn't budge. Ben was so puny, so weak, that he could barely handle Truman's much greater weight. Finally he got down on his knees, in the blood-soaked snow, and pushed Truman's body as hard as he could. The corpse rolled, and since it was on a slight downhill path, turned over again as it gained momentum.

Ben was thrown forward, into the bloody area the body just vacated. When his hands landed in the crimson mess, his cries sliced through the silent night.

And then he felt a set of keys.

"I've got them!" Ben grabbed those keys and held tightly to them, as if they represented the keys to the Kingdom of Heaven.

Nick sagged into the driver's seat of his Tempo. "Great. Now get one more thing. I want you to take the guy's wallet out of his back pocket and bring it to me. I need to know the name of the man I killed."

Ben cringed away from the man's body, but saw the outline of a wallet in the man's back jeans pocket. With two fingers, Ben pulled it out. "That's it, Nick. No more."

Ben ran toward Nick's parked car, cutting through bushes, jumping over logs, tripping several times and falling in the darkness. Still Ben dragged himself up, making the mile or so to the Ford in record speed, especially for him. If Nick said anything over the headset, Ben missed it. He didn't think. Instead, he acted like a robot, cold and desolate.

Yet Ben's impoverished spirit couldn't compare to his broken heart.

* * *

Again Ben sat in the front seat, refusing eye contact with his brother, ignoring Nick's feeble attempts at conversation. When they arrived at Nick's condo, Nick ordered Ben to wipe off the blood spatter on the side of the Ford with some rags from the garage. Ben, zombie-like from shock, rubbed the car then dropped the rag, leaving Rich Truman's bodily fluid on tires and rusted metal.

Nick overlooked the failed clean-up attempt and

helped Ben inside. He directed Ben to the bathroom, where Nick drew a hot bath and stripped Ben of his snow and blood-stiffened clothing. Once Ben soaked, Nick changed from his own crime outfit and loaded all of their garb into the washer. He did his best to clean the blood from Ben's shoes, leaving them in the kitchen to dry. He retrieved Ben from the tub, wrapped him in blankets, and helped him to the couch. Not long after, he moved their clean clothes to the dryer.

Nick glanced at the gold medals hanging on the wall that he'd won for wheelchair racing. That sport had made Nick strong, both physically and mentally. Nick worked his upper body every day, creating sufficient strength to lift Ben, compete with able-bodied cops in wheelchair basketball, or walk on his hands, with Ben holding his legs, all the way down to the lake and back.

Ben, on the other hand, sat like a bag of bones, weighing less than their little sister. Ben had no upper body strength and so little developed muscle, his shoulders clacked together when he slept on his side. Clearly, the little brother with the legs stood as no match against the older, paralyzed brother possessed of both brawn and brains.

For the next four hours, Ben sat on Nick's couch, unblinking, silent, as he rocked back and forth like an autistic child. Likely his brain emptied of thought, as well as the perpetual noise of the televisions. Spiritually, it seemed the young boy named Ben Stagg died that Christmas night.

Nick watched his little brother rock on the couch, as paralyzed from fear as Nick was from his severed spine. He pondered how to silence Ben before the moron did or said something stupid that revealed their guilt.

Nick was not going to prison, of that he was certain. He could blame Ben if they were caught. No one would believe that Nick, the pitiful, helpless kid in the wheelchair, actually killed someone out in the middle of nowhere on Christmas night. Nick played basketball with the cops, and they all believed he was a good guy. They'd never suspect him or his retarded younger sibling of murder, unless Nick pointed them in Ben's direction.

With his back-up plan firmly in mind, Nick replayed every detail during the night's evil deeds. He had no remorse. He actually felt kind of high, powerful for the first time in his life. He could even imagine killing another person, but never again with Ben present. What a mistake to take him along on these escapades.

Lesson learned. Solution to follow shortly.

As he reflected, Nick remembered the gun he'd handed to Ben just after Nick shot the old man six times. He'd demanded Ben shoot the bastard, but Ben had refused.

What did Ben do with that gun?

Oh, fuck! I killed that guy four hours ago. The cops may be there by now.

Again panicked, Nick wheeled into the kitchen, to the table where all the guns lay, about to undergo a thorough cleaning. He counted them, knowing exactly how many he'd taken to the Jaffee house.

And came up one short.

* * *

Nick couldn't believe what was happening. He thought they were in the clear and now it looked like they had to go back to the murder scene yet again, all because his stupid, dumb-ass, little brother had left that gun somewhere. Nick took care to procure guns with their serial numbers removed, but for the life of him, literally, he couldn't remember if the gun he handed Ben could be traced to him. He slowly rolled back to the couch where Ben sat, still silent, not even rocking.

Nick wanted to scream at him, *you scrawny little shit*, but he knew if he did, Ben would freak out again, maybe even run away or go to the cops. So Nick adopted his most persuasive voice and said, "Ben? Hey, listen to me. We left a gun at that house. Remember the one I handed to you to shoot that guy, but you refused? What did you do with it?"

Ben sat silent, as if in a trance. "Ben! Pay attention!" Nick slapped Ben's knee. "This is important. We're missing a gun, and you had it last. Can you hear me, Bro?"

Ben slowly focused on his former hero. "I'm not going back there. You can threaten to kill me like usual. I don't care. Shoot me. Kill me. I'm not going back." He looked down at his lap, covered by a green wool blanket.

Nick, exhausted as the rush of the shooting abated, knew he couldn't get the gun himself. Although he was good at maneuvering on his hands, he wouldn't be able to do that in snow and ice. He needed his hands to search and that meant dragging his body through the murder scene. What kind of telltale evidence would those tracks leave?

"C'mon, Ben. This is our future, our freedom. We could be put to death for this, and you're just as guilty as I am because you were there. The cops and judges won't care that you didn't shoot him. You were there when I killed him. If you don't go back again, they'll find the gun and arrest us. Think what that will do to Mom and Dad, to Megan."

No response.

"We'll never survive in prison. Do you know what it's like? Do you want to be raped by a bunch of thugs? Ben? Answer me, man!"

Mute, Ben simply stared past his brother.

Determined, Nick retrieved Ben's clean clothes from the dryer and somehow got him dressed. Ben's shoes were too wet and cold to wear, so Nick shoved a pair of his own size 7 loafers on Ben's size 11 feet.

Nick herded Ben to the Ford and drove to a different parking spot, this time on a highway across from the Baptist church where their father served as associate pastor. Once again, Nick outfitted Ben with the radio headset. He reached across his zombie brother, opened the passenger door, and shoved Ben out of the car to retrieve the missing gun.

* * *

Bewildered, Ben turned the headset off to shut out Nick's voice. He ran in Nick's vise-like shoes through the snow and ice, his feet rapidly growing numb from the cold. He reached a small pond and ran onto its ice cover, hearing too late the sound from the cracking ice. He knew he could fall through and drown, so he prayed as hard as he could that the ice would break.

At that moment, Ben Stagg wanted the good Lord to take him to heaven because the hell he faced was more than he could bear.

He felt abandoned by God when he made it to the other side without dying but loped ahead to the body of Rich Truman. Almost five hours had passed since Nick killed the man, so Ben expected to see cops. To his great relief, no one was there. Truman's truck lights were still on, faint but affording Ben a dim view of the scene.

Everything was just as he'd left it several hours before. His tears flowed as he again gazed at the corpse, now stiffened and covered in early morning frost. He couldn't remember what he'd done with the gun before he ran away. He approached the front of the truck, hoping the gun had fallen within the weak light rays emanating from the headlamps.

And there it was, right on top of the truck's hood

where Ben had set it down after he refused to shoot Nick's victim. *Thank you, God!*

Ben grabbed the gun and ran, this time along the forest near the driveway. To his horror, he saw another vehicle approach, creeping cautiously up the Jaffee's snowy road. Terrified, Ben crouched behind some rocks, hidden by bushes and trees, and watched as the pickup drove past him.

As soon as the truck passed, Ben darted across the pavement and dove into the forest on the other side. He ran as best he could in the tiny loafers, finally reaching the highway where Nick should have been waiting.

Except he wasn't there.

No Nick. No car.

Panicked, Ben turned on his headset and screamed for Nick, who answered with a tone of annoyance. Nick's voice perked up when Ben told him he'd found the missing gun. Within seconds Nick pulled up, and Ben climbed into the front seat, tossing the gun in the back.

As they drove south toward Nick's condo, a patrol car passed them going in the opposite direction, its red and blue lights flashing. Moments later an ambulance passed, also dispatched as a Code 3, its siren splitting the night. Those emergency lights and sirens signaled more than the discovery of Rich Truman's body.

They tolled a death knell for the Stagg brothers' chance at surrender.

CHAPTER FIVE

The Geography of Normal

New Year's Eve
Beartooth, Montana - 1997

JUST AFTER OUR FIRST CHRISTMAS in the little town of Beartooth, Montana, Jack and I awoke early, let the now giant Bob Dog outside, fought him for the newspaper, and won that battle but just barely.

On this late December morning, snow covered everything as the temperature hit *colder than a well-digger's ass*. Ensconced in front of the fire, the dog munching a bone and the kids asleep, Jack and I sipped our coffee as we skimmed through the local events reported in the *Kootenai Gazette*.

"Holy shit. Did you see this?" That morning Jack grabbed the front page before the sports page, while I looked through the post-Christmas ads.

"What?" I focused on cashing in on the latest bargains. I didn't need a thing, but entertainment was in short supply in Kootenai County, so shopping had become a recreational sport.

"A guy named Rich Truman was murdered in Whitehall on Christmas night. Shot to death. His son-in-law found the body in the snow at a neighbor's house. They think the dead guy interrupted a burglary, but are clueless about suspects. Truman was a well known businessman in the valley."

Jack noted these facts with relish. He loved a good homicide.

Burned out as I was, avoiding the real world as much as possible, the new and reformed me - The Mom - didn't want to hear the details. I was done with blood and guts, done with gore, done with sadness. Now I was a soccer mom, housewife, and an almost reverent teacher of religious education at the local Catholic Church. I'd even given up swearing, more or less.

"Jesus," he continued. "It says the dead guy's wife came across the road and found his body just after the police arrived. She actually held the corpse before the cops took the body away. Christ Almighty! Where have you moved us, anyway?"

I looked up from the small appliance ads. Despite his heretical exclamations, he'd asked a fair question.

"Well, it isn't heaven, I admit, but crime happens everywhere. One homicide every few years is hardly Fairfax or Richland on a daily basis. Besides, it's probably a family member who killed him in a drunken stupor. Typical holiday killing."

"Yeah, true, although your basic holiday homicide usually has one guy stab the other guy with the turkey-carving knife at the kitchen table." Jack picked up the sports page. Right on cue he launched into his next anti-Montana rant. "This fucking newspaper! How do they even call themselves reporters? There isn't one score in here for the Niners or Raiders and nothing about the final results of the Cal game."

Thankfully our daughter emerged from her bedroom just then.

"Dad, what are you yelling about?" Claire asked rhetorically, for it seemed Jack frequently yelled about something during his brief visits from California.

"I'm not yelling. I'm just animated."

Claire rolled her eyes in standard 13-year-old fashion. "So Mom, are we hitting the sales today? Can we leave Dad and Sean here? Where's Bob? Did he get off his leash again? He's just a puppy! He isn't just running through the neighborhood, is he? You know that farmer will shoot him --"

I cut her off before she revved up to turbine whine. "Calm down. Bob's in the kitchen. Yes, we can hit the sales, and yes, we can leave the guys here. I doubt we could drag them to Aberdeen anyway."

And that colloquy pretty well summed up the Defalco family's reaction in December 1997 to the murder of Rich Truman and the devastation of his family. So focused were we on our new life, we gave no to thought to theirs. Besides, for Jack and me, homicide was just that - another murder.

No big deal.

* * *

A few days after Rich Truman's murder in Whitehall, while Bob dragged us behind him on his daily walk around Beartooth, I panted out, "I invited the neighbors to dinner tomorrow night."

"Which neighbors?" Jack queried, barely winded even though he held Bob's leash and served as the 135-pound counter-weight to the dog's 110-pound pull.

"The banker guy and his wife. Here's the thing. I haven't exactly told people I'm a lawyer, so I don't want you telling war stories about the D.A.'s office tomorrow night. These people are normal, and I want them to think we're normal."

Jack managed to stop Bob, who sniffed the ground for anything edible to add to his considerable size. "What's that supposed to mean? We *are* normal."

My turn to do the 13-year-old eye roll. "Oh please. We are so far from normal, we wouldn't recognize it if it bit us in the ass."

"Tell me what's not normal about our family," he

demanded. As Bob took off after a squirrel, Jack nearly fell from the jerk on the leash.

"Let me count the ways. Our careers, for starters. We look at dead, dying, and decimated people all day and then talk about the details with each other at night. You're considered a holy terror at your office, and I finally wigged out at mine. Our friends in California rightly think we're morbid and depressing. Our families are bizarre. You don't even talk to your sisters anymore, your mom's been lying in a vegetative state for the last ten years, and my brothers and I rarely call each other. And my asshole father and I haven't spoken a word in a decade, the son of a bitch."

Evidently, cursing was tough to abandon.

"Our kids are both learning disabled, and Claire is so shy, I'm not sure she'll ever make a friend here. Sean can't read, write, or do jumping jacks, but his teacher says she can read him complicated math problems that he solves in his head. He seems happy, but he also seems to live on a different planet half the time and just pops out with these random, albeit interesting, thoughts."

Bob gained speed in his pursuit of the squirrel, forcing us to jog.

"Our *dog* is out of control," I continued, gasping. "Even this studded choke collar doesn't keep him in line, and that million volt underground fence you installed doesn't faze him. He looks at me, gets zapped, and runs away. We go to Mass at a church that is archaic, led by a priest who is bitter and rants about all of us burning in Hell. And as a family, we sit around the table and argue religion and politics with an eight-year-old and a 13-year-old. The eight-year-old just announced he's a Republican, by the way. I feel like I'm living with Alex P. Keaton in a weird version of *Family Ties*."

Apparently I'd gained Jack's attention. Bob was now running the ditch next to the road, the thin layer of ice shattering under his weight, letting him play in the murky ice-cold water below.

"Sean thinks he's a Republican?" The little Republican's father laughed.

"My *point* is that people here are normal. They don't talk politics or religion, and they certainly don't discuss macerated eyeballs, incinerated corpses, and blood spatter patterns. They don't relish reviewing autopsy reports and crime scene photos or recreating bullet paths through somebody's brain." I paused to draw a breath. "They have normal jobs, like teaching and delivering bottled water. They live humbly, in normal houses, and drive American cars. No one here is pretentious. They eat normal food, don't want to know about kalamata olives and goat cheese, and don't sniff at corks from expensive wine."

I rubbed my gloved hands together. "I want to become normal. I'm tired of not fitting in. I don't want people here to know I'm an over-educated, ex-Berkeley granola-head, at least not until I'm ready to tell them. For once, despite my red hair, I want to blend in, to disappear."

I stood still, giving Jack a chance to respond to my diatribe.

"So we're a little eccentric, Paige. We are who we are. You can't hide behind white bread and Velveeta. We've worked hard for every dime we have and made it as lawyers because we prepare our cases and take risks in the courtroom." Bob lunged at a bird on an overhead power line, launching Jack forward several feet. "Bob! Knock it off!"

Exasperated, Jack turned back to me. "Look, you can try to be normal, however you define that, but you'll never succeed. You're unique. So am I, and so are the kids. You have red hair and freckles, you're tall, you're smart, and you care about people and causes. None of that has changed in the 20 years I've known you, and moving to Montana isn't going to erase your identity."

We were almost home, and Bob could smell the barn, as it were, now tugging even harder on his leash, despite the collar's prongs digging into his neck.

"Fuck it," Jack muttered as he cut Bob loose and watched him race away.

I stared at him, incredulous. "Are you *nuts?*"

"Relax. He'll come home when he's ready."

"Fine. Then you deal with your hysterical daughter when the farmer shoots him." I stormed up the driveway to the house. Still, I made sure to smile and wave at the neighbors so they wouldn't realize how crazy we were, especially the ones who were coming for dinner.

* * *

In Whitehall, Nick and Ben Stagg also strove to blend in. For several weeks, they kept quiet about Christmas night, 1997, Ben hiding in the relative safety of his family home, refusing even to take Nick's repeated phone calls. Nick, undaunted by remorse, planned his next caper. He recognized he would need a new partner in crime, since his stupid little brother would soon meet His Maker, at least if Nick had any input.

So, Nick groomed his little sister, Megan. Megan, just 14, idolized Nick at least as much as Ben did. She longed to help Nick in whatever way she could, even if it meant committing felonies. Yet Nick told her she wasn't quite ready, but soon she'd be trained to take Ben's place. Meanwhile, Nick knew he could force Ben to help him one more time.

As the next month passed, neither the Defalcos nor the Staggs suspected their paths would soon cross, but all would eventually agree on one thing.

Murder isn't normal, regardless of geography.

CHAPTER SIX

Oh Lord, Please Don't Let Me Be Misunderstood

February 10, 1998
Whitehall, Montana

"GERONIMO!" Sean screamed before cannon-balling into the indoor-outdoor pool at a local motel. I ducked the splash and smiled as I watched our son celebrate his ninth birthday with his buddies.

Unlike fancy birthday events in California, complete with clowns, ponies, and expensive goody bags filled with toys, these Montana boys thrived on swimming in a pool surrounded by several feet of snow as they shoveled pizza after pizza into their growing bodies.

Typical mom, I ruminated over how quickly the last nine years had passed. I worried again about Sean's inability to read, but sighed knowing that our move to this hinterland at last allowed Sean to be a kid.

* * *

Thirty miles south of the birthday party, Ben Stagg, another kid who couldn't read very well, laid on his bed while he talked to God. He ignored the insistent ring of the telephone, knowing that Nick waited on the other end to demand that Ben come over to his condo. He tried to ignore his mother's screaming rant at his little sister, the two going at it once again in the downstairs kitchen.

Ben clutched his tattered Bible in both hands,

squeezed his eyes shut, and drifted to that special place in his head where the chaos of every day life never reached.

"Okay, Lord," Ben mumbled softly, "Nick killed that man, and there's no way I can forgive him. I hate him. I can't even believe he's my brother." He paused to take a deep breath. "But I didn't kill anyone, Lord. I know I'm stupid and all, leastways that's what everyone tells me, but I'm not a killer." Another long inhale. "I need your help, God, just like you always promise, that you'll be here for us when we need you most. Well, I need you now more than I ever have in my whole life."

The only response Ben heard came from the second hand of his clock ticking the time at one o'clock. He clenched his hands a bit tighter around The Good Book, as if he could squeeze out a celestial answer. "If I tell Mom and Dad or the police that Nick shot that guy on Christmas, Nick will kill me. If I don't tell somebody, no one will ever know what happened. Maybe Nick will kill somebody else. But maybe he'll kill me anyways."

Silence.

Ben opened his eyes and sat up. Anger knotted his hands into fists. "Are you even listening, God?" He looked at the ceiling, expecting an apparition of an angel to appear or maybe Satan himself. "Nick thinks he's the Anti-Christ! Do you know that? Are you gonna do anything or just let me die like that man Nick murdered?"

Tick. Tick. Tick.

Ben shot off his bed, looked out his window, and stared heavenward. Angry tears dripped off his chin. He shivered at the February chill through the double-paned glass. "Maybe Nick's been right all along, Lord. Maybe there is no God, only the Devil. Maybe I *am* all alone."

Ben closed his eyes at that bleak prospect, but heard his mother stomping up the stairs toward his room, her fury pounding out every footstep. Suddenly, fleeing to Nick's condo carried more appeal, anything to escape his mother when she was "demon possessed," as Nick phrased it.

Just as his mother flung open Ben's door, the ringing phone interrupted.

"Ben," Megan yelled from the kitchen, "Nick's calling again, and this time he says you'd better answer or you're in big trouble."

Ben's mother glared at him, but let him walk past without slapping him. Still Ben flinched away from her. He approached the kitchen and Megan's outstretched hand holding the phone receiver. He noticed the redness and swelling on Megan's cheeks along with the tears drying on her face.

Please, Lord. If you're there, could you just make this right? Will you help me get away from my family?

* * *

As Ben held the phone to his ear, fear congealed in his gut, born as much from his mother's wrath as Nick's. "Hello?" he quavered.

"Benjie, man, what's wrong with you? Why won't you talk to me? You know I need your help. Mom told me you were sick, but I know you're dodging me. We have to talk, Bro." Nick's voice was at once cajoling and deadly.

Ben felt his resolve shrink as Nick barraged him with pleas and commands. After the murder, Nick warned Ben that the police would never suspect someone in a wheelchair, and that Nick was prepared to tell the cops Ben had killed Rich Truman. He even threatened to turn Ben in as the killer.

Ben's mind drifted away from Nick's voice to that less chaotic place in his brain. He heard Nick, observed his sister and mother resume their battle, but to Ben, the scene unfolded on the typical myriad of television screens in his mind, all tuned to different stations, each one with the volume set at high.

So Ben simply switched channels to one that broadcast relative peace and quiet.

Always when Ben tuned out, he'd leave the present moment but later find it difficult to return to reality. That's why his mom slapped him. To get him back, to force his attention to his studies. That's why Nick shook him and Megan punched him. Ben knew he deserved those hits. He just wished he could boomerang back to reality when he wished.

"Ben! Listen to me!" Nick shouted over the wire.

Ben winced as he turned away from the battle between his sister and mother.

"Bro, I'm coming over there right now, and you and I are going for a drive. We need to talk away from Mom and Dad. Don't freak out on me. I'll be right over."

The connection died along with Ben's hope for salvation. Ben knew what Nick would do in the car. Even before the murder, Nick was convinced someone had bugged his Ford Tempo and people watched him, listening to his every conversation. Paranoid, Nick blasted music from his radio while he yelled orders and threats at Ben. Once Nick made the ten-minute drive to their parents' house, that scenario would repeat itself.

Even if Nick didn't yell at Ben, he'd overwhelm him with complicated plans to murder police officers, church officials, even their own family members. Nick frequently shared his dream of becoming a sniper or an assassin. Nick swore he was the Anti-Christ, sent by Lucifer to wreak havoc on the Kootenai Valley.

Ben, his brain scrambled since birth, his scrawny frame no match for Nick's muscled upper body, felt helpless to avoid Nick's demands. He left the kitchen to find his coat.

As Ben waited in his room for Nick, his thoughts drifted again to his own death. Maybe Nick would kill him today, shoot him with one of his many guns, maybe even the same gun Nick used to kill Mr. Truman. In death, the noises in his head would quiet, the fear and shame of his life cease, and the pain of his family's assaults pass away. Sure, he'd never kayak down the river again, or run through the forests trapping squirrels and foxes; he'd never see his few friends again, nor would they know why he suddenly disappeared. He wondered if they'd care.

He heard Nick's car pull up, the horn honk, and Nick shout his name. Like a robot, Ben pulled on his coat, tied his shoes, descended the stairs, and stepped out the front door for perhaps the last time. As soon as he sat in the Tempo's front seat, Nick started yelling at him, so Ben zoned out. His mind flew to another location on Planet Ben, preventing Nick's screeching admonitions from harming him.

When the car later stopped, Ben returned to earth, noticing at once they were parked in front of a strange house.

Nick pushed a radio headset at Ben. "I want you to enter this house through that little vent." Nick pointed. "See it over there? If you can get into a place where nobody else can get in, like that vent, then you'll be the best burglar in the valley. You're so skinny, I know you can fit through it."

Ben looked at his brother blankly and took the headset. Still, he pleaded. "Please don't make me do this."

"You can do it, Bro. I promise it won't be like last time." Nick's brows furrowed as his voice lowered. "I need you to do this for me. If you're too weak, if you're such a stupid bitch that you can't do one more, then you're done. And I'm done with you." Nick slapped his hand on the seat. "I'll get Megan to help me, and you'll never see either one of us again. God damn it, you're such a whiny little girl, you piece of shit . . ."

And in that instant, Ben retreated to the remote part of his own world where he felt safer, more peaceful, calm in the relative silence of that space. He donned the headset, squeezed through the tiny vent, wiggled up the duct into the house, and returned to Nick with some trays, a lamp with a plug (always he looked for something with a plug), and a stuffed fish.

Satisfied, Nick drove Ben home, allowing Ben once again to dodge death at the hands of his older brother.

* * *

Four days later, on Valentine's Day, Ben attended a Christian youth event with his 14-year-old friend, Grace Swanson. After the murder, Nick told Ben more than once never to tell anyone what happened, and warned him, "Ben, never tell a girl anything because she'll tell on us for sure."

Tonight Ben knew what he had to do. He asked Grace to take a walk with him.

As they approached a bridge over a small creek, Grace glanced at him. "Hey, I'm worried about you lately. You're not acting right. You're so sad all the time and nervous." Grace cared for Ben and knew Ben's mom hoped they'd get married some day.

Ben stopped walking and turned to face her, his expression full of resolve. "Okay, now you have to listen to me, Grace. What I'm about to tell you, you can't tell anyone else, okay? Because if you do, we might both get killed. Do you understand?"

Grace's eyes widened in fear. "What's going on?"

"Okay, well tonight I decided to give my life over to

Christ. To make things alright with God and all. But there's one part I can't give over to God because I'd have to tell, and I'm too scared and all so . . ."

Ben's hands shook more than usual as tears pooled in his eyes. Grace stared at him, waiting for him to continue.

"I saw a terrible thing happen awhile back and I don't think God will ever forgive me. I can't . . . I can't . . . there was . . . so much blood and all and . . ."

Grace, frightened, guessed the truth. After all, nothing horrible and bloody had happened in Whitehall except on Christmas night. "Did you see Rich Truman get killed? Do you know who killed him?"

Ben silently implored God to guide Grace to the police. He prayed Nick was right that telling a girl meant she'd tell someone else. Maybe then this nightmare could end. "I watched him get shot. I watched him die, and I had to touch him later and . . ." Ben's voice trailed away.

His mind drifted, but not before he heard Grace beseech him, "Who, Ben? Who killed Rich Truman?"

Ben gazed at a snow-laden pine tree sparkling in the light from the youth center and knew, as he'd known for weeks, that he had to surrender, at least to God, if not the police. "My brother killed him. Nick shot him to death, and he'll kill you and he'll kill me if you tell anyone."

Ben provided no other details, just turned to walk back to the youth center.

* * *

Shaken and confused, Grace returned with Ben to the party, leaving immediately for the safety of her home. She was a close friend to Megan Stagg and fond of Ben, despite his slow ways and silly smile. Nick was much older, so Grace didn't talk to him very often. Besides, he no longer went to their church, so she rarely encountered him. Still, it was hard to believe wheelchair-bound Nick, community hero, would murder someone.

On the other hand, she knew for a fact that Ben couldn't kill a man, probably not even in self-defense. As she lay in bed that night, sleep eluded her. Grace debated the merits of telling her parents, or some other adult, of Ben's confession. What if Ben was right and Nick came after her or her family? What if he killed Ben? Or Megan?

Grace Swanson was no fool, even if she was only fourteen years old.

So, contrary to Nick's dire warning that girls always blab the facts, counter to Ben's great hope for discovery and punishment, Grace decided that night to say precisely nothing about Rich Truman's murder.

CHAPTER SEVEN

The Inception of Defalco & Defalco

Early 1998
Beartooth, Montana

SHORTLY BEFORE BEN STAGG CONFESSED to Grace Swanson in an effort to solve Rich Truman's homicide, I pondered my professional future.

I knew what I *didn't* want: to work as a criminal lawyer, to go to trial again, to experience the nauseating stress that preceded jury selection and returned at the words: *Paige, your jury has reached a verdict.* I didn't want to hang out with criminals, coroners, or court personnel anymore. Ditto for judges, defense attorneys, and prosecutors.

I knew I could reinvent myself working in a different legal practice area, like personal injury, contracts, or probate. I shuddered at that idea. The only reason I suffered through three years of law school as a wife and mother of two was to work as a prosecutor. No other subject I studied sparked the passion that criminal law generated in my soul.

Neither did I long to resurrect my career as a bartender, helpful as those tips were to pay my college tuition. Even the fact that I met Jack when I was bartending in Fairfax in 1978 couldn't entice me to return to those smoke and booze-filled days.

Discerning what I *did* want proved troublesome.

And therein lay the beauty of marriage. Just when I became so flummoxed over a decision of great import, my spouse jumped in to provide the answer.

* * *

Jack at last moved to Beartooth in mid-January 1998. He spent his first few weeks puttering around our tiny rental house, muttering expletives about Montana and unsuccessfully devising ways to prevent crazy Bob Dog's escape from the yard. Yet Jack, the man once likened to a swarming gnat or a hummingbird, was bored. And a bored Jack Defalco agitated my carefully constructed tranquility.

One day while the kids were at school, Jack threw down the newspaper, announcing, "This truly is the world's shittiest sports page." He glared at me. "Paige, we need to get back to work."

I rolled out homemade pizza crust, trying to create perfection in my carefully controlled mountain cocoon, as I listened to the Stone's *Gimme Shelter*. I turned down the volume and stared at him.

"What's this *we*, White Man?" I asked, using a tired but apt punch line.

"*We*," he emphasized, "as in you and me, need to start a law practice here and get back to work. I was walking Bob near the train depot last night and noticed they have office space for rent. How cool is that? We could look at the train yard and listen to the whistles while we work."

"Like a variation on the Seven Dwarfs?"

I didn't want to tamp down his enthusiasm, but there were two problems with his plan. First, as noted, I didn't want to practice law ever again. Second, Beartooth was a railroad town with 30 to 40 trains blasting through every day. That meant a lot of train whistles, even for a couple that loved trains.

"Cute. Look, I'm so bored in this fucking hinterland

we live in, I'm going crazy. I've been a lawyer for 25 years. I can't just stop practicing. It's what I love and what I know how to do. Not to mention we need some money. What if we want to buy a house? No bank will loan us money for that if we aren't working. My retirement isn't enough to fund a house loan."

Okay. He had me there.

I cleared my throat, buying time. "So . . . any chance you could practice law by yourself?"

Since I'd only lasted seven years as a prosecutor before I insisted we relocate to Beartooth, thereby creating a financial crisis, I had to concede that my plan to meditate my way to Zen tranquility was feeble.

Jack took a breath. Then his eyebrows went up, the clear indicator that his patience ebbed. "And you'll do *what* exactly while the kids are in school? Watch soap operas? Do laundry? You won't last six months as a housewife. You're already edgy. Admit it. You're bored, too."

Snap!

Just like that, I once again faced my addiction to criminal law. Through all my months of denial, I still craved the courtroom, the trials, the excitement, the drama, even the nausea and sleepless nights. Yet, like any decent junkie, I tried to resist the idea of returning to the arena.

"I'm not that bored," I insisted, admitting that I was a smidge insentient.

"Yeah, you are. I've known you for 20 years. If you have to chase Bob off the school playground one more time, you'll scream. I know you enjoyed making the reindeer in Sean's classroom," he pointed to a holiday ornament I'd made from a nylon stocking, a wire coat hanger, and a construction paper set of antlers, "but you don't much care for little kids who don't belong to you, and your teaching years were some of the worst in your life."

"Hey, I loved teaching. At the junior college, at least."

"Exactly. Teaching adults. When you taught little kids, all you talked about was the amount of green snot smeared on your clothes."

Right again. "Okay, point taken. Still, you and I opening a law practice won't prevent Bob from escaping to the school to visit Sean. Besides, the staff is pretty good-humored about it when he shows up."

"Yeah," Jack stood, "until he flattens one of those little kids. Then they'll sue us for failure to control our dog. Which reminds me, I have another plan to keep him in the yard."

And off he went, leaving the matter of the law firm on hold.

* * *

Jack Defalco was nothing if not tenacious, so my respite from his plan was brief. The next day he contacted the manager at the train depot, and in March 1998, we opened the doors of Defalco & Defalco, PC. We'd spent our entire legal careers working as salaried public servants, the government handling the details while we hammered the bad guys. Now we had no secretary, no bookkeeper, no clue how to bill clients, or even how to *attract* clients.

I volunteered to do legal work for battered women through the local shelter to get to know the good folks down at the courthouse. The judges commended my effort, but thought I was crazy since 85 percent of the victims returned to their batterers. After a few months, I abandoned that dramatic, but frustrating, exercise.

Jack had gained valuable civil law experience in the Fairfax County Consumer Fraud division of the D.A.'s office and showed a real talent for business law. To meet people and potential clients, he joined every local service group, from Knights of Columbus, Rotary, and Kiwanis, to the Lions. An extrovert with an irreverent sense of humor, he was an immediate hit in the little town of Beartooth.

An ancient neighbor of ours provided our first legal fee in the form of an old baseball hat and a pair of sunglasses that looked suspiciously like the free ones the doc gave away after she dilated his eyes. Soon, more clients trickled through our door. Some actually paid us cash money instead of the more typical offers to barter for knives, guns, antlers, services, and domesticated animals.

The day arrived in late April, however, when Jack excitedly waved the newspaper in my face, pointing to an advertisement to hire public defenders in Kootenai County. "Paige," he enthused, "you need to apply for this. It'll bring in steady income and give us more contact with the judges and prosecutors in Aberdeen."

"Are you out of your mind?" I blurted. "I am not, repeat *not,* going to defend criminals, Jack! I am not sitting in court with a bunch of reprobates who should have been locked up as adolescents. Not a chance, Honeybunch. If you want the job, you go for it."

True to character, he persisted. "They probably won't hire you anyway since you're an ex-prosecutor, but you have a better chance than I do because you're female. C'mon. Just try."

I caved in and completed the paperwork. As I stood at the mailbox on the sidewalk outside the train depot, I held the envelope for several seconds while I prayed for rejection. Confident that God had heard me, I opened the metal slot and chucked in the application.

CHAPTER EIGHT

Russian Roulette

May 1998
Whitehall, Montana

BEN STAGG, STILL FREE from police scrutiny five months after he'd confessed to Grace Swanson, took the only other route to punishment he could conjure.

Suicide.

Two times on two separate days, this day included, he loaded a revolver with only one bullet. Two times he spun the chamber. Two times he wrapped his lips around the revolver's blued-steel barrel. Two times he closed his eyes and pulled the trigger. Two times the empty chamber clicked. Two times he tested God. Two times he failed to die.

So Ben, a lad of great faith and muddled thought, decided that maybe God was telling him he had to live to see another day. He put the gun away in his dresser, choosing instead to kayak down a portion of a local river to practice for an upcoming race. Since purchasing the kayak the year before, he often sought and found peace in the relentless churning of the water. He drove to the river and put in his kayak near an old wooden bridge.

Montana's rivers run fast and full during spring, the water sluicing with ferocity over rocks and around fallen trees. Melting mountain snow fills the waterways with icy runoff, lethal both in temperature and speed for the inexperienced or unlucky boater or fisherman.

Despite those perils, Ben Stagg didn't much care if he died on the river. He felt comfort in the idea of death, knowing it would end the perpetual torment inside his head. He welcomed the challenge of navigating the roiling waters with only his paddle to steer him away from one threat after the next. For moments at a time in his kayak, the roar of the river silenced the chatter in his otherwise noise-filled brain.

His father, Pete Stagg, had recently returned Ben's kayak to him after withholding it for months as punishment for blocking his mother's intended slap. Before then, his dad whipped him whenever he disobeyed his mother. But shortly after Ben's 18th birthday the previous November, when his dad had beaten him badly, Nick called him a baby and ordered him to stand up to their parents, to refuse to allow them any more violence.

The next time Ben knew a whipping was coming, he packed his bags and left the house. The problem was he had nowhere to go, so he returned late that night, certain his dad would flail his hide. Sure enough, his mom demanded Pete punish Ben, and the two headed out to the shed.

Pete removed his belt. "Turn around, Ben."

For the first time in his young life, Ben balked. He faced his father, looking down a few inches at him, wondering if his height and youth could challenge his father's shorter, more muscled physique.

"I won't," he murmured quietly, but flinched away. "I'm done with you beating me like a little kid. I'm 18-years-old and shouldn't be treated like a baby anymore."

Pete's jaw tightened at the disobedience. "I said, turn around!"

"I won't," Ben averred again, louder, firmer, with less shake in his voice. "Dad, just ground me like other kids. Do anything else, but just don't spank me anymore."

Pete breathed heavily for a few minutes, gazed at Ben with an expression akin to respect, and lowered the belt. "Alright, Ben. No more beatings."

Instead, Pete took away Ben's greatest source of solace, his kayak. With no schooling and no job, that left Ben with nothing to do except mess around with Nick, acting as Nick's legs during his brother's crazy crime schemes.

But then Nick had murdered Rich Truman and, in that instant, Ben's life stopped as quickly as Mr. Truman's heart.

Still, just two days after Ben's second stymied suicide attempt with the revolver, praying once again that the river would suck him down, he instead won the competition for his class and age group. He not only lived through the race, he received a prize awarded at the local tavern that evening.

There seemed no end to the ironic nightmare Ben called Life.

* * *

Not long after the race, God answered Ben's call for help, utilizing Detective George Kimber as the messenger. That morning, after five months without a single promising lead in the Truman homicide, Kimber received a phone call from a local attorney who told Kimber a client had information on the case.

Grace Swanson, as it turned out, had at last fulfilled Nick's prophecy, and Ben's prayers, when she told her best friend that Ben witnessed Truman's murder. Her friend shared the news with her own father, who contacted his local attorney, who called Detective Kimber. All in all, a perfect example of convoluted small town gossip intermingling to solve a murder.

When Kimber arrived at their log home, Pete and Laura Stagg were puzzled that a sheriff's deputy sought their youngest son. Detective Kimber briefly explained he wanted to question Ben regarding the murder of Rich

Truman. Ben's parents laughed at that, assuring Kimber that Ben knew nothing about it.

Pete yelled to Ben at the fishing pond below the house. Ben slowly ambled up the hill carrying a fishing pole, his frozen smile slashing his pallid face. His pants, soaked to the knees by lake water, had absorbed the cold moisture as Ben stood on the water's edge, waiting for a catch.

Detective Kimber later said Ben Stagg looked just like Huckleberry Finn, until Ben stuck a fishhook through his own index finger when Detective Kimber mentioned the Truman murder.

Kimber asked Ben to come downtown so they could talk alone and followed him into the house so Ben could change into sandals. Just inside the door, Kimber spotted a pair of Nike ACG shoes, the soles of which had the same pattern as the bloody shoeprints left in the snow at the murder scene. After Ben admitted they were his, Kimber seized the shoes and hustled Ben to the patrol car.

As they drove the few miles to the Sheriff's Department in Aberdeen, Kimber's excitement grew. This kid, although an unlikely killer, clearly knew who had shot Rich Truman. Kimber intended to exact that information from Ben over the next few hours.

* * *

Sitting alone in the back seat of the patrol car, Ben desperately tried to remember what Nick rehearsed with him just in case the police questioned him. The only part that came to mind was that Nick would kill him if he ever mentioned his brother's name. Several times during the last five months Nick had insisted on practicing what Ben would tell the police. Nick relentlessly played the Inquisitor, peppering Ben with questions designed to break him and make him admit his knowledge of the murder. The sessions nearly always ended with Nick screaming at him because Ben was too stupid to remember the right answers.

As Detective Kimber drove past farmland variegated green after the previous month's thaw, Ben wondered if Grace finally told on him, or whether someone else had witnessed the brothers near the scene that night. He figured maybe Nick had called the police to blame Ben, just as he'd promised to do on so many occasions. Mostly Ben sat quietly, drifting off to a better place in his mind, imagining again the silence on the river.

* * *

Detective Kimber placed him in a small room with a table, two chairs, a tape recorder, and a camera. Ben shivered from the cold moisture on his pants and shoes and nervously chewed the skin around his fingernails. He still wore his fishing hat as he slouched in the chair, his long skinny legs spread open.

"A little apprehensive?" Detective Kimber asked as he sat down across from Ben.

Ben smiled to cover his ignorance of the word *apprehensive.*

Coatless, a leather holster crisscrossed over the back of his white cotton shirt, his gun secured against his upper left side, George Kimber donned a pair of readers and began. The detective alternately leaned forward in his chair, his elbows resting on his knees when he asked Ben probing questions, or rocked backward in frustration, arms raised with hands clasped above his head when he disbelieved Ben's answer.

As Detective Kimber peppered him with questions, Ben smiled and replied, "I don't know." He tuned the detective out for the most part and understood little of the questioning. Cold fear clenched his chest when he thought about what Nick would do to him if he screwed this up. He realized he'd probably have to stay at the jail for a while, but he knew he couldn't give up his brother.

That frustrating colloquy replayed for the next two hours, until the cops watching the interrogation via video camera in the next room wanted to shriek. Detective Kimber, however, was a veteran deputy of 18 years and father to his own teenage son. His patience never wavered.

Finally Kimber invoked the ploy he knew might get Ben to talk: God and guilt. Ben was soggy, worn out, tired, hungry, scared, and confused. So when Detective Kimber talked about God and truth, forgiveness and justice, Ben might listen.

"Ben, you need to get square with God," he pressed. "We need to get this behind us. You need to tell the truth, do the right thing."

Ben shifted in his chair and smiled. "I don't know anything."

"Take your hat off," Kimber commanded. Ben removed the silly fishing hat and placed it on the table.

"Now tell me who all your friends are," Kimber ordered. Ben rattled off a few names before Detective Kimber interrupted. "I'm going to leave you alone for awhile, so you can pray about this. When I come back in here, I expect you to tell me who shot Rich Truman. Now you take some time and pray, son."

After Kimber left him, Ben did as he'd been ordered and prayed. He prayed about whether he should tell the whole truth, implicating Nick. He prayed for his folks and his sisters. He prayed for Nick not to kill any cops when they arrested him. Then he prayed for strength.

After what seemed like an hour, Detective Kimber, joined by Detective Mike Matthews, returned to the room and once again asked Ben to tell them what he knew about Rich Truman's murder.

Ben paused and then broke. He told them what he'd witnessed without uttering the killer's name. Detective

Matthews inveigled, cajoled, and pleaded for the identity of Truman's murderer. Neither detective, however, was prepared for the answer when Ben Stagg, sighing, near tears, smiling his lopsided grin, at last blurted out two words.

"My bro."

"Your bro?" came Detective Matthews' astounded response. "You mean Nick? The kid in the wheelchair?"

Ben nodded.

"Now wait a second, Ben. There were two sets of footprints up there, different shoe types and sizes. How could Nick make one set of those prints?" Kimber queried.

Ben explained the multiple trips to the scene, wearing Nick's size 7 boat shoes instead of his own size 11 Nikes, and Nick shooting Rich Truman from the driver's seat of his Ford Tempo.

Ben felt he should warn the officers. "Be careful when you arrest him. You should arrest him at work. He has a lot of guns, and he's talked about killing cops before."

And with that gesture of good will, Ben closed his eyes and tried not to think about Nick or his parents, his friends or family. As different deputies escorted him from the little room, allowed him to use the restroom, booked him, fingerprinted him, replaced his cold wet clothes with bright orange, jail-issued sweats, and closed the door on his new cell at the Kootenai County Detention Facility, Ben Stagg thanked God for the freedom he believed would be his within the next few weeks.

Later, his folks figured the Good Lord blessed Ben with muzzy thinking so he wouldn't understand that he was about to spend the rest of his life in prison.

CHAPTER NINE

A New Voice for Evildoers

May to July 1998
Aberdeen, Montana

THE KOOTENAI SHERIFF'S DEPARTMENT
ARRESTED BEN and Nick Stagg on May 18, 1998 for
the murder of Rich Truman. One month earlier, that
same agency arrested another 18-year-old, Casey
Hennon, for the murder of his best friend. In a bizarre
twist, two days after the Stagg brothers' capture, the
sheriffs arrested the brothers' 14-year-old cousin, Andy
Gifford, who that morning had shot and killed his own
father as he slept.

Jack and I remarked on the various murders
committed in the valley, all by teenagers, but that was the
extent of our interest. Instead, while our kids busied
themselves at school and in sports, Jack and I puzzled
over the intricacies of starting a law firm. We had no clue
that these kid killers and their families soon would enter
our orbit.

While those young men awaited their fates in the
Kootenai County jail, my 19-year-old niece came to live
with us for an indeterminate period. Our landlord sold
the house we rented, so we relocated to a quirky little
home poised on the edge of Beartooth Lake.

My friend, Anne, fought her cancer with a
vengeance. When she left for surgery and further
treatment in Seattle, I loaded her son, along with my kids
and niece, into the Suburban and drove over to the Fred

Hutchins Cancer Institute for Mother's Day.

Donning a scarf to cover her baldness, warmed from the Seattle bay by a down coat, Annie sat next to me on a tour boat, her arm linked through mine. We watched the kids as the tour guide pointed out various sites.

"So, what's new?" Her smile creased her ashen face, now so thin from weight loss.

"Same old shit." I squeezed her hand. I told her about the law firm, our move to the lake house, and regaled her with funny stories of our boys' adventures around town.

"Did you hear," I laughed, "that my son called for a strike against homework in Mrs. Shelby's class and had all the third-graders sign a petition? She had to counsel him in her supply closet."

Annie's smile broke into a grin. "Why am I not surprised? Always the politician, that boy." She looked off in the distance, at everything or maybe nothing. One tear escaped her pale blue eyes. "God, I miss home. I miss my kid. I miss my dog. Crap, I miss my *life*."

Despite my own parka, I felt a chill inside. "You're on your way back. Not too much longer. You're going to beat this thing. And your dog loves ours as only two dumb black labs can."

She nodded then reached for her son as he climbed onto her lap, hugging him so tightly, he squirmed.

"Mom, when you get back, Sean and I are gonna build a fort down by the creek. The labs can sleep inside with us!"

"It's a deal, Sweetie." Annie planted a smacker on his cheek, which he promptly wiped away, giggling. My own boy rolled his eyes.

Anne and I exchanged a glance, then nodded in solidarity to our future and the futures of our other women friends fighting against breast cancer. Later, we took in a Mariners' game, ate some interesting food, and found a toy store with stuffed dogs for the boys, as if their real dogs didn't offer enough entertainment. When we hugged goodbye, we cried.

Cancer, it seemed, hung like a stalactite between us, its stiletto-sharp point threatening to bleed our friendship to death.

* * *

A month later, after our move to the lake, Big Bob, the giant black lab, escaped his fenced area and failed to return. Our new rental sat about 20 feet from the Burlington Northern railroad tracks. After yelling for him, the kids and I scaled the hill to the tracks. A dark spot sat idle a hundred yards ahead of me. I ordered my niece to take the younger kids back to the house, then ran down the tracks toward what I prayed wasn't Bob.

It was a testament to my brain's ability to shut down in the face of gore that I reacted as I did over the next hours. A train had severed in half our beautiful canine, the two parts of his body lying several feet away from one another along the track. I'd seen many horrid crime scenes in my career, but none prepared me for that sight. A nearby construction guy brought me a huge cardboard carton lined in plastic. When Jack arrived, we placed Bob's remains inside and took them to our vet for cremation.

The kids' sobs stoked my own grief, but I swallowed my tears in an attempt to quash theirs. That didn't work. All of us, including my normally stoic spouse, felt Bob's tragic loss of life every second over the next few days. Finally, I accepted the inevitable.

We needed another dog.

We drove to Whitehall that Saturday, the same town in which the Stagg family reeled from the arrests of Ben,

Nick, and Andy, as well as the murder of Andy's father, and from the harsh judgment of their community. At a ranch filled with two litters of chocolate lab puppies, each Defalco kid picked out and named a dog. Thus, Fred and Molly, 11 weeks old, chubby, wiggly, and warm, jumped into the Suburban with their new owners, after which they chewed and licked their way to Beartooth.

The eternal optimist in me, who warred with my inner cynic, believed that after tragedy, one's life should perk up and remain problem-free for the next decade or so. In that mindset, I walked down to the mailbox, only to find an official-looking envelope from the Kootenai County Justice Center. Puzzled, I read the contents of the short missive contained therein.

"Dear Ms. Defalco,

We are pleased to inform you that your application for the position of part-time Kootenai County Public Defender has been accepted. Congratulations! Please contact the Chief Deputy for further details of your new employment position."

The signature read Judge Hank Winston.

I wanted to shriek out a few expletives but noticed my aging neighbor waive from her porch. Instead, I pasted on a smile, waived back, and silently cursed Jack and his stupid idea that I put in my name for the job. More irksome, however, was the fact that God obviously had been channel-surfing the day I chucked my application into the mailbox.

I looked up at the clouds and muttered, "Really? You expect me to muster sympathy for the devils?"

Inside I dodged the puppies as I entered the bathroom, where I stared at myself in the mirror. If God's ransom for the return of my misplaced soul included compassion for bad guys, my ice-encrusted heart would never defrost.

* * *

So it began, my life as a criminal defense attorney for the indigent.

Dutifully, I met with the outgoing Chief Public Defender, took over his caseload, stole his secretary, moved our office from the train depot to a spot above the local health food store, and pondered how I'd defend the very evildoers I'd spent so much time prosecuting in my former life.

I made two resolutions.

First, I decided to cut alcohol from my repertoire of pleasures. Part of it had to do with our daughter's invitation to the freshman keg, as in beer keg. I figured I needed to set a good example for her about responsible drinking. The other reason was my intuition kept screaming at me that a shitstorm was about to hit our lives, and I would need to be at the top of my game to survive the insanity.

Second, in my old county in California, the public defenders exemplified some of the finest legal talent on the planet. When I was a prosecutor, one PD in particular irritated the crap out of me because he defended a traffic ticket as zealously as a homicide case. He did so because he believed that the U.S. Constitution provided all of us, good or evil, with the same rights and guarantees to justice. If the Bill of Rights didn't work for the poor and downtrodden, or those guilty as sin, then it wouldn't work for the rest of us, and American jurisprudence would fail. So I vowed to represent every new client in Montana with as much zeal as that public defender, my former nemesis.

Keeping that promise in mind, I entered the Kootenai County jail on the first of July to begin my new career.

My caseload of clients included two old ladies who

had lied about their income so they could refinance their home, a dumb kid with some pot, another weird kid who broke into the wrong house when he was drunk off his ass, and still another young man who tried to outrun the cops in a car chase.

It seemed as if young men under the age of 25 provided the bread and butter for the criminal justice system. Since there were so many of them, none of whom seemed to be able to answer the simple question, *What were you thinking,* we had an endless stream of clients and guaranteed employment.

Alcohol and drugs explained most of the criminal conduct. The methamphetamine users presented the biggest challenge because they couldn't focus or listen. Instead, they jittered at me, shaking and stammering, as I tried to question them. Invariably they *promised,* if I just got them out on bail, that they'd *never* touch drugs again. Typically, when I did get bail set and the meth client was released, he lasted about four hours before he reoffended.

After a few weeks observing this merry-go-round of brainless kids rotate in and out of jail, I wondered why I'd hated them when I prosecuted them as a DA. They were just kids. Dumb shits, yes, but kids. Most of them came from disastrous homes and families, generations of which passed along all manner of addictive behaviors and questionable genes for intelligence. From birth, these knuckleheads viewed the world through a limited lens, far different than the world Jack and I provided for our own kids.

Yet one fact stood out. These criminals' moms hovered over them like any other mom, most of them standing by their kids throughout the court proceedings. We mothers, I realized, no matter how poor, how young, how addicted, or how intelligent, love our offspring beyond all reason. We defend them, visit them in jail, pray for them, cry for them, plead with them, feed them, clothe them, and give them a million chances to reform. A mother's love rarely falters.

Of course, there were notable exceptions to that observation, like the mother who tossed her 10-year-old son out the door in favor of a boyfriend who regularly beat the bejeezus out of both of them. Or the mom who prostituted her daughter to secure funds for more heroin. But overall, I found that moms turned out to be their offspring's greatest advocate.

Indeed, the clients' mothers who cried in my arms, shredded my Kleenex, and poured out their life stories to me, loved their kids with a ferocity that matched my own toward Claire and Sean. We protected our babes.

Despite the onslaught of others' tears, by August 1998 I figured so far, so good. No pedophiles or wife beaters yet, so how bad could the job get?

* * *

A month later a child molester stared at me across the plastic table that separated us. Alone in the attorney/client contact room, I avoided his gaze, instead focusing on the single table, three plastic chairs, white-painted cinder block walls, and concrete floor that decorated the 8 foot by 10 foot tomb. The rank odor of greasy food and unwashed bodies constricted the air, squeezing my composure.

I wore my ubiquitous navy blue suit and heels, but left the pearls at home. Since I had a closetful of old Nordstrom designer suits, I saw no need to purchase new ones to impress those at the Kootenai County courthouse. In Montana, folks neither recognized nor cared about current fashion.

Introducing myself, I shook my latest client's hand then mentally recoiled at what I'd done. Pedophiles were criminals of the worst sort. Innocent little boys, like this guy's two victims, were good guys. As a prosecutor in California, I'd put bad guys like this in jail. I'd helped the child victims move forward with their lives.

Now, as a public defender, I had to advocate on this guy's behalf. If his case went to trial, I'd cross-examine the innocent little boys, shredding their fragile truths, wresting from them discrepancies in their stories, all to convince a jury to set this child molester free.

The pedophile lowered his gaze as I put pen to yellow legal pad, preparing to take notes of our conversation. I, too, avoided eye contact, instead peppering him with routine questions about his background. I skirted questions about the crime itself, not willing to listen to details beyond what I'd read in the police reports and his confession.

In his twenties, his brown hair mussed from sleep, he wore the shirt of his jail suit half-tucked into his pants. He spoke quietly to my emotionless queries, at least for a time. Then silence ensued.

I glanced at his face and saw tears streaking his bony cheeks. He put fisted hands to his eyes, lowered his head, and sobbed, "I'm sorry, so sorry. I'm such a monster. How can God ever forgive me? I don't know why I did it. I couldn't stop. I hate myself. I want to die. Could they just kill me after I get to prison?" All that spewed forth in a volcanic eruption of seeming remorse.

What the hell? I silently reacted. *You're a fucking child molester! You're not supposed to cry, for God's sake. You're supposed to gloat or defend what you did or at least lie to me. Deny you did it, you son of a bitch! What am I supposed to do when you act like a freaking human being?*

I felt my chest tighten and briefly wondered if I was having a heart attack. I couldn't breathe, couldn't think clearly, and my eyes watered. I noticed the guard staring at us through the window, ready to save me from the evildoer if only I signaled for help. Instead, I stared at this Lucifer weeping across from me and considered whether this was all an act, more bull from another lying sack-of-shit criminal.

My cynical side cast away the droplets melting around my core and the tear that threatened to roll from the corner of my eye. I lowered my lids to shut down the part of my brain that allowed emotion, just as a mentally ill person dissociates from trauma to seek a safe place within his psyche.

Nice try, Paige. You think you can will this guy away? You think if you ignore him and his bullshit feelings that he'll stop crying and act like the monster he is? You have to do something, say something. Get up, damn it! Leave this fucking jail and all its creepy inhabitants. Quit this defense attorney crap and go back to being a housewife, a mom. Tell Jack that he can have the job if he thinks switching sides of the law is no big deal.

I raised my eyes in time to observe my left hand extend toward him, lower itself to his upraised right arm, and wrap my fingers around his wrist. He looked at me, dropped his larger left hand, and hesitantly, gently, covered mine.

I locked onto his ravaged face, his swollen, bleary eyes, and saw a saddened, remorse-filled young man whose inner demons I could never comprehend. I could understand murder. I could understand theft. Molesting children, hurting the helpless, never. Yet inexplicably, I could accept this imperfect human with whom my hand, and now my job, intertwined.

My own tear fell on the legal pad in front of me, blurring the ink, obliterating my callous questions, and his bleak responses. We stayed like that for a minute, sharing the silence of the contact room, ignoring the startled and concerned stare of the guard through the window. I only had one question I needed him to answer.

"Tell me what you'd like me to call you from now on," I urged as he rose to leave.

He turned back and smiled at me, a weak smile, but better than tears. "Leonard," he said. "I like to be called Leonard."

"Okay then, Leonard," I smiled back. "Take a breath. I'm going to talk to the prosecutor, Frank McShane, to see what kind of plea deal we can work out. I doubt he'll go for probation, but maybe we can minimize the actual prison time, especially if you complete the sex offender training early."

His face softened, as did his stance, his shoulders relaxing slightly. "Thank you, Mrs. Defalco, for listening and . . . for not hating me." He placed his hands behind his back for the guard to handcuff him.

As the door closed and I readied myself for my next criminal client to emerge, I considered Leonard's parting comment. Was that true? Did I actually hate him when I entered the contact room and, if so, how could I hate a person I'd never met? Because he was an admitted pedophile?

Could the sum of a person's life be defined by a single bad act? Could the totality of a person be characterized by his conduct? What if, as an infant, he'd suffered some mental or physical disorder that might cause him to act wrongly? Should he be abandoned to die from exposure, as they did in ancient Sparta? Or perhaps institutionalized for life, as sort of a preemptive strike against possible future violence?

As the jailer keyed the door, I reached for my legal pad. Had my hatred disappeared when he wept?

And since when did criminals actually have names?

CHAPTER TEN

With Liberty and Justice for All

September 1998
Aberdeen, Montana

THE NEXT CLIENT met me with the same dejected countenance as Leonard the Pedophile's. A quick learner, I first asked the client what name he'd like me to call him. I looked him in the eye, now conceding that perhaps a human being lurked behind the criminal label, Defendant, bestowed by the prosecutor.

"Rodney," he answered glumly.

"Okay, Rodney," I tried to smile. "Your file says you're here for a probation violation on a case involving felony possession of methamphetamine. The probation officer says he searched your house and found a hypodermic needle with meth in it."

"Yeah, well the probation officer is lying his ass off. The only syringe he found was in a package in the basement, and it was my daughter's that she uses for her diabetes."

Ah ha, I thought, *the old Lying Cop defense.* Criminals always accused cops of fabricating evidence or lying on the stand and in their police reports. I regarded Rodney skeptically.

Jail clothes rumpled, Rodney's blonde hair hung in long, unwashed strands. He wore large, out-of-date glasses that covered intelligent brown eyes. His complexion looked slightly bilious, or maybe it was the fluorescent lighting in the contact room. In his forties, he looked a bit podgy. He spoke with a southern accent. I knew he was a computer nerd and ran a mom-and-pop market with his wife.

"Not only is he lying," Rodney continued. "I've been in custody for nine months for a case I pled guilty to as a misdemeanor a year ago. Four days after I pled guilty and was sentenced to two days time served, the Deputy County Attorney, Frank McShane, charged me with the same crime, only as a felony. When I told my public defender that McShane couldn't do that because it was double jeopardy, he told me it wasn't and I had to plead guilty again. So I did. And that's how I ended up on felony probation, and how they could search my house and supposedly find that needle with meth in it, which wasn't there."

I held up my hand to interrupt, the one holding the pen with which I should have been taking notes but couldn't because of the speed at which Rodney spoke.

"Stop," I ordered. "Let me get this straight. Originally, a year ago, you were stopped in your car and arrested for possession of methamphetamine. The police report states the meth was actually white powder residue found on a spoon inside a velvet bag that had been thrown out of the passenger window of your car. Is all that correct?"

"Correct," he nodded.

"You were taken to this jail and booked on a misdemeanor, possession of drug paraphernalia, correct?"

"Correct," he nodded again and smiled.

"Then you pled guilty to that charge and the city judge sentenced you to two days, with credit for time served in jail, and released you, right?"

He nodded affirmatively.

"Then four days later, you were arrested *again* by the Drug Task Force for the exact same crime, same date, same incident, same powder on a spoon in a velvet bag?" My pitch rose at the question mark.

"Exactly! See what I'm telling you? Double jeopardy." Rodney ruefully shook his head. "It's that McShane guy. He's such an asshole. Have you met him?"

I shook my head.

"You won't believe it when you meet him. Seriously--"

"*Rodney!*" I emphasized his name to interrupt his tirade. "Just stop for a second so I can think." I stood and paced the tiny room like a nervous bobcat. "If that's all true, then your second arrest and conviction on the felony are illegal, and the probation search of your house was illegal, so anything they found can't be used against you."

I paused, turning to face him. "Crap! How long have you been in custody on the probation violation?"

"Nine fucking months is how long I've been sitting here. My old public defender wanted me to admit the violation, but I refused. I did not have a needle with methamphetamine in my house, and I'm not going to prison for something I didn't do." He slapped his hand on the table for emphasis, drawing the attention of the guard outside.

I held up my hand to the guard, indicating I was fine, and there was no need to intervene. I looked at this man squarely in the eye, as if I could see into his brain to determine if he was bullshitting me. He matched my stare, defiantly challenging me to believe him, demanding from me the courage to ferret out the truth.

I gathered my legal pad and pens into my briefcase and pressed the button for the guard to unlock my door to the free world. Anger fueled me as I turned to my client and growled, "Rodney, I'm heading to City Court to check this out. If you're right - and you'd better not be lying - I'll go see Frank McShane to get you released from custody pending a hearing on this. Who knows? Maybe he'll agree that it's double jeopardy and dismiss the felony and probation violation."

"When pigs fly, Paige Defalco!" Rodney yelled over his shoulder as the guards pushed him out his own door to indefinite incarceration.

* * *

After leaving Rodney the Meth Spoon Guy, I headed

to Aberdeen City Court where the clerk confirmed everything Rodney told me. Armed with copies of her paperwork, I marched into the County Attorney's office where Frank McShane was a deputy prosecutor, requested a brief meeting, and took a seat in the waiting room.

Memories flowed from the seven years in California I'd spent doing Frank McShane's job. There'd been so many times my hard-assed, uncompromising, take-no-prisoners attitude had dimmed the lives and hopes of public defenders and their clients.

In those days, there was no crime of violence too insignificant to take to trial, no chip of rock cocaine too small to overlook, no petty thief or drunk driver pitiful enough to dodge the 'three strikes' rule and spend the rest of his life in prison. Even the criminally insane - say, for example, the guy who shot his parents in the head with a cross-bow when they brought home the wrong kind of Chinese food - incurred my wrath at trial.

If the public defenders advocated too hard for their clients, or adopted supercilious airs, I'd retaliate by refusing to lower the charge or make a reasonable plea offer. Once, after she'd bested me at trial, a public defender told me the defendant, her now acquitted client, had drowned. I felt *vindicated* in that 18-year-old boy's death under some sick notion that while twelve jurors had found him not guilty, God had punished him anyway.

Some who worked with me joked that it was my red hair or my Celtic temper that made me so insufferable. Early in my career I was pleasant, reasonable, and maybe had a sense of humor. I bantered with the public defenders, coddled the young law students I supervised into producing their best legal briefs, and laughed at the antics of my testosterone-driven male colleagues. I cared about crime victims and their families and believed in the integrity of the prosecutor's office.

Yet as a D.A., I cared not a farthing for criminal defendants. They had no faces, no names, no families, and no lives. They were just The Bad Guys. That simple. That black and white.

Ironic that now I worked as a public defender, living in a world of gray.

Since I'd touched Leonard the Pedophile and discovered Rodney's illegal incarceration, I reconsidered my former zeal. In theory, prosecutors sought the truth and swore to uphold justice, even if it meant letting a guilty person go free. Their job wasn't merely to win or secure convictions, but to uphold the United States Constitution. They were supposed to play by the rules.

God, I hope Frank McShane is a nicer prosecutor than I was.

The receptionist led me to Frank's office and introduced me. Frank didn't even look up. Finally he muttered, "Have a seat. What can I do for you?"

I sat down across the desk from him, nervously fiddled with Rodney's paperwork, and prepared my pitch to get Rodney released from custody.

Then Frank squinted at me with unflinching, icy-blue eyes. Right down to the fading red hair, the jutting jaw, the high cheekbones, the pale complexion once dotted with freckles, I confronted my former, asshole-prosecutor self in the mirror of Frank McShane's visage.

* * *

"Christ Almighty," Jack muttered before he left for the courthouse the next day. "You'd think we moved to Cuba or communist China the way justice is meted out around here. This place is enough to turn me into a fucking liberal!"

I knew Jack had a client who stood accused of molesting two teenage boys. The guy had a prior child molest conviction from a neighboring state for which he'd failed to register as a sex offender in Montana, a crime carrying a maximum five-year sentence. His jury trial was set just four days away. Earlier that morning, the court clerk had phoned to request Jack's presence in Judge

Winston's chambers. The purpose of this meeting was a mystery.

After court, Jack sauntered into my office and sat in the chair across from my desk.

"What's wrong?" I knew jury trials neither were expected nor welcomed at the courthouse.

"Well," Jack began as he propped his foot on the desk, "when I got to Judge Winston's chambers, I found him chit-chatting about the Grizzlies' football team with the prosecutor, Don Yeager. When I sat down, the judge announced, 'Jack, your guy needs to plead guilty.'"

Okay, nothing too unusual there, I noted mentally. *Even judges in California involve themselves in plea negotiations between the defense and prosecution.*

"So I said, 'Okay, he'll plead guilty to five years state prison.' Then Yeager said, 'No, he needs to plead guilty to 35 years state prison.' So I said, 'Well, he's 58 years old, he says he's not guilty, and 35 years amounts to a death sentence for him.'"

Jack pulled his pen out and clicked it repeatedly until I reached over and took it away from him. "Right, so the judge said . . . ?"

He smiled at the pen in my hand.

"So Winston said, 'The jury will convict him on the failure to register anyway, and when they hear your guy has a prior molest conviction, they'll convict him of everything else.'"

Rapt, I leaned forward and propped my elbows on the desk while Jack continued his tale.

"So I said, 'Judge, I'm going to plead him guilty to the failure to register charge Monday morning before trial so the jury will never know about it."

Good move, Honeybun, I marveled to myself, *a classic defense attorney move back in California.*

Bad guys often pled guilty before trial to certain charges that clearly would prejudice a jury. With Jack's client, 'failure to register as a sex offender' would alert jurors that he not only was a felon, but he'd been convicted before of a sex offense. By pleading the client guilty before trial, the fact of that accusation would be excluded at trial. Otherwise it might cause jurors to conclude that if the bad guy already was a felon with a prior sex offense, he must be guilty in the new case.

"So, Judge Winston said, 'Jack, if you do that, I'll sentence your guy to 100 years in jail for failing to register.'"

"What?" I shrilled. "Failing to register used to be an administrative offense. It only carries a five-year maximum. How does he get to 100 years?" I paused for a breath and then remembered. "Oh, *crap!* A PFO. They're going to hit him with a persistent felony offender enhancement, and that let's Winston add up to 95 years to his sentence. So, what are you going to do?"

Jack shook his head and laughed, a hint of irony flavoring his voice. "We're going to trial, that's what. And I'm not pleading him to anything before trial because 100 years is bullshit for failing to register as a sex offender. Besides, I've got a good case and maybe the jury acquits him of all the charges. The client wants his day in court, and he has a right to that."

I knew Jack's investigator had interviewed several teenagers who would testify that the client's accusers were dishonest. Still, it would be tough to get around the failure to register count, and I said so.

Jack, undaunted, explained, "The client *tried* to register but he couldn't figure out how or where to go to do it. Or so he says and will state to the jury. At least it's something." And with that, he stood to leave. As he walked away he paused, turning back. "You know what Winston's parting shot was?"

"I can't even guess."

Jack smiled again. "He said, 'Well, I guess on Monday we'll show you what Montana juries are all about. And when they convict your guy, I'm gonna give him 500 years in prison.' And then he and Yeager smirked at me."

"And your parting remark?" I goaded, knowing Jack

always got in the last word.

"I told him that even if the jury convicted my guy, and even if the judge sentenced him to 500 years, I felt confident the state prison, within 24 hours of my guy's death, would release his body."

* * *

The following week, the jury acquitted Jack's client of all charges except the failure to register, apparently believing the alleged teenage victims lied about the molestation to punish the client when he refused to fund any more of their activities.

Shortly thereafter, despite the acquittals and the five-year maximum sentence for failing to register, Judge Winston invoked the persistent felony offender rule and sentenced the client to 56 years in state prison. The good judge, in his infinite wisdom, guaranteed the client would die in custody.

As Jack entered our office after the sentencing hearing, his look of disgust spoke volumes. "Welcome to Montana, Sweet Pea, where Lady Justice loves to sneak a peek under her blindfold!"

CHAPTER ELEVEN

Payback's a Bitch

September 1998
Kootenai County Justice Center

A KOOTENAI COUNTY COP summed up to me Frank McShane's attitude toward his cases. "Either he doesn't give a shit or it's personal. If it's personal, he never lets it go no matter how crappy the evidence is."

Would Rodney's case fall in the personal vendetta category? I mentally winced at the memory.

This could get ugly.

Frank, his mouth a grim slash, the sleeves of his white shirt rolled up, sat at his county-issued metal desk in his cluttered, tiny government office, ready to do battle.

"Frank, I'm Paige Defalco. We may have met at the July meeting but--"

"I know who you are," he interrupted. "What do you want?"

Rude.

I explained Rodney's situation and provided Frank the paperwork, fully expecting his complete agreement that Rodney's second arrest exemplified a violation of the Constitution's rule against double jeopardy.

He cast a cursory glance at my documents and asserted, "That's not double jeopardy here in Montana. We can re-arrest and charge a guy with a felony for the same crime. Look at the *Blockburger* case. Your client stays in custody until he admits the probation violation."

My eyes widened as I leaned forward in my chair. "I'm pretty sure the United States Constitution applies here in Montana just like it does in every other state. I've litigated this issue dozens of times as a prosecutor and lost every time. Seriously, at least let him out of custody pending a hearing on the issue."

He sighed impatiently, sat back in his chair, and glared. "You litigated it as a prosecutor in *California,* not Montana. I'm not agreeing to his release." He emphasized California like many Montanans, as if its former residents spread bubonic plague.

Stunned by his dismissive attitude, I stood. "You're leaving me no choice but to go directly to Judge Winston to get Rodney released."

Frank smirked and returned his attention to his paperwork. "Go right ahead," he offered, and pointed to his door.

So I did.

And I received exactly the same response from the judge. "Sorry, Paige, but if Frank won't agree to your client's release, I'm not letting him out."

"Your Honor, with all due respect, what if I show you the U.S. Supreme Court cases that say Frank is wrong?"

He paused. "I don't really care about the U.S. Supreme Court's opinion. You show me a Montana Supreme Court case that says Frank is wrong, and I'll consider it."

So I did.

I walked down the short hall to the tiny law library and found a Montana case less than a year old that overturned Frank's *Blockburger* case. Triumphant, I marched back to Judge Winston's chambers and showed him the case.

"Well, Paige," he replied smugly, "I just talked to Frank about your client, and he wants him in custody. Sorry." His sneer spoke no apology.

"But, Judge," I sputtered, "he's illegally incarcerated! If you won't release him pending a hearing, then I'll have to appeal this to the Montana Supreme Court."

Judge Winston sat back in his big black chair and smirked. "Go right ahead," he goaded.

So I did.

And that act scorched a fire line between the judges,

the county attorneys, my own public defender colleagues - and me.

* * *

I realized I'd blown my goodwill at the courthouse a week later when an irate Judge Winston confronted me in the hallway in front of his chambers. Black robe flying, waiving a copy of the appeal in front of me, he steamed out, *"Mrs. Defalco!* How could you write this? You insulted Frank McShane at the Supreme Court! I hired Frank at the County Attorney's Office, and we're close friends! And why did you tell the Supreme Court that I hire the public defenders?"

I gripped my file a little tighter as I straightened my spine. "Judge, I told you I was appealing your decision two weeks ago, and you told me to go ahead. Maybe I was a little rude when I accused Frank of not knowing the law, but he doesn't. And the fact that you hire the public defenders isn't a secret. It's a conflict of interest."

He glared at me. "I *know* it's a conflict of interest, but did you have to tell the Supreme Court about it? Now they're going to demand we change the way we've done things for the last twenty years and right now, our little system here in Kootenai County works well. No, this is outrageous, and I promise you, you haven't heard the end of it."

He stormed down the hallway, leaving me with the clear impression that he and Frank McShane would guarantee me utter misery during my tenure as a public defender.

And they did.

First, they intimidated my defense colleagues, who needed their jobs like the rest of us need water. They couldn't afford to anger Judge Winston because he had the power to hire and fire them, precisely why such a hiring scheme was fraught with peril and presented a conflict of interest. If a lawyer feared job termination and income loss by advocating too strongly for his client - for example, by filing pesky motions to suppress illegally obtained evidence or trying the client's case to a jury of his peers - that lawyer instead placated the judge. He pled his clients guilty, collected his paltry paycheck, and shut up about injustice in the justice system.

Once the judge and prosecutors chastised my colleagues, I became the bastard child of the courthouse, shunned, and even roughed up outside the jail by an attorney who shoved me into the wall and accused me of trying to get everyone fired.

Second, they punished my clients. Suddenly there were no reasonable plea deals. Frank McShane blocked my every move. He even charged Rodney with a new felony, possession of methamphetamine for the drug allegedly found in the syringe in his basement, and then set a probation hearing in front of Judge Winston for the following week. After the hearing, Frank and Judge Winston planned to send Rodney to prison.

In response, I returned to the Montana Supreme Court, challenging Judge Winston's impartiality toward my clients and me, alleging he couldn't be fair when Frank McShane was the prosecutor on the case since they were such close buddies. That move lit the duo up like a Roman candle, fueling their wrath toward me.

Third, they contacted the local press and referred to me as an aggressive, in-your-face attorney. The reporters also needed the judge and county attorney on their side, or their news from the courthouse would dry up. They dutifully wrote excoriating stories about me, including editorials advising me to return to California since I didn't like the way criminal justice was meted out in the Kootenai valley. One reporter dubbed me "The Courthouse Crusader." Better, a conservative local talk show host spent hours on his show urging me to leave the state.

The net effect of all this publicity on our law practice was a flood of new clients. People tired of the 'good old boy' system in the county were thrilled to have a pair of lawyers who confronted those Courthouse Cowboys and took cases to trial. However, the net effect of the combat on me showed in my graying hair, under-eye bags, cranky disposition, impatience with our kids, and loss of time for volunteering at school or attending social events. I didn't even have time for Annie, or for any of the other women cancer survivors who needed friendship and support.

In short, I'd returned to my stressful life in California without ever packing a suitcase.

* * *

The day for Rodney's hearing arrived, with no decision from the Supreme Court about my challenge to Judge Winston. After the judge yelled at me when I objected to him remaining on Rodney's case, Frank called his star witness who testified about the spoon that he'd found in the velvet bag outside Rodney's car ten months earlier. The officer swore it had a long handle, like an iced-tea spoon, and that a flame used to cook drugs had blackened the bottom of it. After I insisted he retrieve the evidence, now in a sealed crime lab package, he opened the box in front of us from the witness stand.

Rodney whispered to me, "Watch this. The cop just made that shit up."

The spoon had no handle, no blackened area, and the spoon itself was quite large, more like a tablespoon with its handle hacked off. Judge Winston glared at Frank McShane, who in turn glared at the cop, who said truthfully, "This isn't the same spoon I found that day." It was an awkward moment for the prosecution.

At the noon break, Frank called me a jackass and a bitch. I countered with a gleeful, "Temper, temper, Frank."

Two lawyers, two redheads, two ill-mannered, ill-tempered adults acting like children.

After lunch Frank's case tanked even further when the probation officer who supposedly found the syringe in Rodney's basement admitted he'd lost all the evidence. By day's end, Judge Winston sat on the bench, his head in his hands, as Frank McShane tried in vain to repair his case. Frank asked to continue the hearing until the next morning, but Judge Winston refused, telling us he'd let us know when we could proceed. Meanwhile, Rodney returned to the jail.

The next morning the Montana Supreme Court advised me I'd won in my effort to challenge Judge Winston for bias against me. They refused to release Rodney, but ordered a hearing on the double jeopardy issue. An hour later, Frank McShane dismissed the added felony charge against Rodney, but left the probation violation intact, which meant Rodney stayed in custody indefinitely.

* * *

After the Montana Supreme Court ruled he was biased and prejudiced against me, Judge Winston grew increasingly irate every time I appeared in his court. In his late 60s, balding, and plump, he sported a beard that circled the roundness of his face. Whenever he addressed me, usually in a loud, furious voice, his pate turned bright red, suggesting the chance of a stroke at any moment.

Once, after threatening to toss me into custody with my client, another admitted child molester, Judge Winston stormed off the bench to calm down. During that recess, one defense attorney surreptitiously whispered to me that he'd never met anyone with skin thicker than mine.

Why did I continue the fight?

I stared at the American flag in the courtroom. Lofty idealist? Sucker for the underdog? Jerk? No doubt my antagonists voted for the latter. Whether with a hide like an elephant or emotionally detached, my ire toward the inequities of the Kootenai County justice system fueled me every morning and eroded my stomach lining each night.

In our typical puerile fashion, Frank McShane and I quit speaking to one another, reducing everything to terse, formal missives. I gloated when he had to dismiss five of my cases for lack of sufficient evidence to convict my clients. He retaliated by demanding harsh sentences for Leonard the Pedophile, Genny, a drug prescription forger, and Peg Zanto, a young woman who'd confessed to having sex with a 15-year-old neighbor boy. The last of these three clients unknowingly had a future role in the Cowboys' effort to rid the county of Defalco blight.

* * *

In November 1998, the Stagg brothers pled guilty to deliberate homicide and awaited sentencing in February. Meanwhile I'd prepared a murder case for a January trial for 18-year-old Casey Hennon, who stood accused of executing his best friend. Coincidentally, Casey shared Ben Stagg's cell. Rodney, the Meth Spoon Guy, shared Nick Stagg's cell.

By Christmas, I slept little and ate even less. Clients cheered while courthouse folks jeered. Our children grew angry as my time and attention went everywhere but home. The puppies destroyed the wood deck at the lake rental, along with my shoes, some paint tubes, and the carpet.

Casey and Rodney both advised me that law enforcement had approached the Stagg brothers to testify against them in order to force them to plead guilty. In exchange, the Stagg brothers had been promised lighter sentences. The Stagg brothers, however, politely declined the offers.

Casey and Rodney also hinted to me that there was more to the Stagg case than anyone knew, and they believed the brothers' attorneys were ignoring important, favorable evidence. I responded that I didn't have time to get involved since I was up to my ass in my own troublesome cases. *Their* cases, in particular.

I packed the Christmas decorations away and settled at my desk to review additional evidence the prosecutor, Don Yeager, provided me a few days earlier in Casey's murder case. He'd delivered the load of reports and tapes in a donut box, proof of the stereotype that cops survived on glazed, filled, or frosted fried dough.

A previously undetected videotape of an interview between Casey and the police got my attention. In it, the investigating officer, white-haired, with a long handlebar mustache, accused Casey of being a gang member because he had tattoos, moved to Montana from California, and wore a blue Dallas Cowboys' jacket. The old officer opined that gangs wore blue and red.

Casey told the cop many times that he didn't kill his friend, and even asked why the cop suspected murder when no body had been found. The cop jumped from his chair at Casey and yelled that Casey was under arrest for murder, this despite the absence of a victim. He handcuffed Casey to a chair, stretching the kid's thin arms behind the chair's back, forcing Casey to lean forward in the seat. The cop swaggered back and forth for a minute, then bent over and pushed his red-mottled face several inches from Casey's.

That's when he screamed at my little, five foot five inch, 18-year-old client, "Now you listen to me, boy! You weren't even a wet spot in your old man's underwear when I was ridin' with the Hell's Angels! Damn it, you tell me the truth!" Spittle flew from his lips.

Silence.

The old cop, menacing, threatened, "This ain't California, boy!"

To which young Casey replied, deadpan, "Obviously."

The pure theater in that tape, the villainous-looking cop screaming at the wide-eyed young kid, the idiocy of the murder arrest with no body, the crude words about semen, all brought a grin to my heart, the likes of which I hadn't felt in two years, ever since my last trial. That video hooked the fiend in me, gutting me as it released my pent up craving for the courtroom.

CHAPTER TWELVE

Return of the Trial Junkie

January 1999
Aberdeen, Montana

WHETHER IT'S COCAINE, tobacco, booze, porn, or trial, addiction sleeps, awaiting temptation. One scent, one picture, one taste, and it roars back at full throttle, shackling the junkie.

That videotape of the sheriff spewing epithets at my client stabbed like a lance into my Achilles heel. Helpless to stop the adrenalin racing through my veins, just as, years before, I'd relapsed into smoking after only one puff on a Marlboro, I skittered into Jack's office.

"Holy *shit*, Honeybun! Wait until you see this interview!"

He glanced up from his file, curious at my effervescence. "Is this for your murder trial? I thought you dreaded the day you had to pick the jury."

"I did. Now I can't wait. Do you realize in the hundreds of pages of police reports, in all the crime lab analyses, there isn't a shred of evidence pointing to Casey as the shooter? If anything, the physical evidence points to Dino, the other kid in the car besides the victim." My speech raced, my mouth filled with cotton. That I might have interrupted Jack's important work never crossed my dopamine-flooded brain.

Jack knew the basic facts of the case:

Three kids - Casey, 18, Dino, 16, and RJ, the 17-year-old driver - cruised down a remote road looking to score some meth. RJ pulled over so someone could pee. The front seat passenger got out. Then the kid in the back seat pointed a stolen gun and shot RJ in the back of the head one time. At trial, the only issue for the jury to settle was the identity of the shooter, either Casey or Dino.

After the murder, Casey and Dino put RJ's body in the car's trunk, drove to Dino's house, and displayed the body to his parents, who instructed them to bury their dead friend and burn his car. Along with three buddies, they complied.

Meanwhile, Dino's parents burned his bloody clothes, apparently willing to do whatever was necessary to keep their son from prison. No one told the police or RJ's parents what happened. RJ's mom put up missing persons fliers to no avail. Even as they knew that RJ's corpse decayed in the forest, each kid involved lied to that mother when she begged them for news of her son.

Eventually Dino talked to the police but lied his ass off during the first nine interviews. Finally, Dino told the cops that Casey shot RJ. The cops told Dino that, since he talked first, he was the witness and Casey rose to the level of suspect. Casey, however, denied he shot RJ or had knowledge of the murder, hence the videotape depicting the irate deputy, who may not have known how to interview kids, but understood they were all lying to him.

Jack watched the interview, smiled, and asked, "So how are you going to get this tape into evidence?"

Drat the man, always pointing out the obvious flaws in my plan. Only the prosecutor had the legal right to play the defendant's statements to the jury, a quirk of the hearsay rule. If he chose to omit it, I couldn't use it without a good reason.

"This cop is the lead investigator on the case, so he'll have to testify. Once he does, I can attack his credibility through the tape because it shows what a crappy investigator he is." Hope glimmered in my eyes, even as my brows rose questioningly, beseeching Jack not to dash my idea.

He raised his own brows, a sure sign of doubt. "Paige, only a prosecutor who is a complete idiot would let the jury see that cop screaming at your client. It's so prejudicial that even if they like the police, they'll hate that guy. Not to mention Casey looks like a little kid handcuffed to that chair."

Jack had 350 jury trials under his belt as a prosecutor, so he knew the rules of evidence like most people know their own phone numbers. He clicked his ballpoint pen, still his most irritating habit at the office or in court.

"Yeah, you're right," I conceded as I blew my bangs out of my eyes and collapsed in the chair opposite him. My mind spun around other methods of getting it before the jury. "I'll give it a shot anyway," I vowed. "Interesting that they buried the tape in the evidence room. Like they were hiding it," I mused.

"Hell yes, they were hiding it," he emphasized, clicking his pen even faster. "Talk about shitty police work. This is the most poorly investigated case I've ever seen. What cop tells the two guys left alive in the car that whoever talks first gets to be the witness and whoever remains silent is the suspect? Why didn't they charge both Dino *and* Casey and let the jury sort it out? What kind of a deal did they cut with Dino so he'd testify? Did they give him immunity from murder charges?"

He shook his head as he ran his fingers through the top of his hair in frustration. "Having said that," he continued, "I still don't think you can win this case. Not with Dino's parents and his three gravedigger buddies testifying Casey was the shooter."

I jiggled my cowboy-booted foot. "They claim there's no deal with Dino, which I know is crappola. Also, I asked the cops to test for blood on Dino's pants. His jeans are the only clothing item his parents didn't burn up, probably because they're huge. That kid must weigh 300 pounds. Since he claims he drove RJ's car after the murder, the back of his jeans should be covered in RJ's blood." I stood and paced a worn path on Jack's carpet.

Jack leaned back in his chair. "Are they testing Casey's clothes for blood?"

"They did already. Nothing. Not a speck on anything he wore that night." I smiled. "That's another good fact for the defense."

I glanced at my watch. "Yikes." I grabbed my purse and briefcase. "How about you pick up something for dinner on the way home while I get the kids and help them with homework? We'll decide who has to clean up the puppy debris later."

Jack nodded as I raced for the door.

Parenting 101: Divide and conquer.

* * *

The judge agreed to continue Casey's murder trial while I sorted through the other contents in the donut box. I had dozens of other cases, mostly with Frank McShane as the assigned prosecutor, that consumed valuable trial preparation time, so I solved that issue by working 60 hours a week. Each night after the kids were settled in bed, I'd steal upstairs to the room I'd commandeered as a 'war room' to listen to witness interview tapes, taking copious notes of the nuances in each version.

The evidence to support Casey's innocence was thin, so impeaching Dino's credibility was critical. The crime lab analysis of Dino's pants produced no traces of blood, a fact that ate at me. Even stranger than the lack of blood was Dino's statement in one of his many interviews that when he returned to his house, he removed his bloody pants, put soap and *bleach* in the washer, and washed them, along with his tennis shoes.

In one of the gravedigger interviews, one kid who helped bury RJ's body noted that Dino's *white* pants were covered in blood when he arrived at Dino's house. Blood doesn't easily wash out, so I'd asked to see all the physical evidence at the Sheriff's office. Dino's jeans, the ones the crime lab tested, were *black*.

I learned that after Dino fingered Casey as the shooter, a detective took Dino to his house to collect his 'crime clothes' that he wore the night of the murder. When the detective asked Dino to fetch them, Dino handed over the pair of black jeans. That the sheriff's deputy allowed the accused to provide his own evidence pointed to more bungling of the investigation.

More important, if one witness said Dino wore white pants covered in blood, a fact supported by Dino's admitted bleaching of his pants that night, and no blood appeared when the black pants were tested, then Dino deliberately provided the cops with the wrong pair of pants. That clever move showed consciousness of guilt and pointed to him as the killer. Whether the blood-drenched, white pants were hidden, or his parents had burned them, was a question I hoped Dino would answer during his cross-examination.

In another of Dino's taped interviews, he told the detective that Casey asked RJ to pull over so he could pee, not Dino, a statement he quickly amended, saying it was he who had to pee. Whoever the jury believed had asked RJ to pull over likely would be the innocent party, since that kid would be outside the car at the time of the murder.

The identity of the front seat passenger also mattered because the autopsy showed the shot that killed RJ entered the rear of his head and could only come from a shooter in the back seat. As a mom, I knew it was a rare day when our oldest child called 'shotgun' running toward the car and didn't get her way, relegating her little brother to the back seat. Since Dino was 16, and Casey 18, Casey more likely rode 'shotgun' in front - a small point, but important when aggregated with the other evidence.

Regarding motive, not something the prosecutor had to prove, but helpful to a jury, Dino was on juvenile probation, which meant he couldn't possess or own a handgun. Yet he'd sneaked into a neighbor's house and stolen the gun used to kill RJ. RJ had borrowed the gun and then refused to return it, threatening to turn Dino in to his probation officer if Dino tried to reclaim it. That bit of information, gleaned from Casey's relative, provided a motive for Dino to shoot RJ.

Other physical evidence at the burial site supported Dino as the killer. RJ was an averaged-sized kid, much taller and heavier than Casey. Dino was a huge kid and much stronger than Casey. The cops found RJ's body buried quite some distance from the road out in the forest, which indicated RJ had been carried to the burial site. Clearly, little Casey could not have carried him, while Dino easily could. No drag marks were found in the thin snow cover.

With respect to Dino's claim that Casey forced him to help bury RJ and burn his car, given their respective sizes, his claim wasn't plausible unless Casey forced him at gunpoint, and no witness had mentioned that.

Finally, Casey's grandparents would testify at trial that Casey and RJ were best friends who planned on living together. They'd spent hours fixing up a fifth wheel trailer to move into, so Casey had no motive to kill his best friend.

Armed with those facts, I headed to trial in mid-January, our son moaning, "Mom, you *promised* you'd never do this again if we moved to Montana." The adrenalin thrumming through my veins, however, overrode my festering maternal guilt.

* * *

As I questioned prospective jurors about publicity surrounding the case, my senses hummed. When at last we'd selected the jury, I closeted myself in my war room to fine-tune my opening statement.

Jack entered carrying a sandwich for me. "What does your jury look like?" he inquired, setting the food next to me on the desk.

"Uh," I reached for the sandwich, stalling. *He's going to find out anyway so just tell him.* "You might as well know, I left on a fat guy and a cop." I quickly bit into the turkey and Swiss on wheat.

Jack backed away from me as if I'd slapped him, staring while I continued to munch. I swallowed as the silence grew, his gaze never wavering.

I blinked first. "Look, I know that violates two of the big rules of jury selection you taught me, but Casey wanted the fat guy, and the cop is a retired captain from the California Highway Patrol. The investigation is such a disaster, I figure he'll look at the evidence and realize there isn't enough to convict Casey. Besides, I'd settle for a hung jury if the fat juror performs as expected."

All trial attorneys follow certain lore when selecting jurors, rules based on stereotypes but grounded in experience. Jack hammered those rules into my brain early in my career, so I understood his reaction when I'd just broken two big ones.

Rule number one: Never leave the obese on a jury, under the theory that fat people never get any attention, so they will remain the lone hold-out vote and hang the case, merely because eleven other people are focused on them.

Rule number two: Never leave on someone who works closely with the criminal justice system, because those folks will taint the rest of the jurors with their personal knowledge about how things work.

Rule number three: Never leave on anyone whose profession begins with the letter P - as in pastor/priest, psychiatrist, professor, etc., or anyone who is in a helper job - as in nurse, teacher, counselor, etc. - because they will sympathize with the underdog, whether that is a cop on the stand or the defendant.

Other rules lawyers follow: A prosecutor with an African-American defendant throws off black women since they might sympathize with the accused. Defense attorneys dump Asians because they are conviction prone. In any death penalty case, prosecutors toss off Jewish people since they will never vote to execute anyone after experiencing the horrors of the Holocaust.

Jury Selection 1A: The art of utilizing sweeping generalizations.

Following these underground rules is tough because they're illegal. If a lawyer tosses a juror who falls into a 'cognizable group' - for example, women, African Americans, the obese, etc. - without a good reason, and the other side objects, the lawyer gets in big trouble and the case gets reversed. Fortunately, in Montana, the number of cognizable groups is minimal. We have white men and white women, fat people and thin people, a few Native Americans, and that's pretty much the end of diversity in the state.

Jack shook his head. "I hope you know what you're doing, Sweet Pea. You're already way behind the eight ball in this case, and your client is looking at a 100-year sentence."

Miffed, I shot back, "I don't need you to remind me of the high stakes, Hon. I could use a little support here. Although thanks for the sandwich. I was starving." I wiped the last of the crumbs from my lips and pushed the plate away.

Jack took the plate like a waiter at Denny's and added, "If anyone can pull this thing off, it's you, Paige. Let me know if you need anything else." Then he left to check the basketball score.

At that moment I wished I still smoked. Even though I hadn't inhaled a puff in nearly 15 years, I remembered the relaxation nicotine brought. I needed to slow the frenzy of facts racing through my neurons, to sleep undisturbed for more than three hours at a time. I knew from all my prior trials it wouldn't happen. Tomorrow was only an hour away, yet I had more to prepare.

I'd gambled on the jury. If I'd erred in my assessment of those folks, small, vulnerable, 18-year-old Casey was headed to Deer Lodge State Prison for the rest of his life. Glancing at my reflection in the antique mirror on the opposite wall, I saw the sags and bags, the circles, and the gray complexion. The annoying constriction in my chest returned, wrapping my torso like a boa constrictor. My heart pounded, so I held my breath to slow down my pulse, a useless gesture. That's the problem with addiction. The high always ends in a crash.

Yet if I crashed at the end of this trial, I still returned home to my family. For Casey, it meant 100 years in prison.

CHAPTER THIRTEEN

The Trial Ain't Over Till the Fat Guy Votes

Early February 1999
Aberdeen, Montana

ONE TEARDROP. Was that too much to expect from a kid who dumped his friend's body into a trunk, carried it to a lonely burial site in the forest, threw it into a hastily dug hole, covered it with dirt and slash, burned the car, and then lied to his dead friend's mother?

As I cross-examined Dino for hours about the previous lies he'd told, I inwardly shuddered at his detachment from RJ's murder. At sixteen, how could he sit before the judge, jury, press, and RJ's family as he continued to lie?

RJ's mom and sister, sitting in the front row behind the prosecutors, shed more tears than I could bear. Their anguish tore at me, forcing me to view the crime scene photos and autopsy photos as the mother of a son, no longer as the lawyer/addict relishing trial. I winced every time I encountered RJ's mother's ravaged face. I prayed for God to somehow comfort her, to help her find peace one day, unsure if such peace was possible for the parent of a murdered child.

Dino's expressionless testimony, his occasional sneer, ended when we finally arrived at The Pants. Dino looked smug as I held them up for the jury, large and black.

"Did your mom teach you to separate clothes into piles of darks and lights before washing them?" I inquired.

"Yes," he replied, somewhat confused.

I felt confident the prosecutor hadn't caught the

discrepancy in the interviews, nor its impeachment value against this star witness. Dino had no clue what was coming.

"So when you told the detective you added soap and *bleach* to the machine when you washed these jeans, weren't you concerned the bleach would ruin them?"

He squirmed in the witness chair. He looked around the courtroom. He cleared his throat.

"Was I concerned?" he repeated, a classic stalling tactic by lying witnesses.

"Yes, why did you add bleach to wash these obviously *black* jeans, Dino?"

"Uh . . . I didn't. I made a mistake."

"You made a mistake when you added bleach, or when you turned over these black jeans to the detective?"

"Uh . . . when I said I added bleach." He paused, leaning forward. "Those *are* the pants I was wearing that night," he emphasized, with no question pending regarding the veracity of the jeans.

I dogged him, this near-child witness. "Really? Your friend Jason, who helped you get rid of the evidence, told the detective that when he arrived at your house the night of RJ's murder, you were wearing *white pants* that were covered with blood. Is he mistaken?"

Silence.

"Or, Dino, did you intentionally give the detective the wrong pair of pants because you knew RJ's blood covered the white ones you wore that night, and you knew that would make you look like the killer?"

More silence.

Quietly, since I stood at a podium next to the jury box, I inquired, "Dino, where are the bloody white pants you wore the night RJ was killed? Did you burn them along with your other clothes?"

I let his continued silence hang in front of the jury as I stared at him.

Judge Holmes interrupted, "I think this would be a good time to take our evening recess." It was nearly 5 o'clock. "Ladies and Gentlemen of the jury, please do not discuss this case among yourselves or with anyone else. Please do not watch or read any media coverage of this case. Have a pleasant evening. I'll see you and counsel at 8:30 tomorrow morning."

Dino glared or stared at me, I couldn't quite nail the look, as they cuffed him to return him to custody at juvenile hall.

When I returned to the office, now at that point in trial when I didn't pretend to be a parent to our kids, I heard the phone ring through the empty silence. I let it go, intent on preparing for the next day's cross-examination of witnesses. At a knock on the door, I looked up to find a girl outside, a 16-year-old friend of Casey's.

"Hey Shannon, come in. What's up?" Although trial prep beckoned, I needed a break from the evidence.

She sat on the edge of the chair facing my desk. "Mrs. Defalco, I was in court today. I need to tell you something." Fear caused her hands to tremble as she twisted a tissue in her lap.

Well shit. Just shit. What is this kid going to tell me? That Casey really is the shooter? That she was in the car and saw what happened?

I sighed as I asked, "What is it? What do you know?"

Shannon looked out the window then back. "I was with Dino and Jason after RJ's body was found. They told me Casey shot RJ, and then they got rid of the body and other evidence. I didn't say anything to the police. I didn't want to get in trouble. But today when I heard Dino lie about the pants, well, I just thought you should know. Dino said he did have on white pants that night, and he told me he buried them in the backyard of his mom's house. They should still be there."

Bingo!

That was a break I hadn't expected. The pants didn't prove Dino was the shooter, but since Casey had no blood on his clothing, it might sway the jury toward acquittal. At least Dino's incessant lying and destruction of evidence created reasonable doubt about the killer's identity.

I smiled at Shannon. "Honey, I know you don't want to get involved, but I need you to come to court when our case starts and tell the jury about the pants. I have a duty to tell the prosecutor first thing tomorrow, and then we'll see if the sheriffs can dig them up.

I secured her promise to testify, called Jack with this latest development, and headed home. I could work in my war room as easily as the office, and kids, dogs, and food awaited me at the house. At that moment, I craved a state of normal so badly I'd have sold my mother's antique china to attain it.

Driving the short distance to the rental house, I wondered what other surprises would surface before this trial ended.

* * *

The next morning in court, I advised Don Yeager about the missing pants. He looked surprised. "How did you know that? We just found out last night from Jason."

I regarded him warily. "I heard it from Shannon, a friend of theirs. So what did Jason tell you?"

Yeager shook his head and rolled his eyes, looking like a lawyer who knew his case was falling apart. "Jason came to me this morning. He said he and Dino were in the common area at juvenile hall last night, talking about the case. Dino told him, 'That bitch really got me on the pants. Man, how did she figure that out? That I gave the cops the wrong pair?' So we're calling Jason first thing this morning, if you're done with Dino, to tell the jury Dino lied to them."

As I thought how to respond, I noted the ineptitude of housing two kid witnesses together so they could polish their stories before they testified. I also questioned why this kid, Jason, suddenly found God and told the truth for the first time in the case.

"I'm finished with Dino, so put on Jason. Now what

about the pants? You're going to send the sheriff to Dino's house to get them, aren't you?"

His annoyance showed in his voice. "No, I am *not* going after the pants. They're not relevant to my case. If you want them, *you* go dig them up."

We'd been discussing the issue quietly, mindful of the audience filling the courtroom's seats. Now my pitch rose. "You're kidding, right? C'mon! The pants are a key piece of evidence, and Dino's your star witness. The jury will wonder what you're hiding if you don't get them. I can't get them because the information is too old to get a warrant, but your guy can tell you where they are and give us permission to dig."

As the prosecutor turned away, he barked, "Not happening."

So, even now, those big, white, bloody pants likely still rot in the back yard of Dino's old house.

* * *

More witnesses, more cross-examination. The days dragged on. The jurors listened attentively but occasionally snored, the reporters kept the story front page, television cameras rolled, and microphones piped the testimony into a classroom at the local high school. High courtroom drama was rare in Kootenai County, so a lengthy murder trial had folks' attention. Evidently, so did the nasty, California, female defense attorney representing the alleged killer, who had all but been convicted before trial.

To my astonishment, Don Yeager introduced the video of the cop screaming at Casey, under the theory that it would look better coming from him than me. It had the expected effect on the jury, who afterward stared at that cop on the witness stand as if his handlebar mustache accompanied a matching set of horns sprouting atop his ears.

Cop's credibility, zero. Score one for the defense.

Then one morning Yeager again approached me in his

quiet manner. "We need to talk to the judge."

Once in the privacy of the judge's chambers, he began wearily, "More breaking news. We received a call this morning from a mother in Bozeman who claims her 16-year-old son was housed with Dino in juvenile hall a few months ago. Her son asked Dino why he was in custody, and Dino told him, 'You know that case in Beartooth, where they murdered the kid and burned up his car? That was me.'"

The judge sat back in her huge chair, I sat forward in my little chair, mouth agape, and then grinned.

Yeager smiled. "I suppose you want to go to Bozeman to interview him?" It came out as a statement more than a question.

"I suppose I do." I smiled back. "Sorry for the delay, Your Honor, but this is new evidence I had no reason to anticipate. I think we need to take a road trip."

Judge Holmes agreed and recessed court. At counsel table, I explained to Casey why we we'd stopped the proceedings. "You, Casey, must have a guardian angel. If this kid is willing to testify to Dino's statement, that is enough reasonable doubt to set you free. You sit tight, and I'll be back tomorrow."

Don Yeager, two sheriffs, and I drove together to Bozeman and interviewed the kid, who I immediately subpoenaed to court for the following week. He'd just become the premier witness for the defense. And that, I reflected on the return drive, is what I love about trial. You plan and prepare, get your evidence together, and weigh the odds of winning. And, *whamo*, out of nowhere, manna from heaven drops into your lap and the whole game changes.

As we passed a bird sanctuary, I marveled at the Crazyhorse Mountains reflected in numerous snowmelt pools, then thought of RJ's family. If Casey was acquitted, and Dino was immune from prosecution for the murder, what sort of justice would they receive for their son?

* * *

Judge Holmes turned to the foreperson. "Has the jury reached a verdict?" The man nodded and handed the verdict form to the bailiff, who handed it to the judge, who handed it to the clerk. "Madam Clerk, will you read the jury's verdict please?"

We'd sat in trial for three weeks, viewed scads of physical evidence, and listened to hundreds of hours of testimony from dozens of witnesses. The jury had deliberated for twenty hours, taking an evening break late the previous night. Every person in the courtroom exemplified 'haggard', all of us tense with anticipation, but none more so than the 18-year-old kid sitting to my left.

Jack couldn't make it for the verdict, tied up as he was with kids, animals, the law practice, shopping, dinner, coaching Little Guy Football, and handling my other cases that he'd covered for three weeks while I lived at the courthouse. I sat alone with Casey, keenly attuned to RJ's family sitting to my right, weeping, while cops poured into the courtroom to maintain order when the verdict was read.

Our defense witnesses had testified well, and no jurors slept through closing arguments, so I placed our odds of winning around 40%. After all, liars or not, five people swore that Casey was the shooter. The prosecutor and I knew from the jurors' responses to Judge Holmes' inquiry the night before that eleven jurors had reached one conclusion, while a lone holdout refused to change his or her opposite vote. We hadn't a clue whether the eleven were for or against Casey's guilt.

When the bailiff told me the jury had a verdict, and the judge would allow twenty minutes for the families and press to arrive, I'd waited outside in the cold for Casey's family. I told them that whatever the outcome, we would handle it quietly and with dignity. We had reasonable appellate issues if the jury convicted him. None of us was confident of an acquittal.

The jurors looked grim as they took their seats, some

staring at Casey, others focused on their laps. One woman cried quietly. As the clerk stood, I patted Casey on the shoulder, but he was wooden - terrified, yet without visible emotion.

The clerk, stoic as ever, read from the verdict form. "In the matter of the State of Montana versus Casey Hennon, regarding count one of the Information - murder - we the jury find the defendant . . . *not guilty*."

The air pushed from my lungs as I sat back in counsel chair, my right hand reaching over my heart. My eyes closed briefly, my lips pursed, and I grabbed onto Casey's arm with my left hand. For his part, he hung his head in relief, then smiled. I heard Casey's family behind us, crying, laughing, and sobbing. He went to them for long-awaited hugs as jurors walked by and patted me on the shoulder.

"Good job," one said.

Don Yeager and RJ's family walked quickly from the courtroom as the press descended on me for comments. One juror also talked to the press, the lone holdout who, after twenty hours, had finally changed his vote to not guilty.

Yeah, it was the fat guy, yet again vindicating Jack's trial instincts.

On the other hand, my retired highway patrolman led the charge for acquittal so I, too, triumphed. Or maybe I just got lucky.

I'd been warned that RJ's brothers threatened violence if Casey was acquitted, and to take precautions for his safety and my own. Casey's family, at my insistence, had arranged for him to leave town the next day. The sheriffs escorted me to my car, but I assured them I'd be fine on the way home.

I stopped at the office to drop off my trial files, when suddenly Jack appeared at my desk on his way from the grocery store. Since I was on the phone he mouthed, "What happened? Did you get a verdict?" I nodded, mouthed back, "Not guilty" to which he shouted, "Alright! I can't believe it! I can't fucking believe it!" And he hugged me.

Once home, the kids celebrated, especially our daughter, who had endured months of questions and comments from kids at the high school, most who knew Casey, Dino, and the others. I fell into a chair to watch the news, realizing for the first time the magnitude of the verdict.

While my reputation as a lawyer rose in some circles, my trial victory cinched the noose around my neck, preparing my courthouse critics to kick away the stool on which I precariously balanced.

Meanwhile, alone now in his jail cell without the comfort of his friend Casey, Ben Stagg, ignorant of his own imminent demise, played with a hackey-sack ball he'd fashioned from his sock.

CHAPTER FOURTEEN

Amazing Grace

Ash Wednesday – February 1999
Beartooth, Montana

IN THE MINUTE IT TOOK THE CLERK to enunciate two words, "not guilty," a seismic shift launched 18-year-old Casey from *murderer* to free man. From a future flashing *lifetime inmate* to a path spread endlessly before him with potential and hope.

The next morning as he prepared to leave Montana, we walked on the road where he'd been arrested nine months before.

Casey glanced at his family home one last time. "You know my cell mate, Ben Stagg?"

I nodded. The wind howled around us as if seeking asylum under my down-filled parka. I shivered at the cold, but also at Casey's imminent departure to an unknown location, alone, without friends, family, or work, at 18.

He kicked at a stone barely exposed through the early February snow drifting on the road. "I'm worried about Ben. He's different. Not tough enough, and he can't think very well. The weirdest thing is that he *flinches* all the time. If you come near him, he ducks away from you. It's like he's a beaten dog, but he won't say why. He's afraid of his brother, too." His blue eyes implored me. "I was thinking you should tell his lawyer."

Casey had known his share of brutality, his stepfather's fist used as a common bludgeon against him as he grew up. Now he'd witnessed a murder and covered it up, at the demand of Dino's parents. His compassion for the friend he left at the jail touched me. I promised him I'd mention it, although with my colleagues shunning me, the odds of that conversation occurring were slim.

I hugged Casey fiercely and watched him walk away, my mom-sadness evident in tears that froze to my cheeks. My lawyer pragmatism sighed, knowing I'd done all I could do for him. His future loomed, but he had to step forward to take it in his own hands.

* * *

Later, as I drove to the warmth of our home and the chaos inside, I recalled that Rodney, who currently shared a cell with Ben Stagg's brother, Nick, described scarring on Nick's back from a beating when Nick was 11, just after he'd returned home from the hospital in his wheelchair. Nick also refused to talk about his past or his family.

My prosecutor's instincts screamed that the Stagg family had a dark side, especially after I'd read that their 14-year-old cousin, Andy, shot and killed his dad just two days after the Stagg brothers' arrest. The clan lived close to one another in Whitehall, sharing genetic material and, evidently, an urge to kill.

Not my assignment, I reminded myself as I pulled into the garage, chocolate labs scattering and yipping.

"Hey, Mom!" my son shouted as he ran to me, giggling. "I peed off the balcony while Heather was smoking down below and the pee hit her and she screamed. It was so great!" His words couldn't spill out fast enough to alert me to his older cousin's distress. "And the puppies ate the deck. You should see it. There are wood chips everywhere. Dad's mad. And Claire . . ."

As his little voice sailed through the day's

adventures, it yanked me into the present, back to normal life, whatever that was. The foreboding and sense of gloom surrounding my heart eased. I dropped my briefcase in my war room.

Not my case.

I shed the endless navy blue of my suit.

Not my clients.

I sautéed chicken for that night's dinner.

Leave it alone.

I cut out construction paper heads of U.S. presidents for the fourth grade history project.

Let it go, Paige. These lost boys, these accused killers, thieves, and drug addicts, they're not your kids.

I read *Harry Potter* to our son and dozed with him in the chair, finding silence from the cerebral chatter.

Not . . . my . . . problem.

* * *

"Let us share with one another a sign of peace," the priest intoned.

At 5 o'clock Mass on Ash Wednesday, two weeks after the jury acquitted Casey of murdering RJ, my family prepared to shake hands with our fellow parishioners. I turned to the pew behind us, extended my hand, and looked into the grief-stricken face of RJ's mom. Her daughter, RJ's older sister, stood next to her mother as if to protect her from further trauma.

I winced, unsure what to do next. Should I murmur words of condolence? Apologize? Leave the church to prevent them additional pain? For the last two weeks I'd expressed my frustration at the family's dearth of justice, both privately and in the press. As I faced their sadness, with my own healthy kids standing next to me, I choked on my voice.

I pictured the crime scene photos of RJ's body

buried in a shallow grave. A white sock covered his big toe, which protruded from the thawing ground, providing the search and rescue team with their only clue to the body's location. This woman's beautiful, blonde-haired boy had died on his 18th birthday.

Those seconds of reflection ended when RJ's sister reached out her hand to mine, shook it, smiled, and murmured, "Peace be with you, Mrs. Defalco."

Her mother did the same.

The forgiveness in that simple gesture spoke volumes about the kindness in their character. Through the warmth of their touch, the boulder compressing my chest rolled away.

"Peace be with you," I whispered as I returned the squeezes from their clasped hands.

I prayed that their faith would deliver them to a place of healing, to that point during grief where we never forget, but we don't remember quite so often. Looking at my own children, I wondered if such a place existed.

* * *

"This is the attorney I told you about who kicked our ass in court three weeks ago in that murder case." Detective Gayle Overcast thus introduced me to her dinner companion, a gothic-looking fellow with a dyed black Mohawk. Leaving a local restaurant with my family, I'd spotted her and stopped to say hello.

Gayle, the commander of the Sheriff's Detectives Division, who'd done considerable work on Casey's case, was a legend in the valley. She'd begun as a dispatcher 20 years before and worked her way up through a sea of male deputies to lead the detectives, with a stop along the way to train and teach at the FBI academy in Quantico.

She was one tough broad: plump, silver-haired, her twinkling blue eyes always ready for laughter or mischief-making. She'd raised her two sons alone and knew the wiles of teenage boys. Testifying at Casey's trial, she'd proved a formidable witness for the prosecution.

In the midst of Casey's trial, Gayle had driven with me to Bozeman to meet the kid who became my star witness. There, while we awaited the meeting, Gayle and I killed time together shopping at the local mall while the prosecutor and deputy ate lunch. Nothing like a little female bonding to turn adversaries into amigos.

Fascinated by the Mohawk, I shook hands with her companion, a reporter for *Rolling Stone* magazine who'd come from London to cover the Stagg brothers' sentencing that had taken place earlier that day.

"So," she continued around a bite of Cajun gumbo, "did you hear the sentences for the Stagg brothers? I noticed you weren't in court."

I shook my head as I responded, "I don't go to the courthouse unless I have to, Gayle. In case it's escaped you, I'm pretty much a pariah."

She laughed. "Yep, you sure have rocked the boat downtown," she enthused. Her smile vanished as she grew serious. "Judge Winston gave those boys 100 years apiece, with no possibility of parole for Nick. What a circus. The Winston family and friends sat ringside in the jury box. The spectator gallery was packed. *NewsTime*, *CBS* filmed the whole thing, and the rest of the media recorded it or wrote it down." Her fork hovered over a slice of andouille sausage as she pondered the event.

"Holy crap," I muttered so as to avoid nearby patrons overhearing. "That's crazy! Neither of those kids has any record. They confessed. They cooperated with you so all the stolen goods could be returned to their owners, and they've been model inmates at the jail. What did they get in return for pleading guilty and saving the county the cost of a trial? Or the Truman family the stress of one?"

Gayle put down her fork. "They got out of a death sentence, Paige, and that's a lot. Besides, it's probably the right sentence for Nick since he was the shooter, but it seems a little excessive for Ben." She stabbed the chunk of andouille and added, "You're just turning into a bleeding heart since you switched over to the Dark Side."

Her companion nodded agreement, devouring his shrimp etouffe'.

I ignored the barb, but wondered if she would agree with Nick's sentence if it were her own son's life hanging in the balance.

"A death sentence? I've got news for you. The younger brother wasn't even eligible for the death penalty under Montana law." I ran my fingers through my hair in frustration, separating my bangs. "Besides," I continued, "these are *kids,* Gayle. Ben was barely 18 at the time of the murder and has obvious learning problems, and Nick was 19 and bound to a *wheelchair.* What judge would condemn those kids to death?"

Gayle pointed a roll at me, which she was about to butter. "Hank Winston and half the people in this valley wanted to kill those kids." She turned to her companion as he picked up his wine glass. "She's from *California,"* Gayle noted, *sotto voce,* from the side of her mouth, as if that explained away my legal qualms.

"Which means," I addressed the reporter, "that I don't understand Montanans and their lust for vengeance. Did you know," I continued rhetorically, "that this state just outlawed *hanging* in 1997 because there were too many lawsuits when they used it as a form of execution?"

The reporter gazed down at his half-eaten meal, wisely saying nothing. Just as his silence grew annoying, my daughter interrupted, politely smiling at Detective Overcast while she tugged on my sleeve. "Mom, can we *go*, please? I've got homework."

I bid the detective and reporter goodbye and headed home for the nightly whining session over algebra.

* * *

The next week when I entered the foyer of the courthouse, I heard my name called. As I turned toward the voice, Detective Gayle Overcast jumped out from the doorway of the Sheriff's office, holding a camera, and quickly snapped my picture. Laughing, she announced, "For our dartboard!" and skittered back inside. I chuckled as I headed into court.

Not long afterward, I heard from a local attorney that, indeed, she'd blown up that photo and drawn a target around it for the cops' daily dart competition. Rumor had it that my likeness would next appear at the shooting range.

Adversaries or amigos, I knew Gayle and I could be both, but not at the same time. As long as I worked on the Dark Side, representing the accused, I had to expect pushback from law enforcement. I no longer dwelled upon or cared why I'd switched sides. Like it or not, that train had left the station. I strained to stay on track, violating the railroad's golden rule to slow or blow a warning at the crossroads to avert any oncoming disasters.

Then again, I'd never much cared for rules.

CHAPTER FIFTEEN

Cardiac Meltdown

March 1999
Beartooth, Montana

A FEW MONTHS BEFORE the Stagg brothers entered the perdition of prison, when Casey Hennon still anticipated a similar fate, as Rodney and I battled Frank McShane and Judge Winston, I'd quietly violated a big rule of small town living. Already having snitched off the public defender hiring scheme to the Montana Supreme Court, I next ratted out the entire criminal justice system in Kootenai County.

To the ACLU.

The American Civil Liberties Union, that bastion of Commie Liberals who trash nativity scenes and snuff out the rights of the Evangelical Right, who pursue justice for everyone accused of anything - including Nazis desiring parade permits - symbolized Rodney's lifeline to custodial release.

At Rodney's pleading, I'd called the ACLU's only legal representative in Montana and met with her secretly to advise her of the multitude of injustices I'd encountered in Kootenai County. This, after regarding the ACLU with scorn my entire career. Even after meeting with her, I doubted the national organization would actually fight a battle for justice in Montana. Still, the guys at the jail needed far more help than any single lawyer could provide. We needed the ACLU's power and resources.

The local attorney contacted the ACLU's main office in New York to relay my concerns. The New York lawyers phoned me to discuss the local criminal justice system. They assured me that if I agreed to help, they could make a difference in the state's indigent defense system.

Agreeing to help the ACLU meant professional suicide. The legal community downtown would never forgive me. I considered declining, since my public defender career already had careened off a cliff. On the other hand, how much worse could my life get at the courthouse?

So, with a nod from Jack, I agreed to help them.

Eventually, true to their word, the ACLU arrived in Beartooth to work out of the law office of Defalco & Defalco while they investigated my claims. After several days and numerous interviews with our jailed clients, my public defender colleagues, and the two judges, the ACLU's lead attorney shook his head as he sat at our conference table.

"You're right, Paige, this is about as bad a system as I've seen, and I've seen a lot. The guys at the jail added more details that support your claims. On the other hand, the judges and public defenders denied there's any problem and advised us, in no uncertain terms, to go back to New York and leave them alone." He smiled.

Still dubious, I queried, "So what can be done? Rodney sits in custody while we wait for another judge to accept his case, now that the Supreme Court dismissed Judge Winston. Judge Holmes won't take the case, so that means an outside judge needs to agree to hear the double jeopardy motion. Meanwhile, more and more defendants head to prison because their lawyers are afraid or incapable of going to trial." I sat back in frustration, rubbing a spot on my Levis.

The ACLU lawyer looked weary but confident.

"What can we do? We can sue the State of Montana for failure to develop and fund an adequate indigent defense system, that's what we can do. We'll investigate some other counties, and if their defender systems are similar to Kootenai County, we'll put the lawsuit together and file it."

My skepticism showed in my arched brow. "You've done this before and it actually worked?"

The lawyer nodded. "It works. We make the lawsuit bullet-proof, and the legislature eventually capitulates because otherwise they violate federal constitutional law. The consequences for that are severe, like losing massive amounts of federal funding, so states change their systems."

"Yeah," my inner cynic blurted out, "well, welcome to Montana. These guys can stonewall change like nothing I've ever encountered."

"We've never lost a lawsuit like this," he assured me. "Ever."

So, the ACLU attorneys at last toured the state, confirmed the endemic nature of the problem, and returned to New York prepared to save the condemned. Buoyed, I awaited the imminent arrival of fresh troops to bolster the Defalco army of two.

And waited, and waited, and waited . . . for the next several years.

* * *

In the meantime, after Judge Winston destroyed the future for Ben and Nick Stagg, Frank McShane and I fought fifty or a hundred more fights.

My children inflicted a thousand pangs of guilt.

Then one late-March afternoon, as rare sun sparkled in the windows of my office over the health food store, Stormy ushered in Pete and Laura Stagg, whose sons' conduct had divided Kootenai County, Montana and destroyed Rich Truman's family. They'd made an appointment in a desperate effort to help their sons get out of their 100-year prison sentences. Since I'd won Casey Hennon's trial, and stood up to the Courthouse Cowboys, they figured I could help them.

They were wrong. I had no interest in jumping into the middle of that cesspool.

As I listened to them, I maintained a perfect facade of calm competence. My ubiquitous dark suit and white blouse shouted efficiency. The pearls at my ear lobes and neck bespoke quiet conservatism. Red curls framing my face blended with green eyes and freckles to warm the charged space across my desk that separated me from the couple.

What a bullshit artist you've become, Paige Defalco. I reached for pen and paper.

The Staggs held hands as they sat across from me, Pete wearing a short-sleeved western shirt and jeans, Laura in her long skirt, white blouse, and sensible shoes. Pete's own rusty red hair and mustache set off his azure eyes and white, straight smile. His lean build testified to many hours of heavy labor spent as a logger in the forest.

Laura's softer shape reflected thousands of meals prepared for Pete and their four children, of clothes washed and mended, and homework completed. Her waist-length gray hair belied her 40-something age, yet her own blue eyes shone with hope.

They looked like cardboard figures cut from a coloring book of western ranch families - surreal, stiff, and fake - their facade as firmly in place as my own. Their persona of perfection repelled me like the aliens' force field repelled America's missiles in *Independence Day*, our son's favorite movie.

I sat with pen poised above yellow legal pad, unmoving, my face frozen into an expression of detached interest. Yet my heart started the telltale slow but steady rise to arrhythmia, as they explained that Don Yeager, the prosecutor, had promised their boys one sentence, then reneged at the hearing and recommended a much longer one. The boys' public defenders let it happen without objection. So now the Staggs wanted me to go back to court for both sons to try to reduce the length of their sentences.

I didn't write down a word. *Why am I talking to these people as if I might actually try to help them when I know I can't? No lawyer can. It's a hopeless case.*

Two sets of tear-moistened blue eyes beseeched me across the desk. I glanced down at the empty lines on my legal pad, avoiding their hope. I dreaded contamination from their abiding faith that God would answer their prayers for their sons' salvation. I reeled at their suggestion that I should accept a role in that Passion play.

I don't want to see dead bodies anymore. I don't want to see dead children. I don't want to see murder victims, rape victims, or assault victims - ever again. I don't want to see their families crying or their parents wailing as they beat the earth for their dead or decimated loved ones. I'm tired of the blood, the scattered tissue, and the protruding organs. I'm tired. Just that. So . . . fucking . . . tired.

The weekend before, I'd watched a retrospective on the massacre at Jonestown

And *Dead Man Walking.*

And *The Shawshank Redemption.*

And now what I screamed in my head to everyone, except that they couldn't hear me, was, *"I'm done!"*

So when these people, these parents of killers, showed up at my office, three weeks after their sons had been sentenced to life for the murder of Rich Truman, and wanted me to help their boys, I said, "No!"

Because I wanted them to go away.

And when they begged, I said "No!"

Because I couldn't bear the parent-tears that would follow my inevitable failure to free their sons.

And when Baptist pastor Pete Stagg promised me that God would help me so, *please*, could I just try to reduce their sons' prison sentences, I said, "No!"

Because I didn't trust God to do shit, even though I prayed for him to do a lot more than that when I went to Mass every Sunday.

And then I said to them one last time, "No!"

And added, "You people! There isn't a chance in hell that we'll win. Your boys confessed to murder! It's over!"

Because I didn't want to take on another battle with Judge Harold "Hank" Winston, or leave my children and Jack for the smelly bowels of Deer Lodge State Prison.

And when Laura wept and Pete's eyes turned down in defeat, I pulled off my reading glasses and rubbed the aching spot between my eyes. I tried to quell the rising acid in my stomach, to staunch the flow of blood reeling through my head. I wanted to get these people the hell away from me. I looked up and noticed rays of sunlight shining on the Staggs. It seemed as if God wanted to warm their dampened spirits from the arctic air gusting from my lungs.

So I paused, for just a minute, to take a breath and punctuate my denial.

Then I remembered that in *Dead Man Walking*, at the end, when the anguished mom talked about the last thing she'd ever said to her daughter, I'd wept, because what if that had been *my* daughter?

And when Sean Penn's character, Matthew Poncelet, succumbed to the relentless pleas from Sister Prejean, when he'd confessed to the murders at the moment of his lethal injection, I'd cried for that bad guy, because what if that were *my* son?

Suddenly I needed to wrench the strangling pearls from my neck, the strand I'd inherited from my own mother at her death, but terror froze me because I knew the fragile string would break, exploding iridescent beads across the office and my life.

I eased back into the cushion of my chair and stared at the sun, at those parents, at the picture on my desk of my daughter, at age five, holding her newborn baby brother in her arms, and felt the numbness in my arms tingle with circulation.

I'd always figured, whenever I thought about it, that when my heart burst, at least I'd know. That at least I'd hear the crack of the encasing ice or feel the splintered shards as they sliced through my soul.

Yet when those Born-Again-Christian parents, whom I suspected of child abuse, once again pleaded with me to represent their sons, I felt no pain at all.

Instead, despite knowing there wasn't a hope of alleviating their boys' prison sentences, my heartbeat slowed, my lungs sucked in fresh oxygen, and I exhaled one word.

"Okay."

Another intake of breath and then two more words.

"I'll try."

That's when my world shifted as I, like Atlas, shrugged.

PART TWO

CHAPTER SIXTEEN

Table Tennis Anyone?

April 1999
Beartooth, Montana

THE BEDROOM CEILING COLLAPSED in slow motion, sheetrock and plaster filling my lungs as I screamed. I clawed at the debris, desperate to escape, to live.

"Christ almighty, Paige! Wake up!" Jack yelled as he shook me from the nightmare. The light from the bedside lamp burned my eyes, my heartbeat pounded at warp speed, and my mind swam in disoriented confusion. Only Jack's grasp on my shoulders grounded me to our bedroom and the reality of Montana.

My first cogent thought: My professional life sucked.

My next cogent thought: The early April temperature at 2:00 a.m. formed steam from my panicked breath, despite the wall heater's effort to warm me.

"What the hell were you dreaming about this time?" Jack demanded. "I thought we'd left these nightmares in California."

I dove under the down comforter, shivering as much from terror as cold. "The ceiling was collapsing on me and I couldn't breath. It all had something to do with Judge Winston and Frank McShane and a bomb," I chattered out.

Jack snuggled next to me. "Sweet Pea," he murmured, already nodding back to sleep, "I keep telling you. You can't let these bastards get you down. You can't let them win. You can do this. We can do this. Just relax." Soon his soft snores filled the quiet.

You're wrong, I mused. *They've already won. The only question is how much longer I can fight a windmill for the sake of moral principle.*

My breath eased to normal and I, too, returned to slumber, yet I thrashed for hours through visions of courtrooms, angry men, and Rich Truman's bloodied cadaver riddled with bullet holes.

The next morning, showered, suited up, high heels polished and hair coiffed, I drove to the courthouse to face the formidable power of Judge Hank Winston and Frank McShane.

Not even Mick Jagger could lift my spirits.

* * *

Like the plastic ball that players bash across the net in table tennis, the fight between the Courthouse Cowboys and me lobbed back and forth with increasing intensity. When I filed the motion to withdraw Ben Stagg's guilty plea, wrath rolled across the valley like thunder in mid-June.

Ping.

McShane served the first return volley. After housing Rodney the Meth Spoon Guy, for nearly a year in county jail, Frank transferred him to Deer Lodge State Prison, denying me access to my client while I prepared for his double jeopardy hearing. I couldn't call Rodney or visit him for the next thirty days - prison rules - despite the fact that his long-awaited hearing was set in front of a Bozeman judge in three weeks.

Pong.

I returned the serve, accusing McShane of vindictive prosecution, a claim that would allow me to produce evidence at a public hearing showing that McShane retaliated against my clients because he disliked me.

Ping.

In the case of Peg Zanto, the 29-year-old woman who screwed the 15-year-old neighbor boy, McShane refused to consider a misdemeanor plea, even though the client had no record and would lose her kids and her low income housing if she pled to a felony.

Pong.

I blistered the local criminal justice system and its worst players, including McShane, in interviews with inquisitive reporters from *60 Minutes* and *The Atlantic Monthly* who had heard of the controversy in connection with the Stagg brothers' case.

Ping.

McShane, after having one of my clients arrested the day before Christmas in front of her children, heaped on additional felony charges of forging prescriptions, even though the evidence didn't support those allegations.

Pong.

As allowed in my contract with the judges, I requested extraordinary expenses, beyond my meager public defender pay, for 500 plus hours earned during Casey's murder trial and another case.

Ping.

Judge Winston demanded further explanation of the additional money I requested, and announced to the press that I had filed a *false claim* - implying I was a thief - for payment to write an appeal, when I'd instead written a longer, more complicated document for the client.

Pong.

The chief public defender advised me I wouldn't be re-hired when my contract expired in June, so I responded to Judge Winston, in a confidential letter, with additional explanation of my expenses. Like an idiot, I threw in a comment that he'd only hired me because he thought that I, as a former prosecutor, would plead all my clients guilty and not rock the boat.

Ping.

Judge Winston published the confidential letter to his cronies at the courthouse and to the press. His colleague, Judge Holmes, called my clients before her court, ranted about me for 16 minutes, and advised them to fire me, all while I was in California. Afterward, both judges threw me out of their courtrooms - forever - and instead hired a judge from outside the area to preside over my cases.

Pong.

Game One goes to the Courthouse Cowboys.

My normally thick skin dimpled like the rubber on a table tennis racket, while the color of my anger matched the same bright red of the racket's side blade. I didn't care that I couldn't practice before the two Kootenai judges, or that my PD contract would expire. What stunned me was the viciousness of their personal attack, along with the willingness of Judge Winston's fellow Rotarian, who happened to be the editor at the local newspaper, to widely publish their views.

Rally Two.

I served a subpoena to Judge Winston's good buddy, a local news broadcaster, to testify at the vindictive prosecution hearing, along with several other noteworthy witnesses, and elicited from Frank McShane an admission under oath that, indeed, he'd arrested my client on Christmas because he was angry at me. He also admitted that he'd called me a bitch and a jackass in court in front of several law enforcement officers.

Ping.

The judges called in their favorite replacement judge to listen to my remaining cases, a retired cohort who was as deaf as he was nasty, and who blasted me publicly for challenging Judge Winston's ability to be fair and impartial. Judge Winston complained to the press that I was a surly, argumentative, in-your-face-attorney who didn't get along with the folks at the courthouse.

Pong.

I turned the lascivious Peg Zanto's case over to Jack in a failed attempt to convince Frank McShane to let her plead guilty to a misdemeanor. At trial, since she'd confessed, the jury convicted her of the felony. Meanwhile, I hired an investigator to explore Judge Winston's relationship to the murdered Rich Truman, including the fact that they were Masonic Lodge brothers.

Ping.

Judge Winston's deaf and nasty crony denied my assertion of vindictive prosecution, instead ruling that Frank McShane treated my clients fairly. Days later, at Rodney the Meth Spoon Guy's hearing in Bozeman, McShane at last defeated poor Rodney and convinced him to drop his claim of double jeopardy after Rodney wept in court, unable to stomach any more isolation at the state prison. A year of his life in custody, all wasted.

Pong.

The investigator and I interviewed Judge Winston's pastor at the Sunset Fellowship Church, who had socialized with Judge Winston and his family while he 'ministered' to young Ben Stagg at the jail. We also connected Judge Winston to Rich Truman through mutual friends and relatives. I filed paperwork in which I accused Judge Winston of bias against the Stagg brothers that resulted in their 100-year sentences.

Ping.

Game Two goes to the surly, argumentative lawyer.
Rally Three.

To make the point that Judge Winston was biased, Jack, with his extensive jury trial experience, applied for my spot on the public defender list, only to be rejected by the judges' new hiring committee, in favor of a local attorney with far less experience.

Pong.

Just before my contract expired, I subpoenaed records from the courthouse that showed not one public defender had gone to jury trial, nor filed a substantive motion, in the five years previous to my hiring, indicating that my colleagues failed to advocate strenuously for their clients. Instead, every one of their clients pled guilty.

Ping.

McShane had Judge Winston quash my other subpoenas, and advised the head clerk to disregard my requests for court statistics regarding the average length of sentences in Kootenai County, claiming the task of providing them was too burdensome.

Pong.

In the last throes of my public defender contract, I filed a motion in a rape case for the public defenders to release records of their individual trial experience, since one of them would soon represent the client in a complicated DNA hearing and jury trial. A visiting Bozeman judge granted the request.

Ping.

Game Three ties the match.

And so we rallied, back and forth, on and on and on.

* * *

For the first two weeks after my public defender

contract ended in late June, I relished my freedom. I cherished summer hours spent with my children at Beartooth Lake. I read trashy novels and cooked mounds of food. I breathed in the heady aroma of beach, birch leaves, and barbecued hot dogs. I listened, eyes closed, to my children's laughter, to the multiple trains passing just feet from our house, and to the inboard motors on boats pulling skiers and wake boarders. Even the steady hum of bugs and the chatter of birds comforted, instead of annoyed, me.

Yet Ben and Nick Stagg, along with their parents and sister, never strayed from my peripheral vision. They hung there, waiting like apparitions for me to return to the real world of Kootenai County justice. All too soon I again immersed myself in courthouse drama, with their case receiving top billing. They had, after all, hired me in my capacity as a private defense attorney.

Some days, sitting in court awaiting whatever new judge turned up to hear my cases, I questioned whether I'd merely achieved a Pyrrhic victory during the previous year, winning some battles only to lose the war. The icy glares from my colleagues supported that notion.

Considered aloof by some and a loner by others, I'd long ago learned to fly solo and relished solitude. I was an 'across the table' kind of gal, not the type to lunch with the girls or join groups of moms to organize events. Jack was my closest friend, and he and the kids were the sum of what mattered in my life, along with a few friends and family members.

Still, being despised by a bunch of guys who didn't even know me brought its own unique emptiness. In the moments when I faced their disdain, I sometimes wished I could knit, as one lawyer did throughout her court appearances. She knitted and looked down, ignoring all who might incinerate her with their anger. She, I thought whenever I saw her, was cool.

I knew the conflict with the Courthouse Cowboys might simmer for the moment, but eventually it would reach full boil. They wouldn't relent in their effort to rid Kootenai County of the Defalco pox, nor would they forgive and forget.

So, as much as I longed for peace and quiet, for normalcy and knitting needles, I had to stay in the fight.

CHAPTER SEVENTEEN

A Concatenation of Lives

July 1999
Deer Lodge State Prison

I MET BEN STAGG AT DEER LODGE STATE
PRISON in July 1999. I'd gone to that sterile tomb of
concrete and razor wire to get Ben to sign a legal
document so I could try to reverse his plea of guilty to
the murder of Rich Truman. It was my third trip to a
prison as a defense attorney, although I'd made several
such trips when I worked as a prosecutor in California.

Prosecutors receive red carpet treatment at prisons
because they wear the white hats. They're the good guys
who put the bad guys behind bars. On the other hand,
most prison staff view defense attorneys as Commie,
bleeding-heart liberals. Accordingly, defense attorneys
typically are searched, forced to abandon their briefcases,
and required, if female, to remove their underwire bras,
lest the bad guys somehow wrest the wire away from
their lawyer and use it as a weapon.

I'd dressed in a dignified pantsuit, but as part of my
new role practicing law on the Dark Side, I'd eschewed
my former high heels in favor of ugly, but comfortable,
clogs. I processed through the metal detector and pat
search, received the required visitor's pass, which I
dutifully clipped to the lapel of my suit jacket, and
followed a guard to an area of the prison known as Fish
Row. Fish Row was an entry area where new prisoners
spent their first 30 days, while the prison assigned them

to an appropriate cellblock.

The criteria for murderers like Ben Stagg were the same: They all went to the prison's 'high side' where the really serious, long term evildoers lived out their years, as opposed to the 'low side' which was reserved for those who presented a minimal danger to the prison staff, and who would see release from custody before hell actually froze over.

The guards seated me on a bench and surrounded me, their paunches jutting within a couple of feet of my face, their demeanors as tired and cynical as my own. When a door opened, through which even more guards emerged, my new client shuffled forward, dressed in a prison-issue jumpsuit, shackled head to foot in chains.

If not so young and skinny, he could have doubled for Jacob Marley as the Ghost of Christmas Past.

Ben Stagg was 19-years-old that July day. He stood well over six feet tall but weighed just under 120 pounds. He unfolded his skeletal frame next to me on the bench. His guards stood silently, refusing us any privacy, reminding me that this was Montana, where they didn't coddle the lawyers or prisoners by building attorney-client visiting rooms. They refused my request to unshackle Ben, including his hands, which made it difficult for him to hold the legal documents I offered him.

I explained to my new client that his parents had hired me to try to reverse his guilty plea and conviction for the murder of Rich Truman, rambling on a bit about the legal consequences of doing that. I looked at everything but his face. I'd looked in the face of too many criminals lately and concluded that my job was easier if I remained distant and detached.

Hearing only silence, however, I turned to him, and gazed into the face of yet another convicted killer.

This murderer, however, this kid named Ben Stagg,

wore the hairless, baby-smooth face of a child, not a grown man, yet it was smashed, broken, and bruised. I stared at his flattened, purple nose and his puffed up, bloodied lips. I registered two black eyes, one swollen shut. He tried to smile at me, but his smile twisted from all the damage someone had inflicted. I tried to smile back, but my own face froze. I silently attempted to reconcile this visage before me with Ben's picture in the newspaper accounts of the murder.

I remembered that Ben wasn't the actual shooter in the case but had confessed to watching from the forest as his older brother, Nick, shot Rich Truman to death. I recalled that the brothers previously had burglarized some 30 homes and storage units around the valley.

Ben's parents, and all the psychiatrists who examined him at the time, described Ben as 'slow', but not retarded or insane. They said he was easily led by others, but not entirely unable to make decisions about day-to-day events.

His court-appointed psychologist concluded, "This is a boy who could be salvaged." The doctor worried that Ben, if sent to prison, would be vulnerable to predatory inmates, given his youth, his slight musculature, and his profound mental dysfunction. The young man sitting next to me bore out the psychologist's fears.

What particularly unnerved me as I returned Ben's gaze was the light that seemed to emanate from his one very blue, partially opened eye. That light, perhaps in combination with his lopsided smile, bespoke *hope*, and I thought it very odd indeed that this kid could hold out any hope, given his past and present circumstances and his 100-year prison sentence.

I noticed that Ben's hands shook uncontrollably as he tried to peer at the legal papers he held. That trembling, exacerbated by the handcuffs cutting into his wrists, distracted me as I explained the document's purpose. Soon Ben haltingly advised me he couldn't see very well, so I offered to read the documents to him, "because of your eyes," I reasoned.

In an instant, maternal instinct compelled me to impart some bit of dignity to Ben Stagg so he didn't think that I, too, believed he was 'stupid', as so many people had told him over his 19 years. I read to him quietly, stopping here and there to put the legal terms into language I thought he could understand. When I finished, I asked him if he had any questions. He smiled his infectious grin and uttered a simple, "Nope."

I handed him a pen, and he signed as best he could, handcuffs, trembling hands, and all. His signature angled down, far off the line. I noticed his writing looked much like my 9-year-old son's. Ben formed all the letters into different sizes as he forced them to connect in cursive.

He looked embarrassed and apologized. Again I felt the need to reassure him that he was fine, that his signature was fine, that his battered face was fine, and that his life was going to be fine, just *fine*.

Never mind the 100-year prison sentence or the savage beatings that likely would kill him not too far into the future; never mind that he would never have a girlfriend, or a family life, or even *any* life except the dark one in which he now found himself; never mind that the chances of me prevailing in my legal efforts to reverse his guilty plea were pitifully slim, or that even if I succeeded, he still would face a nearly impossible uphill battle to get a lesser sentence; never mind that if we couldn't get a lesser sentence and eventually had to go to a jury trial, he again faced the prospect of the death penalty and surely would be convicted, since there was no defense to the felony murder charge.

Never mind any of that because somehow, like every mom, I was going to fix everything, and it all would work out just *fine*.

I grew irritated because the guards wouldn't leave us alone. In truth, however, Ben elicited emotions from me that I didn't want to feel or face. Panic set in, along with the increasing claustrophobia that I always felt in prisons. I needed to breathe in air that didn't have the stench of old cooking grease and unwashed bodies. My heart hurt as my chest grew tight. It felt like my nerve endings dangled in the air, as if they connected on the outside of my skin, instead of tucked safely beneath the armor of 46 years of calcifying numb.

I stood abruptly, announcing I had to leave. I advised Ben to call the office if he had any questions then told him I'd be in touch when I heard something from the court.

"Okay," he said, returning my glance.

I blinked to clear my vision. For a second I felt certain that, in addition to hope, I'd seen a different emotion. I thought I witnessed joy in his single, blue-eyed gaze. Not the kind of joy one feels receiving a puppy or a new bike, but rather the kind of joy that only springs from a place of faith.

Ben Stagg, I realized, still held to his belief in God, even though God had seemingly abandoned him, betrayed him, and left him to die. That realization humbled an old cynic like me, so I quietly fled.

I knew, after that meeting, that if I walked away from his case, young Ben Stagg could kiss his life goodbye.

* * *

On the four-hour drive home from the prison, thoughts of Ben interfered with the endless cow-dotted vistas of eastern Montana. I sensed that Ben viewed me just as a drowning man regarded a life preserver, and the weight of that belief forced me to pull over an hour into my return trip to Beartooth.

I parked on a road winding through low-growing fescue and wildflower-infused prairie. The hills reached up to puffy white clouds drifting in azure skies. Yet I knew that black inverted anvils could form in an instant, deluging the area with splintering lightening and ear-shattering thunder.

It was a magnificent part of the state, a spot where even I could see God again. I breathed in air so clean, it could have fueled an angel as she winged her way to insure someone's salvation. Ben Stagg needed an angel like that.

Ben needed someone who could perform a miracle because Ben was in deep shit.

The chances of reversing his guilty plea were slim, despite Montana law that favored that result. Since the Montana Supreme Court earlier denied Judge Winston the task of presiding over my cases, he wouldn't make the decision. But Judge Winston could choose his own successor in Ben's case, and whomever he chose would dump the challenge. I considered Ben's broken and bruised face, his youth, his multiple disabilities, and the predatory atmosphere in the prison. If the effort to reverse his plea failed, he wouldn't survive to see his 25th birthday.

A vision of my son, Sean, now ten and burdened by his own learning disabilities, crowded my thoughts as fear grabbed my stomach. What if *he* fell in with a bad group of kids and witnessed a murder? What if *he* lost in court, the victim of a biased, angry judge who sent him to prison for life? What would I do to help him?

What if I were Laura Stagg, faced with a future devoid of my sons, knowing they faced death and destruction every time their cell doors opened? What about the other women who had kids in America's jails or prisons, who wept as many tears as Laura had wept?

What would I do to help myself in those circumstances?

The soft Montana wind blew hair from my eyes as I stared at the horizon. My chest tightened. My pulse raced. I fought for breath, much like I did through the chill of sleepless nights and dreams filled with cloying, claustrophobic panic. I wanted Jack, but hours would slip past before I could reach him. Cell phone coverage in that part of the state didn't exist. Again I longed for the cigarette I hadn't smoked in fifteen years. My car squeezed me like a coffin.

I opened the door and walked up the road. Not a truck or house hinted at civilization. Time stood still, marked only by the birth and death of the cattle that grazed there. It seemed like the right place to pray. Yet when the heavens remained shuttered, and no white doves descended with scrolls in their beaks to provide me with answers, I ambled slowly back to the car.

How could Ben have *hope?* How could he smile at me? Why did he exude such quiet joy and faith, when he had little chance at redemption? What could I do, really, to help him? I leaned against a boulder and wretched whatever meager contents remained in my stomach from breakfast. Then I dry-heaved until I had to sit down on another large rock to recover my balance and silence the ringing in my ears. After rinsing my mouth out with bottled water retrieved from the front seat, I took a last look at the surrounding prairie. I listened to the breeze blowing through the grass and noted the rapid shifting of the clouds.

I sensed, rather than heard, the answer.

I would do for Ben Stagg whatever I would do for my own son to protect him, to free him, and to find justice for him amid the anger and hostility at the Kootenai County courthouse. I would do it as both a mom and a lawyer, because that personal duality was inseparable.

As I drove away, peaceful at last in my decision to fight for Ben, I wondered if an angel had whispered to me. If she brought salvation for Ben, could she give the same gift to me? Did she have the power to silence the nightmares while I slept? Would she stand beside me as I faced the battle yet to come?

My inner cynic returned with a vengeance.

Who the fuck are you kidding, Paige? You're on your own, baby. If you think your dreams are bad now, stay tuned.

That chilling thought followed me past the giant plaster bull at Woody's, the intersection where I turned onto yet another deer-infested death trap, and didn't thaw until I pulled into the driveway at our house. I heard my son's excited shout. "Hey, Mom! Wow, we thought you'd hit another deer! How was prison? Does the bad guy look like a killer? Did you bring me anything? Claire tried to tie me to the table again and stick a sock in my mouth, but Heather saved me . . ."

I grabbed my briefcase from the rear seat and hugged my boy.

Reality check.

CHAPTER EIGHTEEN

An Unreasonable Woman

August to November 1999
Beartooth, Montana

"DEFALCO, LISTEN UP! The Marines taught me there are two kinds of people in this world: shit magnets and shit disturbers. Now I'm not sure which one you are, but I suspect you're a little of both. And I'm here to tell you, you ain't attracting or disturbing NO SHIT on my watch! Is that clear?"

An ex-Marine, my supervisor early in my career as a big city prosecutor, fired off that personality assessment.

He had a point.

I never planned to disturb shit. Generally it happened when I refused to take 'no' for an answer. That stubborn determination stemmed from growing up as the daughter of a military officer who responded to all my requests in the negative. When pushed for a reason, he'd bark, "Because I said so."

My father taught me that asking permission didn't work, so the better plan was to circumvent his edicts by seeking an alternate path to my goal. That lesson later proved to be great training for the courtroom when I wanted to admit a particular piece of evidence - say, a bloody corpse photo or an expert opinion - and the judge refused to allow it because it was "too prejudicial" or "not relevant" or "You don't *need* it, Ms. Defalco." Usually, if I waited, I found a way to get it before the jury.

I never sought to attract shit either. The magnet, I'd decided as a teenager, was the bright red hair that capped my pallid, freckled face. People always noticed it. I could sit on a nearly empty bus, and the one weirdo who boarded inevitably sat next to *me,* not next to the guy with the fluorescent orange Aloha shirt or the blonde with the big boobs. Since I had nothing else that set me apart, deductive reasoning pointed to my hair color.

Shit, apparently, loved redheads.

Frank McShane, my nemesis at the courthouse, had red hair and also had grown up in the military. When he'd first come to the Kootenai valley after law school, he sported long curly locks and tie-dyed shirts. Remembering the ex-Marine's words, I wondered if Frank McShane, too, had been both a shit disturber and a shit magnet.

I wondered about all of that in late Fall, 1999, when I stole a moment to catch my breath and ponder my past. Life at the D.A.'s office had been grand, I reflected, despite my supervisor's continual fretting. I'd successfully tried many jury trials, most of the judges liked me, my peers respected me, and the Domestic Violence Unit I'd created changed in a positive way the manner in which those cases were handled by cops, prosecutors, and the community.

I'd dumped that life for our family and my ebbing sanity. Yet here I stood in my garage, hands and clothes covered in sawdust and gel stain, thinking of an Aberdeen prosecutor who, along with his cohorts, made every day of my new life sheer misery.

To exacerbate the madness, in between my trips to the courthouse, meetings with Pete and Laura Stagg, sojourns to Deer Lodge State Prison, and miles of aisles of shopping at the local grocery, I'd convinced Jack we should build a house. We'd broken ground in March and now were two months from completion. We had no money for extras, so we worked alongside the contractor, laying flooring, setting tile, and any other menial task we could fit in during our spare time. Hence the gel stain and sawdust.

In the midst of hand-rubbing and staining the kitchen cabinets, my ruminations skidded to a halt when I heard screams from the house. The mess on my hands prevented me from racing through the door before my daughter flew out of it.

"I can't get this out! Oh my God, Mom! Help!" she pleaded in a panic.

True to her own redheaded personality, our 15-year-old daughter led the drama parade. I stared at her lovely face, puzzled by an object plastered horizontally across her forehead.

"It's a *comb*, Mom," she spat out. "I curled my bangs around it and now it's stuck and won't move *at all* and I will *kill* myself if you have to cut my hair to get it out." She took a breath and wailed, "And I'm going to kill my idiot brother and his friend if they don't stop laughing! I swear to God, I will *kill* them both!"

Back in the day, I'd acted out my own share of teenage angst, so I didn't take her homicidal threats to heart. If she killed everyone she threatened to kill, including herself, Earth, as we knew it, would cease to exist.

I washed the stain from my hands and contemplated her latest debacle. As she sat on a sawhorse, I gently pulled on the comb.

Her scream rivaled my own during her birth.

"Mom!" Her exasperated tone pointed again to her belief that I was the dumbest parent in the world. "You can't pull it out. I tried that already."

I breathed deeply as I heard little-boy laughter just inside the door to the house.

"Shut UP!" commanded the hair princess, "Or I

really will kill you when I get this out."

Wisely, I managed to quell my own laughter as I carefully removed each hair, one by one, for what seemed like the next hour. When my ministrations succeeded, the princess smiled. Then she laughed. So did I. Her little brother and his buddy joined us as we hooted.

"Wow," her brother effused, "that was great! You haven't done anything that stupid since you glued your finger to your eyelid with Crazy Glue!"

And the race was on to see if the older sister could catch the younger brother before he escaped to the beach to tell her friends about her latest caper.

Left to my cabinet project, avoiding further thoughts of the courthouse, McShane, or chaos, I considered the genetics in my family. Mother: redhead. Brother: redhead. Daughter: redhead. Me? I sighed as I grabbed my sanding block.

Redheads: Shit magnets, shit disturbers.

* * *

To paraphrase George Bernard Shaw, a reasonable woman accepts the world the way it is and adapts to it. An unreasonable woman persists at getting the world to change. Therefore, all progress in the world comes from unreasonable people. If that held true, change was coming to the Kootenai County criminal justice system because no one at the courthouse considered me reasonable.

I'd clamored for months that the county needed to adopt formal hiring standards and criteria to select public defenders. To have a staff of attorneys on the public payroll and not know their work histories was irresponsible at best and could lead defendants to receive inadequate assistance of counsel. Defendants like

Rodney the Meth Spoon Guy, for example, or Ben and Nick Stagg.

In October 1999, I still represented the accused rapist, for free, and I still awaited the production of records the visiting judge had ordered that would show the trial experience of my former colleagues. The public defenders lashed out at the order to reveal their records. They asserted that licensing by the State Bar and selection by the county commissioners, based on the chief public defender's recommendation, should be adequate proof of their competency. A record of their past legal experience, they posited, was no indicator of their future abilities.

In a stunning report to the press, the chief public defender, the same guy who recommended which lawyers to hire, conceded that *he didn't know the qualifications of the attorneys who worked under him, and neither did anyone else.* His staff, he noted, neither kept records of their past work experience nor of their qualifications to represent indigent folks accused of felonies.

That, of course, was hokum, a Montana euphemism for bullshit.

There isn't a trial lawyer on the planet who fails to keep track of his or her jury trials and win-loss record. Even big city prosecutors and public defenders who try cases weekly for decades have a ballpark estimate. My colleagues' claims of ignorance rang hollow, even to the general public.

Meanwhile, Frank McShane and his cronies claimed that my ego was all that fueled my fight against the existing justice system. They told whoever would listen that I was incompetent, ineffective, and difficult to get along with. Judge Winston and the editor of the local paper continued to echo that message.

The accusations rankled.

Actually, they pissed me off.

I agreed that the line narrowed when drawn between ego and righteous indignation, or between self-serving goals and altruism. I'd always admitted that my goal in exposing the truth behind the public defender hiring scheme was aimed at changing the system at large. Also, by insisting on publication of my colleagues' trial experience, I was pushing my point.

I disagreed, of course, that my ego fed my efforts because I doubted that a positive change to the system would benefit my family or me. To the contrary, an improvement in the experience and quality of public defenders would obviate much of the need for the privately paid services of Defalco & Defalco. Besides, my kids withstood a lot of crap at school about their mom being the "Courthouse Crusader," as a Bozeman newspaper dubbed me.

Contrary to Frank McShane's assertion that I loved media focus, I despised the publicity surrounding the courthouse drama, especially when accompanied by my photographs. I'd never sought the spotlight as a prosecutor. I'd even balked at walking down the aisle at my own wedding, since it would draw attention to me.

On the other hand, ego is always an arrow in any trial lawyer's quiver. When I advocated for someone else's cause, I radiated confidence and determination. The whir and flash of cameras faded from my awareness when I spoke for others who couldn't or wouldn't speak for themselves. In front of a jury, I became oblivious to all except the jurors, the evidence, and the crime victim or client I represented.

So, ego-fueled or not, with Jack's ongoing encouragement, I resolved to level the playing field for every accused person in the valley, despite my critics' efforts to stop me. However, I still hadn't heard from the good folks at the ACLU, so I knew I'd have to go it alone.

That fall, as I awaited the Bozeman judge's ruling on my colleagues' refusal to disclose their qualifications, optimism tempered my usual cynicism. Surely the judge could appreciate the dire consequences of appointing an inexperienced lawyer to handle such a complex case involving DNA and rape?

Or not.

After six weeks of whining objections from the Courthouse Cowboys, the Bozeman judge abruptly removed me as attorney of record for the accused rapist. In so doing, he wrote that he had no reason to believe the public defenders weren't qualified to represent the defendant, and assigned him one of my former colleagues to lead the defense at trial.

It appeared Lady Justice had sneaked another peek from beneath her blindfold.

* * *

While the accused rapist adjusted to his new attorney, he also came under the spiritual ministry of Pete Stagg who, having two sons in prison, decided to pastor at our local county jail. Before transferring to state prison, Ben Stagg had roomed with my former client for a short time, so Pete had some familiarity with the case. While I wondered at the alleged rapist's sudden need for Pete's spiritual advice, I concluded any words that comforted him in custody were welcome.

Ben, still at state prison fending off physical and verbal abuse, waited for Judge Winston to appoint his successor judge. Nick Stagg also waited, but for statistics from the Department of Justice that might help to remove Judge Winston's parole restriction, the one that prevented him from ever seeking parole. Nick hoped to avoid dying in prison.

I met and spoke with Pete and Laura frequently.

We'd even interviewed with a crew from *NewsTime, CBS,* for a television special scheduled to air in February 2000. My goal for that exposure was to provide locals with previously undisclosed facts that portrayed Ben and his family in a fairer light. If Ben won the right to withdraw his guilty plea, a jury trial could follow. I needed jurors who entered the courtroom with a more balanced view of Ben than they'd received from the local Aberdeen newspaper.

I even accepted another homicide client. Unfortunately, this fellow had tanked up at a local bar, and then shot his wife of many years multiple times in front of several witnesses, even stopping to reload a second weapon before doing her in. He'd fled the police and, after a high-speed chase, attempted suicide in the woods near the Wyoming border. He failed, instead blowing off part of his face and blinding himself in one eye.

One may wonder at a possible defense with those facts. I certainly did when the family approached me to represent their son, brother, and father. I advised them that the best outcome we could hope for was a plea to mitigated homicide, the old "I did the crime but I had extenuating circumstances that made me crazy-ish" defense.

This killer's extenuating circumstance was his wife's announcement that she was leaving him because, in her opinion, he was a no-good drunk. We defense attorneys have to play out the hand we're dealt, but this particular pile of cards didn't bode well for the client's successful future.

Undaunted, I traveled for months on the four hour, round-trip journey to and from the crime jurisdiction, in the process growing enamored of local rivers, the occasional, rare sighting of big horn sheep, and the many black-eyed Susans dotting the prairie grass along the way.

As homicide cases went, at least this one was scenic.

Driving around the huge state of Montana provided me with time to consider the rapid growth of our legal practice after I'd been dumped as a public defender. Despite the vitriol in the media, at least we had clients. The proverbial silver lining, I supposed, but wondered, again, if the bullets I fended off were worth the money.

* * *

One day in November, staring out my office window at trees long devoid of leaves and a ski mountain lacking sufficient snow to open on Thanksgiving, I wondered what had happened to the lawyers in white hats from the ACLU. Seeking coffee and solace, I meandered downstairs to chat with Jack.

After pouring us each a of cup of cheap swill - Jack's leftover addiction from working in too many county offices in California - I sat across from my beloved, waiting until he put down his pen and gazed at me.

"What's up?" he asked, sipping the blackened brew from his overly-used and rarely washed mug.

I ran my fingers through my hair and sighed. "Do you ever imagine what it would be like if one of the good old boys turned on Winston and McShane and came forward with the truth about what really goes on behind the scenes at the courthouse? Like a whistle-blower, but well-known and well-respected?"

Jack leaned back in his chair as he clasped his hands behind his head. "Sweet Pea, I'm a guy. We don't imagine. We just put our heads down and plod along, fighting like bastards when some asshole gets in our way."

I set my cup on his desk and laughed. "Not exactly the response I was hoping for, but at least it's honest."

A knock at the door interrupted my next thought. Our new law partner took the chair next to me. This poor guy had stood in for me at court when the judges blasted away at my reputation for 16 minutes before they banished me forever. He'd been a prosecutor with Frank McShane, then a public defender until he angered Judge Winston, who fired him, and now worked with us on various cases. His wife, also an attorney, urged him daily to move his practice to a less controversial law firm.

"Sorry to interrupt, but this is important. There's a guy who just phoned for an appointment with you, Paige. He's a millionaire who owns most of the newspapers in the northwest."

I turned toward him, eyes widened in astonishment. "Do not tell me it's that nutcase who repeatedly opines that I should move back to California?"

Our associate nodded and smiled. "Yep," he relished, "Old Chad Hammel himself. Apparently he and his partner are in the middle of a dispute, and he wants you to represent him. But here's the catch. Chad Hammel and Hank Winston are in-laws. Chad's son, Charlie, is married to Hank's daughter, Holly. They have two kids, so Chad and Hank share grandchildren. They're also close friends, and big in the Republican Party in Montana."

Jack released a low whistle. "Holy shit," he murmured. "This has to be a set-up. Winston must have put Hammel up to this to get inside our office, and either plant dirt on us or try to get us disbarred. Don't even return his call, Paige."

Our associate stood as he nodded concurrence with Jack. Since our parish priest had shared with me several of the articles in which Hammel advised me to leave the state, I agreed as well. I returned to my own office and again gazed outside. The late afternoon light faded quickly as winter approached. A call home confirmed the kids were safe and studying. Our move into the new house was just a week or so away. Thanksgiving beckoned from our new kitchen. Other than my professional life, all was well.

I thought of Chad Hammel and his rants against me. I tried to imagine his physical appearance, and whether it reflected the soothing timbre of his baritone voice I'd heard on interviews. How close were he and Hank Winston? Was he buddies with McShane as well?

Screw him, I silently nodded, *and the Courthouse Cowboys he rides with. This is one redhead who isn't attracting or disturbing any more shit.*

CHAPTER NINETEEN

And We All Fall Down
(Stagg Family Memories from 1989)

October 1999
Beartooth, Montana

THE CLEAVING OF NICK STAGG'S SPINE sliced through his family like a scalpel, dissecting hearts from minds, and a little boy's faith in God from his soul, as if his fall from the tree mimicked Lucifer's own fall from grace.

During one meeting at my office, Pete and Laura Stagg recounted The Fall, their euphemism for Nick's 65-foot plunge to earth, in voices grown weary from the telling. A decade had passed since that day in August 1989, the one that forever branded their spirit.

Summer had fueled the breeze that day, filling the air with scents of newly hayed fields. Nick, older by two years, and Ben, just nine, climbed their favorite pine tree to spot their dad when he returned from logging in the forest. They hoped to give Pete Stagg *their* version of why they were in trouble before Laura could give Pete *her* version of why they were in trouble.

They jumped up and down on various branches, just 'messing around' as they always did, high above the ground, like most kids, fearless and ignorant of danger. Nick suggested they break off some limbs so they could clear the way for a future tree house. Ben's tree limb barely moved when he jumped because he was so skinny, so despite his earnest efforts, his branch failed to budge.

"Here, Benjie, let me try it," Nick offered as Ben moved to another tree branch. With his little brother safely clinging to the tree's large trunk, Nick ventured out on the unyielding limb, using his additional weight as leverage to crack it.

"Nick, is that Mom calling us? I wonder when Dad's gonna get here? You know what'll happen if Mom gets to him first."

Ben edged around the trunk just slightly and craned his neck, looking away from Nick, as he searched the forest below for any sign of his father. Ben, like Nick and their sisters, spent most days avoiding Laura's temper, fearing the consequences if she got into one of her moods. Today was no exception. Ben spotted his little sister, Megan, playing in her sandbox several yards away. There was no sign of Pete Stagg.

And then Ben heard what sounded like the crack of a gunshot next to his ear. Startled, he whipped his head around to catch Nick's reaction. Ben always looked to Nick for guidance in how he should act, what he should wear, even when he should eat. Nick was more than his older brother. Nick was his mentor, his protector, his brain, his hero, and Ben needed him as surely as others needed air.

What Ben saw when he looked back, however, was nothing.

No Nick, no branch, and no sound except the wind whistling through the pines and a curious *crack, crack, crack*.

More confused than usual, thinking that Nick had been shot and the shooter was firing more rounds, Ben panicked. He ducked, looked down the length of the tree's trunk, and witnessed his brother's body breaking off the last of 10 to 15 branches. With a sickening thud, Nick crashed into the earth, suddenly motionless. Unknown to either brother, Ben's puny weight had cracked the limb on which Nick had stood. When it broke, Nick plunged toward the earth like a falling star.

Ben slowly worked his way down the tree, screaming as he descended for his little sister to get their mother. He was so terrified he could barely climb from limb to limb, not because he feared he, too, would fall, but because Nick wasn't crying, screaming, or rolling on the forest floor in pain.

Nick appeared to be dead.

In Ben's little boy world, he could contemplate nothing worse than losing his brother. Even his parents' frequent anger and strict punishment couldn't hurt him as much as the loss of that hero.

Ben screamed at five-year-old Megan Stagg, "Megan, get Mom! Nick fell out of the tree! Get Mom, Megan!"

Megan jumped from her sandbox, ran into the kitchen, and haltingly told Laura that Nick was hurt. Laura, busy preparing dinner, half-listened to Megan's news. Nick and Ben routinely suffered minor injuries playing in the woods, none of them serious enough to warrant interrupting her cooking.

Ben ran into the house and breathlessly described Nick's fall. Because Ben was such a tease, Laura sternly admonished him that this was not the time or thing to joke about. Ben promised her he wasn't joking. When Laura finally turned from the pot she was stirring on the wood-burning stove, she noted the fear in Ben's eyes, dropped her spoon, and ran to where her oldest son lay helplessly beneath the pine tree.

During that minute when Ben glanced away in search of their father, Nick's world snapped like the branch on which he stood. As he bounced from limb to limb during his descent, gravity increasing his momentum, Nick hit one branch so hard it severed his spine.

Within an hour the Medic-Alert helicopter flew Nick first to Aberdeen, then to Bozeman. Pete and Laura, facing the long drive south, were forced to leave Ben and his two sisters with neighbors until Laura's parents could retrieve them.

Hours later the doctors in Bozeman performed surgery, but could not assure Nick's anguished parents that their son would survive. So the Stagg family reacted as they always did in dire circumstances. They prayed. And God must have heard their prayers because Nick survived, albeit paralyzed from the waist down, a paraplegic for life, and forever confined to a wheelchair.

In just 60 seconds - with a young boy's impulsive decision to mess around - many lives shattered. When Nick Stagg fell from that pine tree, he innocently kindled a series of tragedies that still echo within many families in Kootenai County. At the time, however, no one imagined that eight years later that same boy's impulsive choices would savage the Truman family.

So much can change in a minute.

* * *

In my office, Laura wiped away tears as she continued to describe the decade-old tragedy. Impotent to alleviate her pain, I handed her a box of tissue and waited until she could speak again. Pete held her hand, sometimes closing his eyes as if praying for more strength.

After The Fall, Pete and Laura coped as best they could, given their young age, their isolation, their limited and sheltered life experience, their meager financial resources, and the restrictions of their fundamentalist faith. Since they didn't indulge in drugs, alcohol, or the mind-numbing escape of film, they utilized the only tools at their disposal: Unending prayer and shock-induced denial.

Much like Rich and Nina Truman, the Staggs had met and married when they were young, just 18. Pete became a woodsman in Montana, logging the old-fashioned way, using a saw and two draft horses to haul logs from the forest. Laura stayed home tending kith and kin. They reared their four children in a devoutly fundamentalist, Baptist house. Eschewing television, the family focused on scripture study, 4-H Club activities, church groups, hiking, hunting, and fishing. In 1995, Pete became an ordained minister who served as associate pastor at the local church in Whitehall.

Their oldest child, a daughter, had no physical challenges at birth, but fought with her parents and ran away when she was 16. Nick, next in line, was born with spina bifida, a neural tube defect that resulted in the surgical fusion of Nick's neck when he was four. Unable to turn his head, Nick instead focused on his legs, running miles with his father by the age of six. Ben Stagg was born with a multitude of learning disabilities, and a body seemingly devoid of any muscle to connect his fragile bones. Megan, the youngest child, also was born with spina bifida, but a minor form that required no surgery.

Despite her children's odd genetics, Laura, like most moms, attempted to make life work out well for her kids. She spoke to me of summer vacations, birthday parties with special cakes, Bible camps, and homework, just like any mother recounted her early years of childrearing.

While I couldn't empathize with Laura's experience - parenting alone in the woods every day with four small children, three of whom were disabled - I felt certain that every good day conferred a challenge just as every bad day rendered a nightmare.

And that was *before* Nick's fall.

After The Fall, even God couldn't explain why a

little boy, who already was physically disabled, would suddenly experience another tragedy before he reached the age of twelve.

After Nick's surgery, Laura the Mom who, like all moms, acted as the fixer of everything - this woman of abiding faith - stayed in Bozeman for a month, while Pete returned to Kootenai County to sell the country home, move the family to town, and cope with three kids who tried to comprehend that Nick would never walk again. Pete worked extra hours to earn precious funds to pay for Nick's medical care. He even drove the siblings to the hospital on the weekends so the family could heal as a group, as if such a thing were possible.

Chaos.

The initial trauma of Nick's accident had mutated into utter chaos.

Months later, when Nick headed home in his wheelchair, Laura resumed her daily routine, with the added role of Nick's nurse. Ben, starting third grade at a new school, in a new town, with new kids who thought he was stupid, finally quit trying to learn. Laura worked with him every day until she concluded home-schooling was preferable to her youngest son's tears and dejection, thereby adding yet another full time job to her repertoire, that of Ben's teacher.

The family moved to the east coast in 1994 so Pete could complete a year of Bible College. Pete and Laura became house parents to their own brood and nine other students. Laura cooked every night, for everyone, after nursing, teaching, shopping, and cleaning each day. Pete studied and prayed.

When they returned to Kootenai County in 1995, they moved into a log house Pete built for them in the forest outside Whitehall, just a mile or two from Rich and Nina Truman and Dr. Sam Jaffee.

As Nick grew more independent, entering numerous

wheelchair-racing competitions, Ben grew more confused and more reliant on Nick to make his every decision. The Staggs settled into their new house and their new life as the wheelchair racer's family, the pastor's family, and the family who had endured the worst that life could offer, yet survived.

In 1995, they believed they had seen the last of life's greatest traumas.

Of course, they were wrong.

* * *

As I listened to their quiet murmurs across my desk, I should have focused more on the image of Laura Stagg sitting all day in a sterile hospital room with her crippled son, while at night lying alone in a strange city, with few monetary resources or friends.

I should have wondered if she ever asked God to explain to her the reason for such a tragedy, heaped as it was on top of Nick's spina bifida and her other children's disabilities.

I should have suspected she blamed herself and Pete for a perceived, but illogical, lack of parental vigilance that might have kept the boys safe from the trees. Surely neither parent entirely circumvented the inevitable self-recriminations, the endless 'what ifs' and 'if onlys' that we, as parents, pile on our souls after tragedy.

I should have asked her how she forgave herself and Pete, but most especially how she forgave God.

I should have presumed that at times she silently raged at this son she loved and his mentally disabled brother, for taking such risks and bringing such catastrophe to their family - for acting, in effect, like kids. How did she mask that anger every day?

I should have opined there were days when she looked ahead to her Golden Years with anguish, terrified that she would never catch a break from the chaos and stress of forever caring for a disabled child.

I should have considered, in her quiet moments of tragedy, that she may have contemplated suicide, perhaps a simple overdose of pills or a gunshot to her head, but understood that, like most of us, the Mom in her prevailed, responding at all hours of the night to the distant calls of her children, devoting her days working on their behalf.

I should have marveled at her strength, at her courage, at her sheer determination to face each day, each year, each decade of her tumultuous life and never falter in that forward momentum.

I should have noticed how this tired woman, her beautiful blue eyes focused downward, gripped Pete's left hand with both of her own as if he were her only connection to earth.

I should have queried if she even remembered the excited young girl who had fallen in love with Pete a quarter century before, whose life was once so filled with promise and hope.

I should have, but I didn't. Not then.

Instead, I chewed the end of my pen like a good Cuban cigar and stared at them. My prosecutor's instincts prickled. Something was off with these people, despite their seeming resilience. Something was wrong about their story, the murder, and these kids.

None of that mattered, however, if Ben couldn't withdraw his guilty plea.

When I asked if Nick received counseling after The Fall, they insisted Nick never cried, not once, after his accident, and never experienced any depression. They spoke then of Satan and their belief that psychologists were 'from the devil.' They demanded I profess my belief in Christianity, but then expressed suspicion that the Catholic Church didn't embrace their one true Lord and Savior. They studiously avoided any mention of their nephew, Andy Gifford, who had murdered his own father, in a supposed preemptive strike to ward off alleged physical abuse.

My years of interviews with crime victims and next of kin convinced me that Pete and Laura Stagg withheld some vital facts that could help their sons. I knew any success going forward, if Ben prevailed in court, hinged on unlocking those secrets.

They left that day with instructions from me to rent and watch *Dead Man Walking* and *The Shawshank Redemption* because their backwoods naïveté demanded a lesson on the reality of prison life. They had to understand the future their sons faced, so they could cope with the nasty legal fight that loomed before us.

Alone at the office, with Jack off coaching some kid sport, and our partner and secretary headed home for the day, I kicked off my heels and lifted my stockinged-feet onto my desk. I leaned back in my new executive office chair and closed my eyes, sending up a silent prayer for the Stagg and Truman families.

Nick had fallen straight from the top of that tree, through a black gap in his soul, and into a perdition where he one day plotted murder. Much like Alice falling down the rabbit-hole, Nick Stagg grew bigger and smaller, taller and wider, stronger and weaker, depending on the potions of words he ingested from his parents, friends, doctors, teachers, community, and of course, from God.

During her trip to Wonderland, Alice never met up with Lucifer.

Had Nick? Was that whose voice taunted him to kill Rich Truman on Christmas night two years before?

CHAPTER TWENTY

A Sport Illustrated

November 1999
Aberdeen, Montana

"JUDGE, A PERSON CAN'T BURGLARIZE HIS OWN HOUSE. Just because my client's wife got mad and locked the doors after he left doesn't mean he can't come back in through an open window later that night. It's his house too."

Jack made that obvious point of law to Judge Winston on behalf of his client, Bill, just before jury selection began in Bill's trial. During the fall of 1999, as we dodged Chad Hammel's calls to our office, Judge Winston still presided over some of Jack's cases, despite my own banishment from his courtroom.

"You're wrong, Jack," Winston declared as he rocked back in the large black chair that sat amid the clutter of files piled in his chambers. "People *can* burglarize their own houses. They *can* be charged with that felony, and I *can* send your client to prison for 15 years. If he doesn't take the plea deal, I'll send him for longer than that once the jury convicts him. I know the law."

Jack sighed in frustration, shaking his head. "I'm sure you do, Judge, but he's not pleading guilty to something he didn't do. I'll see you on Monday for trial."

Jack gathered his briefcase and left the courthouse to return to the relative calm of Defalco & Defalco. He'd been down this road before, different client, same judge.

* * *

Sitting at my computer typing furiously, I didn't hear Jack enter my upstairs office. I'd commandeered that lofty space of the little building in which we practiced law so I could avoid the incessant chit chat between Jack and our law partner. Women, I believed, accomplished more in a morning than most men did in a day, mainly because we were too busy with life to share war stories and gossip about courthouse crap.

"Paige," Jack yelled at the doorway, startling me so I jerked as I let out a "Jesus, Mary, and Joseph!"

"Sorry," he continued as he sat across the desk from me. "I didn't mean to surprise you."

I swiveled toward him and noted his eyebrows furrowed into his *I can't believe you moved us to this damned hinterland full of courthouse nutcases* look.

Uh oh.

He set both elbows on my desk. "So that supreme legal genius, in front of whom you no longer have to appear, just ruled that people can be convicted of burglarizing their own houses and sent to prison forever." Jack removed a ballpoint pen from his pocket and clicked the end repeatedly.

"You mean Judge Winston?" I asked rhetorically.

Jack nodded, gazing out the window. I'd scored the great view when I moved upstairs.

"Let's go across the street for a burger at The Buffalo," I suggested, knowing food could salve most wounds.

Ignoring me, Jack rolled on. "This place is mind-boggling. When I first saw Bill in court a few weeks ago with his public defender, I couldn't believe the PD and Winston had railroaded him into pleading guilty to 15 years in state prison for burglarizing his own house.

Then when he fired his lawyer in court and demanded a trial, I cheered him on. Now that he's my client and we're heading to trial on Monday, I'm worried. What if the jury convicts him, and Winston sends him to prison like he promised?"

My stomach rumbled, maybe from hunger, but more likely from stress. "Jack, that's always the risk at trial. You've won nearly every case you've tried in your career. Bill's case has a viable defense, and jurors here have been very fair to our clients. Besides, it's Bill's decision. If he wants to risk it, that's his constitutional right. At least you've got a winning issue on appeal."

Jack must have noticed the irritated look on my face because he stopped the pen-clicking, instead putting it back in his pocket. He steepled his fingers and sighed. "I never understood as a prosecutor why defense attorneys got so chewed up by their jobs. The problem is you get to know your clients, and while some of them may be guilty or a little strange, you actually start to care about them. And then when you think about them spending the rest of their lives in prison, it makes you feel kind of sick."

Whoa! I paused, stunned. Did Jack Defalco just show compassion for an evildoer? Did he actually feel an emotion besides disdain for a criminal? What the hell was happening to us? First me with Leonard the Child Molester and Rodney the Meth Spoon Guy, and now Jack with Bill who broke into his own house and smashed some plates on the counter.

"Anyone want lunch?" our law partner shouted up the stairs. Jack and I smiled at each other. The guy never missed a meal. He'd even proposed painting the exterior of the building red and yellow to attract clients, like McDonald's, until his wife pointed out that people weren't coming to our law firm to eat.

"You got it," Jack hollered back. "We'll be right

down."

Life's complications eased when inhaling burgers at The Buffalo.

* * *

At Bill's trial, after the lawyers picked a jury, the prosecutor admitted evidence that one night after Bill and his wife argued, she locked him out of the house. He re-entered the house through the living room window. His entry infuriated her, and their argument escalated to Bill throwing and breaking dishes.

Jack countered the prosecutor's case with Bill's testimony that mostly consisted of his repeated assertion, "It's my house, too."

Evidently the jury agreed. After a short recess to deliberate, the jury returned with a not guilty verdict, some jurors even patting Bill on the back as they filed out of the courtroom.

My former PD colleagues, including the one Bill had fired, watched the trial from the back of the courtroom. During Bill's testimony, he offered a scathing opinion of his former lawyer, and then pointed to said lawyer in court for the jury and press to view. Obviously the lawyer was displeased at such a public rebuke and ultimately blamed Jack and me for the hit to his reputation.

Nevertheless, Bill had just dodged 15 years in state prison for a crime he didn't commit.

Finally Jack and I understood the system. Unless we shackled Lady Justice to twelve impartial jurors, her blindfold slipped. Without the wisdom and common sense of regular people sucking it up for jury duty, guys like Bill or Casey Hennon for years would glimpse the world through steel bars that faced a common hallway filled with empty futures.

* * *

"No!" the 21-year-old killer in the wheelchair barked at me. "We are *not* blaming Mom for any of this."

I sat back in my chair, blasted by the vehemence of Nick Stagg's words. That day, in November 1999, I faced Nick in the recreation room of Deer Lodge State Prison. A prison guard sat at a podium a few feet away, pretending to work while he listened to our conversation.

I'd come to the prison at Nick's request to sit in on his interview with a writer from a popular sports magazine, an interview that Nick had anticipated with some excitement. During the previous hour, the writer had interviewed Nick about his career as a wheelchair racer, and his life before he murdered Rich Truman on Christmas night nearly two years earlier.

When they'd finished, I'd asked for a moment with Nick. I sought my own answer to a question raised months before by Rodney the Meth Spoon Guy when he had been Nick's cellmate in Kootenai County. Without warning him, I'd leaned toward Nick and chopped out, "Nick, have your parents beaten you before, badly enough to draw blood or leave bruises?"

Provoked, he'd spewed out his fervid defense of his mother.

I fumbled with my pen, berating myself for missing the fact that for the first moment in two years, Nick Stagg had just spoken to another human being about something *other* than the slaughter of Rich Truman. To the sports writer, Nick had described a time in his short life, before the string of burglaries, before the murder, when he'd spread courage and goodwill to those around him, when he'd *mattered* for reasons unconnected to homicide. I'd watched his blue eyes light up and his smile beam as the writer's questions drew attention to his former decency, to accomplishments earned, and praise readily given.

For indeed, such a time existed, many years of it. Nick had spent his first 18 years overcoming the series of traumas to his psyche that would have felled most grown men. Hampered by spina bifida from birth, his neck fused into permanent stillness at the age of four, his spine shredded and his lower body rendered useless at age 11, Nick's competitive spirit had prevailed.

Yes, he'd raced in wheelchair competitions, but he'd also protected his little brother and sister from others' bullying and teasing. He'd stood up to his parents on Ben's and Megan's behalf, verbally sparring with them from his rolling chair. He'd participated in countless charity events to raise money and awareness for disabled children. He'd reached out to his community and embraced police officers and kids alike.

He'd finished his GED, worked hard at his newspaper job at *The Whitehall Eagle,* and moved into his own apartment. He'd even secured a specially equipped car to insure his independence. In fact, Nick chose his role as a badass outlaw only three months before Rich Truman's murder. Up to that moment, in the police blotter of crimes and in life's blotter of dastardly deeds, his record had been clean.

Yet society had reduced the life of the young man who sat before me to a single event. In the eyes of Kootenai County's citizens, the Nick Stagg who'd existed before Rich Truman's murder had vanished, replaced by Nick Stagg the Killer. No one any longer thought of him as the sum of his prior life experiences. Instead, for two long years, Nick's former comrades had vilified him, their hatred toward him outmatched only by Nick's hatred toward himself.

The mom in me should have considered the

desiccated state of his emotional reserves. At 21, after two years in custody, Nick's heart pumped solely for survival, not love; his brain responded only to circumstance, not to kindness or hatred from his fellow humans; his anesthetized soul sheltered his senses from trauma, while it obviated his angry inquiry into the existence of a kind and just God. Doubtless Nick's conscious response to life had grown as numb as the limbs he dragged around below his waist.

Into that bleak landscape, ignorant of Nick's visceral anticipation of a future spent behind concrete and steel bars, I'd spoiled the one day, the one hour, when he'd shined like the gold-medal star he'd once been. I'd crashed his party and in so doing, I'd crushed his spirit. Ironic given that his parents had hired me to rescue both of their sons from the injustices heaped on them by a broken system.

After my abrupt question, followed by Nick's angry response, we stared at each other across the silence of a two-foot span separating my stationary chair from his mobile one. The guard shuffled his papers. Inwardly I cringed with shame, but I needed an answer. I needed the truth about this family. I had to know if there were past events Nick's public defender could have provided the court, facts that might lessen his culpability and sentence.

I stole a deep breath. When I felt like I could speak, I persisted. "Nick, all I'm saying is that Rodney told me your parents beat both you and Ben. He told me about one beating that happened right after you came home from the hospital after your fall."

Nick's blue eyes seared me as his jaw tightened. "Yeah. So what?"

I took another breath, nervous that he'd simply wheel himself out of the room, back to the safety of his cell and away from my prying affront. "Rodney told me that your mom called your dad in from the forest that day just to beat you. He told me your dad lifted you out of your wheelchair, laid you face down on the bed, and beat you with a belt until you bled. Rodney told me he saw the scars on your back from that beating. That could be important to your case, Nick, to your chance of getting parole."

He sized me up with eyes that belied his disappointment in my question, his lack of trust in me, and the death of his faith in God, country, and perhaps his own family. "How is what my parents did to us important? I shot that guy on my own because I thought he was going to turn me into the cops. I didn't want to get caught because Ben and me getting arrested for burglary would have killed Mom and Dad."

My brow furrowed in confusion at his reasoning. To no avail, I grasped at the aggregate of my college classes to make sense of his words. A period of silence hung between us before I clarified, "Rich Truman is dead because you were afraid of your parents' reaction to your arrest for *burglary?*"

Nick's expression softened, the fire in his eyes cooled, and he slumped back in his wheelchair. He glanced at the guard as if fearful the officer would spread gossip about Nick's past to other inmates. When he returned my gaze, he nodded. "Yeah." A sad smile creased his mouth. "That sounds so lame when you put it that way, but yeah, there was no way I could let that guy call the police to arrest us. It would bring too much shame on our family and my parents . . . so I stopped him."

How, I wondered, could parents engender a fear that was so pervasive, so strong, that it subordinated all logic and provided their child with only one solution to getting caught at a crime, a solution that included the murder of an innocent man?

Again I leaned forward, but now my own jaw tightened in frustration. "Nick, if you want me to help you get out of here - *ever,*" I emphasized, "then you need to answer my question. I need *something,* Nick. I need the truth about what really happened in your family when no one was looking. I need to know how you and Ben got involved in burglary and murder, and how your little cousin could shoot his own dad in the head just two days after you and Ben were arrested. I need to know how in God's name your parents could beat a little kid who just came home from the hospital - a kid *paralyzed in a wheelchair* - until you *bled!*"

My exasperation showed in the increasing pitch of my words. "Do you think that's okay?" I rolled on rhetorically. "Do you think *any* of this is *normal?* Because I'm telling you right now, that kind of conduct is *not* normal, Nick. No parent who beats his kids like that is normal, and being beaten like that as a child will matter to the judges at the Sentence Review Hearing. If you want me to help you, you have to come clean with me on this stuff."

Silence.

Finally, he placed his hands on the wheels of his chair, prepared for flight. "It happened, it's over, and that's not why I killed that guy. I am not blaming Mom for any of this, and that's the end. Ben isn't either, so don't ask him about it. I'm telling you, Paige, *let it go.*"

And away he rolled, leaving me with the guard, who stared at me before he slowly followed Nick to the door.

I collected the yellow legal pad that grew like an appendage from my right hand. "Crap," I muttered aloud to the empty recreation room. As I headed outside to drive the sports writer back to Kootenai County, I frowned at Nick's warning: *Let it go. Don't ask Ben about any of it.*

The writer and I processed through the prison's

salle-porte, that secure area between two locking doors in which the guards returned ID and insured no contraband left the prison. As we escaped to the fresh leather smells of my SUV, away from the unwashed body odor of the prison, I concluded that Nick's veiled threat covered up a cache of relevant secrets.

Yet Nick's admonishment bounced off my thickening skin. More determined than ever, I drove away hell-bent on excavating some hidden artifact that would free Ben Stagg, or give Nick a fighting chance at his sentence review hearing. If the Stagg family intended to dig in their heels and hide the ball, so be it.

My navy blue heels sported three-inch spikes that were a hell of a lot sharper than theirs.

CHAPTER TWENTY-ONE

Rescue Me

Late Fall, Early Winter 1999
Beartooth, Montana

WHETHER OR NOT I DISCERNED THE SECRETS of the Stagg clan, if I succeeded in getting Ben Stagg's guilty plea reversed, I'd need an unbiased jury to listen to Ben's side about his role in the Truman murder.

First, however, I needed a judge appointed to Ben's case who would follow the law and apply fairness instead of revenge. As we neared Thanksgiving in 1999, Judge Winston appointed his successor judge to Ben's case. Of the possible 36 or so judges in the state from whom he could have chosen, Winston selected another crony of his from Bozeman, a former military officer who wasn't known for his fair and balanced approach to defendants.

Worse, I'd already challenged this judge - in other words, I tossed his ass out - in the homicide case where the guy shot his wife and blew out his eyeball, telling the media that I considered the judge "harsh" based on his ruling in another case. It didn't take Johnny Cochran to tell me Ben was screwed. The likelihood that this newly assigned judge would do anything other than deny Ben's motion to withdraw his guilty plea defined *when hell freezes over*.

When I explained the judicial appointment to Ben in a call to the prison, he seemed only to understand it wasn't good news, and then asked me to "fix it." When I explained the appointment to Pete and Laura Stagg in a call to their home, they understood too well the ramifications, and then asked me to "fix it."

Unfortunately, there was just one way to fix it, and that solution lay in filing yet another writ with the Montana Supreme Court.

My theory was simple: Since that Court already ruled that Judge Winston was biased and prejudiced against me, and therefore could no longer preside over my cases, how could he fairly choose a successor judge? The law was ambiguous on the matter and needed clarification, and Ben's life was on the line, so it was an issue on which the Court might bite. Alternatively, the Court could deny the writ without a hearing and leave us at the mercy of Winston's freshly chosen replacement.

I spent several days preparing the legal document and filed it in early December, while trying to decorate the Christmas tree and purchase and wrap gifts. I called Pete and Laura to advise them that we should prepare for the worst. Winning at the Supreme Court was a long shot.

"All we ask is that you *try*, Paige." Kindness and hope infused Pete's tone. "God will take care of the rest."

God.

Right.

Other than my weekly attendance at Mass, I'd ignored God amid the morass of my life at the courthouse. Pete Stagg's assurance of divine guidance and intervention fed my inner cynic, but since it was Advent and Christmas loomed large, I flicked that nasty creature off my shoulder. Meanwhile, I had other clients and cases, kids, a new house needing extensive finish work, and a holiday season for which I needed to prepare.

I also needed a garlic necklace to ward off the

tenacious, larger-than-life, Chad Hammel, whose pleas for help flew through the telephone wires almost daily, insisting to Stormy, our gate-keeper/secretary, that he no longer liked his in-law, Judge Hank Winston. He demanded an appointment with me and promised her he could convince me of his sincerity. She capitulated and set an appointment in early December.

As I walked by her desk, Stormy smiled. "Maybe it will be like *Interview with a Vampire*. Do you think he has fangs?"

I grabbed my heavy coat. "I think, Stormy, that you're turning into a softee who no longer deserves to be called Dragon Lady."

* * *

Chad Hammel stormed our little conference room like the U.S. soldiers who'd invaded the tiny island of Grenada in 1983. I warily shook his outstretched hand. Jack, Stormy, and our law partner hovered nearby in the file room, ready for a rescue. The late December afternoon grew darker by the minute as the temperatures plunged below freezing. My mood, as I met the man who publicly had urged me to leave the state, matched the weather.

"Mr. Hammel," I began as I took a seat across the table from him, "With all due respect, I don't trust you. I think this is a setup by Judge Winston and his courthouse cronies. I find it incredible, frankly, that you and he have parted ways, especially when you share young grandchildren and your kids are married to one another."

"You're wrong, Paige. May I call you Paige?" When I nodded, he pressed his case. "Actually, Hank Winston and I dislike each other, and that has a lot to do with our kids and the grandchildren. Hank and his wife think my wife and I want to buy the grandkids' affection, and they don't have enough money to compete."

Chad spoke with intensity, his deep baritone voice modulated but forceful. He sat forward at the table, his burly forearms resting confidently on the table top, his hands clasped, but relaxed. His shaved head sat atop a broad, white shirt-clad body, the combination adding to my initial impression that he resembled an egg. Tension seemed to emanate from his interior, as if he comprised a large, positively charged atom, its electrons, protons, and neutrons colliding inside to generate heat and energy. Outwardly, he appeared calm, even reasonable, as if to reassure me that he could and would protect me from Judge Winston and the Courthouse Cowboys.

As I listened to his explanations of his relationship with the Winston family, and then to his rendition of the dispute he'd encountered with his business partner, I spiraled slowly into belief. This man, his warm brown eyes locked with my green ones, his smile quick to counter my frown, wore his love and loyalty for his family on his rolled-up sleeves. According to Chad, Hank Winston had interfered in Chad's relationship with his son and grandchildren, insulted Chad's new wife, and covertly sabotaged Chad's standing in the community.

It became clear to me that no one messed with Chad and his family and lived to brag about it.

Chad had grown up as one of the few white kids on an Indian reservation. He'd learned to fight for everything early in life, and those skirmishes prepared him to claw his way to the top of his field in the newspaper industry. He owned nearly every rag in the state, and had acquired a sizeable fortune through hard work and keen business acumen.

Okay, I was wrong about Chad and liked him. More importantly, I believed him about his relationship with Judge Winston, and agreed he needed a lawyer for his business case with some trial experience. Chad evoked adjectives like charming, strong, resilient, funny, and powerful. Yet was he more powerful than Judge Winston and his cronies? Would accepting him as a client help or hurt my law practice, my clients, and my family?

"Okay, Mr. Hammel," I sighed when he'd finished.

"Chad. Call me Chad, please," his low voice soothed as his smile entreated.

"Okay, Chad." I wilted, powerless to turn him away. "We need to send your partner a letter, and then we'll see if he sues you. If he does, and he likely will, we'll face that when it happens. Meanwhile, don't give him any ammunition to use against you in the law suit."

Chad's smile broadened. "So you'll take the case? You'll represent me?"

I nodded, wondering how Jack would react. "You have to understand, though, that I'm pretty busy with the criminal cases I have, especially the Stagg case. This business case of yours might get sidelined if something urgent comes up with Ben Stagg or the Supreme Court. Should that happen, Jack can step in for me and help you with any questions. When you hire me, you also get the benefit of Jack's civil and criminal law experience."

Chad stared at me for a moment as if deciding whether or not to divulge something, then sat back in his chair and crossed one foot over the opposite knee. "That Stagg kid," he cleared his throat. "Do you know what went on behind the scenes in that case with Winston and his buddies?"

"I wish," I replied, looking down as I gathered my notes, pen, and reading glasses.

His silence caused me to glance up.

Chad clasped his hands behind his head as he tipped the conference room chair onto its back legs. Then he grinned like the Cheshire Cat. "I do."

* * *

If my immediate mission focused on rescuing the Stagg brothers from the folly of their fatal conduct two years earlier, Chad Hammel's mission, although he didn't know it yet, centered on rescuing me.

As I faced the millennium New Year with a gathering of friends and family in our new kitchen, I felt the chill from our snowy acreage weigh on me like an avalanche debris field. Even after Chad had appeared at our office with insider information - dirt, so to speak - on the courthouse crew, my days bogged down with defeat.

No longer a public defender, I felt overwhelmed by the sheer number of needy clients who had no cash, but offered to pay with everything from domesticated livestock to guns. Concerned and guilt-ridden at my children's struggles in school, I sagged. My shoulders slumped, my neck skin bunched under my chin, the bags under my eyes multiplied and darkened, even my hair grew listless.

I faced my reflection one January morning before court only because I couldn't apply mascara without a mirror. "I look like shit. And who is that harridan in the mirror?"

Standing next to me at the bathroom counter, looking dapper as always, Jack crooned a chorus of *Cheeseburger in Paradise* as he watched himself fashion a full Windsor knot in his tie. "You don't look that bad, Paige. I keep telling you, don't let those assholes get to you. Besides, now that you've got Chad Hammel as a client, things can only look up. He's probably got dirt on God, and he sure as hell has it on Winston and his cronies." He straightened the tie and reached for his hairbrush.

"I look like a wizened hag, Honeybunch, so don't

sugarcoat it," I shot back. "The bad news is Chad called yesterday to tell me Charlie's wife, Holly, moved out of the house, took the kids, and moved in with her parents. Judge Winston now has control of the grandkids, and neither Holly nor her parents will let Charlie visit them. Chad's furious."

I abandoned the effort to lose ten years off my face, and left Jack to warble his version of *I Wish I Had a Pencil Thin Mustache*.

* * *

Later that day, back from an uneventful morning in court, I entered our office only to face urgent messages from Chad. He arrived within minutes, workout clothes warming him from the arctic air, a huge mug of coffee steaming in his hands. It emulated the heat wafting from his intense expression.

Chad sat forward in his chair at the conference table, looked directly into my gaze, and boomed out, "Two things: Charlie needs to talk to you because his kids have been injured, and he's worried they're being neglected at the Winston's house. My grandson had a black eye at church yesterday, and my nine-month-old granddaughter wasn't there at all. Holly told Charlie she was napping. Then today Holly called to tell Charlie the baby actually had a broken arm. The second thing is: I'm pretty sure I'm about to get sued in the business case."

He sat back and took a sip of coffee, his brown eyes still holding my green ones as if he expected an immediate solution to his legal dilemmas. Instead I frowned at him, puzzled. Chad, I surmised, solved problems in a decisive manner, which is why he'd succeeded at business and made his fortune from nothing but hard work and intelligence. However, this grandchild problem - *thing number one* - held the contents for a nuclear bomb.

"How did a nine-month-old break her arm, and how did her brother get a black eye?" My prosecutor's instincts ratcheted to high alert.

Chad shook his head, swallowing his murky brew. "Holly says the baby fell on her bottom while she was clinging to Holly's pant leg, and somehow her forearm broke. Holly told Charlie she thought my granddaughter's little cast was *cute*. She said my grandson bumps himself all the time, and the black eye is nothing. I think those kids are being neglected. There's a lot of alcohol consumed in that house."

I ran my fingers through the top of my hair and sighed. "Chad, do you know what you're saying? You're accusing a sitting judge who is a big deal in this valley, and a bigger deal in this state, of neglecting his own grandkids to the point where one of them has suffered a very serious injury."

"Look," he put his elbows on the table and leaned even closer. "I'm not accusing him of anything. Those injuries speak for themselves. Maybe Holly's telling the truth or maybe she's covering up for somebody's negligence. All I know is those kids aren't safe over there, and maybe that's the reason they won't let Charlie visit his own children."

Mentally I screeched, *Are you fucking kidding me? You want me to accuse Judge Winston of child neglect? The Courthouse Cowboys will go berserk. Dead meat. I will be dead meat.*

Aloud I assumed my detached-lawyer tone. "I'll talk to Charlie today. He needs to get a copy of the x-rays from the pediatrician so we can have them independently evaluated by an impartial doctor. If that expert thinks Holly's story adds up, we'll let it go. If he tells us there is no way that kind of fracture happens to a nine-month-old by falling eight inches on her bottom, then …"

Then what? I thought, looking down at my notes. *You*

will be a carcass hanging in a local butcher shop. "Then we'll deal with it."

* * *

I ran Chad's versions of the facts by a local doctor in Beartooth who had a family practice and specialized in sports medicine. Although he refused to testify or state his opinion publicly out of concern over reprisals, he confirmed my worst fears as a former prosecutor: Holly's explanation that the baby broke her arm when she fell while holding onto Holly's pants defied medical logic.

A double long bone spiral fracture rarely occurred in an infant under the age of a year, and always signaled the need for a deeper investigation to eliminate possible abuse. The additional fact that Holly failed to report the accident for two days raised another red flag.

Two weeks later we had our answer: two other doctors, one a pediatric orthopedist from another state and the other a local, highly experienced orthopedist, concluded that the fracture resulted from substantial force applied to the baby's arm by an adult. She couldn't have suffered a spiral, double long-bone fracture by falling on her bottom.

Given those opinions, Charlie had two choices: he could leave the kids where they were and hope for the best, or he could finger his wife and father-in-law for child neglect by filing legal papers seeking emergency custody.

Either way, I wanted to wretch. No good could come from ignoring the problem, but publicly calling out Judge Winston and his daughter would both cement the end of Charlie's marriage and my pariah status in the statewide legal community. Still, somebody had to represent Charlie, and I stood alone as his only potential advocate.

Besides, what if the children actually were in danger?

I looked at my stockinged-toes balanced atop my desk and swallowed some ibuprofen. As usual, I gambled my headache would abate before the drug ate a hole through my stomach lining. Then I closed my eyes and waited for any knight in shining armor to materialize.

Nothing happened.

Along with his son and grandkids, Chad Hammel, the guy in the white hat who was supposed to rescue me from my own debacle at the courthouse, suddenly posed the gravest threat yet to my long sought tranquility. If I proceeded with the custody case, my colleagues would relegate me to the status of road-kill.

Too bad Chad wasn't a fanged bat. Having my blood sucked out through my neck sounded a whole lot less painful than a slow death at the hands of the Cowboys.

CHAPTER TWENTY-TWO

The Firestorm

January through March 2000
Beartooth, Montana

"WHAT ARE YOU SAYING, CHARLIE? That Judge Winston burglarized your house?" I lodged the phone between my ear and shoulder while I grabbed a blank yellow legal pad and a pen. His words, along with the gray mid-January sky, darkened my Monday and my mood. Only seven days earlier Charlie had learned of his daughter's broken arm.

"Yeah, can you believe that? Holly called Friday saying she'd be over Sunday to collect her stuff. Saturday morning I left to meet my brother for coffee, locked the house - you know I changed all the locks over a month ago - and when I came back, I found Holly, her dad, and an off-duty Aberdeen cop inside looting the place. They took nearly everything in the house, then threatened to arrest me for having a satellite card."

Over the phone line I heard another guy ranting in the background as Charlie spoke. I tuned out the extra noise as I absorbed Charlie's latest fiasco. "Look, take a breath and tell me what you did when you found them in your house." I cringed inwardly, waiting to hear details of a fistfight or guns drawn, but no violence unfolded in the rest of the tale.

"They told me the cop used a credit card to break in through the front door. They took everything I had to care for the kids, and as they left, Judge Winston told me if I pursued the broken arm and black eye, he'd have me arrested for possessing an illegal satellite card - which Holly took, by the way, so she could use it at her parents' house."

Again I heard a voice in the background, "Tell her about the judge knowing the law," prompting Charlie to add, "Oh, yeah. When my brother accused the judge of breaking and entering, Winston yelled at us that he knew the law, and it wasn't breaking and entering."

It sounded like Charlie took a sip of something, black coffee if he followed his dad's example. Hammels on caffeine, I decided, provoked much drama.

"So, in your legal opinion," Charlie swallowed, "is it or isn't it?"

"Is it or isn't it what?" The vision of the judge looting Charlie's house sidetracked me.

"Breaking and entering, burglary? Can they be prosecuted like the rest of us?"

A fair question. One answer came to mind: Jack's client, Bill, the same guy who Judge Winston had planned to send to prison for 15 years for burglarizing his own house; the same guy who left and returned after his wife locked him out, then came through a window and smashed some dinner plates; the same guy who the jury had acquitted at trial just months before.

In Bill's case, when Jack tried to dismiss the charge of felony burglary under the theory that Bill had as much right as his wife to enter their home, Judge Winston proffered, "I know the law, Jack, and, you *can* be charged with burglarizing your own house." Yet now, that very same Judge Winston claimed he knew the law, and that neither he, nor his daughter, nor the cop could be charged with felony burglary of Charlie's house.

Hmmmm, I gauged, *how should I phrase this* so *Charlie and his family will calm down?*

"Here's the deal, Charlie. Since you grew up here,

you know this is a small town in an under-populated state. By the judge's own ruling in one of Jack's cases, the answer is yes, it's a burglary. However, because the judge and county prosecutors are close friends, and because Winston ran the county attorney's office and knows all the cops, and since a cop was with him, Winston has an unofficial *get out of jail free* card. The chances of him getting arrested and prosecuted are zero."

"What!" Charlie exploded. "That's not fair! What about the rest of us?"

Clearly my calming skills needed work.

"The rest of us," I continued, unhindered by tact, "are screwed. Now let's move on here, Charlie. What do you want to do about your kids? Do you want to file for emergency custody? Because if so, you need to complete an affidavit under oath detailing the possible neglect, and probably all these threats, plus the break-in, before a judge will order a hearing on the facts. Also, it will cost a bundle to have the orthopedic experts testify at a hearing."

Mentioning his offspring sobered his attitude. After a moment, Charlie sighed in confusion. "Look, I still love Holly, and I want our marriage to work out. I don't want a divorce, but I want my kids safe and back in my life. She won't let me see them, and I honestly worry for their safety. I'm sure no one in her family would hurt them on purpose, but Holly's been depressed and doesn't pay attention to them. Her folks adore the kids, but when they drink, they don't pay attention either. I don't know what to do. Chad thinks I should file for custody, and so does my brother."

I tamped down the tension growing in my gut when I thought of publicly airing the Winston laundry, so I adopted my best lawyerese. "This isn't Chad's decision to make. It's not your brother's decision either. It's yours alone, and you have to do what you deem best for your children, first, and your marriage, second. Give it serious thought - *alone* - and get back to me when you make a decision."

Hanging up, I dropped my forehead onto the desk blotter as every expletive I'd ever learned marched across my brain.

* * *

The next day, Charlie chose his kids' welfare over his own reticence, and completed an affidavit under oath that included more details of life in the Hammel and Winston households than the world needed to hear. I attached it to a motion to obtain emergency custody, and hand-delivered it to the courthouse. Within minutes, the place was abuzz. The air stiffened with electricity as clerks avoided my gaze while they whispered through their cubicles. I left quickly, chin up, aware that I'd ignited a firestorm.

Charlie hadn't seen his children more than a few times in the last three months, and his dad hadn't seen them at all. When the process server handed the legal papers to Holly Winston Hammel at her parents' home later that day, I conceded that my world, like hers, tipped a little more out of kilter. Her parents, I knew, would defend her to their death, if that's what it took to keep custody of the children and fend off the charges.

Once I filed the affidavit, a fight ensued between the courthouse crew and me to determine which out-of-area judge would preside at the custody hearing. Once again I prepared a writ to the Montana Supreme Court over the exact issue pending before them in Ben Stagg's case, to wit, whether a judge who was biased against me should pick his or her successor to hear my clients' cases.

Meanwhile, I'd prepared a bill for the 509 extra trial

hours I'd worked in Casey's murder case as a public defender. My contract entitled me to payment for such extraordinary expenses. Judge Winston ignored the bill, but continued to lambast me as a mercenary to the local press, so the County Commissioners denied payment. At Jack's urging, my appeal of that denial also sat at the Supreme Court.

Between all the legal filings, the fights at the justice center, and Charlie's future custody hearing, I found little time to worry about Ben and Nick Stagg. Until the Supreme Court ruled on whether or not a new judge should be appointed to Ben's case, there wasn't much I could do. Still, I wondered daily how drastically my ongoing fight with the Courthouse Cowboys would affect the outcome of Ben's case.

Jack, on the other hand, approached February 2000 still humming his parrot-headed songs. I fretted as usual about the kids, their schoolwork, their social lives, and the disintegration of my legal career in Kootenai County, Montana. After all, it wasn't every day I publicly implicated a sitting District Court judge, both statewide and to the Montana Supreme Court, as a tippler who possibly abused or neglected his grandchildren.

I stretched my spine as I stood up from my desk, unaware that Jack had topped the stairs to my office. "Chum!" I railed at the ceiling.

"You're talking to yourself again," he noted, his voice jolting me. "Chum as in friend or chum as in shark bait?"

"Shark bait." I grabbed my suit jacket so we could head to lunch. "That's what I feel like. As if I'm in the middle of an impending battle between the Hammel and Winston families, but nobody's told me the history or the rules."

"Well," advised my beloved, "then you'd better be the shark."

* * *

"Chad," I followed the arc of his hand as he raised the coffee mug to his mouth, "you knew when you split from your business partner that he'd sue you. He did. You told me it would get ugly. It has. I told you not to mail copies of our lawsuit to people in this county, but you did. Now, you can be prosecuted for blacklisting the guy, and get hit with punitive damages at trial."

My glare pierced him, but his gaze held steady.

"He's out there ruining my business, lying to everyone. I had to do *something*. Besides, I checked with another lawyer who said he thought it was okay to mail the stuff out." Chad leaned toward me across the conference table, his intensity charging the space between us. Charlie, sitting to Chad's left, wisely remained silent as he observed the clash between his father and me.

My aggravation roiled. "That lawyer is also under federal indictment for felony fraud and the theft of millions of dollars. He's on his way to prison. *That's* the lawyer you chose to consult when you didn't like my answer?"

Chad showed the courtesy of looking sheepish for a second, but then the wolf returned. "I'm not going down without a fight, Paige. That's not how I operate. Besides, I just found out from a source at the courthouse that in December, Hank Winston gave legal advice to my former partner on how to screw me in this lawsuit. They think I'll settle and give that idiot a million dollars."

Chad grinned. "That's not going to happen. We'll fight this out to the end. Screw 'em. It's not the money. It's the principle of the thing."

Ah yes, the principle of the thing. The very same principle that forms the fodder of all lawsuits.

I drew a huge dollar sign on my yellow pad and held it up for Chad's inspection. "That," I pointed with my index finger, "is what the principle of the thing will cost you. Lots and lots of money. At some point, if they make a reasonable offer, we need to consider a settlement. Is your secret source willing to come forward and testify against the judge?"

Chad shook his head. "Not a chance. Too scared of the repercussions."

Typical of this town, I silently regretted, *or any town where people want to keep their jobs.*

"Then let's move on to Charlie's custody case." I grabbed the notes of my conversations with the orthopedic and child abuse experts I'd contacted to review the baby's arm x-ray.

"Both the orthopedist and the pediatrician who specializes in child abuse agree with the first doctor's opinion that Holly isn't telling the truth about how your daughter broke her arm. They're both willing to testify at the custody hearing which is set for next week." I paused so they could digest the seriousness of the opinions. "Are you sure you want to go ahead with this?"

Father and son nodded, Chad with more confidence than Charlie. "Okay. I need time to prepare for the hearing, so try not to bug me unless it's important. I'll let you know when I hear the result of our appeal to the Supreme Court about whether or not we're stuck with Winston's hand-picked successor judge."

An hour later, our secretary gleefully phoned me upstairs. "You won! You actually won the appeal in the Hammel case! Not only that, you can dump the current judge and let the Chief Justice appoint her successor."

While I marveled at the win, after reading the Court's order, I realized we faced a dilemma: The custody hearing loomed just four days away, and every day that passed presented more danger to Charlie's kids.

If we challenged the latest Winston handpicked successor, and let the Chief Justice appoint someone else, we delayed the hearing and a change of custody. Yet if we allowed the hand picked judge to preside, we risked getting decimated at the hearing.

Only Charlie could decide.

* * *

Out of concern for his children's safety, Charlie elected to go forward with the hand-picked successor deciding the issue of temporary custody. He reasoned that we had two independent and credible experts who would testify to Holly's possible neglect. He would testify about the burglary of his home and Judge Winston's threats to have him arrested if he pursued any investigation into the kids' injuries, as well as to his wife's refusal to allow Charlie to see his kids.

I agreed that Charlie's decision made sense. No fair-minded judge could ignore that evidence.

Four days later, we presented our case. Our two expert witnesses testified that it would take 100 to 150 pounds of adult pressure to inflict the type of fracture suffered by Charlie's daughter, and that several indicators of child abuse presented the baby's attending pediatrician with a duty to further inquire about potential danger.

The baby's attending pediatrician, the one who failed to report the fracture, testified that he had been Holly's family pediatrician since she was born, and thus he accepted her kids as patients. He'd never noticed any signs of abuse and didn't believe, having known Holly as a patient all her life, that she would abuse her kids. He didn't see anything unusual about the fracture, although he conceded such fractures were rare in children less than twelve months old.

Judge Winston and Chad sat on opposite sides of

the courtroom, presumably to support their children.

The hand-picked successor judge abruptly ended the hearing, and without pausing for breath, immediately ruled that Holly's childhood doctor was the more credible witness. She denied Charlie any visitation with his children unless he visited them in Holly's presence at her parents' house. He couldn't be alone with his kids until he completed a lengthy series of parenting classes.

When we objected that Judge Winston presented a threat to Charlie, as Charlie set out in his affidavit, the hand-picked successor ordered Judge Winston and his wife to vacate their home during Charlie's visits. To exacerbate the injustice of the judicial ruling, the other agencies that should have helped Charlie and his kids failed them. Before the hearing, when Charlie learned of his daughter's fracture, he reported the broken arm and black eye to both Child Protective Services (CPS) and the Kootenai County Sheriff's Department. The CPS agent, citing a conflict of interest because she worked in court alongside Judge Winston, promised to turn the investigation over to an impartial worker in Bozeman.

She didn't.

Instead, she met briefly with Holly and decided there was no merit to Charlie's claims. She didn't visit or inspect the Winston household, nor did she review the available medical evidence or consult with her own experts. She never inquired into the presence of other child abuse risk factors, like post-partum depression, stress from family members, alcohol abuse, separation in the marriage, or the added risk of abuse when a mom or dad parents two young kids instead of one.

In fact, in just a few short hours, that CPS worker, Judge Winston's colleague, accepted his daughter's word that nothing was amiss and closed the investigation. As a result of CPS refusing to investigate any further, the Sheriff's Department also dropped its inquiry.

Case closed.

For Charlie, the devastation of losing his children in such a lopsided, biased justice system evoked both anger and grief. Chad, on the other hand, polished up his armor. He knew we were at the incipient stage of battle, not at the end. All of us looked grim as we left the courthouse.

If satisfied smirks were audible, the one on Judge Winston's face as he left the courtroom that day roared in triumph.

* * *

Three weeks later I sipped a cup of tea and gazed out the window of my office. "If it weren't for the kids, Jack, I swear I'd pack up and leave this god-forsaken wilderness for the sanity of our old jobs."

Jack set his own mug on my desk, raised his eyebrows, and drummed his fingers.

I held up my palm to preempt his rant. "I know. Don't say it. I'm the one who moved us here. We had perfectly good jobs, a great house, and money, all of which I threw away because that life was insane and this one would be different."

Jack straightened out of his slump and sat forward, much like Chad did whenever we argued. "Yeah, you did. You're also the one who got into it with Winston and McShane, although I understand why you had to do it. But shit, Paige, we could be in trouble here. If Winston loses another round at the Supreme Court, he might try to disbar us. If they disbar us here, they'll disbar us in California, and then how will we support the kids?"

I felt anger creep up the back of my neck. "Listen, if I could extricate myself from this morass of crap, I'd do it in a heartbeat, but I'm in too deeply to bail out on my clients, especially Ben Stagg and the Hammels."

I tossed back the last of my tea to swallow my bitterness. "When we were prosecutors, we never saw this side of the justice system. We never saw judges like Hank Winston or prosecutors like Frank McShane. We never saw all this small-town, incestuous bullshit that drives this entire county. *We* were the good guys, damn it! *We* wore the white hats and actually *won* in court most of the time."

"Well," Jack reasoned, "we still win in court most of the time. Besides, I've known judges more bizarre than Winston, and you admit that you and McShane have a lot in common. It's just that you're starting to view the world from the opposite side of the courtroom, and it bothers you that the playing field isn't level. I, on the other hand, see it all as a game, and don't give a shit whether it's fair or not. I just want to win."

Jack didn't exaggerate his take on the criminal justice process. He still believed in the death penalty, viewed criminals with cynical derision, and he detached his heart if it attempted to grip any of his clients.

I reached for the intercom to answer Stormy's page. "Winston and McShane can't be all bad. They both have wives and kids who love them. Then again, so did Genghis Khan."

Stormy's voice squeaked out of the speaker. "You won again! The Supreme Court just agreed to appoint a new judge in Ben Stagg's case. They said Winston was wrong to appoint his own successor, and now the Chief Justice will appoint someone new."

Jack shouted out a "Yes!" and hugged me before heading downstairs to share the news with anyone who'd listen. For a moment Jack's elation filled me, but as I gazed at my image reflected in the window, I shuddered. I felt shadowy, as if a specter perched nearby, waiting to leap at me the moment I exhaled.

I'd always reacted to good news that way, measuring my joy, gauging how bad the news would be that inevitably followed. It proved a safe way to go through life, never expecting rapture nor experiencing disappointment, reaching only for the narcotic stillness of numb.

I dialed Ben's parents to tell them the news.

Before I left for the day, I watched a recorded version of the *NewsTime*, *CBS* special on the Stagg case that had just aired on prime time. The one-hour show painted a sympathetic picture of Ben, an unflattering view of Judge Winston, and concluded with footage of me criticizing the length of the brothers' 100-year prison sentences.

Perfect. This will further flame the judge's ire.

As I drove the short distance to our house, to the sanctuary of kids, dogs, spaghetti, and a blazing fireplace, I considered whether our success at the Montana Supreme Court portended a shift in the balance of Judge Winston's power. Either the victory symbolized a spark of hope or an oxygen-enriched ember about to ignite a conflagration.

At the very least, I should pray for an angel.

In a firestorm, I knew I'd need the magic of a Phoenix.

CHAPTER TWENTY-THREE

Seraphim and Cherubim

March 2000
Beartooth, Montana

HELL'S ANGELS, CHARLIE'S ANGELS, TEEN ANGELS, snow angels, Blue Angels, and even the Los Angeles Angels - those I could believe in. Fallen Angels, Arch Angels, or Angels of Mercy - they evoked a skeptical *maybe.*

Yet by early March 2000, I would have welcomed all of them if only they'd promise to save Ben Stagg from his nightmare in custody. Still, since I expected wings, motorcycles, baseball uniforms, or at least fiery beauties, I listened with distrust to the intense phone-voice of a female shrink explaining to me that she wasn't a nutcase and only wanted to help Ben.

Dr. Sara Berg, forensic psychologist, expert witness in numerous death penalty cases, clinical diagnostician to several bad guys on America's death rows, private analyst for a myriad of troubled patients, author of psychology texts, resident of Columbus, Ohio, doer of laundry, and watcher of *NewsTime, CBS,* phoned our office to inform me that the Stagg family was hiding a big secret.

"I'm telling you, Mrs. Defalco, when I watched Pete and Laura Stagg on television the other night, my first thought was *meshugoyim.*" She paused, awaiting my confirmation of her assessment.

"Uh . . ." Did angels speak in vernacular?

"Oh, sorry," she amended. "At times I lapse into

Yiddish. What I mean is *crazy people*. And they're withholding a huge piece of the puzzle. Boys like Ben and Nick Stagg don't suddenly kill an innocent person, not unless they're enraged to begin with, and that happens mostly to abused kids who feel powerless."

She'd assessed the Stagg family, she explained, while she folded laundry during the *NewsTime, CBS* show.

I cleared my throat to stall my response. "Well, you may be correct, Dr. Berg, but unless I get Ben's guilty plea reversed, the issue of family abuse or craziness is pretty academic. The new judge on the case just set a hearing in late June, so we're focusing on the plea deal between the prosecutor and Ben's first attorney, and the sentencing judge's relationship to various people in the case."

She sighed over the wire. "I understand, and I know you're swamped with other cases. I did a little checking on you, and let me just note, Mrs. Defalco, you're pretty controversial in Montana."

No shit, I nodded as she rambled on.

"Still, I just want to encourage you to hire a forensic psychologist to interview the family before you go to trial. I'm sure there are some reputable ones in Montana. Their insight will be well worth whatever they charge you."

After thanking her for the advice, I disconnected, wondering what prompted a woman with her stellar credentials to contact me from *Ohio*, for God's sake - just to warn me about the Stagg family.

Jack entered my office, interrupting my concentration. "Hey, I just heard the Supreme Court appointed a new judge on Ben's case and set a hearing in June. What's this guy like?" Jack assumed his usual right-ankle-crossed-over-left-knee position as he sat in the chair opposite mine.

I snatched away the mug that held my pens so he

couldn't click as he listened.

"Well, I know he's from Havre, along the High Line. He has a brother who lives here in Beartooth with whom he can stay during the hearing and trial, if there's a trial. And he practiced mostly civil law before he became a judge. He has a fair amount of trial experience for a civil attorney."

Jack, without benefit of a ballpoint, tapped his fingers on the chair's arm to the silent beat of *Cheeseburger in Paradise*. After a minute he proffered, "It probably doesn't matter. With only 37 judges in the whole state, most who graduated from law school with Hank Winston, this guy's going to hammer Ben as badly as Winston or his first pick."

Ouch.

"You know, Honeybun, you could humor me on this. Maybe he's an exception to the rule. At least we have a new judge and a hearing date. Those may be small steps, but we're moving forward." I grabbed my own ballpoint and clicked it as payback for Jack annoying me.

"I'm just a realist. Or maybe a cynic. Probably both. Did you contact that new private investigator Chad Hammel told you about?"

I stopped clicking and reached for the sheet of yellow paper containing my notes. "Actually, I did. Ty Kayman. He's a former Los Angeles police officer who's been doing PI work for several years, mostly out of Seattle. He agreed to work with me on Ben's case. I'm meeting with him this afternoon."

After Jack left my upstairs eyrie, I realized how quickly the Stagg case had progressed after the appointment of The Honorable Jeff Lambert. Judge Lambert was a Catholic father of six and a grandfather. He'd been married to the same woman forever, had a great reputation as a trial lawyer, and most attorneys considered him fair on the bench.

On the other hand, a defense attorney from the east side once complained to the press that Judge Lambert made inappropriate facial expressions in court - rolling his eyes, for example - when he disagreed with the attorneys or with a witness' testimony. If that was the worst I faced, I figured I could handle him. At least he wasn't one of Judge Winston's well-known cronies or friends with half of Kootenai County and the local courthouse club.

I struck him from the roster of potential angels, however, since I felt confident that celestials didn't roll their eyes.

* * *

That afternoon, Ty Kayman arrived for our first meeting. Whatever vision I held of a former cop from Los Angeles didn't fit with the mild-looking man in front of me. The bottom of his round face sported a goatee, while his brow led to a thinning head of brown hair. His blue eyes twinkled when he shook my hand, and his firm grip diverted my attention from his mischievous smile.

"Boy," he opened with a chuckle, "you sure know how to piss off the local good old boys."

I returned his grin. "Yeah, well, don't believe everything you hear. I'm not as bad as they say. Have a seat," I invited as I opened the Stagg file. I commented to fill the silence as I searched for documents. "So, Los Angeles, huh?"

"Yep," Ty nodded. "The City of Angels."

I handed him the police report. He frowned in confusion. "Where's the rest of it? There's only one page here."

"Yeah," I confirmed, "Only one page that pertains to the Stagg brothers. There are several hundred pages that don't, that describe all the wild goose chases the cops pursued before a girl came forward with Ben's confession. For now, all you need to further investigate are some allegations Pete and Laura Stagg have made about Judge Winston and his relationships to certain people and organizations involved in the case."

Ty relaxed back in his chair and stared at me. "Like what?"

"Like the fact that Judge Winston and the murder victim, Rich Truman, were Masonic Lodge brothers. Or that Judge Winston and Ben Stagg were members of the same church and prayed with the same pastor. Or that their pastor visited Ben at the jail and discussed the murder, after which he socialized with Judge Winston at the judge's house. Or that every Saturday morning, then and now, Judge Winston participates in a men's Bible study led by that same pastor, Bobby Rohers. The other members of that little group include a doctor who is one of the Stagg brothers' burglary victims, and Rich Truman's fellow father-in-law, the very same in-law who watched the grandkids after Truman's body was found."

Ty shook his head and laughed. "What's your point? You think the judge had a few conflicts of interest and should have taken himself off the case?"

"Yeah," I smirked. "I think."

"So, you want me to infiltrate the Masons and the judge's church. Anything else? Maybe purloin secret files from the local police departments?" Ty's sarcasm dangled from his smile.

"Just watch your back, Ty," I warned. "These folks are so interlinked, it's impossible to know whether the person you speak to is connected to another player in the game."

Ty stood to leave after accepting the list of witnesses and their contact information. "I'm on it. I'll be in touch."

And off he went to unearth the hoped-for

connection between Judge Winston and the Truman family that would force Judge Lambert to reverse Ben's guilty plea.

Plan A - the one the never worked - raced out of the gate.

* * *

In case Plan A failed, Plan B required that I discover what really happened behind the plea bargain Ben's first lawyer struck with the prosecutor. The written document lacked any mention of a recommended sentence, a glaring omission in a murder plea. Without it, the judge could choose whatever sentence he deemed appropriate, so most experienced defense attorneys never took the risk.

I placed a call to Ben's first attorney who currently hoped for a judicial appointment. Oddly, instead of a callback from him, I heard instead from his personal attorney, who happened to be another Courthouse Cowboy.

"Here's the bottom line, Mrs. Defalco," the Cowboy opened without pleasantries. "Unless you drop the claim from Ben's petition that alleges my client is guilty of ineffective assistance of counsel, I will advise my client to say nothing to you, in or out of court."

Okay.

I sat up in my office chair, defensive. What an arrogant ass! Why did he call instead of Ben's first lawyer?

"You're talking to *me*," he continued, as if reading my mind, "because my client wants that upcoming judicial appointment, and I believe your allegations are hurting his chances. You drop them, and I'll allow him to tell the truth about Ben's plea bargain. You keep accusing him of screwing up Ben's case, and trust me, I'll see to it that he won't remember any helpful details when he testifies."

Hardball. I swiveled toward the window and the view of the mountain. *Welcome to the legal underworld, Paige, where you sell a piece of your soul to gain a benefit for your client.*

"Furthermore, Mrs. Defalco, at my direction, my client will defend his representation of Ben. I will advise him to testify truthfully that Ben tried to fire the shotgun when he hid in the woods, but the gun jammed. If you don't cease your attack, my client will be released from his duty to withhold privileged information, and he will tell the judge that Ben tried to kill Rich Truman."

I sat forward in my chair, slamming my hand on my desk blotter. "Old news, pal. Ben admitted to the cops in his confession that he tried to shoot but couldn't do it. Besides, Ben loaded that shotgun with blanks because he was afraid Nick would kill him with it." I tamped down a "you piece of crap" finale.

"Nevertheless," the Cowboy continued, "you know that my client's testimony will make it look like your client was lying in wait for the victim and had the intent to kill, an aggravator that could result in a death sentence."

I choked back the many expletives waiting to erupt. "I understand," I chopped out. "I'll talk to Ben and get back to you."

I slammed down the phone, yelled out a "son of a *bitch,*" and threw my yellow pad at the wall. "That's extortion! What kind of slimeball demands that choice when a kid's life is on the line?"

Stormy cleared her throat from her defensive position at the top of the stairs. "Problems?" she asked rhetorically. I explained the situation to her. Ineffective assistance of counsel provided a strong claim in Ben's effort to overturn his conviction. On the other hand, to prevail on the strongest claim, that the prosecutor reneged on his promise to recommend only 40 years for Ben instead of 100, I needed Ben's first attorney to testify at the June hearing. He was the only witness to those negotiations.

However, if I didn't drop the claim that impugned his legal talent, his lawyer would advise him to develop amnesia and cement Ben's life in prison. Worse, he'd imply that Ben attempted murder and failed.

Stormy cautiously moved closer to my desk with a handful of phone messages. "I used to work for that lawyer who just called you. He was good in his heyday. Now he's really sick. Maybe that's why he's acting like that."

"Maybe," I rubbed my eyes, "but he has me by the . . . *whatever* . . . so I'm going to have to do what they want. Shit."

Another voice, smaller and giggling, piped in. "Mom! You'd kill me if I swore like that. I thought you gave up swearing when we moved here."

Guilty as charged, frustrated, teetering on defeat yet again, I smiled at my son who'd quietly come up the stairs behind Stormy. "Hey, Sean. Sorry about that," I apologized. "How did things go at school today?"

He took the chair across from mine and crossed his right ankle over his left knee. "It's so cool, Mom. My teacher reads out loud to us every day from *The Hobbit*, and he uses all these neat voices and . . ."

As his little voice droned on, I thought of Ben Stagg as a child. Did Ben tell his mom everything? Did he snuggle in her lap while she read stories to him every night? Did he tell her she was the best mom in the whole world, and squeeze her around the waist as hard as he could?

I recalled how Ben flinched every time a hand neared him.

Let it go, Paige. For now you have to ignore Dr. Berg's

warning and her television assessment of the Stagg family.

"Mom!" my son intoned, leaning across my desk as he waved his hand mere inches in front of my nose. "We have to go. My practice starts at four."

I waved back with my own hand inches from his face, scolding, "That's rude, buddy."

And stopped.

Unlike Ben Stagg, my son didn't flinch.

CHAPTER TWENTY-FOUR

Blowback

March to May 2000
Beartooth, Montana

"THAT DEAF OLD BASTARD FIRED ME as Peg Zanto's attorney this morning at the sentencing hearing!"

I leaned back in my office chair, stunned as Jack, scowling, furious, related the latest courthouse drama.

"We're all in court, ready for Peg to get sentenced to probation for screwing the 15-year-old, and suddenly that fucking judge announces he thinks Ms. Zanto received crappy legal advice before her trial last year - from *you*, Sweet Pea."

He slammed his file notebook onto my desk and trailed back and forth in front of me. "He even said he had no problem with *me*. He had a problem with *Mrs. Defalco*. And Frank McShane and your former defense colleagues sat there smirking. Then the judge set a public hearing to investigate how well you practice law, with you and Ms. Zanto as the star witnesses."

Gazing out the window, I noted how the weather that last day of March muted the sun, just as Jack's revelation grayed my mood. "Well, crap." I stretched, rolling my neck.

Jack stopped his pacing and slumped in the chair across from me. "They're so angry at you, Paige. I'm sure they've hatched this plan to discredit you and likely disbar you. They're not screwing around here. They seriously want you *out*."

Acid flooded my stomach as I took over the family pacing. "Okay, I get why they're mad at me. In the last 18 months, I accused Frank McShane of unethical conduct more times than I can count. I challenged Judge Winston repeatedly for bias and prejudice. I filed innumerable motions on behalf of our clients, several resulting in case dismissals."

I did a 180 at the end of my office and approached Jack. "Then I won Casey's homicide trial, filed to withdraw Ben Stagg's guilty plea, and beat Judge Winston at the Supreme Court on some writs and appeals."

I leaned on my filing cabinet, watching Jack nod as I recounted each of my courthouse sins.

"They're probably fired up because I called in the ACLU and ratted out the public defender hiring system. And maybe because I've given so many interviews to the media about how unfair the justice system is in this county."

Another disbelieving nod from Jack, then, "You think? And let's not forget you just won another victory against them when the Supreme Court ordered them to pay you extra money for Casey Hennon's trial. So yeah, that could be why they're fired up."

I rarely found husbandly sarcasm helpful. I put my hands on my desk and leaned toward him. "You know, Jack," I snapped out, "you're the one who agreed I should represent Winston's arch-enemy, Chad Hammel, as well as his daughter's arch-enemy, Charlie."

I paused for a swallow of lukewarm coffee. "You also approved Charlie's affidavit alleging someone in the Winston house broke a nine-month-old baby's arm. And it's not my fault that the silly visiting judge ordered Winston and his wife to vacate their own house during child visitations."

Jack's eyebrows lifted as he filled in the rest.

"You've also accused Judge Winston of corruption in the Stagg case. He knows you're investigating his church, his friends, his family, and his social connections to the Masonic Lodge. You're about to subpoena *him* to testify at Ben's plea reversal hearing, along with many of his friends and fellow church members." He sighed. "Christ Almighty."

Resuming my seat behind the desk, I winced, fearful that Jack's blasphemy might somehow impede my effort to retrieve my misplaced soul, as if God followed a guilt-by-association theory when deciding our chances at redemption.

On the other hand, Jack used the expression so often the kids and I vowed to carve it as the epitaph on his tombstone. He ran his fingers through his thick, graying hair, smiling. "Shit, Paige. I'd never thought about it all together. You're lucky they haven't shot you.

Silence.

A pause.

His mirth faded to alarm. "This could be dangerous. I need to think." He walked toward the stairs, head down, likely envisioning a bullet shattering my upstairs window.

"Jack, come on. Don't be absurd. They may be pissed off, but they're not violent. Did they set a date for the hearing about me?" I reached for the antacids, popping two into my mouth. Losing my ability to practice law far outweighed any concern for my physical wellbeing.

Distracted, he muttered, "Soon. Probably just in time to interfere with your preparation for Ben's hearing in June. Have you noticed," he turned back before descending to his own office, "that every time something goes well for Ben Stagg, the courthouse guys come after you with a new attack? Almost as if they're trying to sabotage your every effort to overturn Ben's sentence?"

The question hung like fog as he disappeared. Toward late afternoon, edgy, I lowered the blind on my window while I continued to type up my latest drubbing of the Kootenai County legal system.

* * *

As I lay in bed that night, the rest of the family peacefully snoozing, I churned through other dramas that had intermingled with my professional life.

Both kids struggled in school, necessitating many meetings with staff to determine their best course of study. Homework often led to tears or shouts. Their sporting activities ran the gamut from swim team and soccer to baseball and Little Guy football. Jack coached while I cheered. We celebrated their birthdays with a minimum of fanfare, yet each celebration made me gasp at the racing passage of our time with them living at home.

We'd managed to fit in a couple of family vacations during the summers. I thought back to our recent trip to California, only four weeks earlier, to attend my mother-in-law's funeral. Initially, Jack offered to go alone, his mother's death a relief since she'd lain paralyzed from a stroke for the past thirteen years. But a mom's death is tough regardless of age or illness, so I insisted the family attend to honor my mother-in-law and support Jack. Besides, it was a break from non-stop work.

Jack rolled over next to me, ignoring the light I'd turned on to read my latest romance novel. Even the bodice-ripping scenes failed to hold my attention, so I ruminated.

Travel, I reflected, absorbed much of my time. The previous year I'd traveled to and from California to testify in an old case I'd prosecuted. I'd also traveled the great state of Montana. I'd driven to Cut Bank, Superior,

Bozeman, and Polson, once within a four day period, to represent a killer, a cop-beater, and a guy arrested for felony foot-rubbing who'd performed reflexology treatments on some old ladies who paid him with cloth rice bags. The rural prosecutor, who hated the client anyway, charged him with a trumped-up case of unemployment fraud.

I'd also traveled to and from Deer Lodge State Prison more times than I wanted to remember and familiarized myself with jails from Great Falls to Thompson Falls. We finally had to lease a new car because I'd driven so many places situated so far apart. I'd careened off Montana's icy roads twice, as had Jack, and hit a deer when I traveled to Helena for a death penalty meeting. The damage to my little Jeep cemented Jack's belief that I needed a safer vehicle.

Since non-stop work defined my life, and since my professional career in Kootenai County sank slowly into a cesspool, I sought additional work by applying with the Federal Defender's Office to practice as a conflict attorney. In case that didn't fund college for the kids, I applied with the California Supreme Court to represent the condemned on death row. I premised those new employment pursuits on my belief that Ben Stagg would lose his bid to reverse his guilty plea in June, and Chad Hammel would soon settle his lawsuit with his former partner.

As I drifted toward sleep, Jack awakened. "What are you thinking about at this time of night?"

I yawned. "I'm envisioning a day when I wake up and have nothing to do."

"Yep," he murmured. "That'll happen. I think they call that *dead*."

* * *

In late May 2000, as I glanced in an office mirror before I again met with investigator Ty Kayman to discuss Ben's case, I sighed. While I'd so far managed to fend off McShane and his buddies in their effort to excoriate me at a public hearing in the Zanto case, the continuing fight at the Montana Supreme Court ate up valuable preparation time for Ben's hearing.

Entering the conference room, I shook Ty's hand. "Man, Tyrone, I don't know what I'd do without you on this case, or on Chad's case, for that matter. Tell me what you've found out for Ben's hearing."

Ty, ever unflappable, sat across from me and opened his notebook. Then he smiled. "The Masonic Lodge confirmed that Judge Winston is a Mason, but they claim the Aberdeen and Whitehall Lodges have no connection to one another. Rich Truman was a member of the Whitehall Lodge. When I tried to go inside the local lodge, they refused to let me in. So I'm not sure how you show Judge Winston and Rich Truman actually knew one another through their Masonic brotherhood."

I interrupted my note-taking. "I can't believe the members of those two lodges don't know one another, Ty. My dad was the grand poohbah of the Arizona Masons for years, and they socialized between lodges all the time."

Ty nodded. "Yep, but you have to prove it at Ben's hearing, and it's a long shot. By the way, the commander of our local jail where Ben was housed before prison is the head of the Aberdeen Masonic order. The editor of the *Whitehall Eagle,* who employed Nick Stagg, is the head of the Whitehall Lodge where Rich Truman hung out. That editor even tried to recruit young Nick as a member. He also presided over Rich Truman's funeral when they buried him in his Masonic apron. Weird, but not hard evidence of anything."

Purely coincidental? I mused. *Doubtful.* "What else?

Anything about Winston and the church he attends?"

"Now there's some red meat. Judge Winston and Ben both are members of that church. So is one of Ben's burglary victims, Dr. Winkleman. So is Rich Truman's former in-law, Phil Fraser, who took care of Truman's grandkids after his body was found. Winston, Winkleman, Fraser, and Pastor Rohers pray together in a men's Bible Study every Saturday, along with a couple of cops who were closely involved in the murder investigation. One of those cops actually arrested Nick Stagg."

Ty took a sip of water and sat back in his chair. "And guess who took the investigation reports for Chad Hammel and Charlie on the business fraud matter, the kids' broken arm and black eye, and the burglary of Charlie's house?"

"That same cop?" I conjectured. "So that's why no prosecution went forward against Winston and his daughter. Between the prosecutors, the Child Protective Services worker, and the investigating officer who goes to church with him, Winston appears immune from any criminal scrutiny."

I chewed on the end of my pen. "So we have Pastor Rohers meeting Ben at the jail right after the arrests to listen to Ben's statements, and then he talks to Judge Winston and the Bible study folks?" I shook my head. "And here's another weird thing, Ty. That Dr. Winkleman whose shed the boys broke into? Laura tells me he was Ben's doctor back when Ben was 11 or 12. She took him to see Winkleman because Ben has a big dent in his chest."

Ty eased forward and doodled for a minute. "Did he figure out what caused the dent?"

"Negative. The doc told her it was normal. I've seen it, and it sure doesn't look normal to me, but what do I know? In any case, now that same doctor is a witness against Ben. It's odd."

Ty nodded. "I agree it smells bad, Paige. Again, I'm not sure what evidentiary value it has at Ben's hearing, but it seems like Judge Winston knew a lot of the players in the case and should have removed himself. To me, at least, he had a pretty significant conflict of interest."

As if on cue, Chad Hammel poked his head into the conference room, apparently fresh from a meeting with Jack. "I couldn't help but overhear you, Paige. You know I sat in the jury box with Hank Winston's family when he sentenced the Stagg brothers?"

I smiled at him. "No, as a matter of fact, I didn't know. Tell me." I gestured for him to join Ty and me at the table.

Dressed in another designer sweat suit, smelling of citrus scented cologne, Chad typified a successful Montana businessman on his way to his private gym. "Well," Chad's low voice rumbled as he sat forward, "before the sentencing, that strange pastor of Winston's, Pastor Rohers, came into Winston's chambers where we were chatting about something. I can't remember what. Anyway, Pastor Rohers talks with us for maybe 15 minutes, then offers to pray for Winston to do the right thing when he takes the bench to sentence the Stagg brothers."

Ty grinned. "Really? So did all of you pray?"

Chad returned Ty's smile. "Hell, yes, we prayed. Then Winston left to take the bench, and the rest of us sat together in the jury box, watching the show. I knew Winston planned to hammer those boys. Frankly, I think they deserved it, or at least the actual killer deserved it."

Chad sat back. "The other thing you should know is that Pastor Rohers attended Winston's family Christmas party at his house two months before the Stagg sentencing. And the good judge helped him become the chaplain for the Aberdeen Police Department."

I stood to stretch my legs and pace. "Maybe I should talk to the church people and re-interview Pastor Rohers. I also have to decide what to do about Ben's former lawyer insisting I drop that claim of incompetent representation before he'll testify."

Ty laughed. "Forget about interviewing the Right Reverend Rohers and his flock. According to one nice lady from the church, Rohers announced at last week's service that you were 'from the Devil' and forbid all members from talking to you."

I spun around. "You're kidding, right?"

Silence.

"You're serious? What is it with that church? Is it a cult where Rohers exerts mind control over the members?" I grimaced. "And they think Catholics are weird. Well, if they won't let me interview them ahead of time, we'll just subpoena them for the hearing and see what they say under oath."

Chad rubbed his hands together. "Are you putting Hank Winston on the stand at the hearing? This I've got to see. I think I'll cover the hearing live on our media website. What do you think?"

I studied his face, gleaning his humor from his smirk. "I think," I paused for emphasis, "that I don't want this turned into another dog and pony show. The stakes are too high. Serving the church folks with subpoenas might coax them into talking to me, despite Pastor Rohers' prohibition."

Ty collected his paperwork. "I'm on it. They'll all be at court, but they won't be happy. You'd better hope they're not into voodoo." As he walked through the door following Chad outside, he turned back and lowered his voice. "I heard a rumor your partner is leaving at the end of the month. He's only been here a year. Too much controversy and stress for him?"

"Yeah," I sighed. "His wife says we're too infamous

and his association with us is hurting his career. He's not a trial guy, Ty, and they're not a couple who handles notoriety well. She's right. He'll be better off with another firm."

Shaking his head, Ty grinned. "Maybe, but this place is *way* more fun."

I tossed a paper wad at his back as he ducked out the door.

CHAPTER TWENTY-FIVE

Score One for the Good Guys

June 2000
Kootenai County District Court
Aberdeen, Montana

AFTER THE EVIDENCE CLOSED at Ben's hearing to withdraw his guilty plea, Judge Lambert intoned, "Mr. Stagg, I have heard the testimony that's been given here today, and I want you to understand some things, Sir. I want you to understand, Mr. Stagg, that you have filed a motion to withdraw your guilty plea. If the court denies that motion, the sentence shall remain as it is, and there will be no trial, all right?"

Ben nodded as Judge Lambert pierced him with his stare. "If the motion is granted, you have been successful at this hearing. I want you to understand, Sir, that if that happens, the deal is off, the plea agreement is gone, alright?"

Ben cleared his throat. "Alright."

Judge Lambert continued, stumbling over his words. "There might be . . . I say might, I don't know . . . something from the state to charge you with other offenses in addition to the burglaries. If the deal is off, the state might - not saying will, it's not a threat - but the state might request the death penalty. And you have no idea if that request will be granted. Alright?"

Ben responded as if by rote, parroting the judge. "Alright."

"I think there might be some evidence that perhaps

was unknown to Judge Winston and the prosecutor that would be introduced at trial, something your prior lawyer might say. So this is what I want you to consider between now and 3:00 this afternoon, and talk to Ms. Defalco about it. This court is in recess."

As the judge left the bench, robes flying, I glanced at Don Yeager, the prosecutor. Normally affable, he huffed out of court without saying a word.

I turned to Ben. "Don't say a word, Benjie. I've got to talk to your parents and call Jack. Then I'll be down to the jail to see you. It sounds like the judge might reverse your guilty plea, and he's just given you three hours to think about it. Eat some lunch, and I'll see you in a few minutes."

Confused, Ben allowed the bailiffs to secure his handcuffs and lead him away.

I turned to Pete and Laura Stagg. "I don't want to get your hopes up, but it sounds like Judge Lambert is going to let Ben have his plea back and set this case for trial. He's warning us, and giving us three hours to mull it over, that the prosecutor will add all the burglary charges and seek the death penalty. I'm not sure where he's going with the evidence from Ben's former lawyer."

Actually, after talking to the former lawyer's extortion-loving attorney months before, I knew *precisely* where the judge was going. What I couldn't figure out was how Judge Lambert and Judge Winston knew about that *confidential* evidence. Unless, of course, all of the Courthouse Cowboys had held a meeting and shared with each other everything they knew or suspected. Since such a conversation would constitute the height of unethical conduct, I silenced the urge to make the accusation.

Ben's parents blinked back tears. "It's a miracle," Pete murmured. "The judge is an angel sent by God."

"It's what we've prayed for every night," choked

Laura.

* * *

After they left for lunch, my carefully schooled facade of calm gave way to excited terror, mixed with a touch of anger, at what I suspected were the Cowboys' underhanded shenanigans.

I phoned my beloved. "Holy crap, Jack! I think Lambert's going to grant the motion to reverse Ben's plea. He warned us about the additional charges and the death penalty." I inhaled before adding, "What am I going to do if we win? There's no viable defense in this case."

Silence, an intake of breath, then, "Take it, Paige. You take that kid's plea back and run like hell. You can worry how to win at trial later." Jack paused. "This is unreal. Great job, Sweet Pea." I heard his smile before he laughed, "Winston must be *pissed.*" Then he broke the connection.

* * *

Three hours later, after explaining to Ben, once again, the consequences of a plea reversal, I sat next to my young and befuddled client.

"I trust you, Paige," he'd said in the jail. "And I didn't kill anybody, so I don't want to go back to prison for something I didn't do. I want a trial."

Judge Lambert resumed his seat on the bench. He chastised me for attacking Judge Winston's conduct and affiliations with the Masons and Ben's church members before he moved on to his ruling. The heat of my anger at the admonishment crept up my neck, but for once I remained silent.

After clearing his throat, Judge Lambert announced,

"I find that there is a serious doubt as to whether the plea that was entered was voluntarily and intelligently made. As directed by the Montana Supreme Court, this doubt must be resolved in favor of the defendant. Now, therefore, it is hereby ordered that the motion by Mr. Ben Stagg to withdraw his plea of guilty must be and is hereby granted."

Gasps erupted behind us, but whether from family members, the press, or folks in the audience, I couldn't discern. Ben's shoulders slumped in relief. Ever the pessimist, I awaited the inevitable, "However," followed by bad news. It didn't come.

Judge Lambert continued, "Mr. Stagg's plea is now withdrawn. He is facing the original Information that charges him with the crime of deliberate homicide, a capital offense. The presumption of guilt is great. Therefore, Mr. Stagg will remain in local custody without bond at this time."

With a final rap of his gavel, the Honorable Jeff Lambert reversed the course of Ben Stagg's life. I glimpsed him give a small shake of his head as he left the bench, as if he, like Pandora when she opened her box, had unwittingly unleashed madness on the world.

Was he, as the Staggs averred that day, an angel sent by God? Skepticism prevented my faith in that. But was he a fair and impartial judge? Definitely.

Rumors flew that the Honorable Hank Winston, his career-making murder sentence up in smoke, screamed and jumped up and down when he learned of the plea reversal. If true, Ben Stagg and I faced an ever-widening chasm to his freedom.

Still, I recalled the rest of the myth. No question that when Pandora unlatched the lid, she sent forth evil, sickness, and burdensome labor to haunt the world. Yet at the very bottom of her box, beneath all of those horrors, lay *hope*.

And hope, I concluded driving back to Beartooth, would have to fuel our efforts over the next few months, because at the moment, that was all we had.

PART THREE

CHAPTER TWENTY-SIX

Once Again, with Feeling

July 2000
Death Row
San Quentin Prison, California

TWO WEEKS AFTER BEN STAGG RECEIVED HIS GIFT OF HOPE, I sat in a clear plexi-glass box on San Quentin's death row awaiting my newest client, a man convicted of shooting to death an innocent bartender in a failed robbery. The prison guard locked me inside and sauntered off, his grin radiant at the presence of another naive bleeding-heart determined to save a condemned killer from his own execution. That guard, however, erred. He'd mistaken me for someone who cared.

I didn't.

Or maybe I did, but I didn't want to.

The fact that eighteen months practicing criminal defense had softened my heart toward the bad guys frankly pissed me off. Despite Ben's overturned conviction, compassion loomed as the last thing I sought to resurrect from my long-buried trove of emotions.

My client failed to show after 15 minutes. The guard yelled through the plexi-glass, "These guys get paranoid and sometimes refuse to leave their cells. I'll check on him."

I nodded, puzzled that a client would refuse to visit his lawyer. I doodled on a piece of paper. As in Montana, San Quentin disallowed lawyers to enter with pads of paper because the bad guys might snatch the pad, disassemble it, and then use the staples as weapons to escape. Ditto for allowing women lawyers to wear underwire bras, since the evildoer might lurch across the table, rip the bra from the attorney, tear out the wire, and use it as a means to freedom.

Earlier the entry guards nearly had denied my visit because I wore a sleeveless blouse under my suit jacket, as if my partially exposed arms might drive prisoners to sexual madness. "Remove your jacket," they'd ordered. "Now twirl."

After rotating a full 360 degrees, humiliated, furious, and impotent, I seethed. "Look, I've come from Montana to see this new client. If you won't let me in because of my clothes, I want to talk to a supervisor or the warden."

They smirked as they ushered me through the metal detector.

Now in the silence of the plastic cube, I shook my head. Crazy. Crazy prisoners. Crazy staff. Crazy lawyers. Crazy world.

What the fuck am I doing here?

Still no client appeared. Focusing on my doodle, I read one word: *Dad.* And then three others: *such an asshole.* Looking around the area, surrounded by other lawyers chatting with other killers in neighboring cubes, I added a question: *Will he really burn in hell?* If I'd ever told the cops what my father did to me, he, too, could have a prison record.

I hadn't spoken to my old man in decades because of the violence with which he'd shattered my young life. I'd made peace with the past, but felt no obligation to resume a relationship with a sire whose life I'd reduced to the seventeen years he abused me.

I glanced up as a guard moved toward the door, escorting an older bald man wearing tinted aviator glasses. The prisoner shuffled, shackled as he was at his ankles and wrists. He sported a long mustache on a face rigid with suspicion. His pale blue shirt hung loosely over his baggy, dark blue pants. He was my age, but looked a decade older.

"Here he is." The guard removed the ankle shackles, opened the door to my cube, slammed it shut and ordered my new client to stand with his cuffed wrists facing a waist-high opening. The guard yelled out, "One hour!" He clicked open the cuffs before he ambled off.

I sat down across from the client and for the next hour I tried to assure him that I'd take his case seriously and do my utmost to prevent his execution. Toward the end of our visit, another prisoner entered the adjacent cell, nodding at me with a grin.

I returned the man's smile. "He looks familiar."

My client smiled as well. "Richard Allen Davis, the guy who kidnapped and killed Polly Klaas a few years ago. He's my next-door neighbor. We help each other out, talk, you know . . ." The client looked away. "He's a decent guy."

I schooled my face into my most stoic expression. The 'decent guy' in question sat as the most famous kidnapper/murderer in California. He'd ripped that child from the safety of her bedroom in the middle of the night, raped her, and strangled her. After the authorities arrested him, he told them where to find her broken little body, alongside some trash next to the freeway.

I closed my eyes at the memory. Her kidnapping, along with several others over a three-year period, prompted my decision to flee California for the safety of Montana. I'd prayed for each of the parents of those children. Now I thanked God every day that our daughter and son lived freely in a town where they could ride their bikes to school, without the terror of abduction.

When I opened my eyes, the guard stood outside, signaling me that the visit was over. This time when I offered my hand, the client shook it. "Thank you, for coming to see me. For taking my case."

I watched him shuffle back to his cell as I headed for the salle-port and my own freedom. I returned Mr. Davis' wave on my way out. Minutes later, driving across the bridge to the east bay, finally clear of armed guards, razor wire, and metal detectors, I ruminated over the word 'decent.' According to Webster it meant respectable, worthy, not obscene, adequate or fair, kind or generous. But applied to monsters? How could an unrepentant adult who committed heinous acts achieve a state of decency in prison?

Or in life?

I parked in my friend's driveway, where my son and I stayed during this California trip, resting my head on arms draped over the steering wheel. Between Ben's hearing to reverse his plea, the attendant public ire raised when the judge granted him a new trial, the long drive from Montana to California with an eleven-year-old chatterbox, the entire San Quentin visit, and fighting Bay Area traffic, I wanted only to bury myself under darkness and sleep.

Bleary-eyed, I headed toward my son's laughter from the backyard, where he played with his best friend.

* * *

Driving back to Montana just days after that first visit to California's death row, I listened to my son.

"Hey, Mom." He fiddled with the seatbelt. "When

you looked around San Quentin at all those killers, did you feel like Dad when he says he'd shoot them all himself if somebody would let him?"

I considered his question carefully. At eleven, young Sean showed particular empathy toward the underprivileged and weak.

"No, Sean, I didn't."

"Why not? Dad says they deserve to die if they killed somebody."

"Well, I used to believe that, but now I don't. Now I figure that a bad guy is just a guy who started life as an innocent baby and then, because of his family or poverty or just how the guy's made up, he ended up doing bad stuff."

He rolled down the window, opened his mouth, and leaned into the wind. After a minute, he chuckled at me and pointed at his now-desiccated tongue. "Ook it! All dwied up!" For some reason, drying his tongue had become a favorite driving past-time.

When he regained enough saliva to speak, he rolled on with his cross-examination of me. "Mom, how come I've never met your dad? Since Papa died, I don't have a grandpa like the other kids. Don't you think I should at least meet him before he dies? He's really old already. Maybe we should go to Arizona soon. Do you hate him or something?"

Well, crap. Leave it to my boy to cut straight to my heart.

"Sean, I don't hate him. It's just that…" How to explain sexual molestation or a father's beatings with a belt and fists? "Look, your grandfather did some bad stuff when Uncle Doug and I were kids."

"Like the bad guys you see in prison?"

"Yeah, just like the bad guys in prison."

Sean paused as he opened some gummy bears. "Did your dad go to prison for what he did?"

"No, Sweetie. We never told the police."

"Oh." He chewed until orange goo dribbled out the side of his mouth. Swallowing, he continued, "So I guess your dad started out as an innocent baby, too, and then somebody hurt him probably, and so he did bad things to you."

I stared ahead at the two lane road stretching before me through eastern Washington.

He offered me a gummy bear then added, "Mom, aren't you supposed to forgive him for the bad stuff? You always tell us no one is all bad. I bet he must have done some good stuff in his life, like all the years he flew in the Navy and fought in World War II. And he took care of your mom when she was dying of cancer."

I veered into a rest stop and turned off the ignition. "I need a little break."

I stretched. I paced. I looked at the sky and then at the hay fields. I didn't like the direction our conversation headed, but I couldn't seem to argue with my son's words.

Back behind the wheel, I watched him consume an apple, better than candy but still sugar. "You'd better go easy on that stuff, buddy. Remember how sick you got on the way down to California."

He rolled his eyes. "I'm not going to barf again, Mom. I'm fine. So what do you think? Can we go meet your dad?"

As I rolled the Tahoe back onto the highway, I nearly capitulated. "Let me think about it, okay? Besides, with Ben's trial coming up and this new death penalty case, I'm going to be really busy for the next few months."

An understatement.

"You're *always* busy, Mom. Remember how you said things would be different if we moved to Montana? News flash. They're not."

"Gotta make money, Sean. At least I'm only five minutes from your school, and I'm home when you finish classes. And Dad gets to coach all your sports. It's better than California. Plus, you've made great friends there and can ride your bike wherever you want."

My son stared out the window and nodded. "Yeah, it's okay, I guess. So, Mom, is Ben Stagg a bad guy like your guy on death row? He didn't really kill anybody, did he? Don't you feel a little sorry for his brother, being paralyzed in a wheelchair and all? Do you think Ben will have to go back to prison for the rest of his life? That would suck, Mom."

And on and on the questions rolled, to infinity and beyond, as Buzz Light Year famously proclaimed.

I slugged down some antacids and tuned out the little voice in the front seat that had adopted the persona of my shoulder angel.

* * *

The next day I hugged my beloved spouse and stretched legs cramped from a 22 hour drive. My first question: "How's Stormy doing?"

Our secretary recovered at home from a mastectomy and faced months of chemotherapy.

Jack returned the hug before grabbing his son. "She's tough, stoic, and claims to be fine. I told her to take as much time as she needs. The temp replacement the agency sent is okay."

"Dad," young Sean interrupted. "I had the best time in California with Jimmy and the twins. It was so warm there, and we got to drive by and see our old house and my old school. But I *missed you so much!*"

Son clung to father, the weeklong separation too much for both of them.

"And guess what? Mom says she's going to quit

hating her dad so we can go to Arizona, and I can meet him before he dies!" With that unfounded proclamation, our son raced off to see the critters and his older sister, in that order.

Jack again wrapped his arms around me. "He's kidding, right? About your father? That bastard deserves to rot in hell for what he did to you, Paige. We haven't seen him in years, and there's no reason to go now."

I nodded, felt tears threaten, and sighed them away. "I'm so glad to be home."

When our daughter ran into our embrace and the dogs wiggled forth, I smiled. No reason to make a decision yet. At eleven, young Sean's attention would divert elsewhere, especially when school started. I relaxed for the first time in days.

My spouse cleared his throat. "Hey, Claire. Why don't you take Mom's suitcase inside?"

I felt him stiffen as she left. He'd updated me on Ben's case a few days before, so I wasn't sure why he'd tensed up.

"I'm okay, really. You already told me about all the burglary charges the prosecutor tagged on in Ben Stagg's case, like 20 counts for all the storage units they broke into and some other houses? We knew that was coming. At least they're not seeking the death penalty."

He gently pushed me back, still holding my arms. "It's not about Ben. Now don't freak out. We have to be in court at the end of August for a hearing in the Peg Zanto case. The judge refuses to allow us to be represented by other lawyers. We can't represent each other. We can't be present in the courtroom while the other testifies. And Frank McShane and the public defenders are planning to decimate us in the press and with the State Bar on a claim of ineffective assistance of counsel."

I stared back. "So what's the good news?"

Jack shrugged. "That the sons of bitches haven't won yet."

We walked inside to the relative safety of our kitchen.

He turned back to me. "And they won't."

CHAPTER TWENTY-SEVEN

Whoopee, We're All Gonna Die

Late August 2000
Deer Lodge State Prison Infirmary

I ARRIVED IN DEER LODGE, MONTANA the day before Nick Stagg's Sentence Review hearing to prepare Nick for his testimony. Meeting him in the prison library, Nick told me he'd been sick for weeks, but the prison refused to treat him or even allow him to see a doctor. Sitting in his wheelchair, he appeared as pale as a small ghost, his hands trembling while sweat beaded his face.

I tried to persuade him to continue the next day's hearing. "You're too sick to help me prepare your testimony, so let's move the hearing date. This is your only shot for a chance at parole."

Nick merely hung his head, his eyes staring at the floor. "No. I want this resolved. I want to testify tomorrow and get a decision. Let's just do this."

I caved in, all too aware that the client had the final word on whether to proceed.

After dinner with Pete and Laura Stagg, I called the prison to check on Nick's status. Laura had called first, but the nurses refused to reveal Nick's condition.

As his lawyer, I reached the head nurse, whose voice dripped with annoyance. "Tonight we moved him from his cell to the infirmary, but he's fine. There's no reason he can't attend his hearing in the morning. Honestly, he complains all the time about nothing."

Laura, after a decade caring for her wheelchair-bound son, balked at that assessment when I called her room. Since The Fall, Nick never complained except in dire medical situations. To assuage Laura's fear, I arrived early at the prison the next morning to insure Nick's health was as hale and hearty as the nurses claimed. That's when I found him in a separated glass room, lying in a fetal position, bleeding into his catheter.

"Holy Mother of God!" I muttered, anger rising to the forefront of my composure. I fought to pull on my neutral lawyer mask, to disengage my heart. I watched Nick Stagg's hand shake as he held up his sheet to show me his naked, numb lower body. A bloody catheter ran from Nick's urethra into a crimson, urine-filled bag. Gauging his blue-gray pallor, I instinctively accepted that Nick's condition spelled fatal if left untreated.

"Paige, they're going to let me die." Nick, 22, could barely whisper, so I bent closer to hear him. Seconds later, he shed tears for the first time since his fall from the tree a decade earlier. "They won't call a doctor. They won't let me talk to my mom. I'm dying, and that's what they want."

I sensed some logic in his accusation. The cost of care for a disabled young killer, who the system deemed a life prisoner, was staggering. It would be so much easier to turn a deaf ear to his complaints and let God handle the outcome.

My own maternal instincts overrode my lawyerly detachment. I swiped a wet trail from Nick's eye with a tissue, took the sheet from his hand, and lowered it to cover his body. As that paralyzed kid faced his own death, his near-hairless cheeks, pallid and strained, tightened with the terror of dying alone, helpless, and without a soul present who loved him.

Just as his victim, Rich Truman, had died nearly three years before.

Despite the similarity between Nick and Mr.

Truman, I still felt rage creep up my spine, flaming my own complexion. My hands trembled with anger as I inhaled several times before any words of comfort could form. "Nick, I'm going to get a doctor in here. I'm going to get your folks because they're just a few minutes away at the motel." I squeezed his hand. "And these fuckers are *not* going to let you die."

I stormed into the nurses' cubicle. I stood before them and slapped my yellow legal pad on the counter.

"He needs a doctor *now*. If you don't call a doctor *right now*, you won't believe the lawsuit I'm going to file against you for malpractice, wrongful death, and whatever else I can think up. And you need to tell his mother what his condition is because he wants her to know, and she has a *right to know*. Now where is a *doctor?*"

The nurses glanced at each other, nervous at an enraged lawyer shouting demands. One man finally piped up. "We're monitoring him, and we don't think he needs to see a doctor just yet. We can't tell his mother anything unless we have a written release from the patient."

I struggled to still the shake in my voice, to unclench my now-fisted hands, to control the incredulity that urged me to throw something, anything, at them. I lowered my head and my voice, glaring more menace.

"Are you *fucking imbeciles?* His catheter is full of blood! His pulse is weak, he's sheet white, covered in sweat, and he's *telling* you that *he's dying!* And you're letting it happen. Now get a *god damned doctor* in here, or I'll call an ambulance myself!"

I tore the top sheet of paper from my pad. "You people want a written release? You'll have one in twenty seconds, after which you'd better call his parents and let them know their son is about to die. Are we clear on this?"

Armed guards approached at the sound of my shrill threats. I plowed past them into the glass room in which

Nick lay, still weeping, curled up, his life slowly escaping from his body.

"Nick," I urged as I composed legalese on the piece of paper. "This is a release form I'm writing out. You have to sign it so the nurses can tell your parents about your condition. Do you understand what I'm saying to you, kiddo?" He nodded as I placed a pen in his hand and held the paper so he could scratch a signature.

A nurse walked in, apprehensive, checking behind her for backup security. I slashed the release at her. "You need to call his parents *now*," I gritted out. She handed the release to someone outside the door, and then stood vigil as I assured Nick that help was on the way.

Minutes later a doctor rushed in, looked at Nick's bloody catheter, checked his vital signs, and turned to the nurse. "Why wasn't I called in about this last night?" His exasperated tone held urgency. "Get an ambulance here *immediately!* In the meantime, start him on an IV of…"

His words lost meaning as I held Nick's hand, praying behind my expressionless eyes. Soon an ambulance crew whisked Nick from Deer Lodge, the doctor and his parents following closely behind.

Breathing deeply of the fresh summer air outside the infirmary building, I headed to the makeshift courtroom in which Nick's Sentence Review hearing was scheduled to begin in less than an hour, before a three-judge review board.

I saw Don Yeager, the prosecutor, across the common area talking quietly to Nina Truman, the two having driven many hours from Kootenai County that morning. Collectively, they meant to insure that Nick Stagg's life sentence remained intact, including no future possibility of parole.

I shook the prosecutor's hand. "Could I have a moment?" excusing myself from Mrs. Truman.

I cringed whenever I saw her, whether in court or on television. She wrung every emotion from me, from guilt to pity, yet I wouldn't apologize for working to free Ben Stagg. Nor would I apologize for my work on Nick's behalf. That left me to pray for her and her family, and especially pray that someday she might let go of her hatred, so she could find forgiveness for the Stagg brothers. But what could I really know of her sorrow and loss, of her enmity?

Quietly I shifted my body away from Mrs. Truman and explained Nick Stagg's medical condition to the prosecutor.

"So," Yeager concluded, "you're saying you can't go forward today with the hearing? That we drove all the way down here for nothing?" He shook his head. "This is going to be tough to explain." He nodded his head in Mrs. Truman's direction.

"My client has a right to be present for his hearing and give testimony on his own behalf. You know that. Obviously no one anticipated his illness." I ran tired fingers through my hair. "For God's sake, Don. This is Nick's only chance to reduce his sentence. Surely Mrs. Truman will understand that."

She didn't. Instead she seethed at me as her mouth drew tight, her eyes skewering me with unreleased disgust.

Nor did the three judges on the panel understand. "Mrs. Defalco," a Tom Selleck look-alike sneered. "Just proceed without your client. You've continued this hearing too many times."

Which, translated, meant: "We're going to deny his right to parole anyway, so why bother wasting anymore of our time? And, oh by the way, don't let the door hit you on the ass when you leave."

For the second time in less than an hour, I squared my shoulders against the anger roiling up my spine. "I'm not proceeding without my client, Your Honor. He has a right to be present. It's not his fault he's sick. The answer, Sir, is no."

Disgusted with me, but trumped by the U.S. Constitution, the three judges capitulated and rescheduled the hearing.

* * *

Four Days Later - Kootenai County District Court

Smoothing the skirt of yet another dark suit, fingering the ubiquitous strand of pearls circling my neck, I eased down in the cushioned chair and adjusted the microphone. In a departure from my usual role in court, I'd just sworn an oath as a witness in a criminal proceeding.

I sat as the accused, the criminal, so to speak. The Evildoer.

Frank McShane and two public defenders faced me from counsel table, salivating at the prospect of cross-examining me before a sea of curious onlookers. They awaited the moment the daft old judge would pronounce me incompetent as the lawyer who represented the lascivious Peg Zanto.

My anger simmered just beneath my frozen attorney mask. I'd avoided food or coffee earlier that morning, fearing I might vomit before the hearing began. Acid burbled in the hot cauldron masquerading as my stomach, and burned up the back of my throat, leaving me parched. I raised the plastic pitcher in front of me and poured water into a paper cup, pleased that my hands held steady as I drank.

I cleared my throat, clasped my hands together, and stared at my adversaries, their faces awash with the glee of anticipated victory. Frank McShane smirked at the judge, and the judge returned his smile. Ms. Zanto's public defenders gathered their questions and approached the podium.

I turned to the judge. "Your Honor, before we begin, why are we proceeding this morning with this hearing? Mr. McShane failed to object to Ms. Zanto's motion for a new trial, so this court should simply rule in her favor and grant that request. Going forward with testimony when the prosecution concedes the case is a waste of everyone's time and the taxpayers' money."

The daft old jurist paused, perhaps experiencing a brief moment of mental clarity, then turned to the assembled crowd. "She has a point, Counsel. Why are we holding a hearing when no one objects to Ms. Zanto getting a new trial?"

For a second, I entertained the futile notion that justice might prevail, that Ms. Zanto's case could start anew, and that Jack and I would be spared the ordeal of testifying against her.

Sputtering, Ms. Zanto's lawyers shuffled papers as they conferred with Mr. McShane in an effort to conjure up a legitimate reason to proceed. I straightened further in the chair, a slight frown creasing my forehead, as if my stature could intimidate them from their quest.

Finally one of Ms. Zanto's lawyers spoke up. "Well, Your Honor, I've prepared all these questions for Mrs. Defalco and her husband, and we have other witnesses here waiting to testify. We're ready to go. We can't just cancel the hearing."

Mr. McShane chimed in. "Judge, just because I haven't objected yet doesn't mean I'm conceding the case. We need to go ahead, right now."

To his credit the old judge frowned, his doubt showing. However, as if Frank McShane willed it, the judge nodded. "Very well. Proceed, Counsel."

So it began. Four hours, or so it seemed, of

repetitive questions concerning how I made legal decisions, why I chose certain strategies, and when or if I'd lost confidence in Ms. Zanto's case before trial, given her confession.

While I paused before I answered each query, extracting memories that had blurred during the previous two years, I experienced both sadness for their exploitation of my former client, and something akin to hatred for the Courthouse Cowboys themselves. Their smug demeanors, their back-slapping, high-fiving, eye-rolling antics cemented their sexist bias against uppity women lawyers who dared to play - and win - on their field. That message dripped from their every emphasis on *Mrs.* Defalco when beginning a question, as if a refusal to use the more neutral Ms. might insult me.

It didn't insult me. It appalled me, just as their use of my former client appalled me. If she'd been *Paul* Zanto instead of Peg Zanto, if she'd been a kick-ass guy instead of a poor mother of three about to lose her Section 8 housing and her liberty if she didn't cooperate with the Cowboys, they'd never have bullied her into participating in such a farce.

Indeed, if Peg had been a *male* who'd had sex with an almost 16-year-old neighbor, I doubted the Cowboys would have charged him with a crime.

When they'd exhausted their questions, I left the witness stand and walked through the onlookers. One lawyer from Beartooth stopped me. "Paige, this hearing is a joke and, just so you know, there are plenty of us standing behind you."

I shifted my briefcase to my left hand so I could shake hands with him. "Thanks for the support. It may be a joke, but we'll see if they pursue this with the State Bar. Rumor has it they're after our licenses to practice law. Anything to rid the valley of the Defalco pox."

I smiled all the way out of the courtroom, because if

I didn't paste a smile on my face, I'd turn back to the Cowboys and tell them to fuck themselves. I'd rant at them about the real meaning of justice, define for them the term *due process*, excoriate them in front of the crowd with their every misdeed committed against the innocent over the last few decades.

As I slammed open the courtroom door, spying Jack waiting outside for his own turn to testify, I lowered my shoulders, straightened my spine, raised my chin, and vowed I'd never again let the bastards dig into me.

* * *

5 days later - the Defalco's kitchen

"Wow. That's quite a color you're painting." Pete Stagg shook his head and smiled when he and Laura Stagg entered our kitchen that Saturday afternoon, Labor Day, 2000. Their youngest child, Megan, hesitantly trailed behind them.

"It's called poppy orange," I sighed. "This is the third time I've painted the kitchen in the last year. I figured it might brighten my mood a little."

"Hmmm," Pete replied as he picked up a brush. "Jack, I'll just help you out here while Paige takes Megan somewhere to talk. Laura can supervise us and make some coffee."

With that offer I faced their daughter, who glanced from one parent to the other, her eyes darting back and forth, her head hanging. Earlier that morning, Laura had called, her voice pitched to frantic, claiming Megan had to talk to me right away to relate information that might help Ben at trial.

Now Laura added, "Don't believe everything she tells you, Paige. She lies all the time."

I loaded Megan into my Tahoe and drove to a

peaceful spot not far from our house. "Okay, Megan," I turned off the ignition. "You told your mom you were going to kill yourself if you didn't talk to me, so tell me what's up. Do you have information about the murder that might help Ben?"

She drew a breath. Exhaled. Turned to me. "You need to know about our family, Paige, about my mom. She's really violent. She . . . she's beaten us since we were little, but she went after Ben the worst because he's so stupid. She always called him a stupid bitch when she hit him. She'd use a hairbrush, her hands, a spoon, pretty much anything she could get a hold of. She beats me all the time, and she beat Nick until he moved out. She even beats my dad. She's demon-possessed. That's what Nick told us. Nick always tried to defend us from her, but he couldn't."

At her onslaught of tears, I could only hand her a tissue and wonder if she, like my own daughter, didn't dramatize the situation. Still, I recalled the other hints of violence I'd heard from clients who knew the Stagg brothers, along with Nick's own admission the year before that his dad had beaten him with a belt after he'd come home from the hospital, paralyzed. And then there was the fact that Ben *flinched* whenever a hand neared his face.

"Megan, I'm not sure I understand what your mom hitting you has to do with the murder or how Ben acts." I patted her shoulder as she wept and sniffled.

Tissues piled up in her lap. "Because she beat us all so much we turned to Nick, and Nick told us what to do, and we did whatever Nick said to do because if we didn't, he wouldn't protect us from Mom. And so Ben, because he was so terrified of Mom and because he's so stupid, he just does whatever Nick tells him to do, and that's why he helped Nick with the burglaries." She hiccupped. "Because Ben can't think by himself. And that's also why he flinches all the time if you come near him. Don't you get it, Paige? He does whatever Nick says. And so do I."

When I'd parked the car, I'd schooled my face into my neutral trial lawyer expression while simultaneously disengaging my heart. I'd perfected my finest talent, utter emotional detachment. Now suspicion prickled at my neck. "Megan, were you with Nick and Ben when Nick shot Rich Truman?"

She shook her head, her face buried in her hands.

I relaxed my shoulders. If she'd said yes, I didn't want to consider the implications for her, or for her family, if anyone discovered her undetected presence at the murder scene, despite the fact that she'd been only 14 at the time.

"But I knew everything right afterward," she blurted.

Well, shit.

"The next day, Nick told me everything, and he showed me Truman's license and all the bullet shells and he told me . . . he told me that shooting Rich Truman was better than shooting a deer."

My eyes closed as my head dropped. *Fuck.*

"And then he said he was going to kill Ben because Ben acted like a baby all the time and cried whenever Nick took him along on the burglaries. And when Nick ordered Ben to shoot Truman, Ben refused and cried and then threw up. And so Nick told me he was going to kill Ben and bury his body in the wilderness. And Nick said I could take Ben's place and be his partner in crime." She bit her lip then swiped at tears and snot with the sleeve of her sweatshirt.

Another shiver of suspicion raced along my neck. "Did you agree, Megan? Did you agree that Nick should kill Ben, and that you'd take over his part?"

Silent, wracking sobs shook her small body as she

nodded. "I hated Ben. I was so jealous of him, and I wanted him dead because I wanted to be with Nick all the time, just us. Nick promised me all kinds of stuff, and he saved me from Mom a lot. Oh God, what have I *done?*"

The problem with emotional detachment is that it's hard to reconnect when appropriate. I knew I should hug that young girl and reassure her that an abused child makes bad choices at times. No one knew that better than I, given my own father's violence toward me. Instead, I sat there in the front seat, mute.

I started the car. "Okay, Megan. Here's what we're going to do for now. You're going home, but I'm telling your folks that I know about the violence and it has to stop. Then I want to meet with you on Tuesday, along with your sister. I need to confirm some stuff with her, since she's so much older than you and might remember things differently. After that, I'll . . . I'll figure out the next step. Meanwhile, I'll try to keep you safe, okay?"

She nodded, clearly afraid to go home.

I eased the transmission into drive, wondering if it all amounted to nonsense. Could Laura Stagg embody the demon-possessed mother her daughter just described? The words of the psychologist from Ohio who'd called six months before echoed through my head. *That family is hiding big secrets,* Dr. Sara Berg had predicted.

If Megan had told me the truth, if Ben responded to Nick's every command, if Nick truly had planned to kill Ben if he refused to cooperate, such facts bolstered Ben's defense of coercion, meaning he didn't act voluntarily when he participated in the burglaries. The lawyer in me felt a faint glow of promise.

The mom in me, on the other hand, worried over one thought.

Would a demon-possessed mother harm, even kill,

her own daughter to prevent her from revealing to the world a parent's acts of abuse?

CHAPTER TWENTY-EIGHT

Relative Truths

September 2000
Beartooth, Montana

AS I TOSSED MY CAR KEYS ON THE KITCHEN COUNTER, Megan trailing in my wake, I pasted on a tight smile and faced Pete and Laura. Pete set his paintbrush on a bucket and returned my gaze, unapologetic. His back stiffened as if ready to defend himself and his wife of over two decades. Laura grimaced and shook her head.

I held up my hand to ward off their explanations. What I knew with certainty was that someone in the Stagg family had lied to me, either the parents for the last 18 months, or their kids. I tamped down my anger by swilling from Jack's diet coke, but my booted foot tapped out my frustration.

"Okay." I swallowed more soda. "Here's the deal. Megan told me many things, some of which might help Ben when we go to trial. Others might not, but it . . . *disturbs* me that no one has mentioned them in the last year and a half." I walked behind the counter to separate myself from these people I no longer trusted.

Jack set his paint roller in the pan, shooting me a *what the hell did she tell you* look.

I glanced up at the newly painted ceiling. "I'm going to the jail right now to talk to Ben. Then I'm going to meet with Megan and her sister on Tuesday to get more facts. After that," I paused, rolling my shoulders, "We're going to meet." I met Pete's gaze, "And when we meet, I want the truth. *All* of it."

I unclenched my fists and steeled both parents with green eyes that bespoke my fury. "Because without knowing all the facts, the *truth,* I cannot help your son. So if you don't tell me *everything I need to know,* I'll quit. You can hire another lawyer."

Pete stood rigid. He set his expression into what I envisioned as a Baptist pastor counseling the spiritually troubled. Laura's face held a half smile as she continued to shake her head in denial. Her grin reminded me of Ben's when he tackled fear or anxiety. Jack, uncharacteristically, remained silent.

"Meanwhile," my voice rose with menace, "you will *not* physically or verbally hurt Megan." I directed my death stare at Laura as I again held up a hand to silence her protest. "Because if you do, she will call the police, and the police will investigate and likely put her in a foster home. But she *will* tell the authorities what she has told me."

I nodded my head at them to emphasize that threat as I took and released a breath, my leg bouncing in earnest to release my building rage. "And if she tells the authorities, the press will have a field day with your arrests." I paced the four feet along the counter, hands now behind my back, watching the stone floor of our kitchen, adding, "and *that* will *not* help Ben."

I paused, both palms slapping the tile surface. Silence. "So, go home and think about this. Because, folks, now more than ever, *the truth matters.*"

Without comment, the trio left. Jack exchanged his soda for a beer, and sat on a counter stool, waiting for me to explain.

I pointed toward the Stagg's departing auto. "Liars! I hate it when people lie to me, especially when their kid's life is on the line. And Pete's a damned pastor! Don't these people read the Bible? They swore to me there was no violence in their house."

Jack drank deeply, then burped. "Truth changes, Paige, and everybody lies, especially clients and witnesses. What did Megan tell you?"

Ignoring his cynicism, I sat on the stool next to him, slumping over the counter. "Megan says Laura is demon-possessed and beats the crap out of everybody in the family every chance she gets, Pete included, but Ben's received the worst of the abuse over the years."

Jack's eyebrows raised, his mouth quirked up, and after another swig of beer, he nodded. "Not much surprise there. You knew something was weird in that house." After 30 years in criminal law, the man had heard it all. Even demon possession didn't evoke a rise.

Weary, I related the rest of Megan's claims. "We need a damned defense in this case, and I've got shit, more shit, and now crazy shit. Short of a miracle, we don't have a chance for an acquittal." I stopped, closing my eyes as I faced my biggest fear. "What if Megan's telling the truth, Jack? Did I just send her home to more abuse? Maybe to her death? I mean, how crazy is her mom, if she's crazy at all?"

Jack, ever the realist, set his bottle on the counter with a clunk. "Laura's not going to kill her, but if you think she is, you have a duty to report it to the cops, Paige."

I whirled on him. "And if Megan's lying, and there's no danger at all, then what? I create a media circus that further kills Ben's chances for a fair trial." I stood. "I almost kept her. I figured she could stay in the spare room, but I wasn't sure how that would affect our kids. Crap. I need to confirm her story with Ben before I do anything with the authorities."

Jack's eyes widened at the idea of a Stagg child moving in with us. "Ethically, I don't think you get to *keep* somebody else's kid without their permission, even if she is 16. What I can't understand is why Pete and Laura let Megan talk to you in the first place. They had to know what she'd tell you." Jack retrieved his paint roller and applied more orange poppy.

I shook my head with the same question. "Megan's threat of suicide, maybe? Her threat to tell the police? I don't know, but it makes me feel a little more confident for Megan's safety that they know that I know about the abuse, and that I told you. If, and it's a big if, any of it is true."

I grabbed up the car keys and a jacket and kissed Jack. "I'm going to the jail to see Ben."

Jack smirked. "And you'll be the only lawyer in the history of Kootenai County to spend a Saturday evening on a holiday weekend with her in-custody client." He shook his head. "I'll save a wall for you to finish. Dinner will be hot dogs and more beer for me."

As I left the half-painted kitchen, I heard Jack sing along with Jimmy Buffet. I, on the other hand, experienced no urge to sing. Instead, I let fury fill me. I couldn't abide liars. Even my kids knew that rule.

Determined to uncover the truth from Ben Stagg's addled mind, I threw the Tahoe in reverse and headed to the justice center.

* * *

Ben's perpetually goofy smile lit his face when he entered the jail's visiting room, the same smile his mother had donned when faced with her alleged abuse of her children. Staff brought Ben's dinner in and left it for him on the plastic table that separated us. As he picked at his fried chicken and tater tots, chugged his milk, and rejected some green mush that passed for vegetables, he nodded at me. "So," he chewed, "how's it goin'?"

If Ben or the guards wondered at the orange poppy spatters scattered across my old green sweatshirt and hole-riddled jeans, their expressions hid their thoughts. And while the guard who let me in showed surprise when he saw me at the bulletproof glass entry window, he didn't flinch when I produced my ID and asked to visit my client.

I let Ben finish part of his meal before I dropped the bomb. "So, Benjie. I visited with Megan today. She told me your mom is demon-possessed and beat the crap out of you kids since you were little."

Ben smiled as he set his roll on his plastic tray. "I don't know what you're talking about." He slurped more milk.

So, I unloaded on him with Megan's full account. Twenty minutes later, Ben's smile faded, his silence confirming the truth of his sister's words. Nausea roiled around my empty gut, exacerbated by the smell of the fried food, burned grease, and seldom washed bodies.

I leaned toward him across the table. No legal pad or pen formalized our meeting; no navy blue suit or pearls separated our souls. "Ben, if I'm going to help you, you have to trust me. You have to tell me the truth. *All of it.*"

He stumbled over his words. He hemmed and hawed, then cleared his throat. But over the next three hours, he told me of his life growing up with an overwhelmed and seemingly mentally ill mother who thrashed her frustrations on her disabled sons, her prayerful but unresponsive husband, and her beautiful but terrified daughters.

I sat across from Ben as he sometimes cried, sometimes laughed, my boot jiggling to control my churning stomach. My fingers clenched and unclenched as my nails dug deep crescents into my palms, belying the threat of brimming tears. I chewed the inside of my lip, anything to cement my facial features into a studied vision of numb.

When he had exhausted both of us with the details of his abuse, of his sorrow and confusion, his terror of his mother and Nick - oh, yes, especially of Nick - his thin shoulders slumped as he rubbed his eyes with his knuckles. His cuticles swelled around his fingernails, bitten to the quick, scabbed over from blood drawn by repeated gnawing.

I untangled my legs, sat back in the plastic chair, and fought for calming breaths. "Why?" I looked at the ceiling, the fluorescent light searing me back to the present. "Why didn't you ever tell anyone, especially your first lawyer? It *matters,* Ben. Don't you see that Nick's threats to kill you show you were too scared to refuse to help him?"

He lowered fists from reddened eyes, and gripped ever-trembling hands together on the table until his thin fingers whitened. Eyes down he murmured, "Because Dad made us promise not to tell. After we were arrested, he told us we were not to blame Mom, that we had to take responsibility for what we did, and we could never tell." He looked up at me, relief softening the sadness in his eyes. "Until now, I've never told anyone, not in all these years."

I itched to reach for him, to fold my hands over his own, and by the strength of my sheer will, imbue him with comfort and courage. I knew he'd flinch away. I longed to rant at him that he, like Rich Truman, suffered as a victim, not just Nick's victim, but as a victim of his parents, his doctors, his teachers, his church, and his community. I doubted he would understand those convictions. I yearned to explain to him that Ben the newborn, Ben the little boy, hadn't chosen his birth into a crazy family, or the cell formation of his confused, injured brain. Yet I felt certain the biology of his life would confound him.

Instead, my mom side deferred to my lawyer side, just as my sweatshirt and jeans always demurred to suits and stockings. I signaled the guard to open my door to freedom. As I left the jail, still worried about Megan, I convinced myself that, for the moment, her father would protect her.

Except he hadn't protected Ben. Nor had any other adult. Indeed, it appeared that in all of Ben's 21 years, no one had ever stopped to help him.

* * *

Three nights later - the Defalco's bedroom

"For chrissake, Paige, will you give it a rest? I feel like the Stagg family has moved into our house. That's all you talk about, all you think about. What about *our* kids, *our* marriage, *our* home life? What about all of your other clients? The guy on death row, Chad Hammel, the other people in jail?" Disgusted, Jack threw a hand towel onto the pile of laundry on the floor, his words heaping more rubble onto my pile of guilt.

I lay in our queen sleigh bed, staring at the cherry finish, police reports from Ben's case resting on my chest. I'd met with Megan and her older sister that afternoon, the eldest Stagg sibling confirming both Megan's and Ben's tales of abuse, while adamantly refusing to testify to those facts at trial. "I won't do that to my mother," she'd averred.

"Look, Jack, all I'm saying is I'm suddenly in way over my head on this case. I'm a lawyer, not a shrink. I don't know what to do with these crazy people. I'm not even sure how this abuse information fits in with a defense for Ben." As Jack approached his side of the bed, I sat up, facing him. "Obviously Nick's threats to kill him help the coercion angle. But unless I can show that Laura's abuse affected Ben's brain, so that he can't think straight, or that it caused a mental disease or defect, what good does it do me?"

Jack grabbed a book on illustrated tours of great baseball parks - past and present - and snapped, "I don't give a shit. I'm done with the Stagg case for tonight."

"Fine." I gritted out. "By the way, Chad's case is under control, and I can't do anymore on the death case until I finish that week of training in California starting in 10 days." I lay back on my pillows.

Jack shot up off his. "You're going to California for a week? When were you going to mention *that?*"

The fact that his eyebrows drew together, and the skin creased in two vertical troughs between them, alerted me to his growing irritation.

I pulled off my reading glasses and peered at him. "I told you a month ago, when the California Supreme Court sent notice I had to attend." I turned away from the heat of his glare. "Which is another reason I'm worried about Ben's case. Three days after I get back I have to litigate a bunch of motions in front of Judge Lambert, including a motion to reduce Ben's bail."

With that one additional mention of all things Stagg, Jack threw back his covers, grabbed his robe and book, and slammed the door to the bedroom on his way upstairs to the spare room.

I once read that women sigh so they don't scream. So I sighed.

Mentally, however, I shrieked.

Because Jack was correct, as usual, when it came to my professional life interfering with our personal one. I obsessed. I prepared, prepared again, and then prepared some more. I read and re-read reports, labored over every sentence in every legal document I filed, and researched cases and statutes from Montana to California to the United States Supreme Court. Like a crazed and rabid jackal, I sunk my teeth into every nuanced piece of evidence, and wagged it between clenched jaws until every fact unfolded. Then I went to court.

In the Stagg case, at least, I'd managed to hold the entire clan at arm's length, refusing to engage emotionally with any of them in the first sixteen months after I'd taken on Ben Stagg as a client. I reasoned that if Ben lost his bid for a new trial, I'd never see him or his parents again. No need to crack the ice around my heart unnecessarily.

Yet now that he'd won his chance at freedom, indeed within the last three weeks, I'd become 'mother' to three new kids: one who nearly died in his hospital prison bed, another who threatened suicide and risked life and limb to rat out her lying parents, and a third whose brain functioned like a wheezing, sputtering, tractor engine.

Worse, I faced a massive amount of trial preparation, with little time in which to complete the work, hence the late night reading of investigative reports in bed. *Alone* in bed, with no spouse to warm me except with his barely controlled wrath, and with my real children sleeping, unaware that their mother soon traveled, once again, to California's death row for an entire week.

I sat up straight and arched my midsection in an effort to quell with gravity the bile that rose up my throat. A familiar pain drilled the muscle lying just beneath my right shoulder blade. Within moments I downed a few ibuprofen, followed by several antacids, and reluctantly turned out the light.

Closing my eyes, stuffing my self-pity, I twisted the sheet in my hands. I imagined telling Pete and Laura Stagg that I quit. I could taste the freedom after I cast off the shroud of panic that suffocated me, the relief after I heaved off the boulder of guilt crushing my chest. No client deserved a higher priority than my own family, especially my own kids.

Just do it. Screw them if they won't tell the truth.

Except, I made a promise to Ben. I vowed not to quit. I pledged to stay in the fight. I swore to him that I'd stand for him against injustice, protect his life and liberty, and speak for him in court. Ditto for all my clients, as well as the crime victims I once represented as a prosecutor.

And promise, like truth, is unrelenting in its demand for commitment, for fulfillment at any cost. A promise made, a truth uttered, brooks no compromise in loyalty or execution.

I grimaced into the darkness when I remembered who taught me *that* moral code.

An abuser, a molester, a war hero, a Navy commander, a loyal husband, and a life-long community volunteer, all tightly wrapped into the man I called *Dad*.

CHAPTER TWENTY-NINE

Of God, Life, and Liberty

Last weekend in September 2000
Cursillo at Kootenai Lake

"SHIT," I MUTTERED INTO ATMOSPHERE. No cell phone, no car, no escape from the group of women singing, clapping, and playing get-acquainted games in the recreation room of the log building at the lakeside religious camp. I grimaced, stiffening at each 'cluck, cluck, cluck' of the Cursillo tune.

Earlier, my buddy, the nun, explained to me that a Cursillo was a spiritual retreat at which people reconnected with God through music, silence, group discussions, and faith talks. All of that required participants to *share their feelings*, an abhorrent idea to a cynical curmudgeon like me.

Ah, but there I stood, not singing, mouthing the words, throwing the ball of yarn back to whatever well-intentioned female waited on the receiving end, while cursing the good Sister who talked me into this fiasco the week before.

"Listen, Paige," she'd urged. "You're lost." We sat in a downtown coffee shop, she in civilian clothes, me clad in another variation of gloomy court attire. "You have no idea how to help your young murder client, you don't know what to do with the violence and mental illness in his family, and now you're representing a guy on death row when you don't even know if you still believe in the death penalty."

She drilled me with her sternest Catholic nun, *teacher-of-small-children, straighten-up-and-fly-right look.* "You need to talk to God. You need answers that only God can provide. The Cursillo has a cancellation this weekend, and I want you to go. I'll sponsor you."

I sipped my millionth cup of coffee that day, wincing as it hit the acid-pocked lining in my stomach. "I don't have *time*, Sister. That's four days out of my life, away from trial preparation in Chad Hammel's case, and most importantly, away from my family." I drew my fingers through my hair, exhaling. "I just returned from California, after which I spent days in court on Ben's case. I *can't* just leave again."

In true nun fashion, she slapped her palm on the table. "This retreat is to take care of *you* and *you only.*" Leaning toward me, she clunked her mug next to her hand. "If you don't do something soon, you'll fall apart and be useless to your family *and* your clients." She sat back, sipping her tea as if to emphasize the ensuing silence. "You're a train wreck, girlfriend."

The train wreck part I admitted. The lost part I conceded. The retreat weekend I agreed to attend out of sheer desperation, with the faint hope that God might just answer me.

The leaders sent us to bed with the admonition to remain silent until morning. Wearily, I hiked to the bunkhouse, relieved to clear my head of musical ditties, but soon grew appalled at the loud snores emitted by my fellow seekers. I lay sleepless in the top bunk, assigned to me only because I stood as one of the few in the group nimble enough to scale a ladder.

I snuggled into the warmth of my sleeping bag, praying into the darkness. "Two questions, Lord: First, now that I'm defending a guy on death row, does Christianity really approve of killing people in prison? Second, why am I, out of all the lawyers in this valley, the one who has to defend Ben Stagg, and take all this shit from the community, aside from the fact that I promised to do it?"

Answers to those two questions focused my entire spiritual quest. Forget developing compassion, understanding, or a closer relationship to God. Cut to the chase. Get down to the facts. I needed answers, and I needed them fast.

At Mass the next morning, the priest noted that it was 'Right to Life' weekend in the Church and community. Instead of harping about the evils of abortion, however, he chose a different topic - the death penalty. He explained that Christ advised us to love one another and leave judgment and punishment to God. We could lock evildoers away to protect society, but we didn't get to kill them.

As I sat in my chair, a chill rippled across my shoulders. I nodded my head, closed my eyes, and lost myself in that message. *Whoa.* I sucked in breath. Tightened like an angry fist, my heart relaxed, as if encircling fingers loosened their grip. Genuflecting as I left the chapel, I found no words to convey my shock at such an immediate answer to my first question.

I spent the rest of that day mouthing more tunes, talking, and attempting to share my feelings. I marveled at the way guilt clung to our small crowd, just as the smell of America's prisons lingered in my suits. We women, almost without exception, endured unfathomable traumas - childhood abuse, incest, self-medicating with drugs and alcohol, rape, abortion, death of loved ones, abject poverty, mental illness, chronic and terminal disease - all enshrouded in a conviction of failure.

I felt as if I led that parade. I'd excelled at messing up my own life as an adolescent. In those days, I thought of myself as the queen of sin. Even though my brain recognized that my bad choices arose from my own physical and sexual abuse, my mother's death, and my oldest brother's prisoner-of-war status in Vietnam, my heart never forgave me for being such a screw-up.

Yet that night we seekers - we women who'd surfaced from a tour through the bowels of Hell - stood together in a circle of sudden freedom, our arms locked on each other's shoulders, singing, praying, and finally, rejoicing. I quit mouthing the words to the Rosary and music. I spoke out, sang out, in affirmation of our spiritual dawn. In that hour, the death knell tolled for our collective transgressions.

Later, lying within the soft down of my sleeping bag, pounds of guilt melted off my bones. For 30 years I'd nurtured my demons, even grown fond of them as the enemies I knew. They raised themselves as predictably as a sunrise whenever I felt vulnerable. They sat next to me, whispered in my ear, cackled, and exulted when I caved into terror. Killing them off ended a destructive habit, like smoking or sniffing cocaine, and I'd kicked those bad boys long ago.

In fact, I realized, I'd done a lot of tough stuff. Dragged my ass through a protracted undergraduate career at Berkeley, miraculously graduating with honors; finishing a Masters degree; hanging in a marriage for 20 years with a beloved, but slightly crazy guy; birthing two kids while surviving three miscarriages, during my three years at law school; passing the state bar exam after studying 12 hours a day for six weeks straight; succeeding as a prosecutor working 60 hour weeks through trial after trial, as I juggled children, friends, and family.

Then again, as the good nun pointed out, I rivaled a train wreck. I'd moved to Kootenai County to find peace, to discover 'normal,' to spend all my time with my kids and spouse. Instead, I'd once again entangled myself in the sticky web of criminal law. And Ben Stagg's murder trial loomed as the giant, woman-eating arachnid that waited patiently to pounce.

Why me? I tamped down my self-pity, inserted earplugs, and dozed.

The following morning the priest again addressed us at Mass. The theme? Why some were called to take on heavier tasks in life than others. The answer? God only placed burdens on those folks He knew could shoulder them. If we carried a laden load, God planned it that way because He knew we had the strength and talent to succeed in the battle.

For the second time in as many days I exhaled a *Whoa.*

I cut a glance over the priest's left shoulder, to the corpus of the Lord hanging on the crucifix. I knew I should have offered thanks, but instead I yelled a silent, "Shit!" As much as I believed in promises kept, I'd *hoped* for a reprieve from Ben's case. I wanted God to answer, "It's okay. You've done enough. You're tired, burned out. I'll find someone else. Vacation time, my friend."

But no, sniveled my inner Whiner. Good old God granted me no quarter. No opportunity to quit or rest. No shelter. No retreat. Only an implied promise of divine protection. Disgusted, I lumbered back to the cabin, unwilling to hum, talk, or emote.

Still, as the afternoon stretched, my celestial anger abated. I found myself, during the closing Mass, once again singing aloud, smiling along with those amazing women who that weekend, like me, morphed from perpetual victims to survivors. Trust followed that newfound voice. Trust in God, yes, but more significantly, trust in myself.

Somehow I would extricate Ben Stagg from his morass. I'd defend Chad Hammel at his civil trial scheduled only thirty days away. I'd do my utmost to save the guy on death row, be a better mom, and a more attentive wife. I would come out of it all with more stress lines creasing my face, but by God, literally, I'd do it.

As I waited outside for my nun buddy to pick me up, I squared my shoulders, rolled cramps off my neck, and stamped the cold from my booted feet. When I loaded my gear into her Subaru, I admitted, "Okay, so you were right. I needed the Cursillo." Then, in the hush that followed her knowing smile, I ruminated.

With my conscience on the mend and my confidence perked up, I still needed an angel to help Ben Stagg. Only one came to mind - a diminutive, Jewish, forensic psychologist from Ohio. It was time to call Dr. Sara Berg, the one who'd offered her services after seeing the *NewsTime, CBS* show.

Pete and Laura Stagg would balk because she wasn't a Christian, or because for a living she rubbed the lumps on people's heads. Laura had advised me only the week before, when I asked her to rush her daughter to a counselor, that the Devil himself spawned psychiatrists. However, I knew they'd relent to save their son. They'd sacrifice their lives for Ben if I asked.

As for my promise to Ben that I'd hang in and fight, it appeared God had just clanged shut the door to my escape.

* * *

"So, Pete," I ventured to Ben's dad as we sat in the lobby of an Aberdeen bank ten days after my spiritual epiphany, "do you really believe in Hell? Like a place people go forever and burn with the Devil?" Skepticism dripped off my question.

From the identically upholstered chair next to me, Pete Stagg smiled, nodding. "I do."

I expected more, a Baptist rant perhaps, but he

plastered a serene look on his face as he glanced around the lobby. "How much longer do you think this will take, until we get Ben out of jail?" He wiggled the hiking-booted foot crossed over his knee, a gesture that belied the calm tone of his voice.

I pondered that for a minute. Two weeks earlier, Judge Lambert had lowered Ben's bail from a million dollars to a mere $350,000. Since Pete and Laura had no disposable cash, they, along with several close friends, posted their homes and land as collateral for a property bond worth twice that amount. The paperwork that spelled Ben's freedom printed out as we conversed.

"Soon, Pete, maybe even today. Once we get clear title to everything, we have to get the judge to sign an order for Ben's release. It's going to be a media circus, so prepare yourself."

Pete nodded again, sighed, and shifted in the chair. I stood to pace, nervous about broaching Ben's safety once he moved back to the family home. I glanced heavenward, exhaled yet another sigh-so-as-not-to-scream, and pitched Pete my concerns. "How are you going to keep Ben safe from Laura? Or keep Megan safe?"

Caution crept beneath his lowered eyes as his effort to protect his wife warred with his need to protect his children from the lunacy that lurked in Laura's disordered brain. "I'm sending Megan to Nebraska to stay with friends." He returned my stare, the one drilling him with my own worry. "I made Ben a separate room in the garage where he can shut himself away from the family."

My facial expression must have broadcast my skepticism because Pete stood suddenly, his height besting mine by only an inch or two. Nearly nose-to-nose, we squared off in a tense, silent challenge to determine who best could protect his children. I couldn't take Ben home with me, but I figured I could find him a safe place to stay. Two redheads, two square-jawed, chin-jutting combatants, ready to do battle. Neither of us backed off.

"Uh . . . excuse me, Mrs. Defalco?"

I sensed another presence over my shoulder, forcing me to blink first in the standoff. I turned toward the banker clearing his throat. He thrust a stack of papers into my hand. "Everything is here and in order. If any problems come up, I attached my card. Call me." As he walked away he paused to glance back. "Good luck."

Putting our contest of wills on hold, Pete and I drove in silence to the courthouse where I handed the paperwork to the clerk. Soon a local judge, acting on Judge Lambert's behalf, emerged from his chambers, minus his black robe. "Frank McShane objects to Ben's release, Mrs. Defalco. He wants me to raise the bail amount."

Before the judge could utter another word, I flew to my feet and advanced. "You can't do that, Judge. That isn't fair. These people have put this bond together after a huge effort and --"

He raised an open palm to interrupt my escalating outrage. "I'm going to sign the order, Paige, so calm down. I came out here to warn you that you're putting your client in danger. There are people in this valley who want that kid dead, so make sure he's protected."

Pete and I exchanged another competitive look as he minced out, "I will protect my own son, Your Honor. Count on it." His crossed arms reflected his decision to place Ben's safety and freedom before his wife's uncontrollable violence, or anyone else's in the community.

The judge nodded, signed the order, and passed it along to the jailers. Media folks waited outside the jail's rear entrance, anticipating Ben's release through the salle-port. Instead, I arranged for Ben to leave through the front door of the courthouse and jump directly into Pete's waiting pickup.

Just before Ben made a run for it, I grabbed his arm. "Listen to me, buddy." Urgency tore through my words. "If there is *any* violence, any yelling, hitting, or threats, you call me and I'll come get you. Do you understand what I'm saying?"

Ben bent his long, thin frame to meet my gaze. "Yes, Paige. I . . . I trust you. I promise to call."

I arranged my grimace into a reassuring smile. "Then go, kiddo, and remember, don't talk to *anyone* about your case, not even your folks."

As Ben and his dad drove off, I found little comfort at thwarting the waiting reporters. Rather, my lawyer side fumbled to open a bottle of antacids. My terror of someone shooting Ben weighed equally with my fear that Laura might attack him. My mom side breathed back panic as I headed my Tahoe home to my own kids.

After two and a half years behind bars, in October 2000, Ben Stagg at last tasted freedom.

I swallowed back bile.

* * *

A week later, I waited in the emergency room for Laura and Megan Stagg to emerge. Megan had attempted suicide that morning by swallowing oodles of prescription drugs. Once the docs pumped her stomach, she survived relatively unscathed. This day marked her 17th birthday.

Without warning, an ambulance arrived. Suddenly the thin walls of the waiting room failed to silence another woman's screams. That mother's keening, upon learning that her 5-year-old daughter had just died from injuries sustained in a car accident, careened around the little space in which I sat. Unable to absorb more trauma, I searched for a trash bin in which to vomit.

Shit.

I covered my ears, closed my eyes, all in a futile attempt to shut out the reality of a child's death as it shrilled through every molecule of available oxygen, suffocating me. At last, after the mother's shrieks quieted to moans, and weeping replaced her sobs, I rose to search for Laura. I found her sitting outside the heavy doors to the examination area, clasping her fingers in apparent prayer. Her glance when I called her name betrayed the ravages of twenty-some years of motherhood.

I sat next to her, wrapping my arm around her shoulders. "Is Megan okay?" A stupid question when I considered it. Had Megan been okay, she wouldn't have swallowed a plethora of pills to end her life.

Laura added her own tears to the other mother's grief. Tissues balled in her hands as she rocked slowly back and forth, nodding. "But Paige, they sent in a psychiatrist." She looked furtively around the area, whispering, "What if she tells? Will they jail me or take her away from us? Will they make Ben go back to jail?"

Always the mom, I sought to reassure, to fix what was broken. Yet Laura needed more than I could provide. Her brain needed analysis and medication, a possible solution she refused to consider. Indeed, after her children's revelations, she'd simply dismissed them, smiling, "Oh, Paige! I never did any of that. They're exaggerating. I had PMS sometimes, that's all."

She believed her version of the truth.

Laura's denials put her daughters in an impossible situation. If they told the truth, they betrayed their mother. If they lied, they condemned one or both brothers to prison and, perhaps, death. They couldn't escape and they couldn't win. That impossible choice likely fueled Megan's suicide attempt.

Now Laura's fear of getting caught, of public humiliation, battled with her concern for Megan's safety. Still, her swollen eyes, her pallor, the graying hair hanging limply around her face, all bespoke desperation. "I don't know what to do anymore," she murmured.

Lost in the darkness, wandering through another nightmare devoid of hope, any light beckoning her to safety shuttered, Laura Stagg dropped her head into her hands, her utter silence screaming as confusion buried her.

Her emptiness echoed the new-found horror cleaving that other mother's heart.

I stood, a fist at my mouth, my back rounded in the slump that I'd vowed to straighten the previous New Year's Eve. Any moisture that might have produced saliva or tears had earlier landed in the garbage can, along with the remnants of my breakfast.

My impotence to fix any of the mess that spread before me like an overflowing septic field forced me to move. I walked the halls of the hospital - up, down, back and forth - always eyeing Laura for her collapse. Thankfully, I never caught a glimpse of the other mother, or of her tiny daughter's broken body.

As I paused to stare out the window, the afternoon sun warming me, a doctor stomped toward Laura. Protectively, for the mom or the daughter I knew not, I hurried to her side. He looked at us accusingly. "She won't say anything except that she's upset and the attempt was a mistake." Shaking his head he added, "I'm releasing her, but she needs serious counseling, Mrs. Stagg."

An understatement.

Numb, Laura nodded, her own welfare seemingly unimportant now that Megan could come home. Either that or she masked well her relief at dodging detection.

As I walked to my car, I felt a familiar squeeze clench around my heart, serious pain radiating through my chest cavity. Gasping, I balanced on the Tahoe's hood, relieved that the ache failed to travel up my arms. Satisfied no cardiac failure loomed, I keyed the lock and sat behind the wheel to catch my breath.

We women - the mom whose daughter died, the mom whose daughter survived suicide, the just-turned 17-year-old daughter who sought heaven instead of hell, and I, the lawyer-mom-wife who swallowed everyone's offal - frayed around the edges, our safety nets in peril of shredding. Our families, our children, our friends, were left to stare, transfixed, as the gossamer threads tethering us to earth unraveled.

I steeled my spine against the lumbar cushion as I drove, Jack's favorite advice blaring in my head. "Fuck 'em, Paige. Don't ever the let the bastards get you down. Stand up and kick them in the balls."

I readied my boot.

CHAPTER THIRTY

The Counting Game

Late October 2000
Beartooth, Montana

"IF MOST PEOPLE FELT . . . WHAT I FEEL IN MY HEAD . . ." Ben Stagg exhaled as he tried to still his shaking hands. He looked up at me, his confusion evident in the searching gaze from his blue eyes. He finished his thought. "Well, they'd commit suicide."

We sat in my office, me in my large lavender-upholstered office chair, Ben across the desk in a smaller, identically upholstered client chair. He'd savored freedom for only a few weeks, a break during which I'd insisted he spend weekdays at my office working on his defense.

As if one existed.

I also arranged for Ben to talk to a counselor to ferret out his inner terrors. Pete drove him the many miles each way, each day, without complaint.

As I listened to him, I noticed Ben's speech emerged with the same halting insecurity that forced him to lower his head when he spoke, rarely making eye contact, his focus instead riveted on his trembling fingers. Those shakes seemed to rattle his entire, skinny body. He wore baggy jeans and a t-shirt that hung from his lanky frame. His great height edged his pant legs an inch too far above his hiking boots.

Ben cleared his throat. "I . . . like it here at your office. It feels safe." He shifted in his seat, crossing his foot over his knee to jiggle it, much like his dad did when Pete showed his nerves.

I ran my fingers under my pearl necklace and straightened my back, still fighting the slouch. "Ben, can you tell me about that? What happens in your head?" I poised pen over yellow legal pad, then decided to listen without taking notes. Rolling my chair back, I removed my reading glasses and smiled encouragement.

Returning my smile, he began, as always, with 'well' followed by a pause. "Well, like noises that other people can't hear? I hear them. Like if someone walks across carpet, I can hear the carpet crunch under their feet." He nodded to emphasize this oddity.

Crap. I froze my smile to hide my own confusion.

"And I have to count everything all the time," he continued, warming to his subject.

I blinked at him. "Count? What do you mean?"

He smiled again. "Well, take those pictures on the wall behind you." He pointed to five identically framed diplomas that reflected various degrees I'd acquired in my protracted journey through academia. "I count them because they're all square, but since there are only five, I have to rope something else in that is a square to make it so there's six." He met my gaze with another nod. "There's got to be six - *always* - or at least three or six or nine or some such number that includes threes."

"I see." But of course I didn't see at all. "Why the number three?"

He glanced at his hands then out the window at the chilly autumn day. "Well, I don't really know." He pondered a moment. "Three is Nick's favorite number, but I just don't know."

I stood, unable to sit up straight any longer, unwilling to listen to more weird thoughts from my young client. I paced off a few steps.

"See?" Ben smiled excitedly. "I can hear the carpet

crush when you walk! You can't hear it, but I can hear it just as plain as day!"

I stopped short and caught his eye as I shook my head in bewilderment. "No, I don't get this at all. I'm a lawyer. I can't understand what you're talking about."

I feigned interest in a passing truck on the street to buy myself time. As I turned back to Ben, I reached out to pat his arm.

He flinched. I gasped, generating a blush and apology from him. "I'm . . . I'm sorry. It's just . . . you know . . . I . . ." He lifted both hands in bewilderment.

"Hey." I lowered my tone to a croon, hoping to soothe his embarrassment. "I understand about you being hit. It's okay, kiddo." I returned to my chair to give him physical space. "So, this doctor coming from Ohio? Dr. Berg? She'll help us figure this out. She'll tell us what's going on in your brain. But you have to trust me."

Startled, he looked up. "I do trust you, Paige. You're the only person I trust."

"Okay, then," I stood. "Go talk to the counselor. You can trust him, too. We'll talk more tomorrow at the hearing."

After Ben left for his counseling appointment, I called Sara Berg and detailed the conversation for her.

She hesitated just seconds before opining, "Sounds like obsessive-compulsive disorder along with some other stuff. That's why Ben counts. His ability to hear stuff the rest of us cannot indicates several possible disorders."

I closed my eyes at the thought of some incurable major psychiatric disorder imperiling my client's chances at trial.

Sara, however, sounded hopeful. "Hey, Paige, it's a start at unlocking this kid's brain. It gives me something to go on when I interview him next month."

I disconnected, sending up a silent prayer of thanks

for Sara's expertise and her agreement to travel to Kootenai County to help me. Then I headed downstairs to Jack's office. I found him composing an appeal in Charlie Hammel's divorce case, one that detailed the injustice meted out at the trial two weeks earlier. The judge hammered Charlie, limiting his visitation with his kids, charging him a fortune in child support, despite the fact that he was unemployed, and mounting on attorney's fees to pay for his ex-wife's lawyer.

I plopped into the chair across from Jack, waiting for a glance that invited my intrusion into his thoughts. November 1st had marked two decades of our marriage. After 20 years, we sensed each other's moods like old cops intuit danger in the streets. Without looking up, Jack asked, "What's up?" His eyebrows pointed down toward the two deep furrows running between them, emphasizing his anger at the ruling in Charlie's case.

"Fuck these guys!" he spewed, before I could launch into Ben's state of mind. "There's always a hidden agenda around here. An inside track that lets the judges do what they want, no matter how unfair it is to the client. And it's all orchestrated by the Courthouse Cowboys, as you call them."

In full agreement, I sat silently. When at last he stopped writing, I weighed in. "It's not just in this county. Look what happened to Chad, Sr.'s litigation yesterday. We were set for trial in just a few days when that new judge dumped the whole case. Now we have to start over. Chad is furious. He believes Hank Winston is behind his son's crummy deal, as well as his own."

Jack reached for a cup of swill he claimed passed for coffee. "I hate this state, Paige. I hate the cold, I hate the legal system, I hate that there's no professional sports. If the kids weren't doing so well, I'd be back in California in a heartbeat."

A familiar rant. To distract him, I shared Ben's

perception of reality.

Jack appeared as stumped as I. "No clue. When's the expert coming from Ohio?"

Desperate for caffeine, I leaned forward to sip from his mug, pulling a sour face as I swallowed. "Mid-December. Did I tell you she's donating her time and services? All Pete and Laura have to pay for is her plane, hotel, and food."

Jack let out a low whistle. "That's a big break. I hope she's not some nut job." Glancing at the clock, he jumped up. "Shit! I'm late to pick up the kids."

I stood, raising a palm to halt him. "I'm on it. Finish your work." I kissed him on my way out.

As I drove to two schools separated only by a few short blocks, I switched masks. Off with the lawyer, on with the mom. As my son and his friends clambered into the rear seat of the Tahoe, I gazed at my brilliant student who, for some reason, couldn't read well or perform jumping jacks with his little guy football team, just as his sister struggled in math and English.

At my daughter's high school, maternal love riddled with worry shrouded me, crowding out thoughts of Ben Stagg. Maneuvering through the tree-lined avenues of our quaint little town, my mind skittered in neurological chaos.

Paige the Mom, the fixer of everything, likely couldn't fix my children's scrambled brains or Ben Stagg's mental disorders. However, Paige the Lawyer, the never-say-die, never-give-up, never-concede advocate for the underdog, knew that I had to try. The naysayers might sneer, the pessimists could mock, and the Courthouse Cowboys would obstruct.

But the option to give up, to surrender to their machinations, died as my stubborn determination ballooned.

* * *

"These people are fucking nuts." Dr. Sara Berg slid this past me in the hallway of our office, *sotto voce*. Shaking her head, she looked over her shoulder at the Stagg family, who sat quietly assembled around our conference table.

When she refocused her brown, bespectacled eyes on me, craning back her head to accommodate my much taller height, she laughed at my shocked expression. "Sorry. Gallows humor. When you've worked at this job as long as I have, you develop a weird sense of the absurd."

I relaxed my shoulders, stuck my head into the conference room to advise the Staggs that the good doctor and I would be back in a minute, and herded Sara upstairs to my office. Safely behind my desk, I laughed. "I understand about the gallows humor. You should hear Jack and me when we're looking at crime scene photos."

I sipped cold coffee as Sara flopped into the chair across my desk. Coughing from the bitter swill, I drilled her. "So what do you think about Ben?"

She crossed one short leg over the other. "I think he suffers from a number of disorders, including obsessive-compulsive disorder, profound learning disorders, and dissociative disorders."

At my blank look, she elaborated. "He's screwed up, Paige. When he confronts any loud noises - yelling and screaming, for example - or physical violence, his mind spins off to another place where it's safe for him. He's physically present in the room, but he's elsewhere mentally. The counting thing, the efforts to hurt himself, all stem from brain confusion and the abuse he's suffered since childhood. And that abuse includes the physical stuff, as well as incest from Nick."

I nodded as if I understood, but I didn't, except the

part about physical abuse and incest. "Hurting himself? You mean his suicide attempts after the murder?" Ben explained the attempts to kill himself after Rich Truman's murder, the one kayaking unprepared in the whitewater race, and the other playing Russian Roulette with the revolver.

Sara sipped from her water bottle. "Those, yes. But also his incessant chewing on his fingers until they bleed, and biting the inside of his cheek. It's all a reaction to living in chaos at home and using a broken and very confused brain to try to make sense of it all."

My own confused mind struggled to find a legal defense in Sara's expert opinion. I ignored the clinical aspects of Ben's diagnosis, since I only cared if it would advance his acquittal at trial. I still couldn't see a shining light in Sara's words.

Trained to read people, Sara noted my troubled expression. "Paige, this *matters*. When Ben's mind travels away, he acts like a robot and does whatever people tell him. So, if Nick screamed at him that night through a headset, and if Ben thought Nick could kill him if he refused to go along with the burglary and just did what Nick said to do, then . . ." She groped for a conclusion just as I had a *Eureka* moment.

Excited, I completed Sara's sentence. "Then Ben didn't act *voluntarily*, and *that* is a defense to any crime on the planet! It's not a great defense, but at least it's a shot at an acquittal or a hung jury."

I stood to pace the length of my office as Sara scrutinized me with interest. "Uh," she hedged, "how do you convince Pete and Laura that they have to testify to all the abuse they inflicted? They've always refused to let that information become public knowledge."

My thoughts raced ahead of Sara's words. "They won't testify, but they can't prevent you from testifying to those facts as part of your expert opinion about Ben's disabilities." I turned toward the window, noted the snowfall, and twisted back to her. "Besides, Ben can tell the jury the truth."

Sara snorted a skeptical laugh. "You're going to put that kid on the witness stand? He barely makes sense when he talks. How's he going to explain to a jury what's going on in his head?"

I smiled at her as I sat back down in my big office chair and leaned forward. "The same way he explained it to you and me, Sara - slowly, haltingly, looking down at his hands while they tremble and shake. But he'll do it, because if he doesn't take the stand and tell the jury the truth," I sighed, "then he'll spend the rest of his life in prison."

I stared at the improbable angel sitting opposite to me, at a woman armed with a doctorate degree in psychology, loads of experience analyzing kids accused of crimes, and hours testifying about their conditions before juries. Not some quirky, rub-the-lumps-on-people's-heads sort of doctor, Sara Berg entered the Stagg case as the Real Deal, with fluttering wings masking an iron will. And she promised to give the Staggs her services for free.

"Sara, you've just become the star witness for the defense. Without you to figure out Ben and his family, and to testify at trial, that kid's sunk. He'll die in jail. *Thank you* doesn't come close to enough."

She shook her head, rose to her spare five-foot height, and smiled. "Well, I guess I'd better get to work." She turned at the staircase. Her next words tossed me a lifeline. "We'll do this, Paige. Together, we'll keep Ben Stagg out of prison."

With her promise of hope, the gossamer threads lashing me together held fast.

* * *

At the December 2000 hearing in which Judge Lambert would decide what testimony the prosecutor could introduce at trial, the hours grew into an evidentiary nightmare.

After the earlier extortion move in May by the attorney representing Ben's first lawyer, I'd capitulated to his demand to drop my claim of ineffective assistance of counsel, in exchange for his promise to keep quiet about Ben's alleged effort to shoot the shotgun the night of Rich Truman's murder.

However, once I dropped the claim, it appeared I'd been double-crossed. Ben's first lawyer, it turned out, had already blabbed the facts to the prosecutor months earlier, without mentioning that to me. By cooperating with the Cowboys, he received his judicial appointment, while Ben got screwed at the hearing.

To make matters worse, even though Don Yeager and I had agreed not to bother involving Ben's first lawyer, Judge Lambert announced that *he* had subpoenaed the guy for the sole purpose of eliciting the privileged contents of Ben's prior conversations with him.

When he took the stand, that lawyer-turned-jurist revealed everything Ben had told him in confidence, none of which constituted new information, but all of which complicated the defense case.

And I was *pissed off.*

On my way out of the court hearing, I slammed the bar on the fire door so hard, I scared Ben Stagg out of the few wits he possessed. As I entered the women's bathroom and parked in a stall, I forced myself to breathe deeply to summon control. I didn't need to use the facilities. I needed to calm down.

A half hour later, back at the office after court, I fumed at Stormy, Jack, and some poor schmuck who happened by the office collecting for a local charity. "Those fuckers lied to me, they betrayed their ethical oaths to a client, and on top of that, they're just *shitty lawyers!*"

The charity guy beat it out the front door as I paced back and forth in the foyer. "Get this. Ben's lawyer claims Ben *closed his eyes,* squeezed the trigger, and the gun wouldn't fire. Yet at the original sentencing hearing, when Judge Winston asked Ben why he didn't fire a warning shot to alert Truman of a problem, Ben said he couldn't think at all because he was so messed up."

Jack and Stormy nodded, never willing to interrupt me when my personal barometer hit *hurricane storm warning.*

"So I asked Ben's old lawyer today why he didn't tell Ben then, in front of Judge Winston, to talk about this supposed effort to shoot the gun, because it sure sounds like a warning shot to me. I mean, this kid is an expert marksman. Why would he close his eyes, and not even take aim at Truman, if he intended to kill him?"

More head-nodding by my audience, only marked by a bit of confusion.

I rolled on. "The truth is, Ben may or may not have tried to fire that shotgun, but whatever he did, he never intended to kill Rich Truman, and his former lawyer conceded that. But what *pisses me off the most* is the judge's interference in the trial. Neither the prosecutor nor I intended to pursue this issue, but the judge, on his own, went ahead with it, because," I made air quotes with my fingers, "*he* wanted to know what Ben said."

Jack jumped into the fray. "So the judge, instead of ruling the information between Ben and his first attorney was a privileged communication and couldn't be divulged, just demanded to know the contents? How does he get to do that?"

I turned so quickly I knocked over the magazine

rack. "Exactly! Can you believe that? I feel like I'm practicing law in a third world country. So Judge Lambert ruled that the prosecutor can call Ben's old lawyer at trial, if Ben denies he tried to fire the gun, which is no big deal really because Ben's said all along that he tried to fire and couldn't."

Stormy's brow furrowed. "Then why are you so mad, if it's no big deal?"

I sucked in a breath. "Because the judge is playing favorites, and he's better than that. And because the lawyers lied to me and screwed Ben." I headed for the stairs to my office but turned back. "The good old boys will stop at nothing to see this kid sent back to prison for a hundred years, even if they have to cheat, and that approach is contrary to their promise to fight for the truth." I leaned against the wall. "You know the reason Ben gave the cops for his inability to shoot that gun?"

Jack smiled. "What?"

"Divine intervention. God. He thinks God is on his side in this, even after all the crap he's been through. Pretty amazing faith, huh?"

"About the same as yours, Sweet Pea."

Not even close, Honeybun.

In my office I searched without success for an aspirin. I'd handed Judge Lambert another writ to the Supreme Court, hoping they'd suppress Ben's confession. Beyond that, I'd run out of strategies. My luck appeared to have dried up. I felt like garbage, looked even worse, and wanted nothing more than to quit Ben's case. Like a balloon with a slow leak, my energy ebbed, along with my hope.

Okay, Paige, end of pity party. Cut the wimpy whining and get your ass in gear.

That wasn't God's voice in my head. That was my inner bitch yelling at me to put one step in front of the other, and at all costs, keep moving forward. Or as my dad, the World War II fighter pilot, once wrote to me, "Always remember the three rules of flight, Paige Ann. Don't stall, don't stall, don't stall."

Thanks, Dad.

CHAPTER THIRTY-ONE

The Hour I First Believed

Early January 2001
Beartooth, Montana

"HOLY MARY, MOTHER OF GOD, PRAY FOR US SINNERS--" I murmured the prayer, fingering the rosary chain, imploring God to make Ben Stagg's case go away. I sat in our bedroom chair in front of the fireplace, dressed in a casual skirt and boots, prepared to meet Ben's grandmother around noon at the office.

My dad's advice notwithstanding, I'd sunk knee deep in proverbial shit, wallowing in a vat of self-pity that marked the nadir of my legal career. That January day in 2001, screamed out, "Four more days, Paige, before your disabled kid client commences a murder trial that will send him back to prison for the rest of his life!"

As I sat with my rosary beads, I silently checked off my 'to do' list. My suits hung newly cleaned from the laundry, high heels sat polished, replenished hair, make-up, and toiletries filled the cabinets.

Now if I only had *a fucking defense for trial.*

Sighing, I stowed the prayer beads, cancelled the fire, and drove to the office. I awaited a decision on my latest writ from the Montana Supreme Court, a ruling that had the potential to put all of us out of our misery. If the Court agreed with me that the police coerced Ben's confession, the case would end. The prosecutor couldn't win if he didn't have Ben's confession to put him at the scene of the murder.

I knew suppressing the confession was a long shot, but I had to try something. In four days the prosecutor would present a grieving widow, bereft children and grandchildren, an airtight case, complete with gory photos and Ben's confession, and I would present . . . not much.

My entire defense rested on the word *voluntary*. According to Montana law, before anyone could be convicted of a crime, the prosecutor had to prove the defendant's criminal conduct was voluntary. My only hope, through Dr. Sara Berg's testimony and Ben himself, lay in convincing twelve Montanans that Ben's conduct arose from Nick's manipulation of him.

I intended to ask the jury to acquit Ben Stagg of murder, and twenty counts of burglary, because Nick made him do it.

Yeah.

That was plausible. When pigs became pilots.

Christmas two weeks earlier had marked the third anniversary of Rich Truman's death. His family's grief grew every year instead of abating over time. He'd been the family's rock - their source of strength, love, humor, and income. For 40 years, he and Nina shared every secret, every joy, and every sorrow. Healing and moving forward loomed far in the future for his family.

For the Defalco clan, Christmas had held its usual array of presents, decorations, and food, along with midnight Mass at our local parish. Still, it faded to memory within hours as I resumed trial preparations, heading to the Sheriff's Department to look through the State's evidence. Nothing like a few bloody crime scene and autopsy photos to put a damper on any New Year's celebrations.

Ben had assumed it would be his last Christmas at home with his family, before returning to life and death incarcerated at Deer Lodge. His older sister arranged for him to have a massage; someone else bought him soothing music; another loaned him a telescope for a final look at the stars sparkling in perfect Montana night skies.

Since his release from custody at the end of October, Ben's joy had deteriorated. His confidence, fragile at the outset, eroded further each day. Whenever I saw him, his hands shook as if he clung to a jackhammer. He stuttered, smiled even as his brows frowned, occasionally wept or flinched, and at times became so unresponsive, I thought he'd become catatonic. Dr. Berg labeled it 'numbing' and 'dissociation from reality'. I knew it spelled his death at trial if I couldn't get him to testify.

Not long before Christmas, Ben had complained of severe chest pains. Laura, ever the vigilant mom, took him to see a new young doctor in town, Dr. Jason Cotter. She noted that Dr. Cotter was a Christian man, as if that increased his medical competence. Dr. Cotter, at Ben's insistence, had requested my permission to test Ben for a genetic disorder. Ben, it appeared, exhibited symptoms consistent with Klinefelter's syndrome. Clueless, I'd agreed, dismissing any medical diagnosis as irrelevant to Ben's murder case.

Now at the office, awaiting the arrival of Ben's grandmother, Millie Gifford, I perused my phone messages, noting none dangled the promise of divine intervention. At noon Mrs. Gifford arrived. For the next two and a half hours, I begged her to testify to Laura's abuse toward Ben. She refused. "I won't testify against my own daughter. I'm sorry, Paige. It wouldn't be right."

At 2:30 that afternoon, the Clerk called from the Montana Supreme Court. "Sorry, Paige. The Court refused to consider your writ. They said to bring the issue up on appeal if your client is convicted."

By three o'clock I sat at my desk, head in my hands,

once again breathing deeply to relieve my own chest pains. A coughing fit cut off my thoughts. Panic drove ice through my fingers and toes. I craved the soothing effects of a cigarette. Still coughing, I swallowed cold coffee. Over and over, I told myself that I'd done my best with what I had.

Stormy's intercom buzz jerked my head up. "What?" I barked, irritated that she'd interrupted my misery.

"Whoa! Somebody's cranky this afternoon." Her voice floated through the phone.

"Listen, Cruella," I sniped back, using a nickname I reserved for her only when sarcasm ruled my mood, "unless you have God on the line telling me the prosecutor dismissed Ben's case, I'm not taking calls."

"Okay, but it's Ben's doctor, and he sounds very excited. He said to tell you he has news that will change everything for Ben at trial."

I looked up at the ceiling, gathering patience. "Oh for crapssake." Another cough. "Fine. Put him through."

I eased my chair back, put my boot-clad feet on my desk, hiked up my skirt, and dropped my pen on my yellow tablet. Nothing some doctor could tell me would make a difference for Ben, so why take notes? I clicked onto the blinking phone line. "Hi, Dr. Cotter. What have you got for me?"

Jason Cotter's excited voice blurted, "He has Klinefelter's syndrome, Ms. Defalco! Ben has KS!"

My only thought as I swiveled my chair so I could look out the window was, *big fucking deal*. However, in the interest of etiquette, I replied, "Ah ha. And this matters to Ben's defense how?"

"Well, it's huge," he enthused. "KS is a genetic disorder that affects roughly one in every 300 to 500 males born - *worldwide*. The reason it's a syndrome is that all of these boys have frontal lobe damage to their brains.

That means they can't make decisions or foresee the consequences of their conduct."

At my continued silence Dr. Cotter huffed in exasperation. "Don't you *get* it, Ms. Defalco? This is the organic, scientific evidence you need to prove Ben didn't act on his own, that he only did what his brother told him to do when Nick committed the murder and burglaries!"

My chair crashed against the credenza as I stood up. I glanced at the graying skies outside, at the ski runs on the mountain, half expecting the clouds to part and a chorus of angels to chime in with an *Alleluia*.

Masking my own excitement I asked evenly, "Dr. Cotter, can you testify to all of this at the trial?"

"Of course I'll testify. Ben's a great kid, and he's no killer. He was sucked in by his brother, and that's what KS is all about - guys who can't think clearly, who then rely on others to do their thinking for them. Research it on the internet, and we'll talk tomorrow."

After we hung up, I paced. I heard Jack's distinctive footsteps coming up the stairs. As only long-time, beloved spouses can, he noted my agitation. He didn't attempt to sit, instead stopping me with his arms on my shoulders as he turned me toward him. "What?"

His simple question evoked no easy answer. Suddenly rare sunlight filtered through the window onto my desk, reflecting off the empty yellow pages under my pen. I stared into his concerned blue eyes, the truth dawning on me slowly.

"What's happened, Paige?" Jack repeated.

I shook my head, staring at the sunlight. "I think . . . I mean . . . honestly--" At last, smiling, tentative, I returned Jack's gaze. "A miracle, Jack. A damned miracle. *That's* what happened."

* * *

The next day I took reams of research on Klinefelter's syndrome to the prosecutor's office and convinced Don Yeager to continue Ben's trial date. I needed to procure an expert witness to test Ben's brain for KS-related defects that would explain why he followed his brother's commands like a trained seal at Marine World.

As elated as I felt at the new diagnosis and the delay of trial, I sensed a certain doom at the courthouse that morning as word spread of Ben's mental disorder. The staff appeared edgy, as if they knew a giant bucket of crap hovered above me, certain to fall if I pushed on the right door. My defense attorney colleagues glared as they passed me in the hall. Standing at a secretary's desk, Judge Winston clenched his jaw in an apparent effort to contain his anger at my legal victory, his balding pate reddening as his blood pressure rose.

Had I possessed a modicum of common sense, I would have fled to the parking lot without a word. Instead I smirked at the judge, adding a snippy, "Good morning, Your Honor," and sauntered through the foyer door.

Unease swallowed hubris, however, in the safety of my car. Driving back to Beartooth, I remembered, too late, the pending debacle from Peg Zanto's August hearing, when the daft old judge declared me incompetent as a lawyer. We hadn't heard any more in the last five months.

Something smelled.

The Courthouse Cowboys, ever vigilant to rid their county of my pesky person, had a plan. The staff knew it, Peg Zanto knew it, the daft old judge who'd presided at her hearing knew it, but the Defalcos, as usual, walked in the dark. Worse, nary a single courthouse rat emerged to enlighten us about any cabal.

"Well, screw 'em." I dropped my file on Stormy's desk, my random comment startling her from her typing.

"What? Don't tell me they refused to grant the trial continuance?" Stormy still wore a kerchief to hide the hair loss from chemotherapy, but her eyes shone a bit brighter every day that passed from her July cancer surgery.

I stretched my back. "Oh, they granted it. We have until April to prepare the new defense." Blinking back sleep, I yawned. "But something's up with Winston and his cronies. Maybe more bad press, maybe more accusations of bad lawyering--"

Stormy frowned. "Or maybe a referral to the State Bar for investigation and disbarment, based on the kangaroo court in Peg Zanto's case."

Oh. My. Lord.

My bowel tightened along with the muscles surrounding my heart. Acid roiled my gut. I grabbed for the nearest chair and sat, dizzy at the thought of losing my license to practice law. I'd spent *years* in college, grad school, law school, and trial as a prosecutor and defense attorney. Ditto for Jack.

If the Montana Supreme Court forbade us to practice law, the California Supreme Court would follow suit. We'd be left without our chosen profession, or the means to provide income for our family, unless I returned to bartending or driving a truck. I'd let those occupations fade years before and had no interest in renewing my skills.

Jack popped out from his office. "Did you win a continuance?" Seeing my pallor he kneeled in front of me. "Jesus, Paige, you look like shit. Are you sick?"

To my great annoyance, I let the tears flow. "Those assholes are trying to disbar us, Jack. I know it. Winston and McShane, the public defenders, they're using Peg Zanto to go after our licenses to practice law."

Wadding up tissue grabbed from our reception area dispenser - we seemed to have an excess of weeping clients - I wiped at the mascara running down my cheeks.

Jack, rarely sympathetic to female displays of emotion, laughed. "Oh yeah? Let 'em try. We're the most experienced lawyers in this valley, and we've won nearly every case we've tried. If you think I'll let those fuckers take us down, you're out of your mind." He dismissed the idea with a clap of his hands. "Let's eat lunch."

Jack the Warrior: Simple, concise, egotistical, irreverent, and hungry, all wrapped up as my spouse. Well, I had to believe in someone. It might as well be the guy I'd slept with for the last 20 years. Besides, I couldn't control Winston and his boys, anymore than I could dictate the outcome for Ben at trial.

What I *could* do was find a damned KS expert.

* * *

One Month Later -February 9, 2001

"Incredible! Both of these KS experts agreed to testify for free, Jack." I looked at the message I'd just received from Sara Berg. "Dr. Lomax is the leading expert in the world on KS behavioral characteristics in young boys. Dr. Purvis is the leading expert in the world on the neuropsychology of KS men's brains!"

I glanced up at Jack's grim expression. "What? Look I know a mental defense is tough, but it's all I've got. Between Sara and these two experts, I think I have a shot at an acquittal." I expected him to agree with me, but instead he sat across my desk from me, tapping his fingers.

Silence followed, interrupted by the sound of Jack clearing his throat.

"Paige," Jack looked at the ceiling and exhaled.

"You were right about McShane and the public defenders going after our licenses to practice. Today that daft old judge signed an order dismissing Peg Zanto's case, based on our ineffective representation. His opinion will hit the press in the next day or two, and it sets the stage for a full blown investigation."

I dropped my pen, sat back in my desk chair, and swiveled away from Jack's words. "It's the *timing*. I get a break in Ben's trial, a chance at a real defense and acquittal, and suddenly, after five months, that goofball comes down with this decision."

Jack nodded. "It's only going to get worse. They'll file a formal complaint within a month, and then we'll have to defend ourselves before the State Commission on Practice and the Montana Supreme Court." He jumped to his feet, threw up his hands, and clenched out, "Fuck!"

Survival mode kicked in as my emotions flattened into numb. "We need a lawyer, Jack. Someone like us, who isn't afraid to stand up to the good old boys in this state. A lawyer I trust, and one who has trial experience."

Jack's raised eyebrows showed his doubt that such an attorney existed in Montana. "And that would be?"

I reached for the phone. "Craig Fortney, a former public defender from Bozeman. He's got a small private practice down there, and he's tough. If anyone can defend us in court, it's Craig."

After 20 years of marriage, I knew Jack's next thought flew to the cost of our defense, as compared to our meager budget and savings. As I dialed I added, "Honeybun, we have no choice. Whatever it costs, if we lose this, we're done practicing law - *in two states*. We lose our house, our cars, our savings, the kids' college money, everything."

I left a message for Craig as Jack paced, then I stood to follow him downstairs. Uncharacteristically, I initiated the pep talk. "Look, Jack, it's no coincidence that I'm jammed preparing for Ben's trial, and you're swamped with your own cases, so that neither of us has time to represent ourselves in this. As it is, between the kids, the death penalty case in California, that new murder case in Glasgow I accepted, Chad's case, and . . . *life,* we're drowning. They know it, and they'll use it to bury us. But only if we let them. And as you always tell me, screw 'em. We won't let these bastards win."

Jack trailed behind me to Stormy's desk but said nothing.

Stormy kept typing to avoid looking at us, but announced quietly, "The word is out, guys. The Courthouse Cowboys want you two *gone.*" Stormy, a native Montanan and long-time legal secretary in the valley, always had the inside scoop on legal happenings.

Jack and I exchanged sighs. We'd just celebrated our daughter's 17th birthday three days earlier, and our son's 12th birthday arrived the following day. I had many mom tasks to prepare for his party. I also had to call my father to let him know we planned to spend spring break in Arizona, and that we hoped to introduce him to his grandson. Not wanting to fight, I hadn't mentioned that vacation plan to Jack yet.

"Hey," I sought a perky tone. "Maybe this all goes away now that the judge has blasted us in his opinion. Maybe McShane and Peg Zanto's lawyers will give up and not pursue an investigation."

Stormy snorted. "What bubble do you live in?"

I grabbed my keys and heavy coat. "Well, it could happen. In any event, I've got stuff to do for tomorrow's party, plus I need to interview some witnesses in Ben's case. I'll see you two later."

Sitting in the Tahoe, awaiting a blast of heat, I slumped in the leather seat. To no one in particular I shouted out, "Crap!" as I thought, *Really? How much more complicated can my life get?*

CHAPTER THIRTY-TWO

To the Pink Planet and Beyond

February 2001
Beartooth, Seattle, San Francisco

"HI, DAD?" I TWISTED THE PHONE CORD around my middle finger as I stared out the window of our bedroom, aware that my next words would once again re-cement contact with my father. "Hey . . . uh . . . we're all going to be in Scottsdale next month, and your grandson wants to meet you."

There. I'd done it. As a sacrifice to my only son, a kid who nagged me to *death* about meeting his grandfather, I'd swallowed my residual anger at the abuse I'd suffered at this man's hands.

"Really, Paige Ann?" My father sounded pleased by the announced visit. "Well, I'd like to meet my grandson. Only problem is I won't be here. President Bush is sending me to the Pink Planet because I know so much secret information about Al Qaida." He sighed into the phone with obvious regret.

I gave a little headshake and pulled the receiver a few inches from my ear, staring at it as though it could translate my father's words. In Dad's 93 years on earth, he'd toughed his way through poverty, two World Wars, the Great Depression, the United States Navy, 32 years of marriage to my depressed mother, 20 years of marriage to my nutsy step-mother, three kids, eight years keeping vigil for my oldest brother's return from a Vietnamese prison camp, unemployment, and a host of volunteer activities. Never once had he faltered or shown either physical or mental vulnerability.

He failed as my father, yes, but as a citizen, patriot, and spouse, he'd excelled.

"The Pink Planet, Dad? What do you mean?" As if President Bush sending my father *anywhere* made sense.

"The Pink Planet!" Dad's exasperation at my ignorance fired over the line. "Mars! What other pink planet is there, for crissakes?"

Of course, you're going to Mars. It all makes sense now.

"Okay." I coughed to buy a second of logic, but failed. "Listen, Dad, one of the kids is trying to call, so I'll get back to you in an hour or so, alright?"

As we hung up, I reached for my brothers' phone numbers. Apparently good old Dad had lost his marbles somewhere, and that fact required legal intervention. Yet which of the three of us had the guts to tell our father he was demented?

My oldest brother answered my call first. "Well, if it isn't my ever-loving baby sister." His voice sounded tinny, so I figured he spoke from London instead of San Diego. After a heroic 20-year career as a Navy fighter pilot, my brother now flew a private jet for a Saudi Arabian prince.

"Hey, Danny." I paused, unsure how to explain the situation. "Have you talked to Dad lately?"

A delay and then, "You mean about his losing the house for not paying his mortgage?"

I had to think about that news for a second. "What mortgage? I thought Dad paid his house off years ago."

Silence, followed by, "He did, but he refinanced it to pay off the wife's gambling and credit card debts. She just ran up more, so finally he quit paying any of his bills. He won't even open his mail anymore."

I closed my eyes. "Is the bank foreclosing anytime soon?"

My brother sighed. "Yes, as a matter of fact. They've sent Dad notices. Dad told me not to worry because any day now he's going to inherit seven million dollars from a deal his own dead father made back in 1906."

Uh oh. A little worse than I thought.

"Yeah, well, first he's heading to Mars on presidential orders, due to his vast knowledge about terrorists." I waited for Danny's wisdom.

My brother, always the officer and gentleman, groaned. "What can we do legally? I'm stuck in London for several weeks."

My selfish thoughts went to our upcoming family vacation and my intense work schedule. "Can't you tell the prince it's an emergency and come home? I'm pretty jammed, and Dad doesn't trust me anyway. Heck, we've only been on speaking terms for a few months."

Danny, the oldest sibling, the one with the money in the family, hesitated. "I'll take care of it. Can you help out when we get to Arizona? I can meet you there, and hire a lawyer to handle this."

Imagining Jack's reaction to spending one minute assisting my father, I rubbed the back of my neck. *Say no. Let Danny handle it. In fact, don't go to Arizona.*

"Paige, are you with me on this?"

I opened my eyes. "Yep. I'm with you."

Evidently, in answer to my question from the day before, my life could get *much* more complicated.

* * *

February 25, 2001

"Whoa. Back up. You just spent three days in Glasgow on the new homicide, a day in Bozeman for the federal defenders, you're about to leave for another week in California for your death row case, and now you're telling me we're spending spring break with your *asshole* of a father?" Jack's eyebrows seemed to stretch to his hairline as his voice rose to a near-shrieking pitch.

We stood nose to nose in the garage, the wind howling around us, as the kids, unable to hear us from their seats inside the Tahoe, waited for a ride to school.

"I'm *busy,* Jack, and besides, you're the one who hired me out on that new murder case on the other side of the state. Talk about stuck in the middle of nowhere. Not to mention the ride to Glasgow on that pitiful excuse for an airline." I jingled my keys as I huffed icy air.

Jack drilled me with his blue eyes. "Don't change the subject. We are *not* spending our precious few days of vacation with your father. I don't care how daft he is." With that proclamation he returned to the house, while I jumped in the car to chauffeur the kids.

I'd arranged for Ben and Pete Stagg to fly to California the following day so Dr. Purvis could test Ben to determine his degree of brain impairment from the KS. Ben had never flown on a plane or viewed the ocean, so his excitement spilled over at our last meeting. I refused to consider the possibility that Dr. Purvis' test results might indicate a very slight impairment, undermining my entire defense at trial.

Dr. Purvis assured me that Ben couldn't exaggerate his disability, even if he were clever enough to try, because her tests had built-in questions designed to detect 'malingering,' to wit, faking. She promised to call with her initial impressions before writing her report. From a legal standpoint, however, if Ben Stagg's mental disability didn't mimic Forrest Gump, instead of Albert Einstein, he'd board an express train back to Deer Lodge.

During the following days at the office, Jack and I

avoided one another, separated by far more than our vacation plans. At home we conversed about kid events and little else. Yet a common enemy often heals such riffs, and our marriage brooked no exception to that rule.

Three days after Ben flew to California, Jack stopped me near the office coffee pot. "Paige," he poured himself a cup of muddy brew, "two days ago, Peg Zanto and her lawyer signed the complaint against us with the Commission on Practice."

I set my cup on the counter. My silence allowed him to impart more news. "And yesterday Peg pled guilty to a sweetheart deal, I'm sure in exchange for cooperating with the good old boys' attempt to disbar us."

"Well," I faltered as my thoughts skidded to my pending trip to California's death row the next morning, "maybe the Commission will dump it without actually initiating a formal investigation."

Jack grimaced. "Yeah. And maybe an earthquake will level the Kootenai County courthouse." He hugged me. "Get real, Sweet Pea. We've got a major fight on our hands."

* * *

As it turned out, the next day a major earthquake missed the Kootenai County courthouse, but struck at the Seattle Airport as I waited in Terminal Seven for my connecting flight to Fairfax, California. As the building shook, the lights fell from the ceiling, while the sprinkler system doused those of us scrambling for cover. Being a veteran earthquake survivor, I grabbed the stuffed bison I held as a gift for a kid I knew, and clambered under the row of plastic seats I'd just vacated. The shaking lasted several seconds as passengers screamed and employees panicked.

Perfect. Talk about crummy earthquake Karma.

I huddled with the stuffed toy, amazed that I'd moved 2,000 miles from earthquake country, only to find myself trapped in what turned out to be the biggest earthquake in Seattle's history. According to reports, if the movement had worked to the earth's surface, instead of quaking seven miles underneath, it would have flattened the Emerald City.

After failing to escape Seattle, since the authorities grounded all aircraft, I rented the only motel room left in the vicinity, a half-hour-a-stay dive offering stained sheets that smelled of old aftershave and sweat. Still, despite my fear of infection from microscopic bugs, I thanked God I'd survived and had a roof over my head. A meal at the local Denny's perked me up the next morning before I secured another flight.

After landing, I lucked into a rental car, mourned my lost luggage that an attendant suggested might be in Atlanta, and drove north to interview folks on my death penalty case. The prosecutor handling the case, a former colleague and friend from the D.A.'s office, promised me dinner and a look through his file. The stuffed bison sat next to me, awaiting a cuddle from the prosecutor's son.

Once checked in at the local Holiday Inn, considered royal digs in Redding, California, I called my buddy to arrange dinner. His wife, sounding embarrassed, informed me that her spouse not only backed out of dinner, but due to politics, also refused to meet with me - ever. Angry and just a little hurt, I informed her the bison would be waiting at the hotel's check-in desk until she picked it up for their child and hung up on her.

Lying in the bed, exhausted, a latent terror of death-by-burial-under-debris rising up my throat, I resorted to my usual crutch. I called Jack and cried.

Ever loyal, Jack supported my anger about the prosecutor's defection. "What a jerk, Paige. And to think we drove all the way to Pebble Beach for his wedding." He spoke to one of the kids about homework. "You still there?"

I sniveled. "Yeah, I'm here. It's too soon for me to interview the local police in this case, so I'm going back to the Bay Area tomorrow to meet with the client at San Quentin. I'm staying at Tina's to puppy-sit while they're away for the weekend, so at least I won't have to pay for a hotel. The weather is the pits, by the way."

Over the line, I heard Jack yell at the dogs as they consumed some forbidden object. "We miss you, Paige. Stay safe. That was kind of a close call there in Seattle." With that understatement of the year, Jack rang off, leaving me to wallow in self-pity as I watched *I Love Lucy* re-runs.

I spent the rest of the trip either at San Quentin sitting in a plexi-glass box across from my client, or cleaning up mounds of puppy poop. My friend forgot to mention the puppies took worm medicine just before I arrived, so diarrhea abounded. I decided death row offered far greater appeal than the puppies.

I flew home during a March blizzard, hugged Jack and the kids, made some tea, and sat in front of the sizzling fire. "So, anything new at the office?"

Jack sipped his martini and then leveled me with a *sorry to blow your Zen moment* look. "The Commission sent us a letter today advising us they've opened an investigation based on Peg Zanto's complaint. We have ten days to comply with their first demands."

My thoughts raced ahead to our upcoming vacation. "Jack, in four days we're driving to Phoenix." I'd prevailed in that arrangement, but only because I suggested to Jack that he stay in Arizona after the visit with my dad to attend major league baseball's Spring Training. Between baseball and my demented father, or no baseball at all, Jack had capitulated.

He held up his hand. "I already wrote to them for more time, because of the trip and because we need to hire a lawyer. I also talked to Craig Fortney, and he said he'll represent us." Jack's voice echoed calm, but the gulp of gin he swallowed belied his outer ease.

At moments like this, I wished I still drank or smoked.

What I suspected, but couldn't prove, was that the Courthouse Cowboys planned the investigation to coincide with Ben Stagg's trial and my preparation for his case. Jack could handle much of the paperwork while I prepared, but he had his own trial beginning just days before Ben's.

I faced the flames in front of me with new resolve. If they wanted to play dirty, I'd sling back the mud with full force. While they might take us out, they sure as hell would know they'd been in a fight.

CHAPTER THIRTY-THREE

Life Really Is Like a Box of Chocolates

March 2001
Arizona and Montana

AS WE DROVE UP TO THE DOOR OF THE PHOENICIAN RESORT in a wealthy section of Scottsdale, we resembled the Beverly Hillbillies. The Tahoe, packed to the rafters with road trip provisions and caked with mud, lacked only Granny's rocker on the roof to complete the image.

"Wow, this place is *classy!*" our son enthused. "Uncle Danny must be rich to pay for us to stay here."

Our daughter, in that phase of life when her family caused her constant humiliation, crouched lower in the back seat. "Mom, aren't you just a *little* embarrassed? Everyone here drives expensive, *clean* cars. And look at that girl's designer jeans. Oh my God, I'm never leaving our room!"

Jack returned from checking us in, trailed by a uniformed guy with a big cart.

"What goes up to the room, Sir?"

Jack gave me a look that said we couldn't even afford the required tips at this place. "All of it, including the food."

Danny had accumulated resort points from his job flying the private jet for the prince. With those points, he'd booked us a week's stay at this exceptional hotel. Despite the notion that this was my vacation, however, I would spend little time enjoying the amenities. Instead, I needed to take the lead dealing with the attorney Danny had hired to litigate a conservatorship for our addled father.

Danny and I approached the legal maneuver with all stealth, since we knew our dad would fight to maintain control over his remaining money and health decisions. For that matter, so would his wife, our very disturbed stepmother.

Our parents had been married for 32 years when our mom died of cancer. At the time, Danny rotted in prison camp, so was unaware of Mom's death until he returned stateside many years later. After Mom's death, Dad busied himself with his ham radio operator's group, the Masonic Lodge, and various other organizations to which he belonged.

Then one day he moved a much younger woman into the house. She seemed nice enough, just not very bright. After he married her, however, he discovered she was certifiably mentally ill and likely should have been institutionalized. But Dad, ever loyal, remained in the marriage, although their relationship took on the drama of *The War of the Roses.*

In short, from a legal perspective, his wife was no more competent than our father to handle their financial affairs.

I decided to introduce Dad to his grandson *before* the shit hit the fan. They got along well. Our son, ever the inquisitive history buff, quizzed his grandfather about his war experiences. To my amazement, my father brought up stories as far back as the sinking of the Titanic, ones his long-term memory never before conjured. I realized that at 93, Dad's ruminations harked back nearly a century, and found myself captivated by his accounts.

Memories of my mother flooded back as I sat in the family room of the house where I'd lived during my high school years. Since Mom's death three decades before, my dad had allowed few changes to her original decorating choices. The same 1967 orange and yellow plastic globe lighted the Formica kitchen table; the aquamarine drapes hung in tatters over the windows. Smoke from thousands of cigarettes dulled the ancient avocado green appliances that matched the moldering wall-to-wall carpet.

Both of my kids went silent on arrival. Claire finally whispered, *"This* is where you grew up?"

But I understood why Dad resisted any changes. My father loved my mother. He'd shown it when he injected her with painkillers during her days immobilized from cancer, and earlier when her head rested on his lap while they watched television. He even colored her hair for her.

But other memories assailed me from every corner, every picture, every stick of furniture, reminders of my father's disgusting crotch grabs, boob rubs, and attempted kisses. He'd only waited three days after my mother died before molesting me. He'd been drunk, of course, wallowing in grief. He'd repeatedly called me 'Audrey' as he groped, his pet name for my mother. At fourteen, steeped in my own grief, I only knew that the last person on earth who could protect me from the bad guys had himself become a monster. I'd allowed my hatred for him to fester for thirty years. Then, just a few months past, that loathing simply flamed out. In an instant, forgiveness, that key Christian concept, replaced enmity.

Somehow, since switching sides of the courtroom, and thanks to my son's insightful comments over the summer, I'd realized that, like every criminal I'd ever prosecuted or defended, Dad the Child Molester, the one who'd betrayed every vestige of my parental trust, didn't square with the war hero, the pilot, the loving spouse, the perpetual community volunteer, or the devout

Presbyterian. Nor did he jibe with the grandfather currently sharing his past with our kids.

Gazing at my children as they listened to this old man named Grandpa, I considered the implications of that epiphany.

No one's life should be defined by a single act or event, regardless of its evil nature, because everyone's heart beats with an amalgam of particular genetics, environment, inherited family, and life events. And like my father, all people fuck up. Every so often, bad guys even recover and make someone's world a slightly better place for having changed.

I'd accepted long ago that I'd never love my father again, but I respected him. More importantly, I knew I'd be there for him when he needed me - or in the present situation, even when he didn't *want* me. I'd be there because Dad ingrained in us his same sense of loyalty, of doing what's right regardless of personal cost, of defending those who couldn't or wouldn't defend themselves.

Hours later, the kids and I left my former home richer for the visit, although I felt like Judas about to betray the Big Guy. Indeed, the rest of my vacation got lost in the Phoenix courthouse, the attorney's office, and in tense meetings with Dad and his court-appointed guardian. Ugly couldn't convey our father's reaction to Danny and me when we told him our plan to handle his affairs.

Family.

No such thing as normal in that word.

* * *

After a week in Scottsdale, during which Danny and I prevailed in our effort to get control of Dad's bank account to save his house, Jack drove to Tucson for

Spring Training while the kids and I headed north for Montana.

The trip home lasted three long days. By the time we approached Whitehall, deer huddled in groups along the corridor. Since I'd already traveled down the kill-the-deer-and-car route, I forced Claire to sit shotgun so she could alert me to critters, while her brother watched a jerry-rigged portable television in the back seat.

Almost to town, Claire shouted the dreaded word, "Deer!"

I screeched to a halt from 65 miles per hour, causing the television cord to rip loose from the TV, which sent the appliance flying like a missile at my son's head. He dodged serious injury by an inch.

"Where?" My heart revved up, waiting for a body thud. "Where's the damned deer?"

"There," Claire pointed about a hundred yards up the road. "See them?"

Patience.

"Claire," I looked at her innocent blue eyes, "next time, when they're a mile away, just tell me. You don't have to yell and scare the crap out of me."

"Well excuse me for doing what you asked." A huff followed her ubiquitous eye roll. "Besides, what happened to not swearing anymore?"

I pressed the accelerator. "I failed."

We made it home and unpacked. Changing into sweats, I noticed a weird rash developing on my torso, little blisters that banded half way around from front to back. Claire happened into the bathroom as I explored the bumps.

"Geez, Mom, that looks like chicken pox."

I turned in front of the mirror. "Yeah, and they itch, but they also hurt, like someone's squeezing my mid-section really hard. I think I'm too old to get chicken pox."

The next day I called the dermatologist who advised me to come in to her office, pronto. I met with Ben Stagg that morning, tried again to get him to make some sense out of the events on the day of the murder, then drove to the doctor's office. She took one look at the blisters and announced, "Shingles." Eschewing all things medical, I paused for her explanation.

"Paige, it's a virus. People who had chicken pox as a kid contract it when their titer levels drop too much to fight off a new attack. It's rare for people under fifty to get it."

I looked at the spreading rash with disgust. "So is there treatment for this? I'm starting trial on the Stagg case in a week. And why do I have them since I'm not that close to fifty?"

"To your first question, yes, there's treatment. I'm going to give you a shot to stop the virus from replicating. That will arrest it where it stands, but it can't eradicate what's already there. The existing rash will have to run its course, which should only take two weeks. In the meantime, I'll give you some heavy-duty painkillers because the pain will get much worse than it is now."

"And the cause?"

She looked up and smiled. "In a word, stress."

I paused buttoning up my blouse. "Stress? I'm not under that much stress."

Her eyes widened, but she tried to maintain her professional poise. "Really? I read the paper. I know *exactly* how much stress you're under from the Stagg case, and everything else going on at the courthouse. On top of that, you've been through a major earthquake, spent a week with an aging and angry parent, and driven alone over 2,000 miles, on your *vacation*. So, yes, you silly woman, you're stressed out. And need I mention that a young man's life rides on your success or failure at trial?"

No, actually, you needn't.

Wearied just listening to her list of triggers, I gave up. "Okay, Okay. I get it. Just give me the shot, and we'll see if it works." At least she didn't know about the effort by the Courthouse Cowboys to disbar me.

I didn't fill the prescription for narcotics because I figured a rash couldn't hurt that much. I'd given birth twice, after all. How much worse can pain get? Besides, I needed to be at the top of my game as I prepared for jury selection and answered innumerable inquiries by the State Bar investigator. Every minute I took to respond to Peg Zanto's allegations produced one less minute I had to prepare Ben's defense.

I grew more convinced that the timing of the State Bar investigation was a little too coincidental. As someone famously noted, "Just because you're paranoid, doesn't mean they aren't after you." Worse, I still hadn't heard from Dr. Purvis about Ben's test results. With the trial beginning just days away, I needed good news, and I needed it last month.

* * *

As luck would have it, the shingles virus nearly outstripped birth pains on a scale of one to ten. I filled the prescription but waited until bed before taking the medication, under the theory that I could sleep off the drug's effects before I left for work.

As I drifted into oblivion, Jack caught my attention. "Hey, did I mention my sister and her three sons are coming to visit next week? So all the kids can spend time together?"

Normally this would be exciting news. I roused myself from the pillow. "Next week is when you and I *both start trial,* Jack. On huge cases, in adjacent courtrooms. How can we do that with company?"

Unperturbed, my darling spouse shrugged. "You

know my sister. There's no stopping her at this point. But you also know she'll cook, clean, and keep all the kids busy while we're in court. Think of it as a blessing in disguise."

Instead, I thought, *drugs*. And I wanted more.

I went through my mail the next morning and found a report from Dr. Purvis that arrived while we were on vacation. Hands trembling like Ben's, I read her results but failed to understand her conclusion. I called out, "Stormy, can you get Kyle Purvis' phone number for me, please?"

Dr. Purvis picked up on the third ring. After we exchanged greetings I cut right to the point. "Kyle, what exactly will you testify to if we fly you up here? I see the test results. I see that Ben's IQ is average, and that there are few tasks he completed without huge problems. On the other hand, there's all this stuff about his frontal lobe and executive functioning that I need translated, so we regular folks can comprehend."

Kyle launched into a detailed account of the tests, their purpose, Ben's results, various parts of his brain that evidenced impairment, and then took a breath. "In short, Ben Stagg is the most severely impaired Klinefelter's patient I've ever tested, and I've tested hundreds of them. Honestly, I don't know how he functions hour to hour, let alone growing up in such violence."

My breathing hitched. This was it, the break I'd been looking for, Ben Stagg's greatest hope at salvation. "Can you opine whether he had the ability to understand what he was doing when Nick screamed at him through those headphones?"

Confidence imbued her answer. "Of course. There isn't a chance in the world, with his level of impairment, he functioned as anything more than a robot. He followed his brother's commands because he simply did not, and does not, have the cognitive ability to understand or question them."

Were trumpets blaring from on high? Doves descending from the clouds?

Nah.

But between Kyle Purvis' test results, Carole Lomax's testimony on the general behavioral characteristics of KS boys, Sara Berg's expertise on the Stagg family's dysfunction and its effect on Ben's mental state, we had a defense. I hung up the phone and made the sign of the cross.

Yes, Ben Stagg, there is a God, and He appears to be on your side.

PART FOUR

CHAPTER THIRTY-FOUR

Nowhere to Go but Up

Late March to early April 2001
Beartooth, Montana

THE RUN UP TO JURY SELECTION JANGLES THE NERVES of most veteran trial lawyers, including those courtroom junkies like me who, as slaves to our addiction, mainline felonies.

With only days to go, Ben's trial loomed larger than most because of the unlikelihood of prevailing on an insanity defense. Ever since 1979, when Dan White gunned down San Francisco Supervisor Harvey Milk and Mayor George Moscone, and then found freedom in the infamous Twinkie Defense, few lawyers pursued diminished capacity to acquit their clients. Despite my experts, and Ben's KS diagnosis, not guilty verdicts on 22 criminal counts posed improbable odds.

Sitting in my office on another dreary April day in Beartooth, I swilled more of the brew Jack passed off as coffee. All afternoon, I'd meticulously labeled file folders for Ben's case. One file per witness, each one containing my outlined questions either for direct or cross examination, everyone filled with whatever documents or exhibits I needed to introduce through that witness' testimony. I color-coded the files to distinguish prosecution, defense, or expert witnesses, and organized the entire trial box in the same order on which I'd relied through a hundred other cases.

Hearing footsteps thudding clumsily up the stairs, I smiled. My son's head popped around the corner. "Hey, Mom! Guess what happened at school today?" While he regaled me with his latest academic drama, he consumed an entire bag of chips and a can of juice.

"Listen, Sean. I've got a proposal for you." I leaned my chair back as he wiped cheesy residue from his fingers onto his jeans. "You know Ben's grandma, Mrs. Gifford?"

My son nodded.

"Well, the other day she told me about a special vision program here in Beartooth that she swears helped Ben's cousin learn to read."

"Really? What do I have to do?" My boy's eyes squinted his skepticism.

I shook my head. "I don't know exactly, except that the doctor has you do stuff that retrains your brain, so whatever's not working gets bypassed and new parts learn how to read. Okay if I give the doctor a call?"

Sean shrugged scrawny 12-year-old shoulders and picked up his backpack. "Sure, Mom. If you think it will help, I'm willing to try it." And off he went in pursuit of friends and Red's curly French fries. I dialed our local ophthalmologist and set up an appointment for him.

In our last meeting, the one in which Millie Gifford refused to testify against her daughter, Laura, she'd mentioned the vision program after I'd commented on my son's inability to read. Young Andy Gifford, she advised, had the same issue a few years before. But after only ten weeks of reading therapy, a light went off, and he could read at grade level. She termed it a miracle.

Not that Andy's new reading gift had helped much after he'd murdered his dad.

"Make the call, Paige," Mrs. Gifford urged. "You never know unless you try."

What if it worked for Sean? If our son could read, I knew that he'd take off in academics, and his self-esteem would skyrocket. Testing showed his IQ was very high, but because of his visual processing disorder, he couldn't read, write well, or judge where letters or numbers fit on a line.

Sighing, I conceded that this was another problem best left to the experts. I'd set the appointment, and that was the best I could do. Even I, the supermom-fixer-of-the-planet, couldn't rewire my own kid's brain. I could, however, strategize questions for prospective jurors to ferret out those with preconceived beliefs on Ben's guilt or innocence.

* * *

Trial - April 2, 2001

"Your Honor, at this time I'd like to renew my motion for a change of venue in this case." I pronounced those words after another potential juror entered the courtroom, cast Ben the evil eye, and proclaimed he couldn't be fair due to a preconceived belief that my client was guilty as charged.

Judge Lambert looked weary after only a few hours of jury selection. "And if this keeps up, I may have to grant that motion, Counsel."

Due to so much pretrial publicity, we'd agreed to interview prospective jurors in a courtroom adjacent to the one in which we would try the case. The bailiff brought in each person alone, sat them before us, and we asked them questions about whether or not they'd formed an opinion as to Ben's innocence.

Almost to the person, they had, and none of those

opinions boded well for the defense.

I scratched at my shingles, swallowed the pain that tightened across my ribs in waves, and sucked on bottled water. I needed narcotics, but knew that I'd end up in a face plant on counsel table if I took any, so I gritted my teeth as the bailiff escorted another citizen into our area.

Enter a wiry little man in his 50s who glared at Ben, sitting slumped in his chair to my right. "I know he's guilty, and I think he should fry," said the ornery used car salesman before we lawyers could ask a question.

The prosecutor, Don Yeager, unperturbed, smiled and addressed the diminutive fellow by name. Kootenai County's sparse population allowed folks contact with one another through a myriad of opportunities, from church to musical groups, hunting organizations to political parties, and local eating establishments to bridge clubs. Yeager, as an elected official, appeared to know everyone in town.

Without further ado, Judge Lambert excused the man and called a recess in the proceedings. He rubbed his finger over the bridge of his nose, no doubt staving off a headache at the thought of moving the entire trial across the state.

During the break, Ben used the restroom before he whispered to me, "Paige, I can't take this. I'm scared near to death, and everybody already hates me here."

"Trust me on this, buddy. If we don't find some jurors soon, Judge Lambert will have to move your case somewhere else, maybe even Bozeman. We'd have a much better chance to get an unbiased jury panel there."

I didn't want to tell him that even with our superb expert witnesses arriving in a few days, his chances of beating 22 counts, including murder, pushed the parameters of reality.

After the break, the next person entered the courtroom and *insisted* she had no bias for or against either side, despite the fact that she knew Ben, had been the one to loan him a telescope over Christmas to watch the stars, and knew and worked for the deceased, Rich Truman.

Yeager and I exchanged looks with the judge.

Seriously? Not even a tiny bit of bias either way?

She didn't make the cut despite her assurances, so we moved on to the next guy who also insisted he did not favor one side over the other. Except that, after I questioned him long enough, he admitted he was best buddies with the cop in another courtroom who presently was getting his ass handed to him by my husband during cross-examination.

"So Mr. Smith, you spoke to your best friend last night, a cop, and he told you my husband was killing him in front of that jury, but you're not biased in favor of law enforcement?"

To the guy's credit, he looked sheepish and agreed that maybe he might favor the prosecution in our case. We dumped him.

Judge Lambert looked up as he shook his head. "Does anyone know why we've had such a change of heart with these folks since we took a break?"

The bailiff jumped in. "Judge, the crew from *NewsTime, CBS* arrived next door to set up their cameras and sound equipment. Local television and news reporters also showed. I think folks *want* to be on this jury now, like in OJ."

The judge nodded. "That would explain it. Well, let's proceed and see where we get."

Several days later, after we plowed through nearly 100 prospective jurors, we watched the court clerk swear in our jury panel.

Showtime.

* * *

I walked into the house after court, greeted five wild kids and my sister-in-law, petted three dogs and two cats - including one dog visiting from California - then threw my briefcase on the kitchen table and collapsed on a chair.

Jack's sister, a nurse, handed me a glass of water and a painkiller. "Drugs," she laughed, "better living through chemicals."

I gratefully accepted the pill, gulped down the entire glass of water, and breathed to the extent I could with the thousand pound gorilla squeezing my mid-section. Jack had been right about his sister's visit counting as a blessing. Before long, she had the kids fed and dinner on the table for the adults, right down to a nice merlot for herself and her brother.

"Tell me again why you quit drinking in '97?" She turned to me and speared a piece of steak.

I sipped my tea. "Because I wanted to set a good example for the kids. In eighth grade, some idiot invited Claire to the freshman kegger - as in *beer* kegger. I decided to quit drinking alcohol until both children move out after high school. Besides, with all the trouble I'm in downtown, if I still drank, I'd probably be in custody for shooting a prosecutor while under the influence."

The siblings laughed. Jack looked at me. "You're right. With all that red hair and your temper, McShane would be toast."

After we cleaned up the dishes and settled the group down with a movie, I walked upstairs to my home office to resume trial preparations. Jack did the same, only he worked at the kitchen table. Midnight passed into early morning before we both called it quits and grabbed a couple of hours of precious sleep.

Trial.

The ultimate rush.

CHAPTER THIRTY-FIVE

On a Wing and a Prayer

April 3, 2001
Kootenai County Courthouse

THAT FIRST DAY AFTER JURY SELECTION, Don Yeager and I orated our opening statements, agreeing on most of the facts and evidence, but disagreeing on their interpretation. Yeager alleged that Ben, by his presence and participation in several burglaries, including the one on the night of the murder, knew he violated the law and therefore, under a theory of accountability to murder, acted as responsibly as his older brother. In other words, he asked the jury to find Ben guilty of deliberate homicide and all other crimes charged.

I laid the road map for Ben's defense, to wit, not guilty of *anything* by reason of mental disease or defect. Nick Stagg, the actual killer and brains behind the crimes, sat in prison for the rest of his life. Ben, due to his severe brain impairment, deserved freedom.

Ben sat beside me, rigid in abject terror, convinced no human would ever believe in his innocence. His khaki slacks, blue shirt, and loafers couldn't disguise his quaking, skeleton-like body. His hairless baby face seemed to grow paler every day.

The medical treatment for young boys diagnosed early in life with KS remained uncomplicated. At the onset of puberty, if the child received regular doses of testosterone, his symptoms often disappeared, save for his infertility. However, in Ben's case, never receiving treatment, none of our experts could predict the effect of beginning testosterone therapy on a severely impaired lad of 21. Nevertheless, all the docs agreed that Ben should try it.

Sitting at counsel table waiting for the prosecutor to call his first witness, I couldn't ignore the fact that burglary victim and state's witness, Dr. Winkelman, had seen Ben's body at puberty and failed to diagnose the KS. This was the same guy who prayed every Saturday with Judge Winston and his cronies at church.

If only the good doctor had been knowledgeable about KS when Laura brought Ben for a diagnosis at age 11, Ben could have received testosterone treatment before the disorder's symptoms grew worse. If Ben had been treated, his thinking would have been clearer, and his frontal lobe not as compromised. With clear thinking and less dependency on others, Ben likely would have refused Nick's criminal commands, and Rich Truman would be alive.

Would anyone besides the defense connect those dots? Did it matter?

I glanced over at my young client. On this first day of testimony, Ben had used the hormone for a little over a month. Miraculously, within weeks, his thinking had cleared to the point where he no longer counted objects into multiples of three or heard every crunch on the carpet. He complained that he couldn't spell anymore, but in reality, his brain was reorganizing itself. Ben's visual processing actually had improved so much, the world he viewed made more sense than it had before treatment.

Still, from my legal perspective, Ben stood a long way from helping me with his defense, or testifying in a coherent manner. I hoped by the time we reached that point in the trial, the amazing testosterone might improve his mental acuity even further.

The prosecutor called his first witness, Nina Truman, Rich's widow. Press, media, and interested citizens packed the courtroom to listen to Mrs. Truman's wrenching testimony. The prosecutor finally turned to me. "Your witness, Counsel."

As a defense attorney, I'd discovered how dicey it was to cross-examine crime victims. All sympathy flowed toward them, while the prosecutor swaggered around the courtroom as the great protector of freedom and justice. We criminal lawyers assumed the role of evildoers trying to get our clients off on a technicality. Since I didn't want to lose the jury at the first witness in the case, I kept my cross brief and polite. Still, Mrs. Truman's narrowed eyes, the pinch of her mouth, and the venom in her tone spewed hatred toward Ben and me.

It made for a rough start on an uphill march to an unknown outcome.

* * *

"Ben, I've told you and your family that the worst part of trial is the first part, where the jury hears only the prosecutor's evidence and witnesses. He'll just heap it on until you'll all want to give up. You can't." I leaned close to Ben at counsel table during a break in the proceedings.

Ben looked down at his trembling hands. "But they have all that evidence they found at Nick's apartment and storage shed. And now they're going to play my confession, for like three hours!"

True enough. First the jury heard testimony from multiple law enforcement officers who testified that on arriving at the scene, after Truman's son-in-law called 911, they considered the death a suicide. They found Truman's body lying face down in the snow in front of a white pickup truck. Blood stained the snow around the corpse, more blood smeared the tow-bar of the pickup, and additional blood seeped from the body itself.

One officer noticed an open window on the lower floor of Dr. Sam Jaffee's secluded summer home. Peering inside, he saw that someone had ransacked the first floor. Below the open window, lying in the snow, lay a hand-painted saw blade, a wooden duck decoy, a stopwatch, and a roll of quarters - loot, he concluded, apparently abandoned by a suspected burglar.

Further investigation provided numerous clues: a footprint frozen in blood in the snow, a crazy pattern of additional footprints of different sizes and treads that spread from the body all the way to a road over a mile away, and tire tracks similar to ones a detective viewed previously at various storage shed thefts around the valley. Yet no evidence pointed to the identity of the actual killers. Based on the different shoe print tracks, however, the cops were confident that two *ambulatory* criminals transected the woods together. Along with all this testimony, Yeager introduced bloody crime scene photos and diagrams of the area.

Next came the dramatic testimony of the forensic pathologist who provided the jury with a bullet-by-bullet explanation of Truman's shooting. The worst fact, of course, was the *kill shot* to Truman's neck with a .357 caliber weapon, just in case the six .22 caliber bullets from the first gun didn't do the trick. That final shot left a gaping three-inch wound, the bullet from which blew through Truman's body into the ground below the snow.

The afternoon trial session sped further downhill as we all watched nearly three hours of Ben's videotaped confession. There sat Ben in the tiny interrogation room, pants wet up to his knees, floppy hat covering his head like Huck Finn, until Detective Kimber told him to remove it. Ben's lopsided smile remained frozen in an unmoving grin, even as he lied to the detective about knowing who committed the murder.

That videotaped confession is what defense attorneys deem *a bad fact*. Prosecutors know it's gold. Ben's statement, taken out of context from his genetic disorder and mental problems, sealed the prosecution's already airtight case, while it dared the jurors to look at Ben and me with anything other than distrust.

We ended the day with the prosecution's introduction of several more scene diagrams. Coming up the next day, however, was a host of additional evidence further implicating the Stagg brothers in the murder, as well as in over 20 burglaries of storage sheds and summer homes around the valley.

Grim.

That little adjective spelled out our chances of acquittal with four quick letters.

* * *

Over the next few days, more experts cemented Ben's connection to the crime scene. A ballistics expert from the crime lab matched the bullets and casings to the two murder weapons. No surprise there, so I didn't cross-examine the guy much. Another expert matched the tire print evidence from the murder scene to Nick's Ford Tempo, the car he drove the night he killed Truman. Those tire prints closely matched tire prints found at the scenes of many of the storage-shed break-ins. Again, no surprise since Nick and Ben had confessed to *everything*.

The jurors watched as detectives explained diagrams of the strange footprint patterns surrounding the area near the victim's body, but that also led out to a main road over a mile away. Small shoes and much larger ones formed these prints after Ben later returned to the body, hobbling around in Nick's tiny boat shoes. Naturally both pairs of shoes appeared for the jury to inspect.

Detective Kimber testified to the bloody footprint left at the scene that matched up to Ben's ACG Nike tennis shoe, the one from which Nick had tried to eliminate Truman's blood. This was the same shoe Kimber had seized when he picked Ben up for questioning.

Detectives displayed the radio and headsets the boys wore to communicate, diagrams and drawings Nick made for a burglary in an office building, and hundreds of items found in Nick's storage unit that comprised the booty from all the prior break-ins. Everything from guns to lawn chairs, electronics and artwork, eventually sat on a table before the jury, piling on Ben's complicity in the crimes.

The cops testified to a series of newspaper clippings Nick kept that chronicled his brief life as a gangster in Kootenai County, Montana, along with a signed letter confessing to Truman's murder. Nick titled the letter, *Regret, Until Next Time,* and signed it 'Zock.' What became known as the 'Zock Letter' contained a detailed description of the exact events leading up to, and through, Truman's execution-style-murder.

The strangest evidence, however, appeared in the form of two carved out books found at Nick's apartment. Nick had hollowed out a rectangle in a copy of *The Warlord* by Malcolm Bosse and placed Rich Truman's driver's license inside, along with a plastic baggie containing the spent shell casings from the scene. Nick kept the license, six brass .22 casings, and one nickel-plated .357 casing as cherished souvenirs of his first kill.

Weirder still, Nick had carved, in exact shape and detail, a space for one of the murder revolvers inside *Strong's Exhaustive Concordance of the Bible,* a tome in which the author coordinated the word of God between various sections of The Good Book.

Perhaps, as Ben averred, Nick actually believed he was the Anti-Christ.

* * *

Over the weekend I met with Ben to explain, once again, the events of the prior week.

"Paige, I didn't kill that man! I didn't kill anyone! How can they charge me with murder?" My young befuddled client, despite the testosterone treatment, clasped his hands so tightly they couldn't tremble. He still failed to grasp the basics of felony murder - not unusual, even for folks whose brains fired on all cylinders.

I leaned toward him across the conference table. "Okay. Listen again. You and Nick were in the middle of committing a felony. You were burglarizing Dr. Jaffee's house. Whenever a guy gets killed during that kind of crime, everybody present is guilty of the murder. It's just a legal way for the prosecutor not to have to prove who actually pulled the trigger, especially in gang situations."

From Ben's furrowed brow, I deduced he remained clueless.

"Ben, I can't seem to explain it so you'll understand. You're just going to have to take my word for it that the state of Montana can convict you of murder. But here's where *our* evidence comes in." I drummed my manicured nails on the table. "Are you with me, buddy? Or are you zoning out?"

He smiled. "I'm with you. I'm much better now about that."

"Good. So the prosecutor has to prove you made decisions about what you did on each of the thefts and break-ins, including the one at the Jaffee house. Our experts will testify that you can't make those kinds of decisions. If the jury agrees, then they'll vote not guilty." How much simpler could I make it, without getting into the specific mental state required to prove criminal culpability?

Ben nodded, but I knew he only wanted to please me by pretending to understand. At least our doctors pounded *that* idiosyncrasy through my thick skull. "But I never killed anybody. I never tried to kill anybody, and I never shot Mr. Truman."

I stood up. "I know that. So does everyone else. But you were *there*, and that's enough for Mrs. Truman to want you to spend the rest of your life in prison. Ben, I'm doing my best not to let that happen, okay? And what you have to do, kiddo, is get on that stand and just tell the truth."

Another nod before he, too, stood to leave for his counseling appointment.

Afterward, I mulled over the coming week's evidence. The prosecution would rest on Monday, which meant I began with witnesses on Tuesday. Dr. Cotter, Megan Stagg, Ben, Dr. Purvis, Dr. Lomax, and Dr. Berg. After that my quiver lay empty of arrows.

I worked the rest of the weekend, returning home for meals and a few hours sleep. My sister-in-law returned to California with her boys and dog in tow. I noted several missives from the State Bar, but avoided reading them. Who needed more bad news?

I checked in with Anne, whose remission from her breast cancer looked permanent. She'd regained all of her lost weight, styled her growth of blonde hair into a bob, returned to work as a physical therapist at the elementary school, and found love with a man she'd met in Bozeman. We promised each other a long overdue visit when I concluded Ben Stagg's case.

I spoke to my brother, Danny, who slowly worked Dad's finances under control, avoiding the foreclosure on Dad's house. My shingles improved, so my evening narcotic consumption ebbed. Our son met with the vision specialist and loved the exercises she gave him to reorganize his synapses. Our daughter leaned on her core friends for support from the crap some kids dished out at her high school - stuff about her parents letting killers and child molesters loose.

Indeed, as if to prove their point, Jack's jury returned a verdict of not guilty on some of the counts against his client, an accused child molester, while they hung on the remaining charges. The prosecution chose not to re-file the case, so Jack's young client walked into freedom. It was a huge win for Jack, and gave all of us hope that Ben's jury might acquit him after they heard from our experts.

Hope.

Ever elusive, it flickered across a broad distance, beyond a hundred more trial hours, past closing arguments, and into the jury room.

To hedge my bets, or maybe out of sheer desperation, I decided to light a candle after Mass.

CHAPTER THIRTY-SIX

The Perfect Storm

April 10, 2001
Kootenai County District Court

ON MY WAY TO COURT EACH MORNING, I listened to James Horner's soundtrack from the movie *A Perfect Storm*. I hadn't seen the film, since I wouldn't watch anything with a sad ending, but the soundtrack stirred in my heart a vision of Ben's acquittal. The music haunted me at all hours, and when I listened to it, I *believed* that somehow the jury would pronounce Ben not guilty of murder.

My certainty lessened when I thought of attaining acquittals on the other 21 criminal charges. I couldn't imagine a jury cutting Ben loose from all those counts, if for no other reason than the heat they'd take from their fellow citizens if they did so.

On the other hand, each juror had promised to listen without bias or influence. At this point, since I'd placed all my trial cookies in one basket, a mental defense, either the jurors believed it or they didn't. Other than presenting each defense witness to them, and making a cogent closing argument, the case had slipped from my hands.

"Mrs. Defalco, you have a physician in the wings?" Judge Lambert peered over his reading glasses at me from the bench.

Tuesday morning, April 10th, 2001 and it was my turn to bat. "I do, Your Honor. The defense calls Dr.

Jason Cotter."

I'd switched to basic black that morning, but I stuck with my mom's lucky pearls. I hoped my funereal color choice didn't convey despair to the jury, even though I knew I had just embarked on a long-shot defense.

"Dr. Cotter, you're a physician here in Aberdeen?" Affirmative. "And Ben Stagg is a patient of yours?" Another yes. "And you diagnosed Ben with Klinefelter's syndrome?" Again, yes.

For the next hour or so, Dr. Cotter testified to the physical symptoms of KS, including fair skin, slight muscuclature, an abnormal distribution of hair on the body, tall height, thin weight, the presence of *pectus excavatum* – which, translated, means a dent in the breast bone - or conversely, breast development. About one in every 500 boys, *worldwide*, is born with KS.

He told the jury that a simple blood test sent to the Mayo Clinic for genetic testing determined that Ben had an extra X chromosome, giving him a genetic pattern of XXY instead of XY, as is typical with males. That extra X chromosome defined the disorder and explained both the physical and mental symptoms that made up the spectrum of KS.

I stood at the podium next to the jury as I checked questions off my legal pad. "Did you also test Ben for his testosterone levels?"

"Yes, I did."

"All right. What is the normal range of testosterone in an average male?"

"A normal male will have a value between 300 to 700 nanograms per deciliter."

I wrote that number on my pad. "And what was Ben's level?"

Dr. Cotter consulted his notes. "204 nanograms per deciliter."

He went on to explain that testosterone is

responsible for the formation of secondary sex characteristics like hair on the face, chest, back, and legs. It also provides increased muscle strength, sex drive, and personality traits such as aggressiveness or assertiveness.

I introduced a picture of Ben and Nick taken a few years earlier, when neither was wearing a shirt. It clearly showed Ben's dent in his chest, along with his thin skeletal frame. "Dr. Cotter, based on your examination of Ben, the results from the Mayo Clinic that he does, in fact, have KS, your research about the disorder, and his low testosterone levels, have you reached an opinion about whether or not Ben had the ability to resist his brother's orders?"

Dr. Cotter faced the jury. "An individual who has a poor self-image, which these individuals commonly do because they're less strong, have trouble competing with their peers, and have a tendency to be submissive and dependent, would have a very difficult time disagreeing with someone he considered an authority figure or someone above him."

"Thank you, Dr. Cotter." I turned back with one last question. "By the way, Doctor, how much are you getting paid for your testimony today?"

He smiled. "Nothing, Mrs. Defalco. I'm here for free."

I returned his smile. "No further questions, Your Honor."

Prosecutor Yeager made no headway in cross-examining Dr. Cotter because there was nothing to attack. A guy either has Kinefelter's syndrome or he doesn't, just like he either has or doesn't have a big toe.

Next witness.

* * *

"Please be seated, Ladies and Gentlemen," Judge

Lambert invited. "We have the entire jury. Counsel, please proceed."

Once again I stood at the podium, my witness file in front of me. "The defense calls Megan Stagg."

Megan, now 17, tiny, brown-haired, her vivid blue Stagg eyes clear, approached the witness stand with more courage than most cops I'd seen testify. The clerk swore her in, and she seated herself as she smiled at the jury. I glanced behind me at the Truman family maintaining their vigil in the front row, just behind the prosecutor. I hoped to see compassion there for this young girl who risked so much in telling the truth about her family. Yet only bitterness washed their faces. I guess I couldn't blame them.

"Megan, why didn't you come forward earlier to tell the police about the abuse in your family?"

"Well, when my brothers got arrested, we were talking about the abuse that had gone on with my mom, and my dad said we shouldn't tell because it would just make things a lot worse, and I might be taken out of the home, and it would ruin the family even more. And he didn't want that, and he wanted the family to stick together. And so we all agreed that we wouldn't say anything about it."

Here we go.

"Megan, can you describe to the jury what kind of abuse you saw against Ben?"

Megan dumped it all out - the endless smacks from Laura when Ben couldn't answer questions during home-schooling sessions, hitting him, kicking him, grabbing his hair, swinging his head around - every day, sometimes two or three times a day.

"Did she say anything while she was doing this?"

"Yeah, she would call him a lot of names like 'stupid bitch,' and 'idiot,' and like, 'I can't stand you, I can't stand it any longer.'"

I paused for a second as Laura's words came to life. *I can't stand it any longer.* How many women had shouted those words during their lives as moms, wives, sisters, friends, and workers? Didn't they resonate even more from a woman like Laura, mentally ill, alone in the woods with four kids, three who suffered disabilities, and one who had suffered a fate nearly worse than death?

Megan detailed more beatings with belts, hairbrushes, and spoons. She told the jury of the time when Pete hauled young Nick from his wheelchair, laid him face down on a bed, and beat him with a belt until he bled - all because Nick tried to block Laura's blows.

Megan explained that Nick often saved Ben from beatings, but that both she and Ben feared Nick at times. Nick, she said, controlled Ben, even down to the way Ben laughed and walked. She verified that Nick used both Ben and her for target practice, and that he took her along on their early crime escapades. "He made me feel smart. He made everything sound really cool and exciting."

"Did he plan to get rid of Ben?"

"Nick said that 'we will get rid of Ben and we will use you instead.'"

"Are you still afraid of Nick, Megan?" I knew what was coming, but still hated to make her say it.

She looked at the judge. "I'm afraid of him because he's written to me a few times about escaping and wanting me to help him again, and trying to get me back in, control me again. And I'm scared of that because I don't want to be controlled by him again. And I'm scared that if he does ask me for help that - and if I say no - that if he does get out, he will come find me and kill me."

My stomach burned and the remaining shingles squeezed my ribs. "Why do you think Nick would kill you?"

"Because he doesn't have a conscience, I believe. He has threatened before to kill me."

I stopped writing and put my pen at the top of the podium. "When was that?"

"When he told me about the Truman murder, just after it happened."

"Did Nick give you details about the murder?"

Megan nodded. "He was proud, almost bragging about it. He showed me Truman's license, and he had it in his wallet. He said he felt so much power when he killed Truman, and that it was way better than killing any animal, or a deer, and that he'd do it again."

Sobs erupted over my left shoulder from Nina Truman and her family, accompanied by gasps from the audience. Nausea rolled up my throat. I closed my eyes against the emotion flying through the courtroom. Finally I took a breath, and chanced a look at the young girl on the witness stand.

"Megan, did you ever tell?"

Her own tears choked her words. "Nick told me that if I told anybody he'd kill me, but later I told my friend Grace. I told her to be really careful and to not tell anybody."

I closed her witness file. "One last question, Megan. Does anybody else in your family flinch when someone comes near them?"

"Yes, I do, and my sister does."

I turned to the judge. "No further questions, Your Honor."

As I resumed my seat, my own hands trembled, as if jolted by the electric grief emanating from Mrs. Truman.

Before trial, I'd had little time to ponder the bizarre tragedy of Nick Stagg's life. Born with spina bifida, neck fused at age four, paralyzed at 11, physically and verbally abused, brainwashed about a good and gracious, but violent, God, Nick must have realized in his teens that he'd never be the cop, the pilot, or the fireman of his dreams. So he chose to become a sniper, a militiaman, and the Anti-Christ.

On Christmas night, 1997, all those factors coalesced into a perfect storm that snuffed out Rich Truman's life.

CHAPTER THIRTY-SEVEN

Forrest Gump or Albert Einstein

April 11, 2001
Kootenai County District Court

JUDGE LAMBERT NODDED TO THE JURORS. "We are back in session this morning. The defense is continuing. The weather is getting better. We do have the entire jury. Ms. Defalco, further witnesses?"

I stood. "Yes. The defense calls Ben Stagg."

Ben sat on the witness stand, staring at his shaking hands to avoid looking at the lights from the *NewsTime, CBS* cameras and the hordes of people crowding the courtroom. After some preliminary warm-up questions, I hit Ben with his confession.

Trial lawyers strive to elicit the worst facts at the beginning of a witness' testimony, with the hope that, by the end, the jury might overlook the damning conduct. Jurors aren't that dumb, but we who earn our shekels in the courtroom kid ourselves by relying on this strategy.

"Ben, in the first part of your confession, you wouldn't tell Detective Kimber the truth that you were involved. Why was that?"

Looking into his lap he replied, "Well, Nick always said if I ever got picked up that . . . if I ever mentioned his name at all, that he would kill me."

Ben explained that Nick threatened him, especially in the car, where Nick had the music blasting so people listening through bugging devices couldn't hear what he was saying. Ben told the jury about Nick's use of him as a shooting target, how Nick first ordered him to run, but when Ben ran, Nick shot him in the butt with BBs. Nick demanded Ben hold out soda cans so Nick could shoot the can with live rounds from a .22 rifle. Nick also threw knives at Ben, again for practice.

Through it all, of course, my brain-impaired client never considered the consequences if Nick missed. Now aware of how debilitated Ben's thinking was, I took my time on direct examination. His testimony, I expected, would take all day and possibly carry over to the next.

"Ben, did Nick tell you how he'd kill you?"

"He used to talk about how he'd take me up into the wilderness and dump my body up there because the place is so big and there's so many roads that nobody would find me. And he'd put me up there because I was a baby, and I was a threat to him or something."

I asked him why he told Grace Swanson about his knowledge of the murder. Ben explained that Nick told him never to tell a girl anything because they'd tell somebody else. He told Grace because he wanted her to tell someone what he was too terrified to reveal. Besides, he noted, he'd given his life over to Christ the night he talked to Grace, and he wanted to make things all right with God.

I showed Ben the picture of him minus his shirt, flexing his muscles next to a shirtless Nick in his wheelchair. Why did Ben think Nick was bigger and stronger than he was?

"Nick always worked out and he could walk on his hands all over the place - even down to the lake and back, and up and down stairs. He was strong, and I wasn't."

I braced myself for the next set of questions, the ones about the murder. When I'd talked to Ben for the months leading up to trial, he could barely remember that night. I even took him back to Dr. Jaffee's house, walking through the woods with him in an effort to refresh his memory. We viewed the entry gate, the drive up to the house, the spot where Nick parked his Tempo, the place where Truman parked his truck, the window through which Ben entered and left the house, and the site where Rich Truman inhaled his last molecule of oxygen.

We'd hiked the hills, following the footprint patterns to and from the road where Nick picked up Ben after his first return to the crime scene. As we moved through the silent forest, Ben had advised me to look out for wild cats, a warning I brushed off, figuring I could handle a little feline. Then he pointed out a giant paw print from a mountain lion prowling the hills. And I'd left my gun in the car.

I shook off the memory. "Ben, I want to talk about Christmas night 1997, the night of the murder. Why did you go to the Jaffee house?"

"I don't know why I went there, but Nick told me he was sick and tired of me making excuses for not wanting to mess around with him, and he said that he would put me away if I didn't help him out." He continued to look at his hands.

"Was there something on your head?"

"Yeah, he had a headset that he got somewhere that he made me wear every time I went with him, so he could tell me what to do, what to get."

"What kinds of things did he want you to get?"

"Just anything, so I just grabbed anything I thought was neat."

The jury could see what he took from the previously introduced evidence through Detective Kimber. And what Ben stole at the Jaffe house exemplified a short-circuited brain - a wooden duck, a stopwatch, a saw blade sporting a hand-painted picture of Kootenai Lake, and some quarters.

Those items also represented the pittance gained in exchange for Rich Truman's life.

* * *

After a recess, I returned to the podium near the jury and flipped the yellow page of my file. "Ben, what did you do when Nick said someone was coming up the Jaffee driveway?"

"I was scared to death. I got out of the house and just took off running, said I was out of there. And Nick was screaming at me to get back there. And . . . so I came back to the vehicle, and then I started heading off the other way, and I started running different directions. And he yelled at me, 'come back,' so I ran back to him, and he threw a shotgun in my hands, said, 'run in the woods,' and so I just took off running."

The jury followed Ben's narrative, some nodding as they glanced at the diagram of the crazy footprint patterns in the snow surrounding the area.

"Once you were in the woods, did he want you to shoot that shotgun?"

Here it is - the question that opens the door for Ben's first lawyer to testify for the prosecution.

"Yeah, he told me to shoot. I said I couldn't do it. He told me he could just talk his way out of it, if I couldn't handle it. And when Mr. Truman walked down to his vehicle, I hadn't a clue that Nick was really going to shoot him. I saw Nick raise both hands, like he surrendered."

"What did you hear?"

"Well, I thought they were firecrackers. I just . . . I was just running. And then I ran up to the vehicle, and there was Mr. Truman. So I threw my shotgun in the vehicle. I couldn't believe Nick actually shot Mr. Truman."

Ben looked at me but only briefly. "Nick was yelling at me to shoot him. I was yelling at Nick . . . I was saying . . . I was going, Nick, what did you do? And he had another gun, and he gave it to me, and he was ordering me to shoot him. And I couldn't do it, not a chance, and I just set the gun down on the front hood of Mr. Truman's pickup truck."

"So what did Nick do?"

"Well, I thought he was going to shoot me, but he drove up and he shot Mr. Truman. And he was screaming at me to get in the vehicle and to pick up his wallet. I didn't understand except that Nick's wallet was flung everywhere. It was spilled everywhere." Ben inhaled a panicky breath. "So I opened the back door of the vehicle and I . . . there was a gun on the ground, too. I didn't know where that came from, and I just grabbed everything, snow, and I just - because it was spread out everywhere - and just grabbed handfuls of snow and cards and his wallet and I just threw it on the floor of Nick's car."

I wanted to look at the Truman family to see if Ben's honesty mattered to them, but I couldn't force myself to turn around. "Ben, later on did you find out that you had scooped up an envelope?"

"Yeah, Nick told me later that there was money in an envelope that I picked up. He told me there was $390 in there."

I realized Ben once again relied on multiples of three when he didn't know the right answer to a numerical problem.

Fact after labored fact poured from Ben's beleaguered memory. He returned twice to the body, once for Nick's car keys, a second time for the gun he'd left on the hood of Truman's truck. On the first return, Nick dropped Ben off about a mile from the house, forcing him to cross a thinly-iced pond before he arrived back at the crime scene. The ice cracked as he crawled across it on his hands and knees, but he didn't care if he died or not, so he finally got up and ran.

At the body, with Nick screaming at him through the headset, Ben couldn't find the key. He had to move Truman's body to search for it. Meanwhile, Nick ordered him to steal Truman's wallet so Nick could identify whom he'd killed. Confused by Nick's demands, Ben reached into Rich Truman's still-running pickup and turned off the engine.

Finally, with Nick's key and Truman's wallet, Ben ran back to the drop off spot.

I tried to hurry Ben through those facts, yet more needed to come out. "Ben, did your shoes have blood on them?"

"Yeah, on my Nike ACGs."

"When you got back to Nick's condo, how did you feel?"

"I was shaking, trying to throw up. I was crying all over the place. Nick . . . I don't know, he wasn't . . . he wasn't doing nothing, really. He made me clean up his car. I don't remember. He gave me some rags or something, maybe. I didn't get it all because I was shaking and freaking out a lot."

Ben relayed to the riveted jurors that, once inside Nick's condo, Nick put him in the shower because Ben was deeply in shock. Later Nick dressed him and sat him on the couch for the next two hours.

"I wasn't sleeping or nothing, I was shaking a ton and scared to death, and Nick was very pissed off and yelling at me that I had left the gun. And he made me go back again. He told me the cops were going to pick him up in the morning anyway, so he might as well kill me right there. And I said I'd go back."

Ben told the jury that this time Nick drove him to a church parking lot on the highway. Ben wore Nick's smaller boat shoes because Ben's Nikes were bloody, and he didn't want to put them on again. Ben didn't touch Truman's body that time because he found the missing gun on the hood of Truman's truck. He grabbed the weapon and raced into the woods. Ben had to hide behind a stand of trees when he saw Truman's son-in-law drive up Jaffee's drive. He waited for the man's truck to pass by, and then took off running. Most of that time, he wore the headset that allowed Nick to scream orders at him.

* * *

Later that day, after covering some details about the numerous burglaries, I moved on to the topic of Ben's brain to see if he could describe for the jury how he functioned every day.

Regarding how he read: "I have never learned, like, to read. I think most people see letters. I don't really see that way. I just see pictures. Like E and C, unless I really concentrate and look for a difference, I just see two, like, squiggly lines. So it's hard for me to figure out . . . and remember what sound goes with what picture."

I asked about the noises in his head, before they abated with testosterone therapy.

"Well, thank God it ain't like that right now, but it used to be, like, talking to anybody . . . it would be like a thousand TV sets right behind them, and each TV set would be, like, switching to another station. And I'd see the person talking, kind of, and I would hear them, but I'd just keep on switching all over the place."

He explained how he used to count everything into multiples of three, that he couldn't stop himself, but with testosterone treatment, he no longer counted.

I asked him what happened when people yelled at him or spoke quickly.

"Well, I just try to zone out. I . . . my mom used to yell at me. I'd just zone out and just try to do what she says. A lot of times, it's like talking, I don't have a clue what people say if they say it quickly, especially in the courtroom and all."

He confirmed his sister's account of his mother's constant abuse, including a hairbrush blast to the face that left indented blood patterns from the prickly bristles that penetrated his skin. He described self-mutilation by chewing his fingers and picking his gums until they bled. He explained he flinched because he was so used to ducking away from his mother's slaps.

He described how, shortly before the murder, he finally told his dad to just ground him instead of beating him with a belt like a child. Pete agreed and took Ben's kayak instead, the one source of peaceful pleasure in Ben's otherwise torturous existence.

Before that, Ben explained, Pete sometimes beat him with the belt because Ben couldn't wake up in the morning. Ben's single effort to call the police for help ended with his father's threat that, "at least he [Pete] and his wife cared for me and if I ever did that, told someone, they'd come back and kill me some day or another."

Lovely, I thought, standing at the podium. Ben referred to his mother as his father's wife and lived with the notion they'd kill him if he told the authorities about their abuse.

I had one more area to cover: Ben's suicide attempts. "Ben, a couple of days before you were arrested, did you do something to yourself with a gun?"

He nodded as he stared into his lap. "Well, it was like a week and a half or maybe two weeks before, I don't know, I just . . . I was . . . I couldn't live with myself and everything because there was too much pressure from Nick, and then I just knew I couldn't live with myself at all. It was killing me. So I put a gun in my mouth. I found out later it was called Russian Roulette, or something like that, and you just put a bullet in the gun and spin the chamber and just put it in your mouth, pull it. And I did that twice, and then I waited a couple more days, then I tried it again, and of course I was still alive, so I thought I was supposed to be alive."

I turned to the judge. "My last question, Your Honor. Ben, you said it was your decision not to have your family present in court for your trial. Why is that?"

Ben looked up. "Because it would just add so much more pressure to me. I don't . . . I don't want any more of that stuff."

I closed Ben's file and returned to counsel table. "That's all I have for now."

Judge Lambert spoke to Don Yeager. "Do you have some questions for this witness?"

"Yes."

And with that simple affirmation, the lawyer for the State of Montana spent the next four hours trying to prove Ben Stagg more resembled a genius Hannibal Lector than a brain impaired kid. After Yeager's lengthy and convoluted cross-examination, the jurors looked as dazed as the rest of us felt.

Still, Judge Lambert pressed on. "Redirect, Ms. Defalco?"

I nodded a 'yes' and moved to the podium with pages of notes. "Ben, are you totally confused right now?"

"Not totally, but pretty much."

"Are you okay to answer some more questions?"

"As long as they're not as confusing as what the prosecutor was talking about."

The jurors smiled, Judge Lambert maintained his neutral game face, and I nearly laughed. The gist of Ben's repeated responses to Don Yeager was, "I just did what

Nick was telling me to do. I just never questioned his authority." He reiterated that he feared Nick, and believed Nick would kill him if he didn't cooperate. I cleaned up a few details, or tried to, since Ben barely functioned after a full day testifying.

Near the end of the day I closed. "Ben, why didn't you tell the police what happened, instead of your friend Grace?"

"I don't know. I . . . I was really stuck in a bind, and I . . . I see maybe . . . I mean I was hoping, kinda, Grace would tell, but I was also scared to death if she did 'cause I didn't know how my life would turn out, or if my life was gonna be at all. Although I hate myself, I still kinda want to live in some ways--"

The prosecutor objected. "Your Honor, this is non-responsive."

I looked over my shoulder at him and then at the jury. Non-responsive meant Ben didn't answer the question that I asked. Wasn't that the whole point of my case? Ben *couldn't* answer correctly because his synapses failed to fire on all cylinders. He did the best he could, but usually only answered the last part of any question he heard.

The experts planned to explain that to the jury the next day. Staring into the thirteen weary faces of our jurors, I wondered if they would understand. And if they understood, would they agree with Ben that he just did whatever Nick told him?

CHAPTER THIRTY-EIGHT

Klinefelter's Syndrome Unraveled

April 12, 2001
Kootenai County District Court

"GOOD MORNING, LADIES AND GENTLEMEN OF THE JURY. Good morning, Counsel." Judge Lambert smiled. "Ms. Defalco, please call your next witness."

"The defense calls Dr. Kyle Purvis."

Onto the witness stand floated a petite beauty, a halo of blonde curls framing a face dominated by huge blue eyes. She wore a fitted, animal-print dress, black stockings, and black heels. She looked like anyone other than the world's leading neuropsychological expert on the effects of Klinefelter's syndrome on the brains of adult men. After she explained to the jury, in a lilting tone, her background, training, and experience, Dr. Purvis underscored the physical symptoms of KS described earlier by Dr. Cotter.

She characterized the cognitive traits of KS men into three subtypes. "We found men who, as adults, continue to have problems in language, another group of KS men who have very normal language skills, but have problems in what we call visual-spatial skills, being able to put things together with their hands. Then there is a third group who show mixed pattern, and they really have some problems in both areas."

I asked her about commonalities between all three groups.

"Across all three groups, they tend to have problems in what we call executive problem solving skills, which means they have difficulty planning, organizing, thinking through the consequences of their behaviors. They have trouble thinking of different solutions to problems and coming up with the best solution. They have trouble stopping inappropriate behavior. They have trouble controlling their emotions, and the incidents of learning disabilities in children with Klinefelter's syndrome is virtually 100 percent."

I paused to let that fact sink in to the jurors. "Dr. Purvis, about a month or so ago, you tested Ben Stagg, who is sitting to my left, correct?"

"Correct."

"Based on your test results, can you tell the jury what you learned about Ben?"

"Ben's full scale IQ score was 89, which corresponds to the 23rd percentile, or low average range. He has language problems, so his reading was at the 8th percentile and his spelling was at the 5th percentile. That means 92 out of 100 people his age read better than Ben, and 95 out of 100 people his age spell better than Ben."

"How about his word retrieval skills?"

Dr. Purvis looked at the jury. "On that test he did particularly poorly, scoring below the first percentile. He has trouble thinking of precise words, precise names of things in his conversation. His mental speed is below the first percentile, so he was much slower than other individuals of his same age in very simple tasks."

"Now, what is . . . you talked about executive functioning. And where in the brain is executive functioning controlled?"

Dr. Purvis explained to the jury that executive skills, or problem solving skills, were tied to the front portion of the brain in the area know as the frontal lobe. In KS men, there was a range in which frontal lobe damage occurred, and Ben's scores fell very much within the lower end of that range. As a result, Ben had trouble stopping certain kinds of behavior not appropriate to a given situation. People like Ben couldn't get organized, and they needed to have other people structure their lives. They sat inertly, unable to come up with things to do.

"Dr. Purvis, did you give Ben any tests to determine if he was faking, or malingering, as you doctors phrase it?"

"Yes. It's very important to make sure a client is doing his best on these tests. So I actually gave him two tests that measure whether or not someone is doing his best, and I invented these tests that now are used by many other neuropsychologists. And Ben passed both of those tests."

The jurors hadn't taken their eyes from Kyle Purvis. All sat glued to the witness as she testified. Although much of her testimony involved highly technical scientific data, Dr. Purvis managed to put it into language the jury could understand.

"Dr. Purvis, among all the KS men you've observed, have you found anyone who functioned at a level lower than Ben Stagg?"

She paused before answering. "Well, I tested some men who have lower IQ scores than Ben, but in terms of these executive problem-solving test scores, I, at this moment, do not recall any scores lower than his."

Perfect. Forrest Gump, not Albert Einstein.

"Any other observations you think might help this jury understand how Ben Stagg's brain functions?"

Dr. Purvis explained that Ben couldn't answer complicated questions because he couldn't keep track of multiple things at once. Thus, he likely couldn't recall the beginning of a question by the time the end of the question was stated. Therefore, Ben answered based on the end of a question rather than the whole of it.

"How is it that a person can have an average to low average IQ, yet be as dysfunctional as Ben appears to be?"

"Most patients with frontal lobe damage actually have normal intelligence. The real problem with intelligence tests is that they don't measure frontal lobe skills. So you can do fine on an IQ test, but still have very extensive frontal lobe dysfunction. What it means is that your intelligence is normal, but you cannot harness that intelligence in a productive manner. It's almost like you have a great engine in your car, but no transmission. You cannot put your intellect into gear if you don't have a functioning frontal lobe."

As I'd come to know Ben Stagg over the last two years, I thought of him like my old 1960, lemon yellow VW bus. Reliable, simple, cute in its own way, but with a lousy transmission that forced me to spend a lot of hard-earned cash on repairs.

Except no one had enough cash to fix Ben's broken brain.

* * *

After the prosecutor's brief cross-examination and a short break, I called my next witness. "The defense calls Dr. Carol Lomax."

Raising her right hand, a woman with long, curly brown hair framing a fair-complected, brown-eyed face took the stand. Dr. Lomax hailed from Maryland. Both she and Dr. Purvis sat on the Board of Directors for Klinefelter's Syndrome Associates, a national advocacy group formed to educate and assist KS families and the general public about the symptoms and remedies for KS.

Dr. Lomax held a doctorate degree in developmental disabilities and specialized in children with neurogenetic disorders, primarily under the age of twelve. She assessed children from around the world to help their families best utilize various therapies to reorganize the child's brain so that it functioned at its highest potential. In children up to seventeen years old, the brain remained very flexible and amenable to reorganization.

"Dr. Lomax, can you tell the jury what is typical behavior in KS boys under the age of twelve?"

She adjusted the microphone. "KS boys have a fairly characteristic pattern. Newborn babies with KS have very soft muscle tone, so they have trouble if you put them on their bellies, difficulty lifting their heads. They may have difficulty rolling over. They will often sit on time, but, without help, will walk late, more typically at eighteen months, when most children should walk by twelve months, certainly no later than fifteen months. They are often described as quiet, passive babies. Some mothers will use terms like 'so laid back that I didn't know he was in the room for hours.'"

Dr. Lomax reached for a paper water cup and drank. She cleared her throat. "They have speech delay that we've been able to identify as a year's difference between them and their normal counterparts. They are shy kids in the sense they are a little slow, so they get distressed at family functions, and occasionally will get overwhelmed by noisy places. They hide behind their moms a little longer because they're a little hesitant to deal with all the hoopla that goes into social situations."

I interrupted. "What about toddlers and older boys?"

The witness nodded. "By three, a typical KS boy would be talking, but there would be difficulty formulating his thoughts, often pulling up the wrong word. By five these kids, without intervention, will have difficulty in social settings because they understand what is going on conversationally, but it's hard for them to formulate the answers as quickly as their normal developing peers, so they often get in situations that are very stressful, and answer with whatever is perceived as the most appropriate answer."

"Can you give the jury an example?" I checked off items on my notes so I wouldn't repeat questions. The jury listened to the witness as attentively as they had Dr. Purvis.

"You show a KS kid a picture of a sheep and he will say, I know, it's an animal and it lives on a farm. The whole time he's talking, he's really searching for an answer. Normal developing kids will look at the picture and say, it's a sheep and it lives on a farm. KS kids do a lot of hunting, which actually is guessing. Parents think, he's so stubborn, yesterday he knew the word, and now he doesn't. In reality, he may have guessed correctly, or he may have recognized it, but not today."

I let her continue talking since the prosecutor hadn't objected.

"By third grade, these kids are in tremendous difficulty because teachers are very indulgent with first and second graders. We perceive them as little. By third grade, teachers start expecting more mature behavior and say, sit down, read a book. And these KS guys are often falling out of their chairs because they are a little motor-disorganized. They know they can't do it, they're hesitant to ask for help, they have difficulty completing directions that are given verbally, and their short-term memory probably is deficient. They get a piece of what's going on, but not all of it. They often miss a big chunk, so they look non-compliant."

"Doctor, can you explain what *topic maintenance* means?"

She nodded. "Right. When these guys are talking, they fill in with inconsequential information. Stuff coming out of their mouth is not pertinent to what you're talking about. So, maybe you're showing them a picture of a mom and a dad and a kid, and what you want them to say is, 'The mom and dad are playing with their son.' And they say, 'I have a ball at home.' There is a ball in the picture, yeah, but the child really is trying to pull together the question you just asked. And it's very hard for the kids to recognize that they're different because they've been this way their whole life."

"Once they get to middle school, where classes are changing and they need to move from room to room, they really are in great difficulty because now they have to plan ahead, they have to anticipate what is going to happen, and they have to remember it. And when they should be diagnosed at puberty, they often get into the most trouble because of the lack of any kind of testosterone."

I swallowed water from a cup underneath the podium. "How about social participation, Dr. Lomax, and doing what others want instead of what the kid knows is right?"

She nodded. "Sometimes in an effort to participate, they may say the wrong thing. I just had this happen. A seven-year-old gave his Gameboy away on the bus because a fifth grader told him he had to. He couldn't figure out how to say, 'No, it's mine, and you can't have it.' And when I asked why, the seven-year-old said, 'I gave it to him because he told me I had to.' And he was very clear that he thought that was the right thing to do. I don't think that's a rare occurrence. I think that's more common with KS boys, more typical."

"Okay. Now, Doctor, can you explain to the jury about sensory dysfunction?" I knew this would explain Ben's ability to hear the crunch of carpet.

"These kids are more tuned into sound, so they hear sounds that often we couldn't hear. And those sounds are really painful to them. They're hyper-aroused because the sounds are there, and they can't turn them off. They can also be very sensitive to how things feel, so that certain clothing feels too tight, or it's too rough for them."

"You've reported that these kids function much better visually. Can you give an example of that?"

"Yes. Visually they tend to be very good and often enjoy visual stimulation. They tend to be very good at puzzles. Some are very, very good on computers, like Nintendo. Often there is an increased development in that area."

I thought about how Nick told me that Ben could sometimes beat him at chess. "Doctor Lomax, how often does KS occur in male babies worldwide?"

She paused. "Well, about 1 in every 500 male babies is born with KS, so it's quite common, but it's markedly under-diagnosed. I have a large population of pre-natal kids, moms who have had genetic testing, perhaps because they're older when they get pregnant. Diagnosed before birth, many of these patients come from enriched environments, higher socio-economic backgrounds, with optimal health services available. So these kids receive a very different outlook from other KS kids because, from the day they're born, they have been given support to optimize their brain capacity."

I turned a page of my notes. "So a boy with KS who grows up in a very enriched environment with a lot of support and appropriate interventions at school, and who gets testosterone treatment at puberty, what is his prognosis?"

"I think the prognosis is excellent for him to be successful both educationally and intellectually, to go on to hold a variety of jobs, even post-graduate work. They will have learning *differences,* but they don't appear to be *disabilities.* So we'd see children who are accelerated in visual and perceptual areas, but have language difficulties, just not enough that it affects function in the classroom."

I knew it wasn't relevant in Ben's trial, but I wanted to ask Carol Lomax how many women aborted their babies when they learned the boy had KS. She'd told me the night before that *a full 75 percent abort the KS kid.* Yet with proper interventions, these guys could grow into amazing, productive individuals. The only KS-related problem for them would be infertility, so they'd have to adopt if they wanted children. Not a major issue.

"Based on your expertise, Dr. Lomax, what would you expect to see from a KS kid who entered the world and grew up in less optimal conditions - into a family that is dysfunctional, where there is abuse, where the learning environment is home-schooling by a parent who doesn't understand, doesn't know about the Klinefelter's, and so is not a supportive teacher?"

Again she nodded. "They would have less ability to adapt - to their parents, to the abuse, to yelling - and they'd likely withdraw and grow more maladapted. I kind of describe these guys as 'gentle giants' because they're tall, but often very sensitive. They pick up when they do something wrong. These little guys will say early on, 'Did I get it right?' and it's an unusual insight. They're more likely to seek approval and react with shame if they fail. They look to others to give them boundaries for what is right and wrong."

I removed my reading glasses before asking the next question. "You met Ben Stagg last night for about an hour. Can you explain how someone like Nick, who was in a wheelchair, could control Ben?"

Dr. Lomax shifted in her chair. "One of the things that happens with kids who are less competent at making decisions is they seek out someone to structure them. They don't necessarily make good choices, but it's someone who will tell them what to do. And the idea is, it makes everything black and white, and the gray area of what to do is taken away. You just follow directions. And for Ben, that's the role Nick provided. And since they were in an abusive family, it's reasonable that Nick would protect him as well."

"Based on your testimony about auditory sensitivity, Dr. Lomax, what would the effect be on a kid with KS, like Ben, who had to hear everything through a headset?"

She paused to look at the jury. "If it was a highly charged situation, he would, by default, become fairly frantic, and it would be easy for him to miss things that he was told to do, to misunderstand things. But most important, he'd want to get it all done, just to get it over with, so that the yelling won't be coming into his head anymore."

Dr. Lomax explained to the jury some other traits she'd expect to see in boys like Ben. In confrontational situations his ability to manage language would diminish as his anxiety level rose. Zoning out, hand tremors, obsessive tendencies like counting to deal with anxiety, all were common.

She noted that there were no good control studies to address the effects of late testosterone treatment of KS men, as opposed to boys who received early treatment at puberty. However, she opined that self-esteem, in those diagnosed later rather than earlier, was compromised, their learning certainly was more compromised, but their physical traits when receiving testosterone later on actually improved. They often gained inches, weight, and muscle mass.

I took a deep breath. One last question from this witness, and we'd break for the Easter weekend. "Dr. Lomax, would you expect someone with good planning skills to leave a gun behind at the scene of a homicide, or leave footprints running around in all directions?"

"No."

"Okay, thank you, Dr. Lomax. That's all I have for now."

After Don Yeager's minimal cross-examination, the judge allowed the jury to recess for three days, and resume hearing testimony on Monday, when I planned to call Dr. Berg as my last witness.

The jurors filed out of the courtroom, stoic, but not glaring at me either. Maybe one or two of them believed Ben acted only as a robot on Nick's commands and couldn't form the intent needed to prove the crimes.

Maybe.

* * *

I hugged Jack and the kids when I entered from the garage after leaving my trial box in the rear of the Tahoe. I needed a break, if only for the evening.

Jack browned taco meat on the range. "How did it go with the psych witnesses?"

I poured myself some coffee. "Brilliantly. Those two women are amazing. They both have young kids, they're both married, they're both at the top of their fields - in the *world* - and yet they took all this time out of their schedules to fly to Montana and testify for Ben Stagg. For free."

I swallowed decent espresso for a change. "And Dr. Berg flies in on Saturday to do the same thing, again for *free*. The jurors seemed riveted when Doctors Purvis and Lomax spoke, just as they did with Dr. Cotter."

Jack checked the tortillas warming in the oven. "And Dr. Cotter also testified for free. You lucked out, Paige."

I shook my head. "No luck involved. According to Ben, it's God, pure and simple. How else would such a diverse group of experts from all over America come together to fight to save one young kid accused of a murder he didn't commit?"

Jack bellowed for the kids to come down for dinner. "Yeah, well, the miracle will be if they had enough impact on the jury so they cut Ben loose, at least from the homicide."

As the air deflated from my happy bubble, I, like Jack, doubted that would transpire.

CHAPTER THIRTY-NINE

An Easter Vigil

Easter, April 2001
Beartooth, Montana

I'D DITCHED MY ROSARY BEADS after Christmas under the theory that God and I communicated better through direct chats, with me yakking while He listened. Reciting an ancient prayer a million times didn't resonate with me, probably because I'd joined the Catholic faith in my twenties instead of at birth.

The next day, Good Friday, I sat in church and mentally talked at God as others prayed with their beads. Some intoned the Stations of the Cross, all of this part of the three-hour vigil the Church held while awaiting the symbolic hour of Christ's crucifixion. Ever inattentive during church, I wondered how the jurors fared, knowing they'd have to decide Ben's fate the following week. I knew Ben waited at his home, hiding out in his room, as he prepared to return to prison for the rest of his life.

Pete Stagg fasted, shedding pounds he should have kept on his lean frame. Megan stayed with friends, Nick sat in his jail cell at Deer Lodge, the oldest sister took care of her own family, and Laura Stagg sank deeper into her quagmire of despair over the loss of her kids and her reputation. At least her spouse intended to stick by her until death parted them.

I gazed up at the altar at the front of our old parish church. I'd traveled a long road to arrive at this point in my life, and, for better or worse, I'd nearly finished with Ben Stagg's trial. I worshipped God with less cynicism, I realized, but still not with as much reverence as I should. I'd also forgiven my dad along the way, although I couldn't summon any love for him. I tried, instead, to honor him in deed and word.

Staring up at the giant replica of Jesus hanging on his huge cross above the tabernacle, I contemplated the slow melting of the ice that had encased my heart for so many years. That beating organ had thawed since I moved to Montana. Sitting among bad guys, hearing their voices more than their words, meeting their families, had allowed me to breathe again. It lifted the burden of constantly judging others, of separating the world into black and white.

I now lived in a world of gray, in which I could hand over dollars to bedraggled, begging homeless souls, no longer calculating whether they'd use it for booze or drugs. I figured it wasn't my job to speculate, so I could give without strings attached. At least in God's eyes, I concluded, bad guys differed little from good guys as far as their entitlement to forgiveness.

With that epiphany, I glanced around the church. No bells rang, no lightening struck, and no angels chimed in. Without a doubt, over the last four years, maybe because I'd switched sides of the courtroom, I had changed.

In that quiet moment, alone in my ruminations, I finally remembered God.

* * *

Moments later, I noticed movement from the corner of my eye as my beloved joined me in the pew. Jack removed his down jacket and whispered, "Do I get a beer after the crucifixion?"

I shook my head and smiled. Anyone who knew Jack, let alone sat near him at Mass, would have a hard time believing he'd spent seven years in the seminary studying to become a priest. Irreverence permeated his humor both in church and out, yet he was one of the most devoutly faithful people I'd ever met.

I mouthed sideways, "Fish, no booze, and work for me, since Dr. Berg arrives tomorrow."

We kneeled together and crossed ourselves as Jack asked, "Isn't she Jewish? What are we going to do with her on Easter Sunday?"

I glanced at him. "We feed her, just like we would anyone else. You made reservations for Easter brunch, right?"

Jack nodded. "Bet *that* will be a first for the good Doctor Berg."

We entwined our fingers during the Lord's Prayer, kissed each other at the sign of peace, and shook hands with our fellow worshippers.

I paused for a minute. In those sixty seconds, a second truth blasted me.

My soul, the one I'd misplaced along with my reading glasses and car keys, had re-entered my body. No wonder I felt a bit heavier, not from PMS, but from the heft accompanying my renewed spirit.

At my confused headshake, Jack assumed I'd reached his own level of boredom. "C'mon, Paige, let's go," he whispered. "The Stations of the Cross never change. Jesus always dies at the end."

Yikes. Please, Lord, hang on to your lightening bolt.

* * *

Dr. Sara Berg arrived at the local airport in a fur coat that hugged her like a huge beaver. At least she'd stay warm during her visit. We dumped her luggage in her room at a local lodge and then worked at the office to get a jump on her trial testimony. She joined us at our house for one of Jack's homemade meals before turning in for a decent night's sleep at her hotel.

As promised, after Mass on Sunday morning, we picked her up for brunch at a golf course where Jack had reserved a table. Both kids joined us, fascinated by Sara's stories of testifying in a plethora of death penalty cases, murder trials, and juvenile crimes. Sara's sense of humor, combined with her compassion, allowed her to face the world with exuberance. Her dedication to Ben's case nearly matched my own. She, like the other experts who had testified for free, cared about whether this disabled kid spent the rest of his life in custody.

Back at my office we plowed through her myriad of notes to answer my questions at trial the next day. By late afternoon, Sara looked exhausted. By dinner, she appeared as if she would collapse.

I fetched her some tea. "Tell me you're not sick?"

She laid her head on the conference table. "I don't know. Yeah, I'm sick. I'm tired. And I can't do this, Paige. I'm sorry. I can't testify for you tomorrow."

Well, shit.

Her ashen complexion and dull brown eyes made me consider how I could proceed without her testimony. I needed her to tie up the loose ends in the case through facts she'd gleaned from Pete and Laura Stagg, their oldest daughter, and Millie Gifford, none of whom would testify on Ben's behalf.

"Sara, look, I understand how much work you've put in on this case, over 50 hours so far. And I know you're exhausted and the pressure in trial is a killer. But I need you tomorrow. If I thought I could finish without you, I'd put you on a plane back to Ohio tonight."

She raised her head, tears moistening her eyes. "I just don't think I can do it. I feel like I've got the flu, like

I'm going to vomit and faint at the same time. I look at all these notes, but I can't remember anything."

Determined, I grabbed her fur coat and my down jacket. "Okay, here's the plan. It's 6 o'clock. I'm taking you back to the lodge where you're going to eat some soup, drink more tea, take a hot bath, and get into bed. You're not going to think about the Stagg case. You're just going to rest until tomorrow morning when I pick you up for court."

She walked to my Tahoe as if an executioner awaited her.

I started the engine. "Meanwhile, I'm going to redo all my questions for you so I can lead you as much as possible. That way you won't have to search through your notes for the answers. They'll be in the question. Got it?"

She nodded before leaning her head against the passenger window. As I parked in front of the lobby, Sara opened her door. "But what if I'm too sick to go to court? What if I barf on the stand?"

I shrugged. "Listen, as long as you tell the jury the few facts I need them to hear, you can puke all over the courtroom. I don't want to sound cruel, but we've come too far to blow this thing now. You're my last witness, but one of the most important. A little sleep, some chicken soup, you'll be fine." As she closed the door I lowered the window. "And no sad movies! Just watch something mindless!"

After dispensing that sage advice, I returned to the office and spent the next 10 hours re-working my previously painstakingly prepared direct examination of Dr. Berg. I managed to work in about two hours of sleep, a hot shower, and strong coffee before I picked Sara up the next morning for court.

* * *

Sara, once again dressed for the Arctic Circle, struggled onto the passenger seat. "You need a step ladder to get into this thing!"

Eyeing my long legs peeking from under my black skirt, I smiled. "No, *you* need a ladder. I have no problem." I eased out of the parking lot. "So, how do you feel?"

"Better." She adjusted her seat belt. "Nervous, but at least I slept and don't think I'll throw up this morning."

After she raised her right hand for the clerk to swear her in as a witness, I elicited her long list of professional credentials. They impressed the jury, so I let her expound more than necessary to warm her up. *NewsTime*, *CBS* cameras whirred in the courtroom as crowds of citizens packed the seats. Anyone would be nervous, but knowing the stakes if she failed to testify credibly added to Sara's stress.

For the most part, Sara complimented the prior testimony of the other experts. I had her add in a few new facts to explain, for example, why Ben turned off Mr. Truman's truck when he returned the first time to retrieve Nick's car keys and gun. Sara explained that the action resulted from Ben's auditory sensitivity. The noise from the headset overwhelmed him, along with the horror of the murder itself. The running engine from the pickup cast one too many stressors, so Ben reached inside and turned the key. He never considered that he might leave prints or other evidence from which the police might identify him.

I'd decided earlier to use Dr. Sam Jaffee's pop psychology books to explain the effects of abuse on a child. When he'd appeared as a witness for the prosecution, his hostility toward me seethed. He and Rich Truman had been good friends, so his anger made sense.

"Dr. Berg, Dr. Jaffee wrote that families are as sick as their secrets. Do you agree with that?"

"Yes, I do."

I adjusted my reading glasses. "And he also writes that some common symptoms of a dysfunctional family are expecting perfection from the kids, the adults blaming the kids for the adults' mistakes, the parents insisting on total control over the child, and families in which parents do not hear or do not allow the kids to express their feelings and needs. Do you agree that those are common symptoms of dysfunctional families?"

"Yes, I do." Sara squirmed in the witness chair as the lights from the cameras heated the courtroom.

I plowed ahead, ignoring everything but my end game. "Finally, he says that if you add in alcoholism, incest, and physical abuse to these symptoms, you get major dysfunction. Do some of these symptoms apply to the Stagg family?"

"Everyone of those except alcoholism applies to my findings regarding the Stagg family."

Before trial began, Judge Lambert precluded details about incest between Nick Stagg and his siblings, but allowed in the fact of that incest.

Sara explained the relevance to the jury. "When you are involved in an incestous relationship with an older sibling or with parents, that sexual abuse starts the basis of a situation of control. One of the problems with sexual abuse, besides the fact that it's a violation of one's body, and that it's morally wrong, is that it sets the stage where that individual has control over you. It also greatly diminishes the self-esteem of the victim."

I switched subjects. "What effect does physical abuse have on a kid like Ben?"

"Physical abuse creates an issue of control, of learned helplessness. Abused children feel they have no way to get out of their situations. Abuse takes away their feeling that they can have an impact on the world around them, because they are literally beaten down. It causes a great deal of fear and anger, and it causes children to leave the world they're in. They have avoidance techniques, they change, and they start to withdraw."

That made sense to my own inner hermit. "Dr. Berg, do you agree with Dr. Jaffee that because violence is irrational and impulsive, often random and unpredictable, that this random quality sets up what you referred to as learned helplessness? And before you answer, Dr. Jaffee defines that as a kind of mental confusion where the victims can no longer think or plan. They become passively accepting of their abuse. Do you agree?"

"Yes, I do."

"And Lenore Walker, author of *Terrifying Love*, identifies five factors that might indicate someone is suffering from learned helplessness, correct?"

I rolled on before the prosecutor objected to the leading nature of my questions, and the judge sustained his objection. "Those factors are as follows: A person who witnesses battering in the home, a person who suffers sexual abuse or molestation as a child or teen, a critical period in which the person cannot connect what they do with the outcome that occurs, stereotypical traditional roles for family members from which one cannot deviate, and a person with chronic health problems. Did you find that all of these applied to Ben?"

"I did. Ben suffered from learned helplessness."

After Sara corroborated Ben's account of the abuse he suffered at Laura's hands, I asked her about the Stagg family's life in New Jersey, when Pete attended Bible school. "Did the abuse get worse there?"

Dr. Berg shifted the microphone. "Yes, as Ben put it, demons possessed his mother. I concluded that, in

New Jersey, the family became more isolated, and Laura Stagg became more stressed. Not only does she have her own mental health concerns, she was left in New Jersey alone with all of these children, and her husband was going back to Bible school. She was trying to take care of all this alone, trying to home-school Ben, and she became even more physically violent with him."

Emotional abuse, Dr. Berg testified, added to Ben's overall mental health decline. According to Dr. Berg, one of the hallmarks of the Stagg family was that they were emotionally abusive to their children, and especially to Ben. She added that Ben frequently watched Laura hit, pinch, kick, and throw food at Pete, and Laura's abuse of her spouse went on throughout their marriage. Ben also watched as she abused his siblings.

Based on her observations, Dr. Berg diagnosed Ben with PTSD, dissociation, depersonalization, obsessive-compulsive disorder, and multiple learning disabilities. She explained why he counted, flinched, zoned out, avoided loud noises, and obsessed over the number three. She opined that he couldn't think, plan, or figure out the consequences of his acts.

Dr. Berg concluded, "Ben had every strike against him that he could possibly have, in addition to the cycle of abuse. This is a boy who had no way out. He had a father who was being abused and battered himself by his wife, who did not stand up to his wife, so Ben could not go to his father to get out of the situation. He had a mother who does have mental illness, who continually abused and battered him. He had nothing in his life except for a brother, Nick, who on some level was his window to the world. Nick was the only way out, because Nick was intelligent, certainly light years more intelligent than Ben."

At the podium I closed my file. "Thank you, Dr. Berg. That's all I have for now."

Don Yeager, unable to refute Sara's testimony regarding the results of her 50 hours of interviews, instead attacked her phone call to me after the first *NewsTime, CBS* show aired. He accused her of unethical conduct by soliciting a patient. Of course, he ignored the fact that six months after our first phone call, *I* was the one who contacted *her* for advice. During the intervening six months, we had no communication. Sara's testimony lasted the rest of the day.

Afterward, I turned to Judge Lambert. "The defense rests, Your Honor."

Judge Lambert excused the jury until 9 o'clock the next morning, but kept the prosecutor and me until much later reviewing jury instructions. One more witness, the prosecutor's rebuttal psychiatrist, and Ben's case was over. Closing arguments would follow the judge's reading of the instructions. The bailiff would swear in the jury and off they'd go, carrying Ben's future in their hands.

Driving home to Beartooth, one day after Easter, I looked at the mountain looming ahead of me and said a quick prayer for Ben, the Trumans, our community, and my own family. In that moment, I understood Ben when he said the outcome was up to God.

CHAPTER FORTY

The Verdict

April 16-17, 2001
Kootenai County District Court

DR. ROBERT FOLEY, PSYCHIATRIST TO MONTANA LAW ENFORCEMENT for most of his career, took the witness stand in an effort to refute the testimony of Doctors Purvis, Lomax, and Berg, by questioning their impartiality and skills. He claimed he was neutral, entering the Stagg case without bias or prior knowledge of the facts.

Oops.

When Judge Lambert allowed me to cross-examine the witness, I leapt to my feet. "Dr. Foley, you didn't come into this case with no knowledge whatsoever, is that correct?"

The witness smiled. "I had very elementary . . . very little knowledge when I was asked by the prosecutor to come into this case."

"You were the doctor who examined Nick Stagg for his sentencing, correct?"

The witness' smile faded. "I don't know that I can talk about that."

"Well," I continued, "it's a yes or no question. Did you or did you not evaluate Nick Stagg for purposes of sentencing?"

Judge Lambert stared at the witness, obviously understanding where I was headed with my next set of questions. "You have to answer that one," he ordered.

Dr. Foley wiggled in his seat. "Yes."

I pressed on. "And as part of that evaluation, did you do everything that you accused Dr. Berg of *not* doing?"

"I haven't looked at that evaluation since I did it."

"Right. But my point is, Doctor, if you did everything that you say you should have done, then you were very, very familiar with this case before you were ever asked to work for the prosecution, correct?"

Again he hedged. "I haven't gone back to look at the evaluation, and I've never met your client."

I persisted. "Right. But as part of your evaluation of Nick Stagg, did you not read the police reports?"

"Yes."

"Okay, you also read Nick's confession, correct?"

When he couldn't remember, I handed him a copy of his report. "Does that refresh your recollection about what you did with Mr. Nick Stagg?"

"Yes."

The good doctor recalled the confession, meeting with Pete and Laura Stagg, visiting with jail personnel, giving Nick some tests, and said he believed Nick was an honest person. Indeed, he relied on built-in questions to detect if Nick faked the results, the very part of Dr. Purvis' testimony he'd just criticized as inaccurate. When the prosecutor saw his witness flailing, he objected.

Judge Lambert overruled the objection. "The purpose of the question, in the court's view, is impeaching the doctor by saying he didn't do what he said somebody else maybe should have done."

Dr. Foley's credibility tanked further when he testified that he didn't contact Dr. Purvis because he wasn't smart enough to talk to her or to ask her good questions. Yet he managed to talk to a buddy at the University of Montana, another neuropsychologist, who provided him with talking points for his testimony.

Admittedly, this part of Ben's trial stood as the only portion that fed the junkie in me. Prosecutors, or even ex-prosecutors, love to cross-examine shrinks, to beat them up in front of juries, and make them look like quacks who merely rub the lumps on people's heads before phonying up a diagnosis. Jack had trained me well when I was a D.A., but now, on the opposite side of the courtroom, I needed psychologists and their testimony like a Bedouin needed water. However, I neither needed nor respected Dr. Foley.

I relished the next question. "Well, Dr. Foley, I suppose this is the million dollar question. If Dr. Berg's report is flawed and she's unethical and can't be relied upon, and Dr. Purvis' test results are questionable, why did you not meet with Ben, which you have an absolute right to do by law, and test him yourself or evaluate him yourself?"

"I wasn't asked to do that. I was only asked to be a rebuttal witness . . ." and on he labored, attempting to explain to a tired but attentive jury why he never bothered to meet Ben or contact any of our witnesses. The prosecutor ended the doctor's testimony on that low note.

However, just before Don Yeager rested his case, he approached me, leaning near my right ear. "The back row prosecutors," he jerked his head behind us to the rear of the courtroom where Frank McShane and several of my defense colleagues huddled together, "are telling me to call Ben's first lawyer to testify about Ben's attempt to fire the shotgun from the forest."

I glanced at the Cowboys' smug grins slashing their faces. "Go ahead, Don. I think if it ever happened, that with Ben's eyes closed, aiming at nothing but air, the jury will believe it was a warning shot."

To my amazement, Yeager nodded. "Me, too." He turned to the judge and jury. "The State rests, Your

Honor."

Judge Lambert called for a short recess. I turned to Ben, humor creasing my lips into a smile. "Now *that* cross examination was the most fun I've had in ages."

Ben stared at me, hands shaking, shoulders stooped. "You thought that witness was fun? You're kinda weird, Paige."

I stopped gloating as I considered the torture this ordeal presented to Ben every hour, every minute, of every day. "I'm sorry, buddy. I know how hard this is for you, but honestly, I think we're holding our own with the jury. Some of them look sympathetic."

Ben lowered his head to block out the news crews and noise. "But I'm still goin' back to prison, more than likely." He paused to look at his shoes. "Whatever happens, Paige, I know you tried your best. That's all I wanted. For you to try."

I squeezed his thin forearm that, until then, I'd been unaware of holding. "Hey, Ben, you're the one who always tells me to have faith." I swallowed back sympathy because I knew I had to stand before the jury soon to make my closing argument. "You have to believe that God's going to figure this out. Maybe the best we can get is a hung jury, but even if that happens, you'll stay out of custody until they reset the trial – *if* they reset the trial. They may plea bargain the case at that point for no prison time."

At his silence I added, "You just never know. Hang in with me. It's almost done."

* * *

After Judge Lambert instructed the jury, he turned to Don Yeager, who began his closing argument. Since the prosecutor had the burden of proof, the law allowed him to argue twice. I, on the other hand, had only one last shot to convince the jury to cut Ben loose on 22 criminal charges, including murder.

When Yeager finished, I spent an hour covering the law as it applied to each accusation, the meaning of the term *beyond a reasonable doubt* and what it meant to have a mental disease or defect. I implored the jury to consider that Ben had no control over his thoughts or actions because the aggregate of his physical and emotional abuse, his genetic disorder and its effect on his frontal lobe, and his learning disabilities, prevented him from acting as anything other than Nick's personal robot. I emphasized that Rich Truman's killer, Nick Stagg, sat in prison for the rest of his life. I begged the jury not to create another victim in this tragedy by convicting Ben of any of the crimes charged.

After the jury adjourned, I stared at my reflection in the ladies' room mirror. Dressed in a designer suit and pearls, my hair coiffed, nails manicured, three-inch pumps polished, I realized I'd come full circle from my days as a prosecutor. The only difference over the last four years occurred when I switched sides of the courtroom. Instead of pleading for a conviction, as Don Yeager had just done, I urged the jury toward acquittal.

Worse, for Ben's trial, my work hours approached a hundred a week, no different than in California. Our kids vied for my attention and fought against my workaholism, just as they did in California. My marriage, while much stronger, suffered from neglect, the same as it did in California. Ditto for my friendships, especially with Annie.

What exactly had I accomplished by moving my family nearly 2,000 miles from their home and friends? Was I a nicer, more understanding, less judgmental person? Had I developed compassion? Had I become a more patient parent and wife? Okay, so I'd found my soul. Was my laundry any whiter? My house any cleaner?

"Hey, Paige. Are you in there?" Jack's voice cut through my questions and the bathroom door. I dried my hands and emerged into the courthouse foyer where Jack waited to take me home. The jury had decided to come back in the morning for a fresh start at their deliberations. I kissed him, and then looked outside to keep from folding into his arms in defeat.

Wisely, Jack said nothing until we settled into the Tahoe. "Why are you so glum? I thought your argument went over pretty well with the jurors." He smiled. "At least none of them fell asleep."

My silence told Jack that I'd run out of words. I had nothing more to say about the Stagg case, my life, or our family. I needed to sink into the glorious land of unconsciousness.

Besides rest, however, I needed a miracle on the order of Lazarus rising from the dead. In fifteen hours the jurors would return to the courthouse, enter their deliberation room, complete with his-and-her bathrooms so they had no excuse to leave, and decide Ben's fate. Despite their sympathy toward his genetic disorder, his life of abuse, and the fact that he didn't kill Rich Truman, they'd have to stretch to find Ben not guilty of murder and all of the burglaries and thefts. The stakes stood at all or nothing, full acquittals on every charge, or prison. Because if the jury found Ben guilty on even a single count of burglary, the judge, I felt convinced, would sentence him to prison for 40 years, or the rest of his natural life. With odds like that, tomorrow loomed as a futile culmination of more than two years of effort.

And possibly the legal world's biggest waste of time.

* * *

"Paige?" The next afternoon the bailiff stuck his head in the door of the attorney's room where I sat paying overdue bills. He then uttered the words that struck terror in every trial lawyer. "We have verdicts on all counts."

My hands tensed around the mail I sorted. Nausea again chewed at my stomach lining. I took a shaky breath and nodded. I looked at him, knowing that he likely knew the jury's decision, but ethics precluded him from supplying the answer.

I asked anyway. "What do you think?"

He shook his head and retreated to the courtroom.

Shit!

I phoned Ben, who'd elected to spend the last nine hours of jury deliberations at his sister's house only a few minutes away. "We've got verdicts, buddy. The judge wants you here within 20 minutes. He's giving some time for the press and the Truman family to arrive as well."

Moans in the background from his family and friends interrupted Ben's silence. "Okay, Paige. We'll be right there." His neutral tone belied his defeat.

Next I called Jack so he and Dr. Berg could speed down from Beartooth. My watch ticked five in the afternoon. I hid in my tiny workspace on the third floor as court personnel, interested citizens, and media people flocked into the courtroom.

When I saw the Stagg clan enter the foyer, I stepped out to greet them. Ben sat near the window as he removed his watch. He next emptied his pockets with trembling hands. He knew the drill. After the guilty verdicts, the guards would take him into custody, tighten the handcuffs, issue him a two-piece prison outfit that would forever replace his street clothes, and release his personal belongings back to his family members.

I looked from Pete Stagg to his son, from Stagg sister to Stagg sister, Stagg friend to Stagg friend. Although Laura Stagg hid elsewhere, fully 30 people stood beside Ben for support at this most critical time in his young life.

I cleared my throat. "Okay, everyone. Listen up. We're going to walk into that courtroom with our heads held high and accept with dignity the jury's decision. No crying, no yelling, and absolutely no interaction with the Truman family." I eyed the group as they nodded. "Whatever happens, if it's guilty, we have grounds for appeal, and we'll keep fighting."

I wanted to hug Ben, to hold him as I'd hold my own son were he ever to face such a calamity. But my lawyer mask held firm. I needed to remain calm, impassive, and professional.

The whole world seemed to watch us as we approached the courtroom doors. Before we entered, Pete stopped everyone with a raised palm. He looked gaunt from his fast. "Let's pray." We formed a circle and placed our arms on one another's shoulders while Pete urged God to grant mercy. For once, even my inner cynic shut up and I, too, begged God for justice for this kid client of mine.

Inside the courtroom, sitting at counsel table, Ben and I watched the jurors enter and take their seats. One woman looked at us and sobbed. The other jurors' faces remained impassive. I knew from watching juries in a hundred trials that somber demeanors spoke well for the prosecution, but boded poorly for the defense.

Ben seemed to sense my defeat and said quietly, "Paige, will you please hold my hand?"

I entwined my left hand with his right and squeezed. I stared into his blue eyes and assured him, "Faith, Ben. I won't quit, no matter what. I'll be here for you, okay?"

He lowered his head.

Judge Lambert took the bench. "Ladies and Gentlemen of the jury, have you reached a verdict?"

The foreperson nodded and handed the verdict forms to the clerk.

"Madam Clerk," Judge Lambert intoned after perusing all 22 slips of paper, "Please read the verdicts."

My right hand held a pen poised over a blank yellow tablet. I planned to record each decision, count by count. My grip on that pen threatened to break it in half.

And so began the litany of decisions that shaped the rest of Ben's life:

"Count One," the clerk spoke firmly, "Not Guilty."

I wrote that down with a hint of relief.

"Count Two," she continued. "Not Guilty."

I circled the number two followed by 'NG', but tamped down hope.

"Count Three." She paused. "Not guilty."

I allowed a tiny bit of excitement to swell.

"Count Four." Another pause. "Not guilty."

I heard a rush in my head amid the sounds of weeping behind and next to me. As the clerk continued to read count after count, charge after charge, not guilty verdict after not guilty verdict, I held my breath. Count 17 marked the burglary of Dr. Sam Jaffee's house on the night of the homicide. Count 18 addressed the murder of Rich Truman.

"Count Seventeen, Burglary," the clerk continued. "Not guilty by reason of mental disease or defect."

Ben's grip tensed against mine. Was it possible? Could these twelve people actually buck the Kootenai County community to find Ben innocent of murder?

"Count Eighteen, Deliberate Homicide." The clerk looked at me. "Not guilty by reason of mental disease or defect."

Ben's body slumped forward as he laid his head on counsel table. Sobs from the Truman family mingled with joyous exclamations from the Stagg family. I tossed my reading glasses on the table, withdrew my left hand from Ben's, and placed my arm around his thin, shaking shoulders while I listened to the last four 'not guilty' verdicts. I held him, forcing air into my lungs. My own tears trickled down my cheeks. I lowered my head and exhaled a prayer of thanks.

Ben Stagg.

Acquitted on all counts.

A miracle.

CHAPTER FORTY-ONE

A Kibbutz in Israel

May 2001
Beartooth and Back to Court

RIGHT AFTER JUDGE LAMBERT THANKED AND EXCUSED THE JURY, Jack grabbed me into a fierce embrace, his own radiant smile matching mine. "I can't fucking believe it, Paige! You did it! Not guilty on everything!"

I relaxed against him as we walked to the parking lot, media interviews behind me, elated and devastated families following in my wake. "Not exactly perfect, Jack, since the judge can still send Ben to the state mental hospital for an indefinite commitment. Not guilty by reason of mental disease or defect opens that door."

Jack eased me into the driver's seat of the Tahoe. "A risk worth taking, as you knew before trial. Besides, why would the judge send him there when they can't fix the genetic disorder?"

I shrugged. "I don't know. This just seems to good to be true."

He laughed. "Always the worrier, but not tonight. Tonight we celebrate with the kids and forget the Stagg family for a few hours. I'll meet you at home."

After the verdict, Judge Lambert allowed Ben to stay at his parents' house, but announced that he wanted Ben independently evaluated by a neuropsychologist of the judge's choosing. He randomly chose a doctor in Bozeman, and asked me to arrange for the appointments.

I made the call the next morning as flowers arrived at the office and messages of congratulations poured in from various sources, some from strangers in other states.

Sitting in my upstairs office, clad in jeans and a sweatshirt, hiking-booted feet on my desk, I looked out my window as I tried to grasp that Ben Stagg was free. The case, for the most part, had ended. Of course, my next homicide case, in Glasgow, sat in boxes next to my credenza, awaiting my perusal. My death penalty case from California beckoned from well-organized shelves across the room.

No rest for the exhausted.

"Hey, are you awake up there?" Stormy's voice flew over the intercom.

"Yeah, but barely. What's up?" I sat forward, feet on the floor, and swiveled my chair back to reality.

"I've got a preacher on the line who says he wants to offer Ben Stagg a safe place to stay and maybe a job." Stormy's skepticism over the goodness of mankind dripped off her words.

Even though I'd felt my soul re-enter my body over the Easter weekend, I, too, balked at such an offer of kindness. "You think he's legit?"

She sniffed her response. "You want to talk to him?"

I rubbed the area between my brows. "Yeah, why not? Maybe I'm on a roll with religious miracles."

And apparently I was.

Young Pastor Jeremy and his wife were newly married and recently installed to minister at a small church in Beartooth. They weren't much older than Ben, but they had a house with an extra room and bath in their basement, a private entrance, and more love to give to humanity than the rest of our community combined.

Ben moved in with them the next day, meeting the couple who later would become two of his closest friends. Between the new living arrangement away from his folks, the testosterone treatments, and the counseling sessions to address the effects of his abuse, Ben changed over the next few weeks. He grew hair on his face, he stood a bit straighter, he developed some muscle, and his self-esteem crept upward. Ben smiled, not in confusion, but rather from that place of faith that rested within him. I'd seen that same joyous light emanate from his blue eyes at the end of our first meeting at Deer Lodge State Prison two years earlier.

As I promised Judge Lambert, I drove Ben to Bozeman several times to meet with the court-appointed neuropsychologist. On those trips, with me driving the Tahoe and Ben riding shotgun, he talked my ear off. We explored every subject from child abuse to ice caving in the Crazy Mountains. Both of us grew confident that the court would allow Ben to remain at the pastor's house while he sought work at any menial job he could find.

Hope, that elusive angel dancing over our heads, primed our hearts as we neared Ben's next court hearing. In that hour, before Judge Lambert, Ben's life as a free man could begin.

Or end.

* * *

I received the Bozeman doctor's report with his recommendation for an appropriate placement for Ben Stagg. "Jack, check this out." We stood near the coffee pot at the office. "This doctor tested Ben, came up with the same results as Kyle Purvis, and recommends a non-custodial placement for him."

Jack sipped his swill. "That's a good thing, right? It excludes Warm Springs Mental Hospital, since that's a lock-down facility much like the prison."

I nodded. "I guess. Except he thinks Ben should be placed in an Israeli kibbutz." I looked up at Jack, my eyes twinkling. "I wonder how the Baptist folks will feel about that? They weren't so happy that Sara Berg is Jewish, or that I'm Catholic. Imagine if the judge bought Ben a ticket to Tel Aviv?"

Jack shook his head and spat out, "Shrinks! Bah!" before leaving for the conference room.

I knew the kibbutz plan wouldn't happen. This was Montana, where no active synagogue existed in the state. Still, I liked the guy's thinking.

With Ben settled in at the pastor's, on his way to an independent future, I focused on my own kids for a change. Claire, a junior, stressed over every grade in each class, determined to pull a GPA that would allow her admission to an out-of-state university. Combined with 17-year-old hormones, she drove me mad for a good portion of each week, but I admired her tenacity. When she focused on a goal, she achieved it, whether it was a medal for swimming, saving for a pair of jeans, or getting into college.

Meanwhile, Sean launched into the vision improvement program recommended by Ben's grandmother. Among other activities, the doctor gave him an exercise where he read words from left to right, then up and down a page, all while a metronome beat out every word he read. She increased the metronome's speed after each successful journey. The words spelled out colors: red, black, blue, yellow, green, and they repeated throughout the exercise.

Once my son succeeded at the fast speed, he had to read the words again, only this time each word was printed in the color it described, blue in blue ink, red in red ink, and so on. Again, once he mastered reading the now-colored words at the fast speed, the doctor changed the exercise. She handed him the same page, but the ink colors for each word *differed* from what the word spelled. The word green was printed in red ink, for example, and the word red was printed in blue ink.

Sean now had to read either the word or say the color of the ink, depending on the doctor's order. I recognized from my grad school days that such a task required a multi-operational brain function, since one part of Sean's brain read the word, but another portion saw the color. He had to concentrate to stick to one or the other task.

"You know," I mentioned to the ophthalmologist, "this test seems so familiar to me." I puzzled over that suspicion as I watched my son complete the exercises from another room.

The doctor sat next to me. "It's based on neuropsychology, Paige. Using these standard tests in a different way, we think they force the kid's brain to reorganize itself. With enough practice, the eye-to-brain signal bypasses whatever circuits aren't working and creates new pathways that allow the child to read. Kind of a simplistic explanation, but you get the idea."

Click!

Dr. Kyle Purvis had described this exact test in court when she testified about evaluating Ben Stagg. Only one month later, one of the same tests she'd use to conclude Ben Stagg was the most brain-impaired KS patient she'd ever known allowed my son to retrain his brain and read for the first time in his life.

Indeed, after ten weeks working hard at the program, Sean's reading level sailed from zero to college level. A new world opened for him, giving him freedom to explore everything from Plato to the political theories of Che Guevara. His grades at the junior high zipped to straight As, so the school removed him from all special classes.

Only his small motor skills failed to improve, leaving his handwriting and artwork rather difficult to interpret. If those represented his only academic weaknesses, he could keyboard a computer and go to medical school.

As Sean finished the program, I marveled that Ben Stagg's family provided mine with a priceless gift, my son's ability to read. And all because some neuropsychologist like Dr. Purvis figured out how to rewire a kid's brain.

Now I needed to return the favor by insuring Ben walked out of the Kootenai County courthouse to freedom.

* * *

Before Ben's placement hearing, I hedged my bet and traveled for hours to Warm Springs State Mental Hospital for a tour of the facility. The director took me to the criminal ward where Ben, if sent there, would have his own room, share a bath, and wear civilian clothes instead of a uniform. The idea, the director assured me, was to treat people as patients in a hospital setting, not as prisoners.

I viewed the state-of-the-art gymnasium, eating area, exercise areas, and common areas with interest. All of it seemed very impressive and much different than the snake pit I'd expected. The patients, however, appeared seriously mentally ill, far more bizarre than Ben Stagg acted on his worst day before his trial.

I nodded toward a group watching television. "How will you protect a kid like Ben, if he's sent here, from violence by the other inmates?"

The director corrected me. "Patients, Ms. Defalco, not inmates. And the answer is we have excellent security people who maintain vigilant watch over everyone. We're fortunate not to have many fights here among our residents."

After the tour, as I walked toward the entrance with the director, he turned to me and shook my hand. "Thank you for coming. Do you know you're the very first attorney who's ever come to Warm Springs for a tour?"

I smiled, thanked him for his time, and drove the long road back to Beartooth.

The next day, I called Ben to report my findings and assure him that if worse came to worse, Warm Springs looked like a vacation resort compared to Deer Lodge.

"Thanks for going, Paige. I guess we'll just leave it all up to God, like always."

Hanging up, I hesitated at Ben's faith-filled attitude. I figured if God didn't send Ben in the direction I wanted, to a life outside of custody, I'd help Him out by filing a few motions with the Montana Supreme Court. I remained convinced that Judge Lambert would follow his own expert's advice and find that custody in Warm Springs was inappropriate.

* * *

At the hearing, I called as witnesses the judge's expert as well as the head psychiatrist from Warm Springs, both of whom testified that the mental health facility was not the appropriate setting for Ben Stagg to spend his time recovering from the traumas of his past. Don Yeager, the prosecutor, didn't seem to care where Ben went, as long as he left Kootenai County.

Judge Lambert looked worn out. He shook his head at the kibbutz theory, listened attentively to the psychiatrist from Warm Springs, and took a recess to contemplate his decision. When he returned, I pleaded once again for Ben's release back to the young pastor and his wife.

"Mrs. Defalco," he looked down at me from the bench, "the law requires me to place your client into the care of the Department of Public Health and Human Services, and that is what I'm going to do. It is up to the experts in that agency to decide where you should be placed, Mr. Stagg." The judge closed his notes. "So ordered."

Then he left the bench, and our beautiful area of Montana, desperate, no doubt, to put the entire Stagg matter behind him when he returned to his own family.

Ben looked at me. "What just happened, Paige?"

I glanced at the court clerk. "Well, the judge turned you over to another mental health agency." At his nod I continued. "The head of that agency will decide where you should live for awhile. Since the lead psychiatrist at Warm Springs says you're not a candidate for that facility, I can only guess that the agency will let you live where you are now, as long as you continue to go to your counseling sessions." That scenario seemed logical to me.

Ben looked befuddled, but left with the pastor and his wife, believing that God had his back.

Logic, however, rarely prevailed in the Wild West.

Two days later, on May 24, 2001, after a jury acquitted him of 22 criminal charges, Ben Stagg once again placed his hands behind his back as an armed guard handcuffed him. Along with Ben's sister and grandmother, I stood by helplessly as the public health van drove off with Ben sliding around in the back during the long drive to the criminal ward at Warm Springs State Mental Hospital.

Ben Stagg.

Back in custody, perhaps for the rest of his life.

What the *hell* just happened to our miracle?

CHAPTER FORTY-TWO

Justice Delayed

May 2001 through July 2002
Kootenai County, Montana

"STAGG TAKEN TO HOSPITAL: LAWYER FIGHTS" read the headline in the *Bozeman Gazette's* May 26, 2001 edition. The article detailed the motions I filed when the mental health people carted Ben off. I alleged civil rights violations, illegal incarceration, and virtually any theory that remotely applied, in order to secure Ben's release from Warm Springs.

I failed.

Unless someone at the hospital determined that Ben was no longer dangerous and free of mental illness, he'd reside near the town of Anaconda, Montana, in lockdown, indefinitely.

At home reading the sports page, Jack tried to console me. "Maybe this won't be as bad as you think. Maybe the shrinks down there can help Ben get past everything he's been through." His raised brow undercut his confident tone.

I sat across the kitchen table from him, my hands cradling my face like a forlorn three-year-old who'd lost her kite up a tree. "An indefinite stay, Jack. Do you know there's one guy who has spent the last 25 years at Warm Springs? So what did I accomplish with all my legal maneuvers, my experts, my investigation, and all my trial prep?"

Jack sat back. "You got Ben out of life in prison and

a death sentence, Paige. You listened to Dr. Cotter about the Klinefelter's syndrome and helped Ben get the treatment he needed for that. You took all the information about abuse from Ben's family, combined it with expert opinions about complicated brain functions, and turned the whole mess into 22 'not guilty' verdicts. Shit! You accomplished more for that kid than most lawyers do for a lifetime of clients."

"Yeah, but now where is he? In custody in a mental hospital, for crapssake, and there's not a damned thing I can do about it." I stood to pace.

"Look, you're the one who always preaches that we're not in charge of the world, Sweet Pea. You need to take your own advice and get out of God's way so he can handle this." Jack sighed at me in frustration. "Meanwhile, I hate to sound like an asshole, but you've got other cases that need your attention. Let the Stagg family go for awhile and get back to work for your other clients."

Jack meant my other *paying* clients, like Chad Hammel, the kid in Glasgow, and the prisoner on San Quentin's death row.

Two years earlier, when I'd agreed to represent Ben Stagg, his parents promised to pay me $50,000. Back then that sum seemed sufficient to get us through the investigation and to a hearing on the reversal of Ben's plea. We never dreamed that effort would succeed, nor did we anticipate the amount of work that followed. Certainly we never figured the case would go to trial since at the time, it seemed like a slam-dunk for the prosecution.

We didn't figure on all the post-trial proceedings, the trips to Bozeman with the court-appointed neuropsychologist, my trip to Warm Springs, or the hearing and subsequent motions to release Ben.

I turned to Jack, my guilt warring with

defensiveness. "Look, I know this case cost a fortune to pursue, and we'll never get paid for it. I know what it's cost our family, especially the kids, and I know what it's done for our reputation in the community. I get the same hostile looks you do, believe me."

We heard the kids stirring upstairs as Jack set the sports page on the table. "Paige, I counted up your hours on the case. Before trial began, we had over $120,000 into it. Minus the $50,000 the Staggs paid, we lost seventy grand before you ever picked the jury. Now, with nearly a month of trial and all the crap afterward, we're well over a hundred and seventy five thousand in the hole. I need you to get back to the real world and earn some coin. Claire's graduating next year, and we haven't saved nearly enough for out-of-state tuition."

I swallowed the lump of guilt rising up the back of my throat. "Okay, I get it. I'll move on. I can't just forget Ben, but I'll get back to the other cases on Monday."

Footsteps pounded down the stairs as our son emerged, pajamas crumpled, hair mussed, and mouth moving. "What's for breakfast, Mom? Bacon and eggs? Could you make mine scrambled really hard? Wow, Dad, wait until I tell you about this book I started reading on astronomy . . ."

I rose to fry bacon.

Life in the fast lane.

Could the Defalco family travel any other way?

* * *

To my surprise, the State chose to pursue the death penalty against my 20-year-old client in Glasgow, accused of murdering his best friend. No county in Montana had charged death in over ten years because of the expense of those trials. My client had no record, no prior history of violence, and claimed his co-defendant shot their buddy and burned the body. Since he swore to his own innocence, he refused to plead guilty to murder. When he refused the State's plea bargain, the prosecutor upped the ante with the threat of execution. My client still refused to plead.

Glasgow is as far to the east as a person can travel in Montana without running into North Dakota, another hours long drive. Every time I had to litigate anything, I had to make that tedious journey, which cost the client a bundle and my family time without Mom. As the case progressed, evidence surfaced in strange places, and my erstwhile investigator, Ty Kayman, insisted the cops planted it. Eventually I had to agree with him, but that's another story.

My co-counsel on the Glasgow case, Craig Fortney, also represented Jack and me in our fight in the Zanto case before the Commission on Practice. In September 2001, the assigned investigator cleared us of all charges, helped by the fact that Ms. Zanto admitted lying under oath to the old, deaf judge presiding over her earlier hearing.

The California death row investigation blossomed into a full-scale legal ride. Despite the accusations against him, I liked my client. He'd sat on the Row since his conviction in 1993 and in all that time, not a single person had visited him. I bought canteen items for him at each visit, sent him a television, a CD player, plus some music he chose, and finally a typewriter so he could communicate. I knew his case would take years to resolve. I only prayed it wouldn't be by lethal injection.

My conversion to a bleeding-heart liberal appeared cemented.

Chad Hammel's lawsuit progressed at a glacial pace, as most civil cases do, but Chad became my favorite client during that time. His intelligence, his sense of humor, his loyalty to family and friends, and his startling business acumen placed him high on my list of interesting people. He rarely saw Charlie's children, thanks to the machinations of Charlie's ex-wife and the Winston family, but Chad remained close to his other grandchildren.

All three cases kept me on the road far more than I would have liked, but that was the nature of my law practice. When I remained in Beartooth, I spent every spare moment with the kids and Jack. The Kootenai County community either supported my work in Ben's case or condemned me for it. There were some veiled threats, nasty letters to the editor, and a blatant interview between the local paper and Judge Winston in which he announced that he didn't care about Klinefelter's syndrome. Ben Stagg had gotten away with murder.

One astonishing event occurred that gave Jack and me hope that change might come to the Kootenai County justice system. After my long-ago phone call to the ACLU in 1998, and my work with them through 2000, I'd heard nothing regarding any effort to establish an independent statewide public defender system. Then, in February 2002, the ACLU filed its lawsuit against the state of Montana, alleging every inequity I'd cited to them and more. They named seven counties as particular examples of the most egregious constitutional violations, and Kootenai County came first.

I wasn't sure how the lawsuit would play out, but the ACLU lawyers had assured me years earlier that they never lost, once they filed their paperwork. Jack and I didn't hold our breath because the Courthouse Cowboys still reacted with venomous denials to all who would listen. It promised to be an interesting conflict.

Meanwhile, I talked with Ben regularly by phone, visited him at Warm Springs a couple of times, and sent him clothes and tennis shoes as needed. He sounded better each month and looked healthier than he ever had before. At Ben's request, his parents kept their distance. They sold their house in Whitehall and moved out of Kootenai County to find peace and anonymity elsewhere in the state.

Ben's progress at Warm Springs heartened me as he worked his way through the motivational steps necessary to move from the criminal ward into an independent living facility on the Warm Springs property. In that environment, Ben tried to learn to cook, balance a checkbook, and keep house.

In February 2002, I traveled to Arizona to put my dad in assisted living, since he resisted proper nutrition and refused to stop driving. I stayed in the hospital with him as he fought pneumonia. He told me he'd reached the end. He no longer cared about any of his possessions or even remaining in the home he'd owned for many decades.

It took me a couple of weeks to sort through nearly 95 years worth of stuff, relocate the deranged wife, sell the house, and situate Dad in his new room. After only 30 days, the care facility phoned to tell us Dad was dying. He'd refused to eat for the last month. I grabbed my son, who wanted to say goodbye to his grandfather, and hopped a plane to Phoenix just two days before Judge Lambert announced he intended to release Ben Stagg from Warm Springs State Hospital.

On March 19, 2002, with Jack appearing for me in court, Judge Lambert ordered Ben's release. Only one obstacle blocked Ben's freedom. No mental health facility would agree to supervise him. Rumor had it that a whisper campaign flooded fax machines and emails throughout the state to discourage anyone from accepting Ben. Without a supervisor, Ben had to remain in custody at Warm Springs.

For all the effort to reach my dad before he died, we didn't make it. He passed away with my brother, Danny, at his side keeping a vigil, just as our dad had stood vigil for Danny through nearly eight years of prison camp in Vietnam.

I assured myself that we honored Dad in death, as we couldn't in life. By the time I returned to Montana, Warm Springs still had failed to find an agency to supervise Ben, frustrating me, my client, his family, and the staff at the state hospital.

Three months later, our daughter graduated from high school after achieving the necessary grades for an August acceptance into a university in Seattle. I mourned her imminent departure, but between trips to Glendive and California, along with extensive work on the Hammel case, I swallowed my grief. Court dates came and went, judges continued trials, legal papers amassed into organized piles filling my office and our file room.

Work, as always, fascinated yet overwhelmed me. Ever the trial junkie, I knew the fiend in me could never quit. Criminal law would either propel me into old age or kill me. I figured as long as I ate enough antacids, I'd make it a few more years.

* * *

One day, in late June 2002, I received a call from a mental health agency in Bozeman. They agreed to accept supervision of Ben Stagg for the next five years, a legal requirement after a verdict of not guilty by reason of mental disease or defect. Afraid to get my hopes up, I confirmed arrangements with the staff at Warm Springs, learned they'd secured an apartment for Ben, as well as a construction job with a friend of Ben's father, and that he'd be released immediately.

The press called for comments, the crew from *NewsTime*, *CBS* phoned requesting a follow-up interview, while some nasty people in Kootenai County wrote letters to the editor decrying Ben's release. I fended off all inquiries with vague answers as I prepared to help Ben move into his new apartment.

As it turned out, I did very little. Ben, excited at age 22 to have his freedom and an independent place to live for the first time in his life, procured furniture from various places and decorated the place as any young bachelor might. A bed, a recliner, a table, some chairs, and a few kitchen utensils, all used, but all his. What more did a guy need? The good folks at the local mental health facility oversaw the results and assisted Ben in every way.

When Ben emerged from his year at Warm Springs, he looked like a different young man. His hair, now longer, parted down the middle and looked almost trendy. His skin glowed tan, making his blue eyes and white teeth radiate in his smiling face. He'd gained valuable muscle in his arms and torso from playing basketball and working outdoors. He'd grown sideburns and developed hair on his face, arms, and legs.

What struck me most, however, was his maturity. He'd developed from a dependent little kid to a man, in just thirteen months. Part of this growth, I knew, arose from testosterone therapy, including his increased mental acuity.

But the rest came through the efforts of the staff at Warm Springs. From the caseworkers to counselors, psychiatrists to medical personnel, those people had given Ben the gift of a new life. They helped him forget the details of his past tragedies, overcome his nightmares, and forgive himself, as well as his parents.

Ben now possessed the inner strength of someone who had been to hell and back, a man who could survive anything life dished out. He would never speak to his brother again, nor understand what made Nick do what he'd done, but someday, I suspected, Ben would find it in his heart to forgive Nick as well.

I'd been wrong when I'd objected so strenuously to his hospital placement. Jack had been right. I had to get out of God's way, so He could heal Ben Stagg.

Through it all, Ben never lost his faith in God. Even when my own faith faltered during the three years leading up to Ben's release, his stood fast, humbling me whenever I thought about it. Once settled in his apartment, Ben attended church and considered becoming Catholic because he loved the priest who'd held Mass every week at the hospital. One of Ben's first trips into the outside world of Bozeman, Montana involved finding the nearest Christian center at the local university, a worship group filled with kids his own age.

No longer his lawyer, but always his friend, I made a visit to Ben's apartment in Bozeman. I gifted him with a television and DVD player, took him to lunch, wished him great happiness, and hugged him until he, like my own son, patted my back and pulled away. "I'll be okay, Paige. Really." He smiled his infectious grin and sped outside to his future.

I settled into my Tahoe, noting that, like its owner, it looked older and a few miles worse for wear. I returned to a life filled with kids, murder, and mounds of paperwork.

For the next couple of weeks, Ben fared well, and we spoke daily by phone. I asked, as I would of my own kids, if he ate well. I wanted to make sure he didn't lose any of the precious weight he'd gained during the last year.

"Well," he hesitated, "yeah, I've lost a bunch of weight, I guess."

Exasperated as only moms tend to get, I queried. "What are you eating every day?"

I could hear him ponder that question. "Bagels and lunch meat, mostly."

I sighed out my frustration. "Ben, you need to eat some hot food, three meals a day. I thought they taught you how to cook at Warm Springs."

He laughed. "Well, kinda, I guess. But I don't remember a lot of it."

I closed my eyes. The mom in me, the fixer of all things, formulated a strategy because I knew Ben still couldn't plan for himself. All the hair on his chest wouldn't make up for the damage to his frontal lobe. I wanted to make sure he'd be fine on his own. "Okay, buddy, I want you to hang up and go the store. I want you to go to the frozen food aisle and buy some microwave dinners that look tasty. When you get back, call me."

He agreed and my phone rang an hour later. "Okay, I went to the store just like you said, and I bought five dinners. But Paige, there's no directions on how to cook this thing. I'm looking at the front of the package, and there's nothing but a picture."

Klinefelter's syndrome. Unable to plan ahead, to strategize, to anticipate outcomes, and see what's coming down the road. Be patient, Paige. "Right, Ben. So turn the package over and look at the back or along the sides. Do you see directions now?"

In Bozeman, his excitement zipped over the phone line. "Okay, yeah, I see them. I'll call you back after I've eaten."

In Beartooth, I stuck chicken on the barbecue to feed my own family. So what if Ben suffered permanent frontal lobe damage? He'd shown huge progress in spite of that. Besides, after everything he'd been through, if planning menus posed Ben's biggest problem in the future? Well, for once the mom and the lawyer in me agreed.

Ben Stagg would be just fine.

Five minutes later, my phone rang again. "Hey,

Paige? I did everything that it said, even took off the plastic and all, and threw away the package."

I grabbed some lettuce from the fridge. "Okay. So what's the problem?"

He paused. "Well," I could picture him scratching his head. "See, the thing is . . . I don't have a microwave."

ENDINGS

BEN STAGG DIDN'T STARVE TO DEATH. In fact, he flourishes as a missionary to troubled kids, the homeless, and the elderly. He met and married a quiet, young Christian woman with whom he shares his life. Since his release from Warm Springs, his record remains unblemished. In March 2007, at the end of five years of mandatory supervision, Ben walked away from court a free man.

Pete and Laura Stagg remain married, their life together more relaxed after Ben's acquittal. Empty nesting seems to suit them.

Megan Stagg earned her degree in nursing and lives out of state.

Nick Stagg successfully sued Deer Lodge State Prison for taking away his wheelchair as part of their behavior modification program. After crawling around in his cell, through his own urine and feces, he contacted the Montana Supreme Court, who agreed the punishment exceeded Nick's minor rule violation. Nick requested a transfer to prison in another state where he serves the remainder of his life sentence.

Judge Winston still dispenses his own version of justice at the Kootenai County courthouse, running unopposed in each election. I've never again appeared in his courtroom. Frank McShane, after taking over the helm from his former boss, now serves as the elected County Attorney, running unopposed in each election. Don Yeager has a small local law practice.

Chad Hammel sort of won his lawsuit, but rarely sees Charlie's kids from his first marriage to Judge

Winston's daughter. She remarried and so did Charlie. Each couple had additional children and now live several hours apart, happy in their new families.

I'm not sure what became of the other clients from that time. I hope they're well and free from custody.

Investigator Ty Kayman continues his superb efforts on behalf of our clients.

In July 2006, nearly eight years after I first contacted them on behalf of Rodney the Meth Spoon Guy, the ACLU forced the state of Montana to establish its first independent statewide public defender system. Judge Winston and his cronies battled so hard against it, the Chief Justice of the Montana Supreme Court finally had to order him to comply with the new hiring standards. The local public defender's office is understaffed and underfunded, but at least it's a start. I applaud their efforts.

The tiny law firm of Defalco & Defalco carries on, seeking justice for clients who sometimes pay, but more often don't. As my dad used to say, seeking truth and making money rarely mix. However, Jack and I have a great set of mounted elk antlers above the fireplace in our office. The plaque underneath reads, "Jack and Paige, The best attorneys around. Thanks for everything. Pete, Laura, and Ben." Jack many times points to *The Horns* as the reason we shouldn't take on more *pro bono* work. But we always do.

Stormy, our erstwhile legal assistant, still runs our office with efficiency, wit, and a healthy dose of skepticism about the innate goodness of mankind. She makes a terrific gatekeeper, even though some clients refer to her as The Dragon Lady. I don't know what we'd do without her.

The Defalco children have grown up, gone off to college, and now pursue their lives with gusto, knowing that any second, everything can change. Neither kid completely forgives us for scaring the bejeezus out of them about bad guys during their childhood, but as they get older, at least they understand our fears. They both make noises about going to law school.

Hmm. The Defalco Family Law Offices? It kind of has a nice ring.

Nah . . .

ACKNOWLEGEMENTS

TO MY FELLOW WRITERS known as The Graces: Dawn Peterson, Sue Purvis, Becky Lomax, Jess Owen, Patty Kogutek, Christine Hensleigh, Betty Kuffel, Abby Smyers, and Deb Burke: Thank you all for your edits, suggested changes, advice, understanding, compassion, humor, champagne, and friendship. This one's for you, Ladies!

To authors Robin Simon, Dennis Foley, Ann Rule, Cathy Scott, and Larry Brooks: Thank you for your exceptional advice and talented suggestions. How blessed I am that you took time from your busy lives to answer some very basic questions.

To Annie, my Montana soul mate, who died from breast cancer on December 7, 2005, eight years after diagnosis: Thank you for being there for me. You joined our other dear friends who, like my mom, also lost their battles with breast cancer. Annie, Shari, Jesse, and Dawn, I wish I had an Erin Brockovich law firm to get to the bottom of your disease.

To the angels who helped Ben Stagg: You continue to excel in your professions, helping so many who cannot help themselves. Doctors Jason Bechard, Kyle Boone, Carol Samango-Sprouse, and Jolie Brams, words of thanks don't begin to express the miracle you helped bring about. But thanks anyway, guys.

To Ty, the world's best private investigator: Mr. Grumpy, you made this and many other cases turn into winners. Now smile for a change.

To Stormy: You are the very best at what you do. You earned your nickname, along with our eternal love and respect.

To my former U.S. Marine Corps colleague in the D.A.'s office: You were right. Evidently I'm both a shit disturber *and* a shit magnet.

To 'Lucifer' and his wife, dear friends from my days in the D.A.'s office, who inspired and encouraged us to move to Montana: Your advice and support saved our family. Again, mere thanks seem so inadequate.

To Mike Potter, whose digital expertise, creativity, enthusiasm, and patience launched this project when other efforts have failed: To the e-universe and beyond, dear friend.

To my daughter Lyndsey, for her expertise in business, marketing, and design: I know you've got my back on this one, Sweetie!

To my family, once again: Jack the Elder, Jack the Younger, Lyns and Justin: You are my whole world. You made this happen, all of it. I owe you guys a ton of pot roast.

For more information on Klinefelter's syndrome, or to contribute to further research and outreach on this treatable genetic disorder, please visit:

www.thefocusfoundation.org
www.genetic.org

ABOUT THE AUTHOR

P.A. Moore (her maiden name), wife, mom, author, and lawyer, lives in a small town in Montana, having fled there with her family from Big City, California in the late 90s. Her goal to achieve a peaceful, quiet life never materialized (does it for any parent?), but she's learned to embrace the chaos that comes with loving her incredible family, her work, and her ongoing effort to provide a voice for those who cannot speak for themselves.

Look for her next novel in Fall 2012.

Contact Ms. Moore **at p.a.moore.inc@gmail.com,** follow her on Facebook at **P.A.Moore**, check out her website at **www.courthousecowboys.com**, or follow her blog at **www.TheQKnowsLaw.com** - where, with her law partner, Ms. Moore offers every day law for every day people.

Made in the USA
San Bernardino, CA
29 October 2013